CHICAGO BLUES

EDITED BY
LIBBY FISCHER HELLMANN

BLEAK HOUSE BOOKS
MADISON | WISCONSIN

Published by Bleak House Books,
an imprint of Big Earth Publishing
923 Williamson St.
Madison, WI 53703

ISBN 13 (cloth): 978-1-932557-50-3

Library of Congress Cataloging-in-Publication Data has been applied for.

Printed in the United States of America

11 10 09 08 07   1 2 3 4 5 6 7 8 9 10

Set in Calisto MT

Original photograph copyright © 2007 by Sharon Lomasney
www.sharonlomasney.com

Cover and Book Design by
Von Bliss Design — "Book Design By Bookish People"
www.vonbliss.com

FEATURING

FEATURING (CONT.)

INTRODUCTION
RICK KOGAN

I AM NOT SURE WHEN IT HAPPENED, exactly, at what page in this stunning gathering. But while devouring these stories, I was transported back to the June day in 1988 that I spent with Koko Taylor.

It was a revelation. She was then, and remains thank God, the undisputed Queen of the Blues. But visiting her at her South Side home told me immediately and for keeps that there is no other segment of the entertainment world in which stardom is mirrored less glitteringly than it is in the real life of a blues star. The things one might normally associate with stardom—a fancy house, minions for various chores—were absent from Taylor's life.

It was ten AM and she had chores to do: "Usually I'm up by six. Look at this. I haven't even washed the dishes. I haven't even made the beds." In the den, in a red shirt and even redder suspenders, was Pop, Taylor's husband, whose real name was Richard. Koko's real name is Cora. "Momma," Pop said to his wife, "you forget to bring me my coffee?"

The Taylors lived in a pleasant house, an ordinary Chicago bungalow not much different from the others along a tree-shaded block in Gresham. They had lived there since 1967. It was a bust and crowded house, filled with mementos. The most serene room in the house was Koko's bedroom, done completely in shades of blue.

"And a bed that's a mess," said Koko. "But you wanted the real Koko."

"Real" is, of course, an elusive word. But so, these days, is "blues."

An old blues man once told me, "You've got to know the blues to play the blues."

But do you have to know the blues to write the blues?

All of the writers in this collection have been inspired by that word/music, and by meanings that have nothing to do with music, such as cops, depression, Code Blue or even the Blue Line. They have crafted tales that are as dark as an Austin alley at four AM, and often as ominous. There is danger and death on the following pages but so, too, is there a kind of life. You can feel the pulse of Chicago on these pages.

It is something you will feel is real, even if you have never felt the urge to steal or harm or kill. These are crime stories, and the nature of the crimes is as complex and compelling as a strand of DNA. In the shadow of the blues (whatever your definition), the lines between good and bad, right and wrong, life and death can blur. These stories explore the demons and dangers that lurk in those shadows.

Some of these stories take you into neighborhoods where you've never been, some to times long gone. One of them—again I can't remember which; how miraculous—took me back decades to Theresa Needham. I was watching her cry. She had once operated one of the city's most famous blues clubs, simply Theresa's. But she had been forced out of one spot, then another and another, and at the time appeared to be out of the scene for good.

"They don't ever call me anymore," she said of the performers whose careers she helped jump-start. Her apartment was teeming with cats. "None of them call."

She would die in 1992, by which time the blues was big business in Chicago and some people had a hard time remembering that the music was born not in a Grant Park festival or a North Side club. Its roots are ever in the smoky, ramshackle South and West Side bars and, further back, Memphis and the Mississippi Delta.

For many of us of a certain advancing age, who first heard the blues in places such as Theresa's or the original Checkerboard Lounge, on a Maxwell Street sidewalk or in a place that had no name, the music seems milder now, the crowds a little more chic. Such has been the price of increased popularity. This is good for the performers. After years of playing, as one of them once told me, "for nothing more than bus fare," they are getting the dough they deserve as the blues has finally made its economic migration.

But when you read these stories you will not think about legacy or loss. You will think about life. There is, as in the best blues, something raw and wrenching about words effectively strung together; hard-hitting and passionate in execution, but disciplined in form. There are no holds barred in these pages.

At the end of that long-ago day I spent with Koko Taylor, we were outside behind the Norris Center at Northwestern

University. It was night. Big Daddy Kinsey and his band were on stage; behind it, on a folding chair, sat Koko.

"Something magic happens when I get to a club or get on stage," she said. "The crowd, the musicians … Even if I'm in a bad mood, I gotta smile, and that gets me in a better mood. I put everything behind me when I perform. My problems don't belong to my fans. I don't put a burden on my audience. I give them 100 percent of my energy. I get tired; sure, I get tired. Some days I'm sick, don't feel like getting on stage. Some days there are bills coming that I don't want to see. But I never bring that onto stage with me. That's not for my fans. I don't want them to know that the sun don't shine around here everyday."

The sun don't shine much on the following pages, but the effect, the literary show, is magic.

Named Chicago's Best Reporter in 1999 and inducted into the Chicago Journalism Hall of Fame in 2003, **RICK KOGAN** is currently a senior writer and columnist for the *Chicago Tribune*'s Sunday magazine and creator and host of "The Sunday Papers with Rick Kogan" on WGN-AM. Kogan has written 10 books, including, in collaboration with his father, *Yesterday's Chicago*, and in collaboration with *Tribune* colleague Maurice Possley, the best-selling *Everybody Pays: Two Men, One Murder and the Price of Truth*. His *America's Mom: The Life, Lesson and Legacy of Ann Landers*, was published in October 2003 by William Morrow, Co. In 2006 his *A Chicago Tavern*, the history of the Billy Goat, was published by Lake Claremont Press, and Northwestern University Press published a collection of the "Sidewalks" columns he writes for the *Tribune* magazine, embellished by Charles Osgood's photographs.

PREFACE
LIBBY FISCHER HELLMANN

I HAVE A PROUSTIAN ASSOCIATION TO the Blues. Somewhere, someplace, a memory of the Blues must have seeded itself in my psyche, making me feel safe and secure and whole. When I hear the twang of a wailing guitar, the funky blues beat, or a harmonica riff, I feel like I'm home. I'm where I'm supposed to be.

Strange, given that the Blues are largely about loss and despair. I first experienced this *petite madeleine* soon after I moved to Chicago and discovered there's no better place in the world to hear the Blues. Whether it's Legends, Rosa's, Kingston Mines, BLUES, or even Bill's in Evanston, you know from the instant you hear that first chord that you're in for a ride. But it's a sobering one—you're listening to people tell you about the lover who did them wrong, trouble on the job, dreams that will never come true. In that sense, the Blues are the Noir of music. You know you're on a journey to a bitter end, but you don't want to stop.

Which is why, when Bleak House offered me the opportunity to edit a crime fiction anthology set in Chicago, I knew instantly it would be *Chicago Blues*. Brazen, urgent, unrepentant, and passionate, Chicago is the perfect backdrop to blend the noir of the Blues with the noir of crime fiction. The city's dark heritage is more than a cliché—it's a dramatic representation of the competing forces that define urban culture: good vs. bad, light vs. dark, crime vs. punishment. And when those forces are paired to the minor chords and sevenths of the Blues, the result is a match made in heaven with voices that come from hell.

Some of the twenty-one dark, edgy stories in *Chicago Blues* are about people who sing the Blues. Some are about people who have the Blues, and some are about people who wear the Blues. All of them are written by crime fiction authors whose Muses lurk in dark alleys, Lake Michigan, Lower Wacker, Lincoln Park, the "L," the South Side, even Wrigley Field.

But let them tell you in their own words.

"FIRST TIME I MET THE BLUES"

Edgar Award winner **STUART M. KAMINSKY** was named a Grandmaster by the Mystery Writers of America in 2007. He is the author of more than sixty-five mystery novels and sixty short stories, as well as five produced screenplays and television episodes. Kaminsky writes the Porfiry Rostnikov, Chicago detective Abe Lieberman, Lew Fonesca and Toby Peters mysteries. Although he lives in Sarasota now, Stuart was born in Chicago, "and my heart and soul remain there. Both my grandfathers got off the boat and headed straight for Chicago. We were as firmly planted on the West Side as ever a pilgrim was at Plymouth Rock. Were it possible, I would give serious consideration to being buried in the right field corner of Wrigley Field or the entrance to Navy Pier. In Chicago, I have personally known and been inspired by mob hit men, brave cops, corrupt politicians, Nobel Prize Winners, Chicago Cubs and Studs Terkel. Chicago is home."

WWW.STUARTKAMINSKY.COM

BLUE NOTE
STUART M. KAMINSKY

I WAS SITTING IN THE BLUE NOTE LOUNGE on Clark Street, just down the street from the Clark Theater. The Clark was the only place in town that had a new double feature every night, sometimes three features. I spent a lot of time in the dark at the Clark Theater, usually waiting for the Blue Note to open.

Maybe it was 1955 or 1957. I know it was winter. I was twenty-four or twenty-six. One of those. I may not remember the year, but I remember that night when I heard Count Basie and Joe Williams and Sonny Payne going wild for a fifteen minute drum solo.

My name? Pitch Noles. Behind that name was another, the one I was born with, Mitchell Nolowitz. I made my living gambling, but not your ordinary gambling.

I can hear the Count at his piano, lazily running his chubby, delicate fingers over the keys in that tiny, dark room. And that's Joe Williams inside my head belting a baritone, "Oh well. Oh well. Oh well." Keeping it up. "Oh well. Oh well. Oh well. Oh well."

Audience, most of them white, a few of them black, me in the middle with a Jewish, fight-promoter father and a beautiful black mother with a voice that could bring tears. They hadn't lived together since I was fourteen, but Izzy would call her every once in a while just to hear that voice.

Mae would be coming by later. She would touch my face and be waved up on the low platform by the Count and she would sing. She would turn any song into the blues. She did a "Don't Sit Under the Apple Tree," low tempo, deep voice, melancholy voice. Everyone went silent when Mae sang, everybody. Even Joe Williams closed his eyes and smiled when Mae sang. She wasn't Billie, Dinah, Ella or Sarah. She was Mae. She would be coming.

But now Joe was doing the singing, "Every Day I Have The Blues," and Mae hadn't made her appearance. People were moving their shoulders, dreamy or smiling; maybe both. Sonny Payne was drenched with sweat, his head turned at an angle as if listening to the now almost silent rapping of his own sticks against the taut skin. The blue light of the room quivered with wisps of smoke. I was at home.

I nursed a beer and wondered, with my genes, why I could appreciate music but couldn't carry a tune.

Then Terrance "Dusk" Oliver sat down and placed a book on the table, face down. He was compact, black, dressed in a $300 blue suit, a white shirt, and a red and blue silk paisley tie. He folded his hands on the table so I could clearly see his heavy silver skull-faced ring. I glanced at him. Dusk Oliver didn't look at me. His eyes were on Joe, but his soul, if he had one, which many doubted, was somewhere else.

When Joe finished and the Count decided on a break, I looked toward the entrance over the heads of the people seated at the tiny, round tables.

"She's delayed," said Dusk, his voice high, but don't let that fool you.

I looked at him slow, cool, blue in the Blue Note because Dusk Oliver was not a man to be questioned if you wanted to go through the rest of your life with both your ears and all your fingers.

"She'll be in, in …," he looked at his watch, "two minutes."

Terrance's face was round, unblemished, hair cut short, eyes tiny and dark. I wondered, as I had before, what he did for fun. I knew he had studied philosophy and literature at Howard University. He was one of the few people who had turned philosophy and poetry into a practical business asset.

"We sit," he said, "here in the Blue Note, at the epicenter of delusion in the middle of the twentieth century."

Dusk Oliver was always giving out epigrams and books he had read in the hope of finding someone with whom he could talk as an equal. This was a difficult quest since he did not move in the circles of the highly literate and curious. I, with two years at Wright Junior College, was about the best he could do.

A drink appeared in front of him. It dervished with little bubbles. Terrance looked at it and bit his lower lip.

"You know who James Mason is?" he asked.

"The actor, English," I said, not looking at the door but joining Terrance in his fascination with the glass of ginger ale.

"I'd like to meet him. That voice. I'd like to meet him. My bet is he read the fucking *Marble Faun*."

I nodded again. The possibility of James Mason having read Nathaniel Hawthorne opened no new areas of conversation for me.

"You see that movie where he slammed the piano cover down on that skinny blonde's fingers because she couldn't get the song right?"

There was a point to all this. I wasn't sure what it was and I didn't like what it might be.

"Saw it at the Clark," I said. "*The Seventh Veil*."

Dusk Oliver unclasped his fingers and pushed the book he had placed on the table toward me.

"*The Fountainhead*," he said. "Read it."

It was said softly, but it was an order. I took the book. It was hard to believe this educated numbers racketeer and supplier of street drugs with little patience for those who owed him money or homage had come to the Blue Note to give me a book.

There was a flurry near the door. Mae appeared. I knew it had been two minutes. I didn't have to look at my watch. If Dusk Oliver said my mother was coming through the door in two minutes, you didn't have to check your watch.

She nodded to a few people, wended her way through the tightly packed tables. She was wearing a black dress and something tight and glittery around her slim, brown neck. She was a beauty. No doubt. She came to my table, touched my cheek and looked briefly into my eyes with eyes like my own. She didn't look at Dusk. There was something soulful in her smile that said all was not well in the smoke-filled demi-darkness.

She turned and made her way around the small, low stage and through a dark curtain to the left.

"Beautiful lady," said Dusk.

I nodded again. Maybe I would spend the night nodding until Terrance decided to ask me a question or simply disappeared.

"She owes me," he said, inching toward the point and leaning toward me. "She is beautiful, misbegotten, a wisp, a waif, Cleopatra, a waft of gardenia freshness when she enters a room. Mae is a piece of work."

This time he paused and looked at me for a response.

"A piece of work," I agreed.

"Elegant."

"Elegant."

"Somewhere about six in the morning, that elegance will be marred by a missing finger," he said.

There was no sign of sympathy and I knew better than to look for one.

"Unless …," he went on.

"Unless?"

He looked at his watch again and said, "You go to a house in Hyde Park with ten thousand dollars of my money and sit in on a poker game. You walk out of that poker game with a minimum of forty thousand dollars by five in the morning. You get in a car that will be waiting, hand the driver the money and get a ride back home or wherever you want to go with half of everything you make over the forty thousand."

"And …?" I asked.

"Mae's debt is repaid," Terrance said.

It wasn't a request or a proposition. I was going to that game. Terrance was counting on my reputation. I was the Prince of the Tell, the Duke of the Giveaway. Some of it was conscious. Some of it was intuition that came from observation, a lot of it from my father. Once I picked twenty-three straight boxing matches correctly, both under- and overcards. I missed twenty-four because the guy I had picked suddenly got a pain in his stomach, doubled over and took a desperation left uppercut that broke his jaw.

I never bet more than a few hundred dollars on a fight and I never won more than a few thousand max at a poker table. I stayed below the lights. I liked Chicago, day or night. I haunted the Brookfield and Lincoln Park zoos, communing with the gorillas and chimps. Once in a while, I spent a night in a poker game with out-of-towners who saw a kid with a smile and more than ordinary luck. It had little to do with luck. Sometimes, much of the time, it had nothing to do with luck. When I wasn't going to Marigold or Soldier Field or the Coliseum for a fight night, or sitting in a hotel room or the back room of a bar on Elston or Division, I hit the Blues bars.

"When?" I asked.

"When Mae finishes," Dusk said.

Basie and the small traveling band came out one at a time and took their places. The audience kept talking.

Joe Williams didn't appear. The band settled itself and Mae entered—serious, beautiful, dark and smokey. She looked down, moistened her lips. The crowd went quiet.

She looked at me. I knew what she wanted. I couldn't turn her down. I couldn't refuse Dusk Oliver.

We listened to my mother sing "You Don't Know What Love Is," "St. Louis Blues," "Blues for a Lonesome Child" and more. I had the feeling that she didn't want the set to end.

Neither did the audience. Shaharazade in black and glitter putting off the inevitable.

Finally, she stopped and bowed. The audience went well beyond polite. The Count clapped his pudgy fingers and Mae came out for another bow, but no encore.

It was up to me.

"Let's go," Oliver said.

I sat with him in the back seat of a black Chrysler. The driver was alone in the front. I recognized him: Kelly "Two Punch" Jones, heavyweight, great black hope who started by being the man who could put away almost any man with two punches to the man who could be put away by almost anyone with two punches. He never developed even a three-punch combination. He went downhill fast. That was the pros. Now he had another profession and Two Punch was not to be trifled with by civilians.

Dusk took a bundle of bills out of the pocket of his chestnut camel hair coat, peeled off some of them, tucked them in my jacket pocket and handed me the rest.

"Put them away," he said. "Leave the book in the car."

I put *The Fountainhead* down.

We drove down Lake Shore Drive. The night was winter cold. Ankle high mounds of dirty snow ran along the curbing. Late night traffic was light, the windows were closed, Lake Michigan was quiet.

"Three players," Dusk said. "They think you're my nephew."

The family resemblance would best not be questioned.

"You don't know any of them. They don't know you. You walk up to the door by yourself, knock. Don't give your real name. No reason to. The players? Tall, skinny Negro pushing seventy years is Wallace Livingstone. Dapper. He's Elder. Some kind of doctor from Detroit. Been around Wheel City tables longer than double your life. First time in Chicago in twenty years or something. Second guy is younger, maybe fifty, white, bad skin, bad breath, thin hair brushed over. Name is Dunwoody. Nervous little guy. He plays with cash belonging to a New Orleans trucking union local of which he is both treasurer and recording secretary. And that brings us to the Russian. I don't like the guy. He fucking smirks."

Dusk paused as Two Punch made the turn at 53rd and headed west.

"The Russian's no Russian," said Dusk. "He's a Hungarian or something. Maybe not even that. Who cares where he came from. All three of them conned me into a game on Monday and took me for twenty thousand dollars and change. It was rigged. I want it back."

He paused, waiting for an answer to a question that hadn't been asked.

"With interest," I said.

"You know what Hank Sauer said? The only way to prove you're a good sport is to lose. I'm not a good sport."

I could see Dusk Oliver nod in minimal satisfaction as passing street lights flickered across his face.

"House belongs to a former alderman with bad habits. He gets one percent from every pot and makes himself invisible. The man with the gun who'll open the door for you is a cop.

I don't know his name. Don't care. He's there to keep out the unwelcome."

He sat back and said, "You'll like the book. We'll talk about it. We'll pick up some Jew hot dogs at Fluky's and talk about it."

Woodlawn south of 53rd was a line of stone and brick two- and three-story houses. Inside the houses dwelt the dwindling ranks of Hyde Park's old wealthy and the latest wave of University of Chicago administrators and better-paid professors. The wealthy and the educated locked their doors to keep out the poor and the uneducated Negro kids who lived five minutes away across the snow-covered Midway in Woodlawn to the south and the huddled ghetto of Kenwood to the north.

The whites and a few blacks who bolted the doors at night on Woodlawn Avenue honestly proclaimed their oneness with their banished, low-class neighbors. That didn't stop the comfortable but wary of Hyde Park from closing those doors.

Two Punch pulled up in front of a three-story white stone house on the right. There were no lights in the first floor windows. There was a light behind pulled drapes on the second floor.

Dusk reached past me and opened the door for me to get out.

"Two Punch will be back out here before five. Think about Mae's future, but don't let it get in the way of your play. I want what's due me kid."

I got out.

Before he closed the door, Dusk added, "Just imagine James Mason's voice telling you to be calm and concentrate and you'll be fine."

The door closed. The car pulled away and I spent no more than two seconds wondering how James Mason's voice was going to help me.

I patted the bills in my jacket pocket and the backup stack in my other pocket. Then I stepped over a knee-high pile of black snow, stepped in front of the door and used the heavy knocker.

A shadow flickered across the small glass peephole.

The door was opened by the cop, in slacks and a jacket with a tie that didn't come near matching anything either he or I was wearing. The tie was knotted clumsily to the left. It didn't matter. What did matter was his jacket was open enough to make his holstered gun clear.

He led me up a wooden stairway that creaked and, in one or two places, sagged. He didn't ask my name.

The cop with the gun opened a door, let me step in and then closed the door and stayed outside.

Handshakes and introductions all around. The thin, old doctor introduced as Elder, the jumpy New Orleans union fund thief Dunwoody and Serge, the Russian. I smiled. The doctor examined my face. The thief wanted to get started. The Russian, who wasn't a Russian, cocked his head to one side slightly to examine me. The Russian was about forty-five, lots of neatly brushed hair with gray sideburns and a salt-and-pepper, neatly trimmed beard.

An antique sideboard against the wall held a variety of alcoholic drinks and sandwiches. I was hungry and dry. I took a Goebel beer, used an opener, put two sandwiches of something that smelled like ham on a plate and took my seat at the table.

The other three: Wallace Livingtone the Elder on my left, Dunwoody on my right, and Serge the Russian across from me. I took the small stack of cash from my jacket with one hand and worked on a sandwich with the other. The Elder took my cash and expertly measured out five thousand in chips of red, white and blue.

The game was five-card stud. Period. One card dealt down and one card turned over for the first bet or fold. Then three more cards, betting on each card.

I started reading the table before the first card was dealt.

The Elder knew his tell. I could see it from the way he stayed erect, not blinking, hands as steady as he could hold them; but they threatened to betray him when the ante went in. The Russian was up for the deal. The Elder was struggling to keep away a tiny tremor. I wasn't sure what it meant. Dunwoody and the Russian hadn't paid any attention.

The Russian didn't say much, but what he did say was open for a tell. Sometimes he dropped his t's. Sometimes he didn't. Sometimes he pronounced his o's as u's. "Long" became "lung." His knowing smile was frozen, less knowing than a truly confident smirk.

The hardest one to read before that first card was dealt was Dunwoody. He kept talking, kept moving his hands, fidgeting; more moves than a third base coach. He didn't have a tell. He had dozens of them.

And then the cards came. We didn't start till almost one in the morning. Four hours wasn't much time.

I started by checking, folding or staying in only when I had a pair. I bet into players knowing I would lose, just to see what they would give away when they were sure to pretty certain they were going to win. Dunwoody always reached eagerly to look at his hole card. Then he would put the card down and tap it. The Elder held the hole card for no more than an instant, not even lifting it from the table, just peeling it back enough for a glimpse. The Russian held his card in front of his eyes, touched his nose, smiled, turned his card in a circle and placed it face down on the table.

By the time I was down by almost four thousand dollars, I could see how they were trying to hide every read. The tells took a while to spot. All three of them were good. I wasn't about to make any mistakes. I couldn't afford to. The clock was ticking toward Mae's fingers.

By the time it was almost three thirty I had a good idea of what kinds of hands each man played, how and when they bluffed. That left only luck of the draw, but even that could be overcome with smart bluffing.

The problem was that it can take time to wear down a player you could read who was drawing lucky and betting recklessly.

Dunwoody sometimes bet with no chance of winning on the table. The Elder came in hard when he had something, but came in just as hard about one hand in six when he had nothing. Sometimes he did it twice in a row. Sometimes he didn't do it for a dozen bad hands.

The Russian always bet to kill.

I was down to four hundred of the five thousand I'd put on the table, when I pulled out the backup stack of five thousand at four thirty.

I knew now that when he had something, the Elder let his hands rest lightly on the table, so lightly that they were almost not touching. When he had nothing, the hands came down just a touch heavier, maybe the width of a butterfly wing, but I saw it.

Dunwoody was down even more than I was. It wasn't his money any more than it was my money at stake. He had nothing to lose but other peoples' money and his arms if he got caught. He didn't go out till all was hopeless. If he had a good hand, that was the big tell. He ran his tongue gently along his upper teeth with his mouth almost closed. It was hard to spot, but it was there.

The Russian held his chips about half an inch higher when he bet with good cards.

My father had taught me that everybody has a tell—boxers, betters, bankers, every blind man and Catholic Bishop. Even if you cover your head and eyes, keep a stone face, keep your hands flat on the table and always count to exactly thirty-two before you bet or folded, something would give you away.

I started to win. Slow at first. I would have won less and a lot slower if I didn't know Dusk Oliver was probably sitting across a table from my mother somewhere, with a small but sharp garden pruning shears in his hand. By four fifteen I was almost fifteen thousand over the stake Dusk had given me. I passed the deal and gave up position so I wouldn't be accused of manipulating the cards.

"Lucky fuckin' ...," Dunwoody said.

Larry the Elder shrugged.

The Russian allowed himself a serviceable frown.

I was going to make it. Table rule was you could not quit when you were ahead until the last hand of any hour.

Then something went wrong. I started to lose and the Russian started to smile and I started to worry. I ate sandwiches. Nobody else did. I ate an egg salad, a ham salad and two shrimp salads, all on white, no crusts.

Dunwoody went bust at four thirty. The Elder bowed out a few minutes later, though he was almost even. I met the Russian's eyes and didn't like what I was seeing. Confidence.

I was still five thousand short of Dusk's demand with twenty minutes till five.

And then I knew. The Russian was reading me. He saw a tell. I thought mine were covered. They weren't.

Then it got even worse. The tells the Russian had been flashing for almost three hours disappeared. He had played me, probably the way he had played Dusk.

I lost four more hands going over my movements, finding nothing. Dunwoody and the Elder watched with interest. I was sure I hadn't been doing something I'd done before.

Then I got it. Big pot. Figured it out. Asked myself the question. Why did he wait so long to nail me? Answer: I was doing something now I hadn't done earlier in the game.

"Bet two thousand," the Russian said.

He had a Jack in the hole and a pair of Jacks. I had a pair of fours. It was almost five o'clock. Two Punch was parked in front of the house. *The Fountainhead* was lying on the back seat. In an hour, Mae would lose a finger. She wouldn't scream, wouldn't let herself make a sound, not Mae. It wouldn't kill her, but she would never be the same.

My right eye stung.

I didn't reach up to wipe perspiration away.

That's what was telling the Russian all he needed to know.

I bet a bad hand. He raised me.

It was a few minutes to five. I went to the drink table for a last sandwich and came back. I wasn't hungry but I ate.

I looked at my watch and the Russian said, "You half somewhere to go to?"

"Yes," I said. "To see my mother."

"At this hour?" asked the Russian.

"She works nights."

The cards were dealt. I had a nine in the hole. I bet it. The Russian raised. I stayed with him. He turned two spades, one a queen, one a king and then a third spade. I turned a second nine to match the hole nine I'd been dealt.

"Last hand?" the Russian asked.

"Looks that way," I said.

"Make this interestin' perhaps?"

I wiped my upper lip with the back of my hand and said, "Why not?"

"How much you wanting to bet?"

"Ten thousand," I said.

Dunwoody paused, a glass of watery Scotch almost to his lips. The Elder shook his head at the folly of the much younger generation.

"Ten thousand," the Russian agreed, stacking his chips in the center of the table.

"Cash?" I asked.

The Russian opened his palms to show he was a sporting man. I put in ten thousand dollars and the last card was turned over.

"Two nines," said the Russian, showing his hole card.

"Two tens," I said, showing mine.

I'll give the Russian this. He didn't break. I was sure he didn't understand, not yet. I had let him read my last tell, but it had been a sham. When I was getting my sandwich, I had palmed a small chunk of ice and brought it to the table. When the last game started, I touched my upper lip. It was moist when I had made my final bet. The Russian, meanwhile, overconfident, had inadvertently touched his thumb to his finger.

I pushed all the chips toward the Elder, who was the banker.

I didn't meet anyone's eyes. I half expected the door to open and the cop with the badly knotted tie to come in and say I wasn't leaving. Or maybe the Russian was going to reach into his jacket and come up with a sharp or explosive surprise.

But nothing happened. The Elder counted his remaining chips and handed me the cash. Dunwoody looked at the draped window and shook his head. The Russian waited for me to look up and nodded at me.

I forced myself to calmly gather and fold the bills before I said my good nights, thanked them all and escaped.

The car was waiting. It was ten minutes after five.

I got in the seat next to Two Punch and handed him the money. He turned on the dashboard light and slowly counted.

"Forty thousand, six hundred and ten," he said looking at me.

"If you say so," I agreed. "Let's go."

We got to Dusk Oliver's current headquarters, the Rib Emporium on 82nd Street, at ten minutes to six. The sweet smell of barbecue sauce made me wish I hadn't eaten all those sandwiches. The place was dark. Two Punch had a key. I followed him in, trying not to stumble in the dark as we went through a door in the rear of the restaurant.

Dusk was seated at a table in the small kitchen, an iced tea clinking in front of him. Two Punch handed him the money. Dusk stacked it neatly in front of him.

"It's a good feeling to get back at those who cheat you," he said.

I nodded.

No one had cheated Dusk Oliver; not the Elder, not Dunwoody, not the Russian. No one had cheated at the table for the four hours I had played. I had seen Dusk play poker.

The Russian in an all night game could have taken Dusk without cheating. No contest. Dusk's high opinion of his skill was not merited.

I said nothing.

He pushed a pile of bills in my direction. I took them.

"You think I'd really cut off one of Mae's fingers?"

"Yes," I said.

"Yes," he said. "You're right. I would have. Consider her debts canceled."

I knew Mae's debts would start up again in a day or two. Not owing money to a dealer didn't get you to suddenly quit taking. If anything, it gave the taker a breather and the feeling he or she could start over, that they had bought time. Dusk Oliver was a lousy poker player but a smart drug dealer. He understood.

"Don't forget the book," he said.

"I won't."

"Two Punch has a big bucket of ribs and chicken for you. Julius doesn't sell day-old."

"Is it Christmas?" I asked.

"Don't be a smart-ass. You look into the mouth of a gift horse and you're liable to get your dick bitten off."

The metaphor was mixed but it could turn into a reality if I didn't shut up.

"We'll do more business now," he said.

Nothing to say.

The Blue Note was closed for the morning. The sun was coming out. Two Punch dropped me at Stella's on Diversey Avenue just off of Western. I recognized all four of the musicians playing. Three were black, one was a redheaded white kid with a cigarette dangling from the side of his mouth and burning his eyes. The redheaded kid was a music student at Northwestern. He was coaxing the guitar on his lap. They were playing "Blue and Sentimental."

Five people, all male except for my mother, were seated on folding chairs, listening, smoking, wandering into a back room to take something for the edge, something to bring on the dreams and hold back the nightmares. I laid out my tribute, a bucket of chicken.

Mae's legs were crossed. She looked up at me. I nodded. She understood. Her fingers were safe for a while. Why didn't she look tired? Bored maybe, but not tired. I sat next to her and listened to the music. She touched my hand.

"Thanks," she said.

And then the song stopped and without being told or invited, Mae walked forward and started to sing. I had never figured it out. I wasn't a musician. If there was a tell, I never spotted it. Musicians like my mother and the Count didn't need words. They knew what to play, what to sing. Two notes, just two notes from Mae, were enough for the musicians to start.

"I'll never smile again," Mae sang, almost just spoke, looking at her hands.

Then she looked at me and the sad voice of my mother sang, "Until I smile at you."

I felt rather than saw someone sit in the chair Mae had vacated. I didn't look but I sensed and then was sure.

"She is good," the Russian whispered.

"She's the best," I answered.

"Dunwoody knew someone who knew where I'd find you. He knew who you were when you sat down at the table with us."

Nothing to say, at least not on my part.

"You gave it all to Oliver?"

"All," I said, which was true though he had given some of it back to me.

"I couldn't leave this dark and glorious city without letting you know."

"Part of the game," I said. "Sometimes when it's over, going over the game is the best part."

We both looked at and listened to Mae. Before she started "Love for Sale," the Russian stood.

"Ice on the upper lip," he said. "You must have been desperate."

"Lady singing is my mother. Dusk said he was going to be unkind to her at six if I didn't win."

"I know. We knew it when you sat down."

"You let me win," I said.

It wasn't a question.

"Leaving the game ahead of Mr. Oliver seemed like a bad bet," said the Russian. "He is obviously a very bad loser. We didn't know how bad a loser he could be until after we took him for the twenty thousand and people let us know. Letting him have his money back with a little interest seemed like a good idea. Letting him think he had taken us seemed like an even better idea. Never again sitting down with him is the best idea of all."

The Russian reached over and offered his hand. I took it.

"If you're ever in Dallas, look me up. Marty O'Brien. Leave a message at the Texas Independence Restaurant."

"I will," I said.

"I look forward to playing you Even Steven across the table, Pitch Noles."

"Me too, Marty O'Brien."

Then he was gone and I settled back. I should have been in bed sleeping, but I was young and Mae was singing and this moment would be gone. I wanted to hold onto it for a while, at least till the sun came up.

I'd get around to reading *The Fountainhead*, but not for a while.

END

Published in more than fifteen languages, **KEVIN GUILFOILE'S** debut thriller, *Cast of Shadows*, has been called "gripping" by the *New York Times*, "a masterpiece of intelligent plotting" by Salon.com, and was named one of the "Best Books of 2005" by the *Chicago Tribune* and the *Kansas City Star*. He lives in La Grange, Illinois with his wife Mo, and their sons Max and Vaughn. About Chicago, Kevin says, "I write about Chicago for the same reasons I choose to live here: I love the people, I love the history, I love the sense of place in every neighborhood, and I love the way Chicago's lakeside skyline is a testament both to human resilience and to the beauty man can create."

WWW.GUILFOILE.NET

O DEATH WHERE IS THY STING?
KEVIN GUILFOILE

YOU ASKED WHAT KIND OF RECORD could be worth killing someone for, and if you were smarter you would know the answer is an old blues record. A mythical, pre-war, American blues record. A mythical, pre-war, American blues record by a Mississippi cook named Jimmie Kane Baldwin who had a scar from throat to ear and three fingers on his left hand. You've never heard of him and I can't even prove he existed, but I've spent some part of every day of the last thirty years thinking about him.

Is there anyone you think about every day? Besides your mother? Not that my mother ever thought much of me. And all because of a round piece of black wax.

Nobody ever killed nobody over a damn CD.

See, twenty years ago almost every house had dozens, and sometimes hundreds, of obsolete vinyl records stacked up in basement rec rooms like fossils in layers of shale. All I had to do was knock on the door and offer to haul them away. If the owner looked savvy, sometimes I'd pay a couple bucks—maybe five dollars for a hundred—but most people just wanted them gone. If they were pop or disco albums, or *showtunes*, I threw those away. But frequently I'd find a minor treasure, which I slid into a plastic sleeve and brought home.

Collecting isn't about buying a record that some store clerk's set out on a rack. Any record somebody else wants you to have isn't worth having. Collectors are *explorers*—Balboas and Vasco da Gamas. We're looking for lost Mayan gold. A record others don't even know exists. Or, like Ponce de Leon and the Fountain of Youth, a record other collectors don't *believe* exists. That was what Jimmie Kane Baldwin represented. Hell, if you had asked me twenty years ago for the odds of finding Jimmie Kane Baldwin's voice—or *guitar*—on an actual vinyl record, I'd have told you it would be like finding proof of Bigfoot in the middle of a snuff film.

And Jimmie Kane could play guitar, too. Lordy how they said that three-fingered sonofabitch could play guitar.

So December, 1987. There'd been some Thanksgiving snow followed by a mild thaw and there were just patches of the stuff around—dirty drifts of rock-hard crystals pushed up to the ends of driveways and curbs. I'd stopped cold-calling on houses and by this time I was relying on tips. I'd given my cable guy an extra fifty and told him if he was ever in a house with records lying around he should call me. This particular week he'd phoned with word of a mother lode. An old lady who had no idea what she was sitting on inside her little Hyde Park apartment. *Easy pickings*. That Saturday I drove my Subaru down the LSD from Edgewater, parked over by the museum and went to the brick six-flat matching the address.

The name H. Walker was label-makered next to the buzzer, and I rang but she wasn't there. I hoped she was just at the Jewel around the corner, so I walked four blocks to Blues Island Records, which was owned by an arrogant prick named Paul. For a few minutes I looked around the stacks—all of which might have been interesting stuff to a newbie—with Paul following steps behind. He asked if I was out scavenging and I lied and said *no, don't do that anymore, just browsing,* and behind the counter he had this black-and-white television tuned to WGN and they were predicting a storm in a couple days. Maybe a foot or more. I thought to myself, *good.* I could use a snow day. Teenagers were driving me crazy.

I left the store and walked back to the old lady and her mother lode, and this time she was there. I told her I was interested in records and, maybe because I was wearing a nice shirt and a teacher's tie, she invited me in. She was seventy or so. Round in the middle with wattle in the neck and fat under the arms. Lonely. Loved to talk. Just had her hair blued. She waved me to one wall of her living room and backed into the kitchen to make some tea.

Then I turned to the piles of records and tried to make sense of what I saw.

Thousands of discs lined up across shelves and stacked neatly on one of those ancient console entertainment centers with built-in RCA phonograph and television. Good records. *Christ,* great ones. Robert Johnson's *Sweet Home Chicago.* Early Marion Abernathy. Original *Stack O'Lee Blues* by the Down Home Boys. Hundreds of rare records, all in excellent condition. I didn't think undiscovered stashes like this still existed. And I felt for my wallet because I wasn't sure I had even a hundred bucks on me—this was not a collection that anyone, even a clueless old lady from Hyde Park, would let me walk away with for nothing. This was *auction* material. Library of Congress stuff.

I started to wonder how much of it could even fit in my car.

She came from the kitchen with two cups of hot tea and I wore my poker face, trying not to let her know what she had. I was easing the jackets out with fingers at the corners, adding their value in my head, and the old lady was prattling on about her husband (dead since the seventies) and her son who lives in Mesa, Arizona where the Cubs go each year for spring training.

I tried to listen, I did.

It was the best private collection I'd ever seen, even better than mine, and that was before I found it. I found it and it sucked the breath from my lungs, as sure as if you had just punched me in the chest.

It was in a brown paper sleeve with a hole in the center revealing a plain, white and red label with the legendary Cicero Records logo and the famous Cicero motto: *Nature herself makes the wise man rich.* There was no song title or artist printed on the label, but someone had scribbled across it in pencil, "DEATH NO. 2." Beneath that word were three initials, "JKB."

Now I'd memorized a description of this label and I'd probably seen a half-dozen fakes. Back in the 70s a fellow tried pressing a record of what was *supposed* to be Jimmie Kane Baldwin's *Death Where Is Thy Sting*, but even to the ears of a non-expert it was obviously inauthentic. Too slick. And the screams the counterfeiter added to the track weren't any more realistic than haunted house sound effects.

That's what I said. *Screams*. Sorry, I didn't mean to leave that out, but this is the kind of story that gets released in a slow leak. There are just too many whos, whats, wheres, whys, and hows. See, the thing that makes this record so *mythical*, so extraordinary, the reason it's obsessed blues fans for seventy-odd years, is that between the chords and the notes, between the words and the grunts, between the guitar and the piano, between the chorus and the bridge, it allegedly contained the sound—the *screams*—of a woman being murdered.

Let me back up. In August of 1938, Jimmie Kane Baldwin walked into the offices of Cicero Records—down by where Midway Airport is now—and demanded an audition. He had no money to make a vanity record, and like I said, he only had three fingers on his fret hand. But Cicero had already made a star or two out of walk-ins and that was part of their reputation, so Marvin Pounder, the sound engineer, asked Jimmie to play a few bars in the lobby. Just for grins. Marvin didn't let Jimmie pick for more than half a minute before he brought in Irving Dunn.

Dunn was the infamous president and founder of Cicero Records—as well-known for turning poor black musicians into household names as he was for stealing their royalties. Dunn sat down and allowed Jimmie to play his song all the way through. Jimmie had written it himself and as he played, Dunn and Pounder knew they were in the presence of genius. Pounder would say years later that he had goosebumps listening to Jimmie play. *This is what it must have been like to discover Robert Johnson. Or Son House,* he said.

They even whispered that Jimmie might be possessed by Johnson's ghost, who had died at a crossroads in Greenwood, Mississippi just days before.

They recorded Jimmie that very day. Dunn wanted to release the record before the summer was out. He was already on the phone boasting about his latest discovery while Pounder arranged things in the studio with a couple Cicero regulars called in to back Jimmie up on piano and horn.

And Jimmie Kane was in a hurry, too. See what Jimmie hadn't told anybody—*and why would he?*—was that he had traveled all the way to Chicago to make this record because he was wanted in Lafayette County, Mississippi for the murder of his girlfriend, Betty Sharper, whom Jimmie Kane had stabbed thirty-seven times in the chest. Apparently he hoped his song would be worth a few hundred dollars cash, which he could use to start a new life under a new name.

Oh, and Jimmie Kane killed his girlfriend on the very day Robert Johnson died.

Pounder once gave an interview to *Rolling Stone* and he claimed that during the actual recording session he heard nothing unusual. Jimmie and his ad hoc band played the song four times and Marvin thought the last take was acceptable. Jimmie was itching to leave, but Irving Dunn was taking his time pulling the cash from his safe or the bank or wherever he needed to get it, while some other functionary prepared the boilerplate stripping Jimmie of any future rights to the recording, so Jimmie stuck around and listened as Marvin pulled the master disc and played back *Death Where Is Thy Sting* for the first time.

That's when things got spooky.

The screams began at the end of the first verse, like she was joining in early for the chorus. Jimmie glanced at the others; he seemed just as confused as they were. At first Pounder thought it must have been a radio that had bled through the walls into his session. He cued the discs from the other takes. On each one, the wailing began on the same beat.

They listened twice more. They heard screams of pain. Horror. Betrayal. The intensity increased to about the midway point of the song and then diminished into moans and sobs and wheezes. The last thing you could hear on each recording, in the repeating silence after the final note, was a long, ghostly gasp.

Jimmie, at first stunned into quiet, became agitated while the Cicero men searched for the origin of the sound. Marvin was just about out of theories when Jimmie suddenly began to whisper *Betty Betty Betty* over and over. Marvin asked who Betty was, but he just kept repeating *Betty Betty Betty* and then he was pacing the room and then he was crying and he had his hands to his head shouting *Betty! Betty! Betty!* He called this Betty a witch and a ghost and a whore, and Marvin sent for Chesterfields and whiskey to calm Jimmie Kane down but he wouldn't have any of it and he lunged for one of the masters and he smashed it against the wall and he called her again a ghost and a whore and then he grabbed his guitar and ran out onto Cicero Avenue—and as far as Blues aficionados are concerned, that was the last time anyone ever saw Jimmie Kane Baldwin.

They had three masters remaining, including one of the final take, and Marvin played them for Irving Dunn. The boss was furious. The recording was unreleasable. He ordered Marvin to check for Jimmie in every Chicago flophouse and men's hotel that would take negroes, and stormed from the room. Marvin kept the best master and the broken pieces of the one Jimmie destroyed, and the other musicians each took one of the other masters as a memento of the oddest, eeriest day of their professional lives.

Within a week the piano player and the trumpeter were both dead. One from too much morphine; the other either fell or jumped from a roof onto State Street. Marvin thought it was the record that drove them mad. That it was cursed. Possessed. He was sure they'd listened again to the recording—perhaps even again and again—just as he had been tempted to do but never had done. Only the nine times he heard it in the studio. So Marvin destroyed his copy and tried to track down the other masters from the musicians' widows, but they didn't know what he was talking about.

You're skeptical, I can see, but I also see that tiny Bible next to your bunk. Let's just say that for me, this too was a matter of faith.

So I tried to be casual and I slid the world's most priceless record carefully back into the stack, about six places from where I found it, and I told Mrs. Walker there wasn't much of value but I'd be happy to haul it away and I might even be able to get her a few bucks for the more popular albums. At first I thought she was going for it, but before she agreed she started telling me a story about her husband that went on for twenty minutes or more without any insight into how he obtained this holy relic, and then I tried to bring the conversation back to the records and she said *Oh yes* and then told another story and finally I said I really have to be going *but about these records* and she said if it were up to her I could have them for nothing but she needed to check with her son in Mesa before she gave any of his father's things away. She would call him that night and I should come back the next day, Sunday. After mass.

I don't have to tell you I didn't sleep that night.

I returned the next day and parked across the street from Blues Island and walked over to Mrs. Walker's apartment. She had tea made and some pastries she'd brought home from a church sale, and I listened to three or four stories about her dead husband, my eyes always going back to that little corner of brown paper protruding from the stacks, and when I thought

I had pretended long enough to be her tea cookie companion, I brought up the records again. *Oh yes*, she said. She spoke with her son but she forgot to ask about the records. She would call him again tonight and I should come back again tomorrow. Monday.

Another night of no sleep.

I called in sick to Senn High School and helped arrange for a substitute to teach my history class. I put on my tie and drove to Hyde Park through the weekday traffic. I didn't get there until about ten AM but I found a spot on Mrs. Walker's street. She buzzed me in and when I stepped over her threshold I felt lead drop into my stomach. Thirty pounds of it at the bottom of my belly. Lead Belly. *Ha.* That was me.

Sitting in Mrs. Walker's living room, three feet from the precious wax I had hidden between lesser records, was Paul DeGregorio from Blues Island. And he was grinning at me like a Maine Coon that had just downed a whole box of chocolate-covered canaries.

Yes, *that* Paul DeGregorio. Around here they call him the *Cold One*. Just last week you asked me what it meant that every time he passed us in the yard I flashed all ten of my fingers at him. Like this. I had been coy then, but you're in luck because that too is part of the story of *Death Where is Thy Sting*.

And what's that? That phrase sounds familiar? It should be to a man who's found God as you have. *Behold, I tell a mystery. We shall not fall asleep, but we will all be changed, in an instant, in the blink of an eye, at the last trumpet. For the trumpet will sound, the dead will be raised incorruptible and we shall be changed. O death where is thy victory? O death where is thy sting?* First Corinthians. By saving us, Jesus Christ has removed the sting of death, which is our sin.

Wishful thinking on Jimmie Kane's part, don't you think?

Now, you've seen the Cold One when he's studying someone intensely, and he was doing it to me that day and I was trying my best not to look at the records. Mrs. Walker said, "Paul's interested in old music, too." And she sat down with a story about her husband working as a precinct captain in the 18th Ward and what a saint that Mayor Daley was, how good he had been to their family, although she had also grown fond of Harold Washington who lived nearby, and what a shame it was about his sudden death last month—*The city's at a crossroads, don't you think?*—and Paul and I were just staring at each other and I was scowling and he was still grinning even though I still wasn't sure if he even knew about the Jimmie Kane yet.

When Mrs. Walker went to the kitchen, I leaned forward and asked him what he was doing here, and he laughed and said the day before he saw me pull up to the curb across from his shop and thought I must be up to something if I was in the neighborhood two days in a row, and so he'd followed me to Mrs. Walker's house and after I'd left he'd buzzed up and introduced himself. The old lady said I was coming back the next day and she invited Paul to come join us.

Wasn't that sweet?

So I tried to look a little disappointed and I said okay, let's split them. Fifty-fifty. He said fine, so long as he got to pick first and I said no way, and that's when we both knew that we both knew and Paul kicked a brass coffee table leg and whispered, "Jimmie Kane Goddamn Baldwin!" and he pointed at me and said, "You sonofabitch!" like I had done something wrong, and I called him a poacher and a parasite and then Mrs. Walker came back in with the tea and we shut up fast.

"I'm afraid my son said he'd have to sleep on it," Mrs. Walker said. "You'll have to return tomorrow." She started another story.

And here's where Paul and I faced identical dilemmas.

You see I wasn't going to leave before him. And he wasn't going to leave before me. So the old lady kept talking and we kept waiting for her to hand us our coats and walk us to the door. But she never did. She just kept talking and talking.

Her son never called.

Around one o'clock she made sandwiches. At six she made dinner. We ate and listened. Around nine she passed out on the couch.

While she slept we tried to come to an arrangement. Shared ownership. Joint custody. But neither of us found these acceptable. You don't collect just to possess something. You collect to keep others from having it. Like a woman, a record is only worth having if it's yours alone. I wanted to own *Death Where Is Thy Sting* and I wanted others to envy me for it.

I wanted Paul DeGregorio especially to envy me for it.

So we stayed, slouching in our chairs, afraid to fall asleep, talking in whispers about the legend of Jimmie Kane Baldwin. How neither of us had ever really believed and yet here we were, up all night, refusing to leave, not giving in.

We both agreed we must be fools.

So foolish in fact that around three AM we realized we hadn't even tried to listen to it. He nodded and I took the record gently from its sleeve, my thumb at the edge and my fingers on the label like a waitress balancing a tray of drinks. Watching me carefully, Paul opened the old record player, set the speed for 78 RPM and took *Death Where Is Thy Sting* into his hands. We distrusted one another completely, but we each knew the other would take care of the record.

Paul dropped it down the spindle and I watched it turn with a shiver. He checked the volume so we wouldn't wake Mrs. Walker, lifted the tonearm and began to bring the stylus down on the opening groove.

Then I shrieked, "Wait!" Way too loud.

We both turned to the couch. Mrs. Walker hadn't moved.

"There's no needle!" I told him. "The stylus is broken."

We could hold it in our hands, make our eyes follow the long, magical groove, but we couldn't listen to *Death Where Is Thy Sting.*

I returned it to the shelf. He turned his back and I think Paul started to cry.

The next morning Mrs. Walker woke up and seemed unsurprised to find us still there. She changed clothes and made eggs and told us more about her dead husband. I called in sick but there wasn't any answer at the school. That was when I looked out the front room window.

The storm had dropped at least four inches of snow overnight and it was still coming down in a fury. Big flakes falling at tremendous speed. The street below hadn't been plowed. Every parked car was buried, which didn't matter because we weren't going anywhere.

Mrs. Walker didn't seem to mind.

"You boys love music," she said. "My husband's brother was a musician. He called himself a bugler, but the trumpet was his instrument." Paul and I looked at each other and nodded. That must have been it. Her brother-in-law was the Cicero session player who had sat in on *Death Where Is Thy Sting.* Over the hours she told many stories about her musical brother-in-law and how he used to play at the old Bismarck on Randolph, but nothing about Jimmie Kane Baldwin and nothing about the unfortunate way in which her brother-in-law had thrown himself off a State Street roof.

The snow kept falling and by midday it was also sleeting and thundering—big, booming blasts of winter thunder that shook the whole building. There would be ten heavy inches on the ground by dinnertime, enough of it to take down phone lines all over the South Side, and so the son never called and at night we were in the same predicament as the day before, with the old lady asleep on the couch and Paul and I each afraid to shut our eyes for fear the other guy would grab the record and run.

I hadn't slept in more than four days, but I couldn't even linger on a blink.

As a teacher I had mastered something I called the Study Hall Snooze. It was a meditative technique where I could achieve a resting state without closing my eyes. My heart rate slowed. Unnecessary parts of my brain dimmed. Sometimes I even dreamed. But I never lost awareness of my surroundings. It was no substitute for sleep but it helped me through long days at Senn.

When I hadn't said anything for an hour, Paul sensed weakness. He stood up in front of me. Whispered my name. Did a silly jig. I watched it all but didn't react. He inched over to the bookshelves and knelt down before the record and eased it into his hands. He didn't move for a long time as he carefully assessed my condition, Mrs. Walker's snoring from the couch, and the distance between him and the front door.

He decided to make a break for it without his parka.

I was up in an instant and my left hand beat him to the door, holding it shut before he could undo the deadbolt.

"Where are you going with that?" I said. "You know I'll just tell Mrs. Walker you stole it. She'll call the cops."

"I have to listen to it," Paul said. "I was coming back."

"No," I said.

"I'll be back in an hour."

"No."

He sighed. "Come with me."

"What?"

"To the store. Come with me to the store. We'll listen. We'll bring it back. Then we'll sort all this out with the old lady and her son."

"That's crazy."

"You want to hear it as bad as I do."

I said, "Do you believe what Pounder said? That listening to it makes you insane?"

He said, "*Not* listening to it is making us insane. Marvin Pounder listened nine times and nothing happened to him."

I nodded. "We listen once."

We found Mrs. Walker's keys and put on our coats and borrowed a plastic garbage bag to protect the record and we crept down the stairs, out into the snow. Paul was carrying it but I was so seduced by the thought of finally hearing *Death Where Is Thy Sting* that I didn't protest. I was already imagining what the first chords would be like. The anticipation of Betty's first scream. Jimmie's voice beginning the chorus, unaware that a supernatural agony had possessed Marvin Pounder's studio lathe and was inscribing itself onto his legacy.

So enraptured, in fact, that I didn't notice when Paul took off running down the deserted middle of the street.

It was a pathetic, winter kind of run, hands far out to his sides for balance, sneakers unsure in the unplowed slush. I broke after him, but my footing was no better and after ten yards I was face down in the ice. Before I could catch him, Paul would be holed up inside Blues Island with Jimmie Kane Baldwin and Mrs. Walker's keys. I could call the police, but what would I say? He hadn't taken anything of mine. And Mrs. Walker probably wouldn't even know the record was missing.

She probably wouldn't even remember us.

Frustrated, I stood up and launched a hastily packed snowball in his direction, missing him by body lengths. I threw another one. Another miss. I heard Paul laugh. I made a third of mostly ice, the anger like a drum in my chest, and threw it as hard as I could.

I missed again. But this iceball hit a Volvo parked just to Paul's right. And back then, if you remember, you hardly had to blow on a car alarm to set it off.

The Volvo lit up like the Sox park scoreboard—*Whoop! Whoop! Ah-naaaah! Ah-naaah!* Startled by the noise, Paul's arms flew over his head and the bag with the record skidded behind him as he fell. I raced ahead, slipping in every direction, and I dropped on it like Richard Dent on a loose ball, my wet body curled around the bag as Paul sloshed toward me and the epithets from neighborhood windows rained down.

"Is it okay?" Paul asked without apology.

I nodded.

"You sonofabitch," he said.

I stood and walked back toward the six-flat. "We're going to wait for Mrs. Walker's son to call."

Paul followed. He said, "What if you don't have to listen? What if just touching it makes you insane? What if it killed Mr. Walker, too?" Seconds later he scowled, "You're going to fall asleep soon, and when you do Jimmie Kane and I will be long gone."

Drying out in the living room we quietly threw trivia at one another the way soldiers fire mortars, each question designed to wound. He challenged me to name five songs with B.B. King's name in the title ("The Day I Met B.B. King" by Louisiana Red, "B.B. King and Jesus" by the B-Team Blues Band) and we argued for two hours about whether "B.B. King Intro," the first track on the *Live at San Quentin* LP, should qualify. I swear if there had been a gun in the room the murder would have happened then and not the next day.

Yeah, the *murder*. I'm getting to that.

I remember it was mid-morning on Thursday and I must have been taking another Study Hall Snooze, but suddenly he was standing over me and he had this weird look in his eyes and he just said, "She's dead." I was a little disoriented and I actually asked, "Who?" And then he motioned to the couch and sure enough Mrs. Walker wasn't breathing. No pulse. Nothing but carbon behind her open eyes. No person. No mother. No widow. Just shuttered capillaries and bones. A bag of lifeless blood and pus and shriveling lungs and undiscovered tumors that would have killed her one day if she hadn't been killed then. I knew it hadn't been natural causes. I knew that Paul DeGregorio—the *Cold One*—was no longer certain he could outlast me and decided to kick Mrs. Walker out of our trio. He must have taken a pillow and pressed it over her sleeping face and, when I didn't stop him because my mind was on a delirious daydream miles away, he kept pressing harder and harder and she must have struggled some. I bet she beat his arms and kicked him up and down as best as her weak legs could manage. I'm sure he felt her face twitching behind the pillow, perhaps even saw her death mask pressed through the fabric, but he showed her no mercy and he didn't stop pressing until she was dead.

And now there was just me to deal with.

The phones were still out so we couldn't call the police even if we wanted. I never could have explained to the cops what I'd been doing during the murder. I wouldn't be able to say why I hadn't stopped it. Then old Jimmie Kane would just be handed over to the son, who hadn't cared enough about these precious artifacts to even call his mother when she was alive. I owed it to history to make sure that *Death Where Is Thy Sting* never fell into the hands of an ignorant sonofabitch, and by that I meant Paul DeGregorio as well as Mrs. Walker's son in Arizona.

The old lady didn't smell like Carolina peaches when she was alive and her corpse was fouling the sealed apartment by the minute. Around midnight Paul and I dragged her body into the bathtub and we walked down the back steps, quietly across her neighbor's junk-strewn porches, and hauled up buckets of snow, packing her body tight into her cast-iron coffin. Then we emptied bottles of perfume and air freshener into the front room. We were doubly exhausted, *triply exhausted*. We could hardly move.

They would be coming now. Friends. Neighbors. Cops. Landlords. Someone would be coming to check on Mrs. Walker and we couldn't be here when they did.

So I knew an escalation was inevitable. Nevertheless, I let Paul strike the first blow.

He'd taken an empty pot from the stove and swung it at my temple. But at this point he was barely strong enough to elicit a musical clang from the collision. I pulled myself up to the coffee table and tried to get my fingers around a huge gardening book, but I was either too weak to lift it or years of immobility had naturally adhered it to the glass underneath. Paul took another slow-motion swing with the pot that I managed to just avoid, but with gravity's help he was able to create enough force to smash the coffee table into bits. A fortuitous event because now, just beside my head, was a long glass shard, so sharp that even I wasn't too weakened to press it into the flesh of another man's neck.

I turned on Paul and swung my arm. He threw up his hands and exhaled, the sharp edge of the glass missing his belly by inches. At just that moment the snow thunder started again, exploding like a bomb above the building. I felt the vibrations in my teeth and the impact sent me back on my heels as Paul advanced with the pot. He swung it once against my temple, twisting my head hard into the mantel of the fake fireplace. I dropped to the hardwood and Paul was on me again, hitting me once, twice, three times, and now he had adrenaline pumping through him and the impacts were more painful.

They say your life flashes before your eyes when you know you're going to die. That didn't happen to me. The only thing flashing through my mind was that shitty back room at Blues Island with posters of young Buddy Guy pinned next to centerfolds of some long ago Miss September, and Paul hunched over his Bang and Olufsen turntable—which cost as much as his car—and on his head were those padded Koss headphones which would have been adequate protection in a Harley accident and although I'd never actually heard it for real, I swear in that moment I could hear Jimmie Kane Baldwin on guitar, and Mrs. Walker's brother-in-law on trumpet, and Miss Betty Sharper on screams, and although my body would have been perfectly happy to give in, I repeated to myself that I had a duty to history and as his hand came down for what he must have thought was the killing blow, I reached up and stabbed Paul in the meat of the forearm. He yelped and the pot clanged to the floor and Paul fell backward onto hardwood, shrieking obscenities and nonsense.

And we both rested.

The police arrived about two hours later, led by the landlord and tailed by Mrs. Walker's son.

He was a pitiable man. Not at all sorry his mother was dead. But as the police handcuffed me and knocked my swollen, bleeding head against the fireplace tile, I could see guilt in his shaking knees; in the way he washed his hands repeatedly in the kitchen sink; in the way he refused to look at his mother's body for more than an instant; in the way he'd abandoned her to a life alone; in the way he'd abandoned his inheritance, these precious circles of wax.

Paul told them I had killed Mrs. Walker and then tried to kill him. I, of course, told them the opposite. Neither of us hinted at motive. It seems Mrs. Walker had lied to us. She had never asked her son about the records and so he had no idea who we were or why we were there. The papers figured out we were collectors and gathered that we must have killed for her husband's collection, but there would be no mention of Jimmie Kane Baldwin. We both went to trial for her murder and since neither the judge nor the jury nor even the prosecutor could divine the truth, we received identical sentences for second-degree murder and attempted burglary.

Thirty-five years.

Of course they empty this place every time the state blows its budget, and after two decades of good behavior it happens to be our turn. But because of that incident in the yard last month between Paul and the skinhead one cell over, I'll be getting out ten days before him.

Paul thinks I had something to do with it. That I paid our Aryan neighbor or did him some favor so he'd provoke Paul. Put a blemish on his record. Whatever.

This time next week I'll be on a bus to Mesa, Arizona. With a ten-day head start. Just ten days between us after more than twenty years.

I've used all this time inside to imagine what will happen when I get to Mesa. To consider every angle. How to find Mrs. Walker's son. How to find out if he still has the record. How to find who has it if he doesn't. Everything I need to get that recording after being so, so close in that apartment all those years ago. Before Paul walked through the door and screwed everything up.

And when I get it I'm going to listen to it only once and never again. Owning it will be so much more important than *hearing* it. Nevertheless, I'm going to savor those three minutes, alone with that record, savor the expert playing of Jimmie Kane Baldwin and the trumpet horn of Mrs. Walker's relation and the exquisite cries of Miss Betty Sharper and after it's told me every one of its secrets, I'm going to wait for Paul DeGregorio, who sure as shinola will be on the same bus exactly ten days behind me. And with plugs in my ears and a gun to his head, I'll make that ignorant sonofabitch listen to it again and again and again and again.

As many times as it takes.

I have an obligation to history, after all.

END

LIBBY FISCHER HELLMANN, editor of *Chicago Blues*, writes the award-winning Ellie Foreman series. She has been nominated for an Agatha, two Anthonys, and has won the Lovie three times. A transplant from Washington DC, she says of Chicago, "They'll take me out of here feet-first. Chicago is a city that's made for dark crime fiction—with real corruption, real graft, real rackets. And it's been this way over a hundred years. I'm proud to honor that tradition."

WWW.HELLMANN.COM

YOUR SWEET MAN
LIBBY FISCHER HELLMANN

"Who's gonna be your sweet man when I'm gone?
Who you gonna have to love you?"
—Muddy Waters

1982: CHICAGO

CALVIN WAITED FOR THE MAN WHO'D been convicted of killing his mother. Outside Joliet prison the July heat seared his spirit, leaving it as bare and desiccated as a sun-bleached bone. Sweat ringed his arm pits, grit coated the back of his neck. Almost noon, and not a shadow on anything.

He extracted a Lucky from the crumpled pack on the dash and leaned forward to light it. The '74 Chevy Caprice never failed to start up. As long as he kept enough fluid in the radiator, the engine ate up the highway without complaint. Even the lighter worked.

He took a nervous drag. He hadn't seen his father in fifteen years. His granny had made him come when he graduated high school to show his father that Calvin had amounted to something after all. Calvin remembered clutching his diploma in the visitors' room, sliding it out of the manila envelope, edging nervously up to the glass window that separated them. He held it up against the glass, hating the sour smell of the place, the chipped paint on the walls, the fact that he had to be there at all. He remembered how his father nodded. No smile. No "atta boy—you done good." Just a lukewarm nod. Calvin imagined a yawning hole opening up on the floor, right then and there, a hole he could sink into and disappear.

Now, the black metal gates swung open, and a withered man emerged. Calvin was still wiping sweat off his face, but his father was wearing a long-sleeved shirt and beige canvas pants. Even from a distance, his father looked smaller than he remembered. Frailer. The cancer that was consuming him, that had triggered his early release, was working its way through his body. He walked slowly, stooped over. His skin, a few shades lighter than the rich chocolate it once was, looked paper-thin, and he blinked like he hadn't been in sunlight for years. Maybe he hadn't. His father looked around, spotted Calvin in the Caprice. He took his time coming over.

Calvin slid out of the car, tossed his cigarette on the dirt, and ground it out with his foot.

"Hello, Calvin …"

Calvin returned his greeting with a nod of his own. Cautious. Polite.

"Appreciate you coming to get me, son."

A muscle in Calvin's gut twitched. He couldn't remember the last time someone had called him "son." "Son" was a word that belonged in the movies or TV, not in real life. Calvin gestured to the gym bag his father was carrying. "Let me take that."

His father held it out. Calvin threw it in the back seat. His father stood at the passenger door but made no effort to open it. Calvin frowned, then realized his father was waiting for permission. Twenty-five years in prison did that to a man. "Just open the door and get in."

His father shot him a look, half-embarrassed, half-grateful, and slid into the car. Calvin waited until his father was settled, then started the engine. As they pulled away from Joliet, he said, "Thought we'd go back to my place."

"You still in Englewood?"

"Hyde Park now. Got ourselves a house near 47th and Cottage Grove."

His father's eyebrows arched. "Well, that's mighty fine."

"Jeanine fixed it up nice. Even got a little garden out back. She's a *good* girl."

His father didn't seem to notice. He should have. It was Jeanine who shamed him into picking him up in the first place.

"He's dying, Calvin" she'd said. "And he's paid his dues. Twenty-five years of 'em."

Now his father turned to him. "How's that job coming?"

"What job?" Calvin made his way back to the highway.

"The one you was talking about when you come to see me. Janitorial supplies."

"I opened my own company six years ago. I got five people working for me now."

"Well that's mighty fine, son. Mighty fine."

But it didn't feel fine. Calvin imagined that black hole opening up wider. That was why he never wrote or visited his father, except for the Christmas card Jeanine made him sign every year. Any time he thought about him, even a stray fragment, the night his mother was murdered flooded back into his mind. He couldn't help it. Better not to think about it at all, his granny would say. "Just go on and live your own life."

But Granny was dead, and the people at Joliet called *him* when they found the cancer. Calvin stole a glance at his father. He was quiet. Just staring out at the road, a dreamy look on his face. Calvin remembered that look. His father's body might be in the front seat, but his mind was miles away. Calvin knew he was thinking about his mother.

He tightened his grip on the wheel. How dare he? "So ... You feelin' okay?"

His father pulled his gaze in and looked at Calvin. "For the days I got left, I'm doing jes' fine."

Calvin turned onto the interstate. "You sure? Jeanine talked to our doctor. He can see you tomorrow if you want."

His father gave him a sad little smile. "Appreciate it son, but don't go to no trouble." His father went back to looking out the window. Calvin turned on the radio. The all news station was blaring out something about Israeli troops in Lebanon. His father just kept gazing out. He seemed somehow smaller, less distinct than he'd been just ten minutes ago. Like his shadow was slowly fading from black to gray. At this rate he might disappear altogether.

Calvin snapped off the radio. For a while the whine of the air conditioning was the only sound in the car. Lulled by the air blowing through the vents and the rhythm of his wheels on the highway, Calvin was startled by the abruptness of his father's voice.

"You start making the arrangements?"

Calvin cleared his throat just loud enough. "Not yet." He wasn't sure what to expect. Would his father lay into him? Cuss him out?

But all his father did was to wave a weak hand. "I guess I got to do it myself."

"Why don't we talk about it later?"

His father's shoulders sagged and he closed his eyes. "I ain't got many laters, son."

###

1950'S: CHICAGO

The hot breath of the blues kissed Jimmy Jay Rollins when he was little, leaving him hungering for more. His mama—he never knew his daddy—took him to church in the morning and the blues joints at night. By the time he was seven, he was playing guitar licks with whoever his "uncle" of the moment happened to be, and by the time he left school at sixteen, he knew he wanted to play bass guitar.

The bass wasn't as flashy as the electric slide guitar of Little Ed or Muddy Waters, but it was the glue that held everything together. No one could play a twelve-bar chorus without him; no one could start a lick or riff. The bass was there through every number, from beginning to end, setting the pace. Steady. Unrelenting. The lead guitar, saxophone, even the drummer could take a break; not so the bass. Willie Dixon became Jimmy Jay's personal hero.

By day, Jimmy Jay worked in a steel factory near Lake Calumet, but at night, he bounced around playing gigs on the South Side. You could smell stale cigarette smoke and yesterday's beer in the air, spot a few guns and knives if you looked real close. But none of that mattered when the music started. The Blues flowed through his veins, transporting him to a place where he could let go, soar above the world, tethered only by an electric guitar, wailing horn, or harmonica riff.

He was jamming at the open mike set in the Macomba Lounge one hot summer night, a thick cloud of smoke, perfume, and sweat choking the air, when a wisp of a girl—she couldn't have been more than eighteen—came up to the stage. She was wearing a red dress that skimmed her body just right. A curtain of black hair shimmered down to her waist, and her skin looked pale blue in the light. She tentatively took the mike and asked them to play in G, then launched into a bluesy version of "Mean to Me," an old Billie Holiday song.

By the middle of the second verse, people set their glasses down, stubbed out their cigarettes, and a hush fell over the room. Her voice was raw and unpolished but full of surprises. At first a sultry alto, she could hit the high notes in a silver soprano, then dip two octaves down to belt out the Blues like a tenor. At first he thought it was a fluke—no one had that range and depth. He tested her, moving up the scale, changing the groove, even throwing her a sudden key change. She took it all with a serene smile, bobbing her head, eyes closed, adjusting perfectly. Her voice never wavered.

After a few numbers, the band took a break, and Jimmy Jay bought her a whiskey. As he passed her the drink, he noticed the contrast between her face, soft and round, and her eyes, dark and penetrating. Her name was Inez Youngblood, she said, and she'd just moved here from Tennessee. She was part Cherokee, once upon a time, but mostly mountain white.

"A hillbilly?" Jimmy Jay joked.

She threw him a dazzling smile that made his insides melt. "A hillbilly who sings the Blues."

"Why Chicago?"

"I listen to the radio. Chicago Blues is happy Blues. You got Muddy Waters. Etta James. Chess Records. Everybody's here. Sweeping you up with their music. There just ain't no other place to sing." Those dark eyes bored into him. "And I got to sing."

By their third drink, he began to imagine the curves underneath that red dress, and what she looked like without it. She had to know what he was thinking, because she smiled and started to finger a gold cross around her neck. She didn't seem put off. More like she was teasing him.

Another set and half a reefer later, a fight broke out in the back of the bar. Inez, who was singing "Remember Me, Baby" took it in stride, even when knives glinted and someone pulled out a piece. She just pointed to the fighters, asked the bartender to shine a spot in their direction, and leveled them with a look. The brawl moved into the alley. Jimmy Jay was impressed.

It was almost dawn when they quit playing. Someone bought a last round of drinks, and Jimmy Jay was just thinking about packing up when Inez came over.

"You're pretty damn good, Jimmy Jay."

He grinned. "Thanks, Hillbilly. You got a set of pipes yourself."

She laughed. "We ought to do this again."

Jimmy Jay suppressed his elation. "I could probably get us a couple of gigs."

She nodded. "I'd like that."

He nodded, just looking at her, not quite believing his good fortune.

She offered him a slow, sensual smile. "Meanwhile, I got a favor to ask you, baby."

Jimmy Jay cleared his throat. "Yeah?" His voice cracked anyway.

She turned around and lifted her hair off the back of her neck. "Help me take off my cross."

She ended up in his bed that night. And the next. And the night after that. She might only have been eighteen, but she was all heat and fire. All he had to do was touch her and she shivered with pleasure. When he ran his fingers slowly up her leg, starting at that perfectly shaped ankle, past her knee, stopping at the soft, pliant skin of her thigh, she would moan and grab him and pull him into her. Sliding underneath, rocking him hard, like she couldn't get enough.

"You are my sweet man," she would whisper when they stopped, exhausted and sweaty. "My sweet, sweet man."

They were a team for almost ten years. Inez, the hillbilly, soaring like an angel in one number, moaning like a whore in another; and Jimmy Jay, steadfast and sturdy, setting the beat, making her look good. Inez drove herself hard, and her sophistication grew. Her timing was impeccable. She rolled with the band, but could carry the show. If someone missed a chord, she covered them, and if they messed up their solo, she'd make light of it by singing scat, humming a chorus, or talking to the crowd.

Before long they were headlining at places like the Macomba before it burned down, South Side Johnny's, and Queenie's. Their only disagreement was over Chess Records and the two white owners who wanted to sign them. Jimmy Jay was all for it—not only did his idol Willie Dixon work for Chess, but a record contract was something he'd dreamed about all his life. Inez kept saying they should hold out for a better deal. So far they had.

Even Calvin's arrival didn't slow them down. Calvin was a good baby who turned into a good boy. The same face and nappy hair as his daddy; the high cheekbones and coffee-with-cream skin from his mama. Inez seemed thrilled. She cooed and sang to him all day, but if Jimmy Jay figured she might retire, he figured wrong. Calvin came with them to the clubs on the South and West Sides, even to Peoria and East St. Louis. They'd bring blankets and put him to sleep in the back room on a ratty sofa, sometimes the floor. When he was older, Jimmy Jay or Inez would drop him off at school before they went to bed themselves. Jimmy Jay didn't mind. His own mama had brought him to all the Blues joints.

Inez started calling them both her sweet men. Jimmy Jay would grin. They were happy. Real happy. Until the gig at Theresa's.

It was late autumn, and a chilly rain had been falling for two days, flooding the viaducts and lots of basements. Jimmy Jay and Inez were headlining at Theresa's Lounge on South Indiana. The place wasn't as upscale or as large as Macomba's, and the regulars, mostly people from the neighborhood, treated the place like home, dancing and talking with the players during the set. Tonight the smell of wet wool mixed with the smoke and booze and sweat.

A promoter from Capitol Records was in town and supposedly coming down that night. Inez was excited—Capitol was huge, much bigger than Chess. Jimmy Jay was glad he'd talked a new lead guitar into playing the gig with them. Buddy Guy had just come up from Baton Rouge, and everyone was saying he was gonna change the face of the Blues.

It was a knockout performance. No one missed a chord and the solos kicked. There were no amp or mike problems. Jimmy Jay and the drummer locked into a tight groove, and Buddy Guy's guitar was by turns brash, angry, and soulful. Inez's voice was as rich and mellow as thick honey. Even with the lousy weather, the place was packed, everyone swaying, dancing, bobbing their heads. It was like great sex, Jimmy Jay thought. Hot, sticky sex that trembled and throbbed and built, and ended in a long, fiery climax.

During the break, a white guy came up to the stage. He'd been at one of the back tables, smoking cigarettes. With his baby face and eager expression, he couldn't have been much older than Jimmy Jay. But his tailored suit and hair, slicked back with Bryl Crème, said he was trying to look well-off. He bought the band a round of drinks and nodded to Jimmy Jay. Then he turned to Inez and started talking quietly. She looked from him to Jimmy Jay, then back at him. When she nodded, he took her hand and covered it with thick fingers. She didn't pull away. After the next set, Jimmy Jay caught them talking behind his back. By the last set, Inez was favoring him with the same smile she'd shot Jimmy Jay the first night at Macomba's ten years ago.

By the time Inez left town with him a week later, the rain had changed to snow. Jimmy Jay went to fetch Calvin at school. When he got back, she was gone. At first he thought she was at the store, picking up something for dinner, but when she didn't come home by six, an uneasy feeling swept over him. He checked the closet and drawers. Most of her things were gone. Except her gold cross.

Word got around that she'd run away with Billy Sykes. He hadn't worked for Capitol, it turned out. He did work in the record business, but dropped out of sight after he shorted some men who'd been financing a label with mob money. He reappeared a year later as a promoter. No one could say who his clients were.

That winter Jimmy Jay sat for hours on the bed, running Inez's gold cross and chain through his fingers. His mother moved in to look after Calvin who, at nine, was just old enough to realize his world had shattered. Word filtered back—someone had seen her in Peoria, someone else heard she was in Iowa. Jimmy Jay tried to play, but he sounded tired and flat. Inez was inextricably bound up in his music and his life; with her gone, it felt like part of his body—worse, his soul—had shriveled up and fallen off.

One day Calvin came in and saw him on the bed, fingering the cross with tears in his eyes.

"Don't be sad, Daddy." He came over and gave Jimmy Jay a hug. "I know what to do."

Jimmy Jay gazed at his son.

"Mama just got lost. She don't know how to get home. All we got to do is find her."

Jimmy Jay smiled sadly. "I don't think she wants to come home, boy."

"Granny says every mama wants to come home. All we needs do is find her. Once she sees us, it'll be just fine. I know it."

Jimmy Jay tried to discourage him, but Calvin clung to his idea like a leach to a man's skin. He talked so much about finding his lost mama that after a while, his intensity infected Jimmy Jay. Could it really be that simple? Maybe Calvin was right. Sure Inez wanted to be a star, but she had a family. If they went after her, maybe she *would* realize what she'd given up and come home.

The following spring Billy Sykes brought Inez back to Chicago for a show on the West Side—no one on the South Side would book her. She was singing with some musicians from St. Louis, Jimmy Jay learned. They were staying at the Lincoln Hotel, a small shabby place near the club.

Jimmy Jay waited until Calvin was home from school and had his supper. Then they both dressed in their Sunday best and took the bus to the hotel. Jimmy Jay slipped an old man at the desk a fiver and asked which room Inez Rollins was in. The man pointed up the steps. Jimmy Jay and Calvin climbed to the third floor and knocked on #315.

A tired female voice replied, "Yes?"

"It's me, Inez. And Calvin."

The door opened and suddenly Inez was there, her body framed in the light.

"Mama!" Calvin ran into her arms.

Her face lit, and she clasped Calvin so tight the boy could hardly suck in a breath. When she finally released him, she turned to Jimmy Jay.

"Hello, Jimmy Jay."

She looked washed-out, Jimmy Jay thought, although it gave him no pleasure to see it. Gaunt and nervous, too. Her eyes were rimmed in red, and her black mane of hair wasn't glossy. He thought he saw a bruise on her cheek, but she kept finger-combing her hair over the spot.

"Hello, Inez." He looked around. "Where's Sykes?"

"He's at the club. Getting ready for tonight."

Jimmy Jay nodded. He got right to the point. "We want you to come home. We are a family. Calvin needs you. So do I."

At least she had the decency to look ashamed. Her eyes filled. She gazed at Jimmy Jay, then Calvin. Then she shook her head.

"Why not?"

"Remember what I told you the first time we met?"

"You told me a lot of things."

"I need to sing, Jimmy Jay. And Billy's gonna make me a star."

Jimmy Jay saw the determination on her face, as raw as the first time he'd met her. His heart cracked, but he struggled to conceal his grief. *He* might have lost her, but Calvin didn't have to. "Take the boy. He needs his mama. I'll—I'll pay you for him, 'ifin you want."

"I'll think about it." Inez looked down at Calvin, trailed her fingers through his hair, and smiled. Calvin snuggled closer. "I'll talk to Billy when he gets back."

Jimmy Jay nodded. "I'll leave the boy with you. I'll pick him up at the club when you start your gig. We can talk more."

Inez looked sad but grateful. Calvin looked thrilled.

Two hours later, the band had finished setting up but there was no sign of Inez. Or Billy Sykes. Or Calvin. Jimmy Jay saw the uneasiness on the musicians' faces, heard one of them say, "Where are those damn fools?"

He retraced his steps to the Lincoln Hotel.

No one was behind the desk when Jimmy Jay got there. He went up the stairs and down the hall. Music blared out from Inez's room. The radio. Benny Goodman's orchestra, he thought. He was about to knock on the door when he saw something move at the other end of the hall. Something small. He wheeled around and squinted.

"Calvin? Is that you?"

The figure trotted toward him. Calvin, looking small and lonely.

"What you doin' out here, son? Where's your mama?"

Calvin didn't say anything, just shrugged.

"Is she inside?" Jimmy Jay pointed to the door.

Calvin nodded.

"Is Sykes back?"

Calvin nodded again.

Jimmy Jay turned back to the door, leaned his ear against it. The music was loud. He knocked. No one answered. Probably couldn't hear him above the music. He knocked again, and when no one responded, started to push against the door.

"Inez, Sykes ... Open up!"

Nothing. Except the music.

Jimmy Jay looked both ways down the hall, then threw his weight against the door. It almost gave. He backed up, turned sideways, and rammed himself against it again. This time the door gave, and Jimmy Jay burst into the room.

###

He was still holding the gun when the police arrived. Inez's body was at the foot of the bed, but Sykes' was halfway to the door. A pool of blood was congealing under each of them.

1982: CHICAGO

Three weeks later, Jimmy Jay no longer had the strength to get out of bed. Calvin was putting in twelve-hour days. He knew it was an excuse for not dealing with his father, but he couldn't bear to come home to a place where death hovered in the air.

One night, though, was different. As he trudged inside, Calvin heard music from upstairs. And laughter. When he climbed the steps, he saw that Jeanine had moved their stereo into Jimmy Jay's room. An old album revolved on the turntable. His father was in bed, eyes closed, snapping his fingers. Jeanine was sitting in the chair smiling, her head bobbing to the music. Calvin peered at the album cover. Chess Records. Muddy Waters.

His father opened his eyes. "Hey, Calvin." His face was wreathed in smiles. "There ain't nothing like Muddy for an old soul. With Willie Dixon and Howlin' Wolf on back up. Lord, it makes me see the gates of heaven."

"Don't talk that way, Dad."

Jimmy Jay dismissed him with a wave of his hand. When the song came to an end, Calvin lifted the needle and turned off the stereo. Jeanine went downstairs, claiming dishes needed to be washed.

"Calvin," his father said, "we can't put it off no more. It's time to talk about the arrangements."

Calvin dug in his pocket for his Luckys, pulled one out, and lit it. He sat in the chair. "I don't know why you want to be buried there."

His father eyed him. "She was my wife, Calvin. And your mama."

"She was white trash!" Calvin exhaled a cloud of white smoke. "White trailer trash."

"Don't you ever talk that way 'bout your mama!" His father's voice was unexpectedly strong. "And she was from the mountains of Tennessee, boy," his father added. "The Smoky Mountains."

But Calvin wasn't mollified. "She ran out on us. You and me. She left us. And for what?"

His father just looked at him. Then he turned his head toward the window. "She was my woman," he said quietly, his burst of energy now dissipated. "And I was her sweet man."

Calvin felt his stomach pitch. The black hole was opening up again, and all he wanted to do was jump in and let it consume him. He stubbed out his cigarette, letting the window fan clear the smoke. Jeanine ran it all the time, even though it didn't do much cooling. Beads of sweat popped out on his forehead.

"I still miss her, son."

Calvin swallowed. "Pop, don't."

"I ain't got no regrets." His father said. "And now, in a little while, if the good Lord is willin', I'll see her again."

Calvin's throat got hot. He felt tears gather at the back of his eyes. He tried to blink them away, hoping his father wouldn't notice. But he did.

"Why you crying, Calvin? You're a good son. And Jeanine is a good woman. She been taking good care of me."

"It's not that." The words spilled out.

His father cocked his head. The slight movement seemed to require more energy than he could muster.

"I—I got to tell you something."

His father's body might be wasted, but his soul seemed to expand. His eyes grew huge, taking over his entire face. "What's that, son?"

The black hole widened. Calvin had to take the plunge. "That—that night ..." Calvin's words were heavy and sluggish, as if the hole was already sucking him down. "The night Mama died ..." Calvin whispered. "It was my fault. I killed Mama."

An odd look registered on Jimmy Jay's face.

"After you left"—Calvin's voice was flat and hard—"Mama sang to me. And hugged me. It felt—so good ... So right."

"Your mama had the voice of an angel."

Calvin held his hand up to stop him. "Then Billy Sykes come back. He was pissed when he saw me. 'What's that kid doing here?' he yelled. He and Mama—well, she told him she wanted to take me with them. Sykes wouldn't have none of it. 'Are you crazy?' he said. 'It's bad enough that you're a hillbilly. And part Injun. I ain't taking your nigger kid, too. Get rid of him.'

"Mama begged him. 'He won't be no trouble,' she kept saying and looked at me. 'Will you, sweet man?'

"But Sykes kept saying no. 'I put too much of my money in you to throw it away. What are people gonna think when they see you with a nigger kid?'

"Mama and me were on the bed. She was hugging me real tight. 'I want my son,' she said.

"'He'll be in the way,' Sykes said. 'You want to be a star? You got to make a choice. Me or the kid.'"

Jimmy Jay didn't say anything.

Calvin shuddered. "Mama said, 'Don't make me do that. I'm his mama!'

"'Then I'll make the choice for you.' Sykes says. And he pulls out a gun and aims it at my head." Calvin looked at the floor.

"What happened then, son?" Jimmy Jay asked, his voice almost as flat as Calvin's.

Calvin covered his eyes with his hand. "Mama got up from the bed. She looked scared. 'All right. All right. Put that gun away, Billy. I'll send Calvin back to his daddy. Just put the gun away. Before someone gets hurt.' Then she looked from me to Sykes. She didn't say nothing more."

Calvin pressed his lips together. He couldn't look at his father, but he knew his father was staring at him.

"Sykes started to put the gun away, but then—I don't know, Pop—something came over me. I jumped up and tackled Sykes. Right there in the room." He hesitated. "The gun went off. And Mama dropped off the end of the bed. Just dropped dead right in front of me."

His father whispered. "And then?"

"Sykes was like a crazy man. It was like he couldn't believe what happened. He started screaming, first at Mama. Kept telling her to get up and stop foolin' around. But she didn't, Pop. She never got up." Calvin's voice cracked. "Then he dropped the gun and started for the door. He was gonna take off! Just leave her there." Calvin paused again. "I just couldn't let that happen. I couldn't. When he was halfway to the door, I picked up the gun and shot him in the back."

Calvin felt tears streaming down his face.

Jimmy Jay, his eyes veiled, let out a quiet breath. Calvin heard the hum of traffic through the window above the fan.

After a long time, Calvin said haltingly, "I guess it's time to go to the police."

"You won't do nothing of the kind, son." His father raised himself on one elbow. "I already done the time. For both of us. And"—his features softened—"I figured out what happened a long time ago."

"You knew?" Calvin's stomach turned over. "How?"

"There was no way your mama could do anything to hurt you. Or you her. I knew her death had to be an accident." Jimmy Jay shrugged. "And as far as Sykes goes … well … I don't care."

"You knew? All these years?" Calvin felt his features contort with anguish. "I killed them, and you took the rap for me?"

Jimmy Jay nodded. "I'd do it all over again."

Calvin searched his father's face for an explanation. The silence pressed in.

"You were just a boy," Jimmy Jay finally said, gazing at him with an expression of infinite sadness, compassion, and love. "I done the time for you … so you would grow up and turn into her sweet man. Now …" He paused. "We got to get back to that plannin'. The Lord'll be givin' Inez back her first sweet man, and I need to be ready. We still got music to make together."

END

JACK FREDRICKSON'S debut mystery, *A Safe Place for Dying*, got a starred review in *Publishers Weekly,* and is now in its second printing. Jack's next mystery comes out early in 2008. Jack lives west of Chicago with his wife, Susan. He says, "I love Chicago because there's not much nuance to it. The whip-snap of the winds off the frozen lake; the high-up clatter of the elevated trains, loud and loose; the stink of that part of the river that's called Bubbly Creek where, on wrong days, the water still percolates from the cattle carcasses dumped there decades earlier—Chicago comes at all your senses strong, and straight-up. It's a fertile place, indeed, for the crime novelist."

WWW.JACKFREDRICKSON.COM

GOOD EVENIN', BLUES
JACK FREDRICKSON

HELL, YES, I'D BEEN MINDFUL OF ROBERT
Johnson when I named my tap "The Crossroads." Chi-Town's a blues town; lots of folks know the old Delta legend about Johnson meeting the Devil at a crossroads in Mississippi, to bargain away his soul in exchange for becoming the greatest bluesman that ever lived. With me being a mile west of what's fashionable in Chicago, underneath elevated tracks that shudder enough to make a dead man wince every time a train rumbles overhead, I was scrabbing for any advantage I could get.

But "The Crossroads" was just a name. And bargaining with the devil is just a myth.

Or so I would have said when I opened the place.

###

My sister's husband, Ralphie, had the bright idea. His cinder block building under the tracks had suddenly gone vacant when a tenant, after sponging three thousand dollars from Ralphie for plastic-topped tables, bentwood chairs, and a cheesy back bar, made of angled mirrors to make the liquor stock look big, had decided the incessant thunder of trains, sounding about to crash through the roof, would never be conducive to creating a restful watering hole. He split, leaving Ralphie bereft of the three thousand, and with an empty bar. Ralphie, who needs money like Florida needs oranges, moaned to my sister. My sister, who's never given up on me, snapped back: Jimbo's available. I'd just been retired from a screw machine factory south of the Loop.

Ralphie called the next day. "I got a business proposition for you. I got an empty bar. I'll give you a break on the rent." Always charitable, that Ralphie.

"I might have trouble getting a liquor license."

"That mess at the screw machine factory?" he asked, like it needed to be asked.

"Tell you what, Ralphie—you get the liquor license, I'll work for you."

"I'm thinking two grand a month for the rent."

"I'm thinking ten percent of the gross with you paying all the utilities."

"Who pays the taxes?"

"Who owns the building?"

He had to think some more on it, but he dropped by the next day with the key. The liquor license came the next week—greased; we're talking Chicago here—and I was in business.

I stocked the juke with what blues records I could find—Johnson, of course, and Bukka White, Mance Lipscomb, Brownie and Sonny and Gary Davis. Being mindful of the new order of things, I took care to add in some Memphis Minnie and Ma Rainey for the ladies who came to bask in my slice of cinderblock heaven.

But nobody came. Except the trains, of course; they came every few minutes, shaking the joint about to pieces. After eight months of losing what little kick-out money they'd had to give me at the screw place, I was seriously thinking of following the previous tenant out of Chicago.

That was when Pearly Hester showed up.

He came in one evening about six. A white guy about my age, pale and real thin, he was dressed like an old-time blues-man in a baggy, pin-striped suit, white shirt loose in the collar, and a floral necktie. He set a gray felt fedora on the bar.

"Whiskey, neat," he said, barely above a whisper. "That's no ice."

"I know neat." I filled the shot glass with the house brand, set it in front of him, and turned to polish a glass that didn't need polishing.

A minute later he made some more words, but they were so soft I had to turn back around. "What?"

"Ever think of live music in here?" He pulled an old pocket watch on a chain out of his pants. Late for a bus, maybe.

The 6:14 rumbled overhead. I could have told him the time from that. But instead, I said, "Entertainment for the deaf?"

"Name's Pearly Hester," he said, which made sense, given the shiny paleness of his skin. Then, "You got a juke, don't you?" He nodded at the jukebox in the corner.

I leaned partway across the bar so I could hear better. "Nobody's fed a quarter to it since I opened the joint."

"I can help you," he said.

Whatever it was, I was willing to hear him out, if for no other reason than to pass a few minutes listening to something other than the two gin filters gassing at the other end of the bar. It was rush hour on a Wednesday evening, and they were my only regulars. My clientele.

I set another whiskey in front of him. "On the house."

He touched a finger to his forehead in a vague salute.

"I don't have the money for live entertainment," I said.

"That's the beauty of it," he answered in his soft voice. "Open mike. They'll play for free."

"You mean kids with guitars, coming to play 'Michael Row the Boat Ashore'?" The idea was dimming.

He pulled out his timepiece again, flipped open the case.

Above our heads, the tracks started to shake. "6:18," I said, suddenly impatient. The man talked too slowly. And too softly.

"If they want." He closed the case and returned it to his pants.

"What?"

"What do you care if they play 'Michael Row,' so long as they bring their friends? Thing about open mikes, the performers bring their own audiences." He glanced down at the gin filters. Only one was talking now; the other was resting his head on the counter, like he did every night around half past six.

"Their audiences are out back, sleeping in the alley," I said.

He didn't crack a smile. "What I got in mind, you move back a couple of tables, get a small PA system, hang a couple of dim spots from the ceiling, you're in business. Players come in with their entourages, strum a few tunes, everybody buys drinks, you're a happy club owner."

I had to allow, the man had an idea.

"You know the blues?" he asked, no doubt mulling the name I'd hung on the place.

I waved a hand at the gin filters. "Man, I'm living the blues." Truth was, I used to play a bit, before everything went to crap.

"We'll do blues," he said. "I'll put up flyers, spread the word, manage the night."

"What's in it for you?"

He smiled, but it didn't touch his eyes. "Ten percent of the gross take, which you can more than make up for by adding just a little more water ..." He held up the shot of paled whiskey I'd poured.

"That's all?" Slight dilution was necessary in hard times.

"Maybe I'll make a discovery," he said.

"You think the next B.B. King is going to come through that door?"

He tossed back the whiskey in one gulp, easy enough with the tea I pour. "I got a piece of a little recording operation. We make demos for aspiring crooners, help them develop their careers ..." He let the thought trail away.

I understood. His bite would come from hustling promotional services. I'd heard a demo disc alone could cost a grand.

"Nobody spends like amateurs headed for stardom," I said.

He shrugged, low key and righteous. "They got to, if they want to aspire."

And their friends had to spend money on beer while they encouraged.

The 6:26 thundered overhead, clattering the glasses on the back bar. By the time the glassware stopped vacillating, I had too. "When do we start?"

He pulled out the big pocket watch again. This time I saw it was an old Elgin with Roman numerals on its dial. "Saturday night," he said quickly. Maybe the bargaining made him nervous.

He flipped the watch closed. And then he was gone.

He stopped by the next afternoon with a microphone, a scratched amp, and a couple of dented speakers. Barely nodding at the spots I'd hung on the ceiling—I'd hocked my father's watch to pay for them—he went to tape a flyer on the glass door. "Good Evenin', Blues," it read. He said he'd put up fifty, all over town.

"We're all set?" I asked.

He nodded. And from all appearances, it seemed we were about to be in the live blues business.

That first Saturday evening, it poured rain … and more customers than I'd ever had. They filled the dozen tables, leaving more to stand by the glass block windows facing the street.

Some were underage, of course, but most appeared legal. All in all, it was a fine crowd. Not a mob, but big for me.

Right off, they drank—suds mostly, but also a respectable amount of the tea, keeping me busy behind the bar, pulling and pouring. That was no problem. Pearly ran the evening, schmoozing the ones who'd brought instruments, moving everything right as the U. S. Mail. The music was predictable—Muddy and B.B. and early Clapton for the electric stuff; Robert Johnson, Son House, Gary Davis, and John Hurt for the moans of the Delta. Most of the players were a blur to me, hustling as I was behind the bar, but a couple still stand out from that first evening: A middle-aged guy so good I swear he was channeling Bukka White through a dinged, pre-war National steel guitar; and a boy with brown curls who was struggling to find the few chords of "32-20 Blues" on a big dollar sunburst Gibson the fool had sanded to make look old—struggling, that is, until a girl from the audience, a blonde-haired waif, got up to sing over his tentative fingerings and weak voice. She couldn't have weighed a hundred pounds, wore too much makeup, and had yet to develop the curves of womanhood, but she had the pipes of an angel, and by the second verse of "Come On In My Kitchen," the old Crossroads had gone quiet from people leaving their glasses on the tables. Even the elevated trains seemed to pause their shakings to listen to the waif sing over the curls. When they were done, the applause liked to drown out the next train, the midnight "L." The girl shrunk from the attention, retreated to the shadows by the wall, but Pearly went up to the curls and clapped him on the back, hard, like he'd just brought Carnegie Hall to its knees.

There were a couple more acts following, that first night, but I don't remember them. What I do recall was that I was grateful for one o'clock closing, because I'd run out of beer. I looked around for Pearly, but he'd already split.

Ralphie hadn't paid enough grease for a Sunday liquor tag, so I was closed the next day. On my way to the tap late Monday morning, I whistled in to Three Balls. It's a pawn brokerage, and consequently, the appellation of its proprietor; the name portends nothing concerning his anatomy. Three Balls was holding my father's watch, a fine old Waltham, against the money he loaned me for the spotlights.

"Early to be back for the watch, Jimbo," he said.

"Good fortune has begun smiling. I'm bringing in live talent."

"Ain't that pricy?"

"Open mike. They perform for free. Better yet, they bring their own admirers, who drink while they clap." I peeled off the principal and the vig from the wad in my pocket.

Three Balls smiled as he slid my father's watch through the window.

Leaving, like always, I looked up at the row of guitars hanging from the ceiling. One of them had been sandpapered to dull a sunburst finish. I stopped like I'd hit a wall.

"Fancy that one, Jimbo?" Three Balls said from behind his fenced window.

"Unusual guitar for you," I said, trying to sound conversational. Mostly Three Balls hung junk from his ceiling, Korean knockoffs he caught falling off trucks. I reached up, turned the guitar so I could see the headstock. Gibson, it read, in gold leaf.

"Just get this?" I asked. Damned right he just got it; that guitar had been playing in my place just two days before. The brown-curled boy must have had a sudden, dire need for money to have hocked that Gibson.

"Not two hours ago. You interested, if the owner doesn't come to fetch it?"

"Might be."

"I'll keep that in mind, Jimbo."

Pearly walked in just after two o'clock.

I set an envelope on the bar. "Ten percent of Saturday night's take."

"Very grateful, my friend; very grateful." He snapped open his gold Elgin to check the time.

"You don't want to know how much?" It was a little over a hundred, against receipts of a grand.

"I trust you." He put the watch back in his pocket.

I set a neat whiskey—Jack Daniel's, not the house tea—on the counter next to the envelope. "You've worked other towns?" I asked, meaning open mike nights.

His eyes widened for a second. Then he relaxed, and gave a little shrug. "This burg loves the blues, and you got lots of colleges: DePaul, Columbia, Illinois, Chicago, Northwestern. You're on prime turf, my friend." He tossed back the Jack, winced appreciatively at its undiluted warmth, and set the shot glass down hard on the bar.

I poured him another. "Print more flyers, Pearly. 'Good Evenin', Blues,' every night, save Sundays."

He shook his head. "Saturdays only, my friend. Otherwise, you'll wear out your new clientele. Let them anticipate."

"Why not at least add Wednesdays, double our take?"

He studied my face, no doubt saw greed. "Don't you go second-guessing Pearly Hester."

"Meaning there's other Crossroads where you could bring your magic?"

He pulled out the chain to consult the Elgin. "I best be going," he said, snapping it shut.

It was only after the door closed behind him that I noticed he'd forgotten to take the envelope.

So many folks came the next Saturday they jammed The Crossroads like sardines snuggling in tin. Once again Pearly moved among the ones lugging instruments, chatting them up, assigning them turns to play. And all the while prospecting for promotion possibilities, though he was so smooth, I doubted any of them suspected.

The pre-war National was back, and led off, sounding as good as the previous week. Curls didn't show, understandably since he'd hocked his sandpapered Gibson, but there were plenty of other sour-noters to take his place. Luckily for all the ears in attendance, Angel Waif, the frail blond songstress, had also returned. I remember being particularly relieved when she got up to help a bald guy—dressed in suit pants and a white button-down shirt, like an accountant slumming—with a scratchy voice and fingers unable to find one true note on his guitar, an expensive Martin Herringbone 28. Angel Waif rode over some of his bad notes, shorted him out on the rest, enough so they actually made me weepy on "Beulah Land," Mississippi John Hurt's song about heaven.

When they were done, Angel Waif retreated from the applause, as was her custom. Pearly gave the accountant the full wax, like he'd done with Curls the week before, clapping him on the back as he escorted him back to his table.

A few minutes later, Pearly sidled up to the bar for another taste of Jack.

"What about that guy with the pre-war National?" I asked. "Great chops."

He tossed back the shot, shrugged slightly.

"O.K.," I went on, letting his indifference slide. "What about that blond girl ...?"

"She can sing, that one," Pearly allowed, but he was looking at the bald-headed accountant. He'd made him for the plumpest fish in the pond, that night.

"You got to get the National and the blonde to do demos, Pearly. There's future there."

He slid off the stool, headed for the accountant.

Pearly didn't show up during the next week. But on Friday, two detectives did. Big guys in tight suits, I'd been expecting them for months.

"A little north of your turf, aren't you, Jablonski?" I asked. South Side cops, they'd been assigned to the difficulty at the screw machine company.

"Me and Murph," he said, gesturing at his partner, "we pulled strings, told the brass we had excellent rapport with you." Jablonsiki looked around, making a show of taking in the place. "Safer than working a scaffold," he said, as they sat down at the bar.

"Better class of people, too," I nodded, "at least usually."

Jablonski made his eyes big as he pretended his brain had just caught up with the insult. He'd been slow to talk at the screw machine factory, but I'd learned not to underestimate him. Enough so that when I left the screw place, I never fooled myself into thinking I'd left Jablonski. So today was no surprise.

Murphy pulled out an enlargement of a driver's license belonging to a guy with a bald head. "Ever see him?"

There was no sense being fancy over this one. "He was in here Saturday night."

"What do you remember about him?"

"He looked like an accountant. And he brought a guitar, a new-looking Herringbone Martin, that must have set him back three grand."

Jablonski spoke. "He came here to play?"

"We have open mikes, Saturdays."

"What else do you remember?"

"What's this about, Jablonski?"

"What else do you remember?"

"Thinking he should stick to doing people's tax returns. He was lousy. What's this about?"

"He got choked to death."

My own throat suddenly tasted like chalk, but that could have been dust, being kicked up from the past. "Choked when? Saturday night?"

"No. Day before yesterday. Wednesday."

"Around here?"

Murphy shook his head. "Way north, close to Evanston."

"Even more off your turf." I got the words out smooth, but my ticker was pumping like there was a fire.

"You're our turf, Jimbo." Jablonski set down one of Pearly's flyers. "Especially seeing our vic had this in his pocket."

"Word's getting around. People have been coming in. I didn't talk to the guy."

"So who talked to him?"

"The people at his table, I suppose."

"Nobody in particular?"

I saw Pearly, hustling. But I also saw Jablonski and Murphy using the choke victim to gnaw some more at the screw machine factory. I shook my head. "Just them."

Jablonski set his cop card down on the bar. "You probably got a drawer full of these, right, Jimbo?" They started to leave, but Jablonski stopped at the door. "Ever wonder about your habit of being close to people who get killed?"

I met his eyes. "I was never charged."

"Your bosses knew. They canned you quick."

"They were stupid."

"I feel better, now that we're back in touch," he said.

I took it as coincidence when Pearly came in, not two hours later. I handed him the envelope with his cut for the last two Saturdays. This time, I motioned for him to put it right in his suit.

"Remember that bald-headed guy, Saturday night, played a Herringbone Martin?" I poured him a shot and refilled my own. I'd taken a couple after the cops left.

Pearly shook his head, puzzling.

I leaned just a little over the bar. "Not much of a guitarist, looked like an accountant?"

"White button-down shirt, suit pants?"

I nodded. "No talent, but you spent a lot of time with him. He left looking excited."

He raised his eyebrows. "You're saying what ...?" he whispered.

"Cops were here, Pearly."

"Guy was interested in making a demo, was all," he said in that maddening soft voice.

I handed him Jablonski's card. "Call this cop, tell him you talked to the accountant."

He put the card in his pocket without looking at it, came out with the Elgin. Fast open, fast close; he was in a hurry. Maybe it was just a tic.

"Saturday," he said, getting off the stool.

It wasn't a minute after he'd left that I realized he'd never asked what happened to the accountant. I hustled to lock the door, started hoofing down to the pawn shop. My gut was queasy, churning oil.

"Come to park that Waltham watch for a spell?" Three Balls asked.

I shook my head, looked up at the row of guitars.

"I told you," Three Balls went on, not minding my silence, "I got to hold that Gibson for awhile, Jimbo. Man's got the right to reclaim his guitar if he gets the money."

I finished my scan, relieved. There was nothing new hanging behind the sanded Gibson. "Just thought I'd stop in, see what else you had in a wood body," I said to be sociable.

"Got something nice you haven't seen, Jimbo."

The words came like shrapnel through the mesh window.

I walked up to the counter, made my mouth work. "How nice?"

He bent to snap open a case on the floor. "This kind of guitar I know," he said, holding it up.

It was shiny and glossy and new. A Martin Herringbone. The dead accountant's guitar.

"When did you take it in?" I managed.

"Yesterday. With your new prosperity, I've got you in mind if the owner doesn't find his way back."

There was no sense telling him the owner of that Martin would never find his way anyplace again. "Did a thin guy, a fancy dresser about my age, hock it?"

"In my business, we don't talk about who's selling," he said.

"Come on, Three Balls."

"Some kid hocked both of them, a boy."

I wanted to be relieved, but it meant nothing. Pearly could have paid a kid a few bucks to run the Gibson and the Martin into the hock shop.

"How much you pay out?"

"Five hundred each."

I tried thinking that was chump change, too small to kill for. But it wasn't, not in Chicago. Besides, the accountant probably had also been packing big cash, for demo discs and promotion.

The right thing was to call Jablonski; tell him about Pearly, and two guitars, and that he ought to start hunting for the corpse of a kid with curls. But such righteousness was for somebody who didn't have a question mark already hanging over his head, tossed there by a guy tumbling off a scaffold at a screw machine factory.

I left the store on rubber legs.

###

The next night, whispering across a table, Pearly caught me watching him. He gave me a slow smile, and turned back to motion his new mark, a red-faced guy who looked like he'd spent time on a tractor, to get up to perform.

The farmer ripped at the steel strings of an old Harmony Sovereign like he wanted them out, for chain link. Not even Angel Waif's vocals could disguise his angry inabilities, and he gave up to weak applause, after only three songs. As I watched him walk back to his table, I wanted to take comfort from the fact that his Harmony wasn't worth much, but my gut told me that Pearly must have otherwise made him for promotion dough, for all the time he'd spent with him that evening.

After the farmer sat down, I looked for Pearly. He was nowhere to be seen. I figured he'd hit the can, but when he hadn't reappeared after fifteen minutes, I began to worry he'd gone outside. To wait, to walk the farmer to an ATM.

I spent the thirty minutes left until closing watching the farmer, making sure he sat safe within his circle of friends. Such was my inattention to serving suds that, more than once, I got a raised eyebrow when somebody, stepping up for a refill, got back a short fill, and that mostly foam. My eyes were elsewhere, twitching to warn the farmer if he got up to leave, that evil might be waiting outside, in the shadows under the tracks.

At ten to one, I began moving people out. I started at the back, purposefully avoiding the farmer's table until his small group was all that was left. When they headed out, I followed, and tapped the farmer on the shoulder.

"Best you try another form of music," I said.

He looked at me like I'd slapped him, then turned angrily to catch up to his friends moving down the sidewalk. I stayed outside, watching them as they crossed to the next block. Above my head, the elevated tracks began to shake. The 1:09, still a mile away.

"… cops, damn it." The curse, high-pitched, could have come from a man, could have come from a woman, sitting inside an old, white Ford sedan with dark windows, parked across the street.

Car doors slammed in the middle of the next block. The farmer's people were piling into a station wagon. A second later, its engine fired, and the station wagon pulled into a wide U-turn, aiming yellow headlights back toward me. As it charged across the side street, the driver's fist shot out of his open window, unfurling one upraised finger. My mind barely registered the insult. I was staring at the white Ford across the street, seeing the shape of a fedora being backlit by the headlamps of the approaching station wagon. Nobody wore hats like that anymore. It was Pearly being yelled at inside that Ford.

Pearly didn't show up for his envelope Monday morning. That didn't surprise me. But Ralphie, my brother-in-law, did. That didn't surprise me, either. It had taken Ralphie no time at all to acquire a taste for his ten percent of my increased gross.

"You got to schedule more open mikes, Jimbo." He stuffed his envelope into his green suede jacket.

I reached for the house bottle, poured him a shot of the tea. Ralphie didn't much mind the tea; he savored anything he could drink for free.

"I'm thinking about canceling them altogether," I said.

Ralphie made a snorting noise, like a pig. "Them open mike nights are keeping you employed."

I set the house tea back on the mirrored unit, making the bottle once again look like four. "I guess we'll have another blues night, then," I said.

###

Saturday morning, I swung by Three Balls on the way in. All week I'd been avoiding it, but now I'd run out of week.

"Two nice choices," Three Balls encouraged from behind the mesh. The Gibson and the Martin hung from the ceiling, but there was no Harmony Sovereign. The farmer appeared to have survived.

"That's a relief," I said.

He took it as a joke and laughed. "Must be good times. Nobody's been hocking much of anything this week."

"Nothing?"

"Just this." Something rattled on the counter.

I moved closer.

"Used to take in quite a few of these," Three Balls said. "Now they're a rarity."

My eyes registered the round, gold Elgin, attached to a chain, made shiny from being pulled so often from the pin-striped cloth. Pearly's watch. But my gut was seeing what would lie next on that scarred counter.

My father's Waltham, ripped from my wrist.

"Same boy that hocked the guitars?"

He nodded.

I was already half out the door.

###

Eleven players showed up that night. Being that there would be no Pearly to order up the performances, I gave each a number on a scrap of paper, hoping they'd stick to the sequence, not much caring if they didn't. My mind was on the next show, the one I expected would start after closing.

The hands on my father's Waltham watch gave up the minutes slow that evening, like it knew what was coming. Half the performers lost their numbered scraps of paper and bunched around the microphone like boars, fighting for meat. The music was long and loud and bad; there was no blonde waif to help it. The crowd drank well enough, but they intruded into my planning.

Finally, the music ended. One o'clock. After the last customer slow-poked his way out, I started clearing the tables.

"What did Pearly tell?"

Startled, I backed into a table, clattering glasses. Her shape was barely visible in the shadows of the far corner. She must have been there all night.

"What did Pearly tell?" Her shape got longer. She was coming toward me.

I moved to the wall, switched on the fluorescents, the ones I fire up when I need to see what's been spilled on the tile. In the new, harsh light she looked mannish and cheap, a freak painted with too much makeup. No angel. No waif.

Jablonski's card was in her hand. She took another step toward me.

I grabbed an empty, brown longneck, cracked it against the edge of a table. Broken glass scattered to the floor. "You'll be moving on." I waved the jagged end of the bottle in a cutting motion at the door.

Her black eyes didn't blink. She went out into the night.

I bolted the door, put on rubber gloves, and then spent the next three hours scrubbing down The Crossroads. I always mop before I leave; there's nothing worse than yesterday's beer stinking the fresh of a new day. But that Saturday night, I wasn't looking to just clean. I was looking to erase.

I ran every glass, mug, and ash tray, clean or dirty, through the dishwasher—twice. I sprayed Windex like there was a fire, polishing every bottle, mirror, glass block, and door window. I took Lysol to the tables, chairs, walls, toilets, even the urinals, though I doubted they'd been risked. I even mopped the floors until the cracks in the floor tiles bubbled pine cleaner like ooze from an underground spring.

By four o'clock that morning, I'd cleaned every conceivable touchable in The Crossroads. And something better: I'd summoned back the kind of rage I'd known only once before, up on a scaffold at a screw machine company, when one smug son-of-a-bitch told me about my wife. I'd need the sharpness of that rage most of all.

I was ready. I put the spare pants, sweatshirt, and sneakers I keep for nights when drunks spray me with more than spittle into a clean garbage bag, set it just inside the back door. I turned off the fluorescents.

And stepped into the dark of the alley.

He came at me fast, lithe, and low, taking me down like I was made of papier-mâché. Above me, his fingers flailed at my throat. But the furies I'd conjured stayed with me, those demons that had shrieked so loudly up on that scaffold.

Somehow, I kept hold of the knife whose blade I'd greased black so it wouldn't glint in the alley.

I plunged its blade up, and up again, and he collapsed onto the knife, pinning my hand. For a few long seconds we didn't move. Then his fingers went slack around my throat and the breath came out of him, as warm and foul as the breath of hell. It was only after another minute, when I felt the wet seeping into my own shirt, that I dared to be sure.

The 4:27 train, the last one before dawn, thundered above. I pushed him off me, light as devil's dust now. I found his keys, left his wallet.

The white Ford was on the cross street. Tweezing the key into the trunk lock with my thumb and forefinger, not otherwise touching the car, I let the trunk lid rise on its own.

Pearly stared at me from inside the trunk, his eyes still wide from the surprise of the purply finger marks at his throat. I slammed the trunk lid with my sleeve-covered elbows.

The she-outfit was jammed behind the front seat. I took it all, then wiped the keys and left them in the ignition. Nights were right for cars to disappear in that neighborhood, under the "L" tracks. That didn't matter much now. There wasn't room for two in that trunk. I'd have to leave the body in the alley, where I'd cut it.

I set down the outfit well away from the back door of The Crossroads—a lone strand of hair can fry somebody nowadays, even if it's synthetic, from a wig—peeled off my clothes, and reached through the back door for the garbage bag I'd left inside. I changed in the alley, put my bloody clothes in the bag, added the outfit, and started for my room.

I stuck to the dark streets, the plastic bag rustling against my leg in time with the slapping of my shoes against the deserted sidewalks. Each footfall brought back the same pronouncement, slap after slap.

It had all been about bad bargains.

Bad bargains for Curls and the bald-headed accountant, bringing cash to Pearly, thinking they were buying demo discs and promotion and fame, getting instead Angel's fast fingers on their throats.

Bad bargains for Angel and Pearly. They'd needed an unsuspecting proprietor of a fading tap. But with me, they'd bargained wrong. They got a guy who was already roosting under a cloud of police suspicion, a guy who could unknowingly turn Jablonski's business card into a death warrant. Pearly showed the card to Angel. It was enough. Angel killed him, thinking he'd told me something that had brought those cops.

I paused at the new construction site I passed every day. They were going to pour a foundation there, first thing Monday. I dropped into a trench, scooped gravel, then smoothed it back over the garbage bag, and climbed out.

Bad bargain for me, too. More question marks would get hung over my head—by Pearly if the white Ford didn't get boosted; for sure by Angel, who would be discovered seeping behind The Crossroads. Jablonski would never leave me alone.

They were waiting for me Monday morning. I was late, having stopped to watch the concrete being poured. Jablonski and Murphy had brought a warrant, a couple of uniformed officers, and a crime scene technician with a bag of tools.

"Lost another one, Jimbo," Jablonski said as I unlocked the front door.

"Only one?" I asked, making it sound like a joke. The Ford must have been boosted.

Before I could lead them in, the crime scene tech made a show of sniffing the air. He told us to stay on the sidewalk, and went in by himself.

"What the hell is that smell?" Jablonski asked.

"Pine-scented cleaner," I said to his frown, then, "What did I lose?"

"Another dead guy, right up your alley."

Murphy laughed, admiring Jablonski's wit.

"When was this?" I asked.

The 11:51 shuddered overhead, and for a moment, we all paused to watch its shadow on the sidewalk.

"Early Sunday morning," Jablonski said, when it was gone.

"I didn't see anything, if that's what you're asking."

"You close up at one?"

"That's the law," I said to the law.

"This happened around four thirty."

"Long past my closing. Who got killed?"

"A young man, slight as could be." He flashed a driver's license photo of the pale boy. "One of your customers?"

"Who can tell?"

"We can," Jablonski said, nodding at the inside of The Crossroads.

Just then, though, the crime scene technician came out of the door, wearing pain on his face. "Everything's been washed down, floor, walls; everything," he said to Jablonski. "No fingerprints."

"Not even his?" Jablonski gestured at me.

"No fingerprints," the tech said.

"No way of telling who was in that bar." Jablonski turned to look at me.

"I like things tidy," I offered.

He went on. "Funny thing about this victim, the M.E. found traces of a woman's makeup on him."

"Guy was making out?"

"I'm thinking the guy was cross-dressing. He had a tube of mascara in his pocket." Jablonski watched my eyes, waiting for me to blink.

"The devil you say!" I said.

But of course there was only me to admire my wit.

END

"I GOT WHAT IT TAKES"

SARA PARETSKY has been living in Chicago since coming to the city to do community service work in the Martin Luther King era. The city got into her blood that summer—the heat, the passions, the injustices and corruption side by side with a noble tradition of community spirit going back to women like Bertha Palmer and Jane Addams keep her here. Her VI Warshawski novels, closely identified with Chicago, have won numerous awards, including the Cartier Diamond Dagger.

WWW.SARAPARETSKY.COM

PUBLICITY STUNTS
SARA PARETSKY

I

"I NEED A BODYGUARD. I WAS TOLD YOU were good." Lisa Macauley crossed her legs and sat back in my client chair as if waiting for me to slobber in gratitude.

"If someone told you I was a good bodyguard they didn't know my operation: I never do protection."

"I'm prepared to pay you well, Ms. Warshawski." She pronounced it "Warchotsi."

"You can offer me a million dollars a day and I still won't take the job. Protection is a special skill. You need lots of people to do it right. I have a one-person operation. I'm not going to abandon my other clients to look after you."

"I'm not asking you to give up your precious clients forever, just for a few days next week while I'm doing publicity here in Chicago."

Judging by her expression, Macauley thought she was a household word, but I'd been running my legs off the last two days and hadn't had time to do a search on her. Whatever she publicized made her rich: wealth oozed from her dark cloud of carefully cut curls, through the sable protecting her from February's chill winds, all the way down to her Stephan Killan three-inch platforms.

When I didn't say anything, she added, "My new book, of course."

"That sounds like a job for your publisher. Or your handlers."

I remembered going to see Andre Dawson when he was doing a baseball promotion at Marshall Field. He'd been on a dais, under lights, with several heavies keeping the adoring fans away from him. No matter what Macauley wrote she surely wasn't any more at risk than a sports hero.

She made an impatient gesture. "They always send some useless person from their publicity department. They refuse to believe my life is in danger. Of course, this is the last book I'll do with Gaudy Press: my new contract calls for three personal bodyguards whenever I'm on the road. But right now, while I'm promoting the current book, I need protection."

I ignored her contract woes. "Your life is in danger? What have you written that's so controversial? An attack on Mother Teresa?"

"I write crime novels. Don't you read?"

"Not crime fiction: I get enough of the real stuff walking out my door in the morning."

Macauley gave a conscious little laugh. "I thought mine might appeal to a woman detective like yourself. That's why I chose you to begin with. My heroine is a woman talk-show host who gets involved in cases through members of her listening audience. The issues she takes on are extremely controversial: abortion, rape, the Greens. In one of them she's involved with a man whose university appointment is challenged by the feminists on campus."

"I can't believe that would put you in danger—feminist-bashing is about as controversial as apple pie these days. Sounds like your hero is a female Claud Barnett."

Barnett broadcast his attacks on the atheistic, family-destroying feminists and liberals five days a week from Chicago's WKLN radio tower. The term he'd coined for progressive women—femmunists—had become a much-loved buzzword on the radical right. Claud had become so popular that his show was syndicated in almost every state, and re-run at night and on weekends in his hometown.

Macauley didn't like being thought derivative, even of reality. She bristled as she explained that her detective, Nan Carruthers, had a totally unique personality and slant on public affairs.

"But because she goes against all the popular positions that feminists have persuaded the media to support, I get an unbelievable amount of hate mail."

"And now someone's threatening your life?" I tried to sound more interested than hopeful.

Her blue eyes flashing in triumph, Macaluey pulled a letter from her handbag and handed it to me. It was the product of a computer, printed on some kind of cheap white stock. In all caps it proclaimed, "YOU'LL BE SORRY, BITCH, BUT BY THEN IT WILL BE TOO LATE."

"If this is a serious threat, you're already too late," I snapped. "You should have taken it to a forensics lab before you fondled it. Unless you sent it to yourself as a publicity stunt?"

Genuine crimson stained her cheeks. "How dare you? My last three books have been national list leaders. I don't need this kind of cheap publicity."

I handed the letter back. "You show it to the police?"

"They wouldn't take it seriously. They told me they could get the State's attorney to open a file, but what good would that do me?"

"Scotland Yard can identify individual laser printers based on samples of output, but most U.S. police departments don't have those resources. Did you keep the envelope?"

She took out a grimy specimen. With a magnifying glass I could make out the postmark: Chicago, the Gold Coast. That meant only one of about a hundred thousand residents, or the half-million tourists who pass through the neighborhood every day, could have mailed it. I tossed it back.

"You realize this isn't a death threat—it's just a threat, and pretty vague at that. What is it you'll be sorry for?"

"If I knew that, I wouldn't be hiring a detective," she snapped.

"Have you had other threats?" It was an effort to keep my voice patient.

"I had two other letters like this one, but I didn't bring them—I didn't think they'd help you any. I've started having phone calls where they just wait, or laugh in a weird way or something. Sometimes I get the feeling someone's following me."

"Any hunches who might be doing it?" I was just going through the motions—I didn't think she was at any real risk, but she seemed the kind who couldn't believe she wasn't the centerfold of everyone else's mind.

"I told you." She leaned forward in her intensity. "Ever since *Take Back the Night*, my fourth book, which gives a whole different look at rape crisis centers, I've been on the top of every femmunist hit-list in the country."

I laughed, trying to picture some of my friends out taking potshots at every person in America who hated feminists. "It sounds like a nuisance, but I don't believe your life is in as much danger as, say, the average abortion provider. But if you want a bodyguard while you're on Claud Barnett's show I can recommend a couple of places. Just remember, though, that even the Secret Service couldn't protect JFK from a determined sniper."

"I suppose if I'd been some whiny feminist you'd take this more seriously. It's because of my politics you won't take the job."

"If you were a whiny feminist I'd probably tell you to lighten up. But since you're a whiny authoritarian there's not much I can do for you. I'll give you some advice for free, though: if you cry about it on the air you'll only invite a whole lot more of this kind of attention."

I didn't think contemporary clothes lent themselves to flouncing out of rooms, but Ms. Macauley certainly flounced out of mine. I wrote a brief summary of our meeting in my appointments log, then put her out of mind until the next night. I was having dinner with a friend who devours crime fiction. Sal Barthele was astounded that I hadn't heard of Lisa Macauley.

"You ever read anything besides the sports pages and the financial section, Warshawski? That girl is hot. They say her latest contract is worth twelve million, and all the guys with shiny armbands and goosesteps buy her books by the cord. I hear she's dedicating the next one to the vice president. Of the United States, not the Cubs front office."

After that I didn't think of Macauley at all; a case for a small suburban school district whose pension money had been turned into derivatives was taking all my energy. But a week later, Macauley returned forcibly to mind.

"You're in trouble now, Warshawski," Murray Ryerson said when I picked up the phone late Thursday night.

"Hi, Murray—good to hear from you, too." Murray is an investigative reporter for the *Herald-Star*, a one-time lover, sometime rival, occasional pain in the butt, and even, now and then, a good friend.

"Why'd you tangle with Lisa Macauley? She's Chicago's most important artiste, behind Oprah."

"She come yammering to you with some tale of injustice? She wanted a bodyguard and I told her I didn't do that kind of work."

"Oh, Warshawski, you must have sounded ornery when you turned her down. She is not a happy camper: she got Claud Barnett all excited about how you won't work for anyone who doesn't agree with your politics. He dug up your involvement with the old abortion underground and has been blasting away at you the last two days as the worst kind of murdering femmunist. A wonderful woman came to you, trembling and scared for her life, and you turned her away just because she's against abortion. He says you investigate the politics of all your potential clients and won't take anyone who's given money to a Christian or a Republican cause and he's urging people to boycott you."

"Kind of people who listen to Claud need an investigator to find their brains. He isn't likely to hurt me."

Murray dropped his bantering tone. "He carries more weight than you, or maybe even I, want to think. You may have to do some damage control."

I felt my stomach muscles tighten. I live close to the edge of a financial cliff much of the time. If I lost three or four key accounts, I'd be dead.

"You think I should apply for a broadcast license and blast back? Or just have my picture taken coming out of the headquarters of the Republican National Committee?"

"You need a new-Millennium kind of operation, Warshawski—a staff, including a publicist. You need to have someone going around town with stories about all the tough cases you've cracked in the last few years, showing how wonderful you are. On account of I like hot-tempered Italian gals I might run a piece myself, if you'd buy me dinner."

"What's a new-Millennium operation—where your self-promotion matters a whole lot more than what kind of job you do? Come to think of it, do you have an agent, Murray?"

The long pause at the other end told its own tale; Murray had definitely joined the new century. I looked in the mirror after he hung up, searching for scales or some other visible sign of turning into a dinosaur. In the absence of that I'd hang onto my little one-woman shop as long as possible.

I turned to the *Herald-Star*'s entertainment guide, looking to see when WKLN ("the voice of the Klan," we'd dubbed them in my days with the public defender) was rebroadcasting Barnett. I was in luck: he came on again at eleven thirty, so that night workers would have something to froth about on their commute home.

After a few minutes from his high-end sponsors, his rich, folksy baritone rolled through my speakers like molasses from a giant barrel. "Yeah, folks, the femmunists are at it again. The Iron Curtain's gone down in Russia so they want to put it up here in America. You think like they think or—phht!—off you go to the Gulag.

"We've got one of those femmunists right here in Chicago. Private investigator. You know, in the old stories they used to call them private dicks. Kind of makes you wonder what this gal is missing in her life that she turned to that kind of work. Started out as a baby-killer back in the days when she was at the Red University on the South Side of Chicago and grew up to be a dick. Well, it takes all kinds, they say, but do we need this kind?

"We got an important writer here in Chicago. I know a lot of you read the books this courageous woman writes. And because she's willing to take a stand she gets death threats. So she goes to this femmunist dick, this hermaphrodite dick, who won't help her out. 'Cause Lisa Macauley has the guts to tell women the truth about rape and abortion, and this dick, this VI Warshawski, can't take it.

"By the way, you ought to check out Lisa's new book. *Slaybells Ring*. A great story that takes her fast-talking radio host Nan Carruthers into the world of the ACLU and the bashing of Christmas. You'll find it in any bookstore or warehouse. Maybe if this Warshawski read it she'd have a change of heart, but a gal like her, you gotta wonder if she has a heart to begin with."

He went on for thirty minutes by the clock, making an easy segue from me to Hillary Clinton. If I was a devil, she, poor thing, was the Princess of Darkness. When he finished I stared out the window for a time. I felt ill from the bile Barnett had poured out in his molassied voice, but I was furious with Lisa Macauley. She had set me up, pure and simple. Come to see me with a spurious problem, just so she and Barnett could start trashing me on the air. But why?

II

MURRAY WAS RIGHT: BARNETT CARRIED more weight than I wanted to believe. He kept on at me for days, not always as the centerpiece, but often sending a few snide barbs my way. The gossip columns of all three daily papers mentioned it; the story got picked up by the wires, and, naturally, the Net. Between Barnett and the papers, Macauley got a load of free publicity; her sales skyrocketted. Which made me wonder again if she'd typed up that threatening note herself.

At the same time, my name getting sprinkled with mud did start having an effect on my own business: two new clients backed out mid-stream, and one of my old regulars phoned to say his company didn't need any work for me right now. No, they weren't going to cancel my contract, but they thought, in his picturesque corpo-speak, "we'd go into a holding pattern for the time being."

I called my lawyer to see what my options were; he advised me to let snarling dogs bite until they got it out of their system. "You don't have the money to take on Claud Barnett, Vic, and even if you won a slander suit against him, you'd lose while the case dragged on."

On Sunday I meekly called Murray and asked if he'd be willing to repeat the deal he'd offered me earlier. After a two-hundred dollar dinner at the Filigree, he ran a nice story on me in the *Star*'s "ChicagoBeat" section, recounting some of my great past successes. This succeeded in diverting some of Barnett's attention from me to Murray—my so-called stooge. Of course he wasn't going to slander Murray on the air—he could tell lies about a mere mortal like me, but not about some-one with a big media operation to pay his legal fees.

I found myself trying to plan the total humiliation of both Barnett and Macauley. Let it go, I would tell myself, as I turned in the bed in the middle of the night: this is what he wants, to control my head. Turn it off. But I couldn't follow this most excellent advice.

I even did a little investigation into Macauley's life. She was thirty-five, divorced, no children. A native of Wisconsin, she'd moved to Chicago hoping to break into broadcast news. After skulking on the sidelines of the industry for five or six years, she'd written her first Nan Carruthers book.

Ironically enough, the women's movement, creating new roles for women in fiction as well as life, had fueled Macauley's literary success. When her second novel became a bestseller, she divorced the man she married when they were both University of Wisconsin journalism students, and started positioning her-self as a celebrity. She was famous in book circles for her in-sistence on her personal security: opinion was divided as to whether it had started as a publicity stunt, or if she really did garner a lot of hate mail.

I found a lot of people who didn't like her—some because of her relentless self-importance, some because of her politics, and some because they resented her success. As Sal had told me, Macauley was minting money now. Not only Claud, but the *Wall Street Journal*, the *National Review*, and all the other conservative rags hailed her as a welcome antidote to writers like Marcia Muller.

But despite my digging I couldn't find any real dirt on Macauley. Nothing I could use to embarrass her into silence. To make matters worse, someone at Channel 13 told her I'd been poking around asking questions about her. Whether by chance or design, she swept into Coronna's one night when I was there with Sal. We were both enthusiastic fans of Belle Fontaine, the blues singer, who performed there on Wednesdays.

Lisa arrived near the end of the first set. She was the center of a boisterous crowd that included a couple of big men with bulges near their armpits—she'd apparently found an agency willing to guard her body. At first I assumed her arrival was just an unhappy coincidence when she flung her sable across a chair at a table near ours. She didn't seem to notice me, but called loudly for champagne, asking for the most expensive bottle on the menu. A couple at a neighboring table angrily shushed them. This prompted Lisa to start yelling out toasts to some of the people at her table: her fabulous publicist, her awesome attorney, and her extraordinary bodyguards, "Rover" and "Prince." The sullen-faced men didn't join in the raucous cheers at their nicknames, but they didn't erupt, either.

We couldn't hear the end of "Tell Me Lies" above Lisa's clamor, but Belle took a break at that point. Sal ordered another drink and started to fill me in on family news: her lover had just landed a role in a sitcom that would take her out to the West Coast for the winter, and Sal was debating hiring a manager for her own bar, the Golden Glow, so she could join Becca. She was just describing—in humorous detail—Becca's first meeting with the producer, when Lisa spoke loudly enough for everyone in the room to hear.

"I'm so glad you boys were willing to help me out. I can't believe how chicken some of the detectives in this town are. Easy to be big and bold in an abortion clinic, but they run and hide from someone their own size." She turned deliberately in her chair, faked an elaborate surprise at the sight of me, and continued at the same bellowing pitch, "Oh, VI Warshawski! I hope you don't take it personally."

"I don't expect eau-de-cologne from a sewer," I called back at similar volume.

The couple who'd tried to quiet Lisa down during the singing laughed heartily at this. The star twitched, then got to her feet, champagne glass in hand, and came over to me.

"I hear you've been stalking me, Warshawski. I could sue you for harrassment."

I smiled. "Sugar, I've been trying to find out why a big, successful gal like you had to invent some hate mail just to have an excuse to slander me. You want to take me to court, I'll be real, real happy to sort out your lies in public."

Lisa tossed her champagne into my face. "In court or anywhere else, I'll make you look as stupid as you do right now."

Fury blinded me more than the champagne. I knocked over a chair as I leapt up to throttle her, but Sal got an arm around my waist and pulled me down. Behind Macauley I could see Prince and Rover on their feet, ready to move. Lisa had clearly staged the whole event to give them an excuse for beating me up.

Queenie, who owns the Coronna, was at my side with some towels. "Jake," she called, "I want these people out of here now. And I think some cute person's been taking pictures. Empty out those cell phone caches before they go, hear? Ms. Macauley, you owe me three hundred dollars for that Dom Perignon you threw around."

Prince and Rover thought they were going to take on Queenie's bouncer, but Jake had broken up bigger fights than they could muster. He managed to lift them both and slam their heads together, then to snatch the fabulous publicist's bag as she was trying to sprint out the door. Jake took out her cell phone, erased the pictures, and handed the bag back to her with a smile and an insulting bow. The attorney, prompted by Jake, handed over three bills, and the whole party left to loud applause from the audience.

Queenie and Sal grew up together, which may be why I got Gold Coast treatment that night, but not even her private re-serve Veuve Cliquot could take the bad taste from my mouth. If I'd beaten up Macauley I'd have looked like the brute she and Barnett were labeling me, but taking a faceful of cham-pagne sitting down left me looking—and feeling—helpless.

"You're not going to do anything stupid, are you, Vic?" Sal said as she dropped me off around two in the morning. "'Cause if you are, I'm baby-sitting you, girlfriend."

"No. I'm not going to do anything rash, if that's what you mean. But I'm going to nail that prize bitch, one way or another."

Twenty-four hours later, Lisa Macauley was dead and I was in jail.

III

ALL I KNEW ABOUT LISA'S DEATH WAS what I'd read in the papers: Her personal trainer had discov-ered her body when he arrived Friday morning for their usual workout. She had been beaten to death in what looked like a bloody battle, which is why the State's attorney finally let me go—they couldn't find the marks on me they were looking for. And they couldn't find any evidence in my home or office.

They kept insisting, though, that I had gone to her apartment late on Thursday. They asked me about it all night long on Friday without telling me why they were so sure. When Freeman Carter, my lawyer, finally sprang me Saturday afternoon, he forced them to tell him: the doorman said he'd admitted me to Lisa's apartment just before midnight on Thursday.

Freeman taxed me with it on the ride home. "The way she was carrying on, it would have been like you to demand a face-to-face with her, Vic. Don't hold out on me—I can't defend you if you were there and won't tell me about it."

"I wasn't there," I said flatly. "I am not prone to blackouts or hallucinations: there is no way I could have gone there and forgotten it. I was blamelessly watching the University of Kansas men pound Duke on national television. I even have a witness: my golden retriever shared a pizza with me. Her testimony: she threw up cheese sauce in front of my bed Friday morning."

Freeman ignored my attempt at humor. "Sal told me about the dust-up at Coronna's. Anyway, Stacey Cleveland, Macauley's publicist, had already bared all to the police. You're the only person they can locate who had reason to be killing mad with her."

"Then they're not looking, are they? Someone either pretended to be me, or else bribed the doorman to tell the cops I was there. Get me the doorman's name and I'll sort out which it was."

"I can't do that, Vic. You're in enough trouble without suborning the state's key witness."

"You're supposed to be on my side," I snapped. "You want to go into court with evidence or not?"

"I'll talk to the doorman, Vic. You go take a bath—jail doesn't smell very good on you."

I followed Freeman's advice only because I was too tired to do anything else. After that I slept the clock around, waking just before noon on Sunday. The phone had been ringing when I walked in on Saturday. It was Murray, wanting my exclusive story. I put him off and switched the phone to my answering service. In the morning I had forty-seven messages from various reporters. When I started outside to get the Sunday papers I found a camera crew parked in front of the house. I retreated, fetched my coat and an overnight bag, and went out the back way. My car was parked right in front of the camera van, so I walked the three miles to my new office.

When the Pulteney Building went under the wrecking ball last April, I'd moved my business to a warehouse on the edge of Wicker Park, at the corner of Milwaukee Avenue and North. Fringe galleries and night spots compete with liquor stores and palm readers for air here, and there are a lot of vacant lots, but it was ten minutes—by car, bus, or "L"—from the heart of the financial district where most of my business lay. A sculpting friend had moved her studio into a revamped warehouse; the day after visiting her I signed a five-year lease across the hall. I had twice my old space at two-thirds the rent. Since I'd had to refurnish—from dumpsters and auctions—I'd put in a daybed behind a partition: I could camp out here for a few days until media interest in me cooled.

IV

I BOUGHT THE SUNDAY PAPERS FROM ONE of the liquor stores on my way. The *Sun-Times* concentrated on Macauley's career, including a touching history of her childhood in Rhinelander, Wisconsin. She'd been the only child of older parents. Her father, Joseph, had died last year at the age of eighty, but her mother, Louise, still lived in the house where Lisa had grown up. The paper showed a single-story frame house with a porch swing and a minute garden, as well as a tearful Louise Macauley in front of Lisa's doll collection ("I've kept the room the way it looked when she left for college," the caption read). Her mother never wanted her going off to the University of Wisconsin. "Even though we raised her with the right values, and sent her to church schools, the university is a terrible place. She wouldn't agree, though, and now look what's happened."

The *Tribune* had a discreet sidebar on Lisa's recent contretemps with me. In the *Herald-Star*, Murray published the name of the doorman who had admitted "someone claiming to be VI Warshawski" to Macauley's building. It was Reggie Whitman. He'd been the doorman since the building went up in 1978, was a grandfather, a church deacon, coached a basketball team at the neighborhood club, and was so generally so virtuous that truth radiated from him like a beacon.

Murray also had talked with Lisa's ex-husband, Brian Gerstein, an assistant producer for one of the local network news stations. He was appropriately grief-stricken at his ex-wife's murder. The picture supplied by his publicist showed a man in his mid-thirties with a TV smile but anxious eyes. I called Beth Blacksin, a reporter I knew at Channel 13. Beth had filled me in on what little I'd learned about Lisa Macauley before her death.

"Vic! Where are you? We've got a camera crew lurking outside your front door hoping to talk to you!"

"I know, babycakes. And talk to me you shall, as soon as I find out who set me up to take the fall for Lisa Macauley's death. So give me some information now and it shall return to you like those famous loaves of bread."

Beth wanted to dicker but the last two weeks had case-hardened my temper. She finally agreed to talk with the promise of a reward in the indefinite future. Brian Gerstein had once worked at Channel 13, just as he had for every other news station in town.

"He's a loser, Vic. I'm not surprised Lisa dumped him when she started to get successful. He's the kind of guy who would sit around dripping into his coffee because you were out-earning him, moaning, trying to get you to feel sorry for him. People hire him because he's a pretty good tape editor, but then they give him the shove because he starts getting the whole newsroom terminally depressed."

"You told me last week they met up at UW when they were students there in the eighties. Where were they before that?"

Beth had to consult her files, but she came back on the line in a few minutes with more details. Gerstein came from Long Island; Lisa was local produce. The two met as freshmen, campaigning for Reagan's second election in '84. They'd married five years later, just before moving to Chicago. Politics and TV kept them together for seven years after that.

Gary rented an apartment in Rogers Park on the far north side of the city. "And that's typical of him," Beth added, as she gave me his address. "He won't own a home since they split up:

he can't afford it, his life was ruined, and he doesn't feel like housekeeping. I've heard a dozen different whiny reasons from him. Not that everyone has to own, but you don't have to rent a rundown apartment in gangbanger territory when you work for the networks, either."

"So he could have been peevish enough to kill Lisa?"

"You're assuming he swathed himself in skirts and furs and told Reggie Whitman he was VI Warshawski? It would take more—more gumption than he's got to engineer something like that. It's not a bad theory, though: maybe we'll float it on the four o'clock news. Give us something different to talk about than all the other guys. Stay in touch, Vic. I'm willing to believe you're innocent, but it'd make a better story if you'd killed her."

"Thanks, Blacksin." I laughed as I hung up, though—her enthusiasm was without malice.

I took the "L" up to Rogers Park, the slow, Sunday milk run. Despite Beth's harrangue, it's an interesting part of town. Some blocks you see dopers hanging out, some streets have depressing amounts of garbage in the yards, but most of the area harks back to the Chicago of my childhood: tidy, brick two-flats, hordes of immigrants in the parks speaking every known language and along with them, delis and coffeeshops for every nationality.

Gerstein lived on one of the quiet side streets. He was home, as I'd hoped: staking out an apartment without a car would have been miserable work on a cold February day. He even let me in without too much trouble. I told him I was a detective and showed him my license, but he didn't seem to recognize my name—he must not have been editing the programs dealing with his ex-wife's murder. Or he'd been so stricken he'd edited them without registering anything.

He certainly exuded misery as he escorted me up the stairs. Whether it was grief or guilt for Lisa, or just the chronic depression Beth attributed to him, he moved as though on the verge of falling over. He was a little taller than I, but slim. Swathed in a coat and shawls he might have looked like a woman to the nightman.

Gerstein's building was clean and well maintained, but his own apartment was sparely furnished, as though he expected to move on at any second. The only pictures on the walls were a couple of framed photographs—one of himself and Lisa with Ronald Reagan, and the other with a man I didn't recognize. Gerstein had no drapes or plants or anything else to bring a bit of color to the room, and when he invited me to sit he pulled a folding chair from a closet for me.

"I always relied on Lisa to fix things up," he said. "She had so much vivacity and such good taste. Without her I can't seem to figure out how to do it."

"I thought you'd been divorced for five years." I tossed my coat onto the card table in the middle of the room.

"Yes, but I've only been living here nine months. She let me keep our old apartment, but last summer I couldn't make the payments. She said she'd come around to help me fix this up, only she's so busy …" His voice trailed off.

I wondered how he ever sold himself to his various employers—I found myself wanting to shake him out like a pillow and plump him up. "So you and Lisa stayed in touch?"

"Oh, sort of. She was too busy to call much, but she'd talk to me sometimes when I phoned."

"So you didn't have any hard feelings about your divorce?"

"Oh, I did. I never wanted to split up—it was all her idea. I kept hoping, but now, you know, it's too late."

"I suppose a woman as successful as Lisa met a lot of men."

"Yes, yes, she certainly did." His voice was filled with admiration, not hate, for her popularity.

I was beginning to agree with Beth, that Gerstein couldn't possibly have killed Lisa. What really puzzled me was what had ever attracted her to him in the first place, but the person who could figure out the hows and whys of attraction would put Dear Amy out of business overnight.

I went through the motions with him—did he get a share in her royalties?—yes, on the first book, because she'd written that while they were still together. When she wanted a divorce his lawyer told him he could probably get a judgment entitling him to fifty percent of all her proceeds, even in the future, but he loved Lisa, he wanted her to come back to him, he wasn't interested in being vindictive. Did he inherit under Lisa's will? He didn't think so, I'd have to ask her attorney. Did he know who her residuary legatee was? Several conservative foundations they both admired.

I got up to go. "Who do you think killed your wife—ex-wife?"

"I thought they'd arrested someone, that dick Claud Barnett says was harrassing her."

"You know Barnett? Personally, I mean?" All I wanted was to divert him from thinking about me—even in his depression he might have remembered hearing my name on the air—but he surprised me.

"Yeah. That is, Lisa did. We went to a conservative media convention together right after we moved here where Barnett was the keynote speaker. She got all excited, said she'd known him growing up but his name was something different then. After that she saw him every now and then. She got him to take his picture with us a couple of years later, at another convention in Sun Valley."

He jerked his head toward the wall where the photographs hung. I went over to look at them. I knew the Gipper's famous smile pretty well by heart, so I concentrated on Barnett. I was vaguely aware of his face: he was considered so influential in the nation's swing rightward that his picture kept popping up in news magazines. A man of about fifty, he was lean and well-groomed, and usually smiling with affable superiority.

In Sun Valley he must have eaten something that disagreed with him. He had an arm around Lisa and her husband, stiffly, as if someone had propped plyboard limbs against his trunk. Lisa was smiling gaily, happy to be with the media darling. Brian was holding himself upright and looking close to jovial. But Claud gave you the idea that he'd been attached to his ply-board arms by thumbscrews to get him in the photo.

"What name had Lisa known him by as a child?" I asked.

"Oh, she said she was mistaken. Once she got to see him close up she realized it was only a superficial resemblance. But Barnett took a shine to her—most people did, she was so vivacious—and gave her a lot of support in her career. He was the first big booster of her Nan Carruthers novels."

"He doesn't look very happy to be with her in this picture, does he? Can I borrow this picture? It's a very good one of Lisa, and I'd like to use it in my inquiries."

Brian said in a dreary voice that he thought Lisa's publicist would have much better ones, but he was easy to persuade—or bully, to call my approach by its real name. I left with the photo carefully draped in a dish towel, and a written promise to return it as soon as possible.

I trotted to the Jarvis "L" stop, using the public phone there to call airlines. I found one that not only sent kiddie planes from O'Hare to Rhinelander, Wisconsin, but had a flight leaving in two hours. The State's attorney had told me not to leave the jurisdiction. Just in case they'd put a stop on me at the airport, I booked a flight under my mother's maiden name and embarked on the tedious "L" journey back to the Loop and out to the airport.

Lisa's new book, *Slaybells Ring*, was stacked high at the airport bookstores. The black, enamel cover with an embossed spray of bells in silver drew the eye. At the third stand I passed I finally gave in and bought a copy.

The flight was a long puddle-jumper, making stops in Milwaukee and Wassau on its way north. By the time we reached Rhinelander I was approaching the denouement, where the head of the American Civil Liberties Union was revealed to be opposing the display of a Christmas crèche at city hall because he secretly owned a company that was trying to put the crèche's manufacturer out of business. Nan Carruthers, owing to her wide and loyal band of radio fans, got the information from an employee the ACLU baddie had fired after thirty years of loyal service when the employee was found listening to Nan's show on his lunch break.

The book had a three-hanky ending at midnight mass, where Nan joined the employee—now triumphantly reinstated (thanks to the enforcement of the Civil Rights Act of 1964 by the EEOC and the ACLU, but Macauley hadn't thought that worth mentioning)—along with his wife and their nine children in kneeling in front of the public crèche.

I finished the book around one in the morning in the Rhinelander Holiday Inn. The best-written part treated a sub-plot between Nan and the man who gave her career its first important boost—the pastor of the heroine's childhood church, who had become a successful televangelist. When Nan was a child he had photographed her and other children in his Sunday School class engaged in forced sex with one another and with him. Since he held an awful fear of eternal damnation over their heads, they never told their parents. But when Nan started her broadcast career she persuaded him to plug her program on his Thursday night "Circle of the Saved," using covert blackmail threats to get him to do so. At the end, as she looks at the baby Jesus in the manger, she wonders what Mary would have done—forgiven the pastor, or exposed him? Certainly not collaborated with him to further her own career. The book ended on that troubled note. I went to sleep with more respect for Macauley's craft than I had expected.

In the morning I found Mrs. Joseph Macauley's address in the local phone book and went off to see her. Although now in her mid-seventies she carried herself well. She didn't greet me warmly, but she accepted without demur my identification of myself as a detective trying to find Lisa's murderer. Chicago apparently was so convinced that I was the guilty party, they hadn't bothered to send anyone up to interview her.

"I got tired of all those Chicago reporters bothering me, but if you're a detective I guess I can answer your questions. What'd you want to know? I can tell you all about Lisa's childhood, but we didn't see so much of her once she moved off to Madison. We weren't too happy about some of the friends she was making. Not that we have anything against Jews personally, but we didn't want our only child marrying one and getting involved in all those dirty financial deals. Of course we were happy he was working for Ronald Reagan, but we weren't sorry when she left Brian, even though our church frowns on divorce."

I let her talk unguided for a time before pulling out the picture of Claud Barnett. "This is someone Lisa said she knew as a child. Do you recognize him?"

Mrs. Macauley took the photo from me. "Do you think I'm not in possession of my faculties? That's Claud Barnett. He certainly never lived around here."

She snorted and started to hand the picture back, then took it to study more closely. "She knew I never liked to see her in pants, so she generally wore a skirt when she came up here. But she looks real cute in that outfit, real cute. You know, I guess I can see where she might have confused him with Carl Bader. Although Carl was dark-haired and didn't have a moustache, there is a little something around the forehead."

"And who was Carl Bader?"

"Oh, that's ancient history. He left town and we never heard anything more about him."

All I could get her to say about him was that he'd been connected to their church and she never did believe half the gossip some of the members engaged in. "That Mrs. Hoffer always over-indulged her children, let them say anything and get away with it. We brought Lisa up to show proper respect for people in authority. Cleaned her mouth out with soap and whipped her so hard she didn't sit for a week the one time she tried taking part in some of that trashy talk."

More she wouldn't say, so I took the picture with me to the library and looked up old copies of the local newspaper. In *Slaybells Ring*, Nan Carruthers was eight when the pastor molested her, so I checked 1975 through 1977 for stories about

Bader and anyone named Hoffer. All I found was a little blurb saying Bader had left the Full Bible Christian Church in 1977 to join a television ministry in Tulsa, and that he'd gone so suddenly that the church didn't have time to throw him a going away party.

I spent a weary afternoon trying to find Mrs. Hoffer. There were twenty-seven Hoffers in the Rhinelander phone book; six were members of the Full Bible Christian Church. The church secretary was pleasant and helpful, but it wasn't until late in the day that Mrs. Matthew Hoffer told me the woman I wanted, Mrs. Barnabas Hoffer, had quit the church over the episode about her daughter.

"Caused a lot of hard feeling in the church. Some people believed the children, and they left. Others figured it was just mischief, children who like to make themselves look interesting. That Lisa Macauley was one. I'm sorry she got herself killed down in Chicago, but in a way I'm not surprised—seemed like she was always sort of daring you to smack her, the stories she made up and the way she put herself forward. Not that Louise Macauley spared the rod, mind you, but sometimes I think you can beat a child too much for its own good. Anyway, once people saw little Lisa joining in with Katie Hoffer in accusing the pastor, no one took the story seriously. No one except Gertie—Katie's mom, I mean. She still bears a grudge against all of us who stood by Pastor Bader."

And finally, at nine o'clock, I was sitting on an overstuffed horsehair settee in Gertrude Hoffer's living room, looking at a cracked color Polaroid of two unhappy children. I had to take Mrs. Hoffer's word that they were Katie and Lisa—their faces were indistinct. Time had fuzzed the picture, but you could still tell the girls were embracing each other naked.

"I found it when I was doing his laundry. Pastor Bader wasn't married, so all us church ladies took it in turn to look after his domestic wants. Usually he was right there to put his own clothes away, but this one time he was out and I was arranging his underwear for him and found this whole stack of pictures. I couldn't believe it at first, and then when I came on Katie's face—well—I snatched it up and ran out of there.

"At first I thought it was some evilness the children dreamed up on their own, and that he had photographed them to show us, show the parents what they got up to. That was what he told my husband when Mr. Hoffer went to talk to him about it. It took me a long time to see that a child wouldn't figure out something like that on her own, but I never could get any of the other parents to pay me any mind. And that Louise Macauley, she just started baking pies for Pastor Bader every night of the week, whipped poor little Lisa for telling me what he made her and Katie get up to. It's a judgment on her, it really is, her daughter getting herself killed like that."

V

IT WAS HARD FOR ME TO FIND SOMEONE IN the Chicago police department willing to try to connect Claud Barnett with Carl Bader. Once they'd done that, though, the story unraveled pretty fast. Lisa had recognized him in Sun Valley and put the bite on him—not for money, but for career advancement, just as her heroine did to her own old pastor in *Slaybells Ring*. No one would ever be able to find out for sure, but the emotional torment Lisa gave Nan Carruthers in her book must have paralleled Lisa's own misery. She was a success, she'd forced her old tormentor to make her a success, but it must have galled her—as it did her heroine—to pretend to admire him, to sit in on his show, and to know what lay behind his flourishing career.

When Barnett read *Slaybells*, he probably began to worry that Lisa wouldn't be able to keep his secret to herself much longer. The police did find evidence of the threatening letters in his private study. The state argued that Barnett sent Lisa the threatening letters, then persuaded her to hire me to protect her. At that point he didn't have anything special against me, but I was a woman. He figured if he could start enough public conflict between a woman detective and Lisa, he'd be able to fool the nightman, Reggie Whitman, into believing he was sending a woman up to Lisa's apartment on the fatal night. It was only later that he'd learned about my progressive politics—that was just icing on his cake, to be able to denounce me on his show.

Of course, not all this came out right away—some of it didn't emerge until the trial. That's when I also learned that Reggie Whitman, besides being practically a saint, had badly failing vision. On a cold night, any man could have bundled himself up in a heavy coat and hat and claimed to be a woman without Whitman noticing.

Between Murray and Beth Blacksin I got a lot of public vindication. Sal and Queenie took me to dinner with Belle Fontaine to celebrate on the day the guilty verdict came in. We were all disappointed that they only slapped him with second-degree murder. But what left me gasping for air was a public opinion poll that came out the next afternoon. Even though other examples of his child-molesting behavior had come to light during the trial, his listeners believed he was innocent of all charges.

"The femmunists made it all up trying to discredit him," one woman explained that afternoon on the air. "And then they got the *New York Times* to print their lies."

Not even Queenie's reserve Veuve Cliquot could wipe that bitter taste out of my mouth.

END

KRIS NELSCOTT has been nominated for the Edgar Award for Best Mystery Novel of the Year. She has been nominated twice for the Oregon Book Award, and she won the Herodotus Award for the Best Historical Mystery Novel. Her most recent Smokey Dalton novel is *Days of Rage*. This is her first Smokey Dalton short story. About Chicago, Kris says, "I grew up in the Midwest. Chicago wasn't the Second City. It was THE city, good and bad. It was both the most interesting place on Earth and the most frightening. Everything that happened in Chicago felt like it happened only a few miles down the road, even though I was nearly two states away. Now I find myself writing about the Chicago of my growing-up years, and those feelings come back unbidden. I love the City with Big Shoulders. I love it a lot."

WWW.KRISTINEKATHRYNRUSCH.COM

GUARDING LACEY
KRIS NELSCOTT

EVERY OTHER MORNING, MY DAD DRIVES
me and my cousins to school, except he's not really my dad and
they're not really my cousins. My dad—his name is Smokey—he
says we're family, and I guess he's right about that.

He sure guards us like family. When Smoke drives (I known
Smoke since I was three; I just can't get used to calling him
Dad), he lines us up like little ducklings, and makes us walk
hand-in-hand into the school.

The duckling thing is hardest in the winter. It's the beginning of 1970—a decade Smoke says'll be better than the last
one—and there's been ice. We lose our balance if even one
person slips (and it's usually Noreen, who's six, and never pays
attention), and we just look plain silly.

I'm tired of looking silly, but I know the dangers if we don't.

Last year the Blackstone Rangers tried to recruit me and my cousin Keith, and Smoke, he beat up a Stone so bad they ain't bothered us since. Or not much, anyway. Smoke's a big guy and now he's got a knife scar on his face and he can take on just about anybody. The Stones look away when they see him. I think he scares them.

They hang in the playground and smoke cigarettes and they watch us all, especially my cousin Lacey. Smoke says she's thirteen going on trouble, and he don't know the half of it.

Our school is on the South Side, which the news says gots the worst schools in Chicago. Smoke agrees, but he's weird about it; his girlfriend, Laura Hathaway, is rich and white and has what Smoke calls clout and she says she can get me into one of them private schools and she'd even pay for it. But Smoke says we gots to do what we can afford and we don't take charity from nobody, not even if it's from somebody like Laura.

Besides, he says, we got to do for everybody, not just make one of us special, so that's why him and my Uncle Franklin started the afterschool program for anybody who wants to come and really learn.

Sometimes I wish Smoke would come inside our school though, instead of staying out front. He thinks we's safe inside, but that's not true. Some of the gang kids still go to classes just to cause trouble. Last week, Li'l Dan sat in the back of history class and just snicked his knife open and closed. I almost turned around and took it from him, but that would get me noticed, and I been noticed enough.

Lacey and Jonathon, they say it's worse in the junior high part of the school, which is an attached building at the other end. They come in with us, go down the hall, and then go through the double doors that get locked until school's over since the teachers don't want no older kids coming in and "corrupting" us younger ones. But they forget: most of us gots brothers and sisters who're older, or friends or neighbors, and we get corrupted all the dang time.

I don't like school much.

Especially this year, and that's because of Lace. I'm the only one who sees the problem, and I ain't sure what to do.

Ever since she got into junior high, Lace has been weird. I mean, she's always been stuck-up and stuff, and she's always worn makeup and clothes that my Uncle Franklin don't like at all. This year, Uncle Franklin and Aunt Althea, they make Lacey change dang near every morning before school, and they're threatening to ground her.

But it won't do no good.

Once Smoke or Uncle Franklin drops us ducklings off at school and we get inside those dented metal doors, Lace heads to the girls room. If she can't smuggle her clothes out of the house, she takes what she's already wearing and changes it. She rolls up her skirt and tucks the fabric under the waistband so the skirt is short and double-thick. She ties off her shirt to show her tummy, and she puts on so much makeup you can't see her face at all.

Lately she's been gluing on them fake eyelashes and wearing hot pants like Twiggy and big ole clunky high heels. That kinda stuff is expensive, and I know her family don't got that kinda money.

The problem is she looks good in it too. When Lace dresses up, she can pass for eighteen, maybe twenty. Most of her friends look just dorky in the same clothes, but Lace looks slutty-gorgeous. She got big tits last year and a waist and a fine ass, so she looks like a grown-up girl, which is why Uncle Franklin is so worried, I think.

Or maybe he knows what Lace really looks like.

When she dresses up like that, Lace looks just like my mom.

###

I ain't seen my mom in almost exactly two years. She skipped January 8, 1968. I remember because that's one week before my birthday. When I turned ten, my mom was gone and my older brother Joe was out toking with his buddies. That was Memphis, not Chicago, and Smoke, who was just this guy down the block who kept an eye on me, bought me lunch and told me I needed to get to school.

He didn't know it was my birthday, just like he didn't know Mom ain't paid the rent—again. We got evicted—or really, I did—and that was the end for Smoke. He'd been watching over me for a long time, making sure I studied, making sure I ate. But the eviction, that's when he took me in.

Mom ain't got no idea where I am now, not that it matters. She stayed gone from January to April, and even Smoke, who's a private detective, couldn't find her (not that I think he tried real hard). Mom ran off with one of her johns again, or maybe she knew the rent was due. She said she was gonna send money but she never did.

Sometimes I think she's dead. I seen a lot of hookers before I moved to Chicago, and they get hurt lots. Knifed or beat up or worse. Sometimes they get beat so bad they die. That last Christmas, I was mopping up after Mom all over the apartment, she was bleeding so bad from her female parts. I ain't never told Smoke that. He'd give me that shocked look like he does when I mention my mom, like he can't believe anybody would ever do the stuff she did.

But Mom explained it to me and Joe. She said you have the kinda life she had, you gots to do the best you can. And if she had it to do over she wouldn'ta chased all them boys when she was twelve and she wouldn'ta gone with the older guys, and she wouldn'ta never had kids.

Mom, she was only a year older than Lace when she had my brother Joe. She knew who his dad was, but she never said. Me, my dad coulda been anyone. Sometimes my mom would take on four or five guys a night—and that don't count the quickies in the alley behind our apartment.

Sometimes her pimp, this guy named Thug, used to get her to train the new girls. He'd say he could break them in but he couldn't teach them the ropes. Mom was in charge of the ropes. She'd talk to them and by the end, they'd be crying and she'd be yelling at them: *If you're crying now, you ain't gonna make it. You'll die before the year's out. You gotta be tough.*

Lacey ain't tough and she ain't hooking—at least not yet. But the guys she meets in the school yard during lunch ain't junior high boys. They ain't even high school boys. They's men, and they's way too interested.

It's so cold in Mrs. Dylan's classroom that I'm wearing my coat, and I'm glad Laura gave me real sturdy boots for

Christmas. Still, the tip of my nose is freezing and I can see my breath.

Mrs. Dylan's going on about fractions. I had that a long time ago, so I keep doodling on my notepad while I look out the window.

Lace is standing underneath an archway. The graffiti on it is mostly basic crap—Jud loves Susan, stuff like that—but Lace's standing under some spray-paint that says *Blackstones Are Stone Cold*. She's wearing a miniskirt and open-toed high heel shoes and a top tied under her tits. She's teased her hair into a afro—I got no idea how she's gonna get that out before we get to the afterschool program at the church—and I can see her eye makeup from across the yard.

Her hands are cupped as she leans forward to light a cigarette. That's another new habit, and one I'm surprised Uncle Franklin and Aunt Althea haven't figured yet. Lace stinks of cigarettes most of the time.

She's gotta be cold, but she don't look cold. She looks like she's waiting for someone, just like my mom used to do, only there ain't no road here for them to drive up to, and no way for some guy just passing by to ask her into his car so she can make a quick twenty.

I can't tell her none of this. I swore to Smoke I'd never talk about Memphis ever because I might slip and the secret'd be out. And the secret's an important one. I seen something I wasn't supposed to and people tried to kill me for it.

Smoke saved me, and then he brought me here. Thanks to Uncle Franklin, we get to use his last name (and his kids all think I'm a real cousin) and Smoke got fake IDs and stuff. People are searching for me, but Smoke says we're safe if we stay quiet.

Still I get nightmares and I know if we slip we might gotta leave with a moment's notice. Smoke hates it when I even think of Memphis because then I can't sleep and stuff.

But seeing Lacey like that, all tricked out and me not able to say anything for fear of hurting me and Smoke, scares me to death.

I talked to Smoke about it last fall, when things wasn't quite so bad. We was in the car after dropping off Lacey. He'd seen her tricked out—well, wiping the crap off her face anyway— and he tried to tell her what happens to girls who look like that from our part of town, but Lace didn't listen, not really.

After everybody got out of the car except me and Smoke, I asked him, "You don't think Lace'll end up like my mom, do you?"

He looked at me. He's got this measuring thing, where he can see all the way inside you, and he was doing that to me then. He could tell I was worried.

He said, "She won't end up like your mom. Lacey has too many friends and family for that. But she could get hurt."

I remembered how Mom laid in bed for days sometimes with ice pressed on her face so the bruises would go away, or that last Christmas, cleaning up the blood she left all over the apartment because she couldn't afford no doctor. I didn't want none of that to happen to Lace.

"Some trick'll hurt her?" I asked.

"Some *boy*'ll hurt her. He'll think she wants to do what your mom used to do. Lacey won't understand and—"

"He'll just do her. I know," I said real quick, because I didn't want to think about Lace like that.

That's when Smoke gave me that shocked look, like he can't believe half the stuff I know. Then he blinked, and the look went away.

"We can't talk her out of dressing like this," he said. "We've been trying for nearly a year. She'll do what she wants. But if she does get into trouble—if she starts crying a lot, or acting really angry for no reason, tell me okay?"

I hated that. I hated telling on anybody, even for a good reason. There was lotsa stuff Smoke should probably know, but I'd make my friends and my pretend cousins mad at me if I said something, and they wouldn't like me no more, and worse, they wouldn't trust me.

"What if she don't want me to?" I asked.

"Tell me that too."

"Feels like tattling," I muttered.

Smoke ignored that. "If someone just—does her—then she's not going to want to tell her parents. Maybe she'll tell me. We can make sure it won't happen again. We'd be protecting her, Jim, not tattling on her."

Made sense, but it still scared me. I seen them guys with my mom. There was no protecting. There was just getting by, surviving, and trying all over again.

But I didn't say that to Smoke. I don't say a lot of what I think to Smoke. He don't need to know all the details of what happened before. I try to forget a lot of them too.

But it's dang hard when I see Lace standing under that arch, smoking, when she's supposed to be in class. She's just waiting, and I don't know for what. Then some guy comes up and he's tall and thin and wears a long cloth coat. The thin guy puts a gloved hand on Lace's arm, and she smiles up at him like he's God.

Just then, Mrs. Dylan calls on me, and I have to turn away from the window. Mrs. Dylan always looks tired. She's not as old as Smoke, but she has these big bags under her eyes, and even her voice sounds a little wispy, like she can't get enough energy to use it right.

"I'm sorry," I say, trying to remember what she'd said before she called my name. "I forgot the question."

"When I called on you," she says all precise, which makes her seem madder than she probably is, "I asked you to add one-half and one-fourth."

"Three-fourths, ma'am," I say.

She frowns at me, and I realize I answered too fast. I don't want nobody in this school to know how easy it is for me. I feel my cheeks getting hot.

"Maybe I heard the question after all," I say with just enough attitude to make my friends smile, but not enough to make her madder.

"Sometimes I don't know what to do with you kids," she says, and goes back to talking about how when you add fractions you got to make the bottom numbers the same.

I turn back to the window.

Lace is gone.

I hope she's gone back inside, all alone, and is in some class now, shivering and wishing she was dressed proper.

But I know she's with the guy in the coat. And I know she feels cool.

None of this is cool. And I know at some point, he's gonna hurt her.

But what I don't know is when's the right time to tell Smoke? And what if I'm wrong? What if the guy in the coat is somebody nice like Smoke was to me, trying to talk Lace into the right path like the rest of us been doing?

Lace'd never forgive me.

But she'd never forgive me if I wait too long too.

I wish this all was as simple as adding fractions. But it ain't. And I got no idea what to do.

###

The answer comes at lunch. What would Smoke do if this was some case? And that makes the answer easy.

Smoke would make sure he knows what's going on before he does anything. So I gotta know exactly what's going on.

The lunch room is near the back doors. They're locked during school hours, even though Smoke says that ain't legal. There's windows to the right side, but they're marked up with soap so no one can see in.

We can't see much—sunlight or snow or nothing—and the lights overhead are that regular kind, not the fluorescents like in the classroom, so it's pretty dark in here, which is okay with me.

I always sit as far from the windows as I can get. My cousin Keith usually joins me. He's my age. My younger cousins, Mikie and Noreen, they know better than to even smile at us. We don't want no little girls anywhere near us, though I always make sure I know exactly where they're sitting, so I can keep an eye on them.

Keith sits down across from me. He's smaller than me but not by much. Smoke says I'm coming into my growth. I got taller last year and Keith didn't. He don't seem to mind. He thinks I'll get as big as Smoke, not knowing that we're not really blood.

He opens the brown sack his lunch comes in and I do the same. None of the kids here have them fancy metal lunch boxes because you can hide a gun in 'em so the school banned 'em. We check our sandwiches (both peanut butter), our desserts (he's got three homemade chocolate chip cookies that I want and I know he won't trade for my Nilla Wafers), and our extras. I hand him my carrots and he gives me an apple. There ain't much more to trade, so we settle in.

"Lace dating some older guy?" I ask.

Keith frowns at me. "Lace can't date."

"Well, some guy picked her up this morning." I tell him what I saw. He's more upset about the cigarettes because he don't know what I know about the way the world works.

"Can you find out where the guy takes her?" I ask.

"Why's that so important to you?"

"Because he might hurt her, that's why." I don't want him to ask no more because then I'll have to just shut up. I can't explain.

Instead he grins. "You know Lace. Any guy tries to hurt her, she'll just hurt him right back."

And he don't say no more. Me neither, not then. Because Smoke taught me if you want to get something out of somebody, the best way is to not push. So I don't push. I wait.

Just before the bell rings for the next class, Keith crumples up his lunch bag and tosses it into the garbage can across the room. He makes it, and grabs mine to do the same.

But he stops, frowns at me because I don't complain, and says, "If I find out who Lace's with, what're you gonna do?"

I shrug.

He crumples the bag harder. He knows me too well. "You're going to be Smokey, aren't you? You're going after her."

"This guy's too old for her," I say.

"So tell Uncle Bill."

Uncle Bill is Smokey. That's what my cousins call him.

"I don't know what to tell Smoke," I say. "What if the guy's just some minister or something and he's being nice?"

Keith nods real slow. He finally gets it.

"If you cut school, Uncle Bill will kill you."

"Not if he don't find out," I say.

Keith tosses my bag into the garbage and makes that shot too. The bell rings and we stand up.

"If you cut," he says, "I'm cutting with you."

"You don't got to," I say.

"She's my sister," he says. "And she'll kill me if she sees me going through her stuff."

"Is that what you're gonna do?" I ask.

"You think I'm gonna ask her?" He grins at me. "She keeps a diary. In code. And I know how to read it."

The next day, after we get inside the school and Lacey runs off to the girls room, Keith takes my arm and steers us toward the lockers.

"He takes her to the Starlight Café for lunch, every day for the last week now."

The Starlight's just around the corner. It's the restaurant part of an old hotel that's mostly used for drug sales and one-hour rentals. Mostly old people eat in the restaurant, like they probably did when it was a fancy place.

I frown. "That's all her diary says? Lunch."

"Says he thinks she's pretty. Says he's an agent or something and thinks she can be a model."

I let out a small breath. I'd heard that before, lots of times. Mom used to yell at girls who cried in her living room, girls who were always saying they thought they were supposed to be modeling.

"What're you gonna do?" Keith asks.

"I'm gonna tell him the truth. She's too young to be a model."

"Okay," Keith says. "You wanna go to the café and wait?"

I bite my lower lip. I'm not gonna be able to get rid of him. It's his sister after all. But I don't really have much of a plan. I'm still trying to figure out what's going on.

"No," I say. "Let's see if he comes today first."

We skip class. We hide out near the janitor's closet before it's time for math, and then we go outside. I make sure we stay as far from that arch as we can and still see it. And I tell Keith to just stay quiet.

He thinks it's all a game, and Keith is really good at games. So he's so quiet next to me that if I didn't see the white from his breath, I wouldn't know he was there.

Sure enough, about the time math starts, Lacey comes outside and stands under the arch. She's wearing another short top tied so tight around her tummy that I can see the red mark it's making from where I'm standing. Today she's wearing a skirt so short that if she bends over, she's not hiding nothing, and a pair of white go-go boots she had to have borrowed from somebody.

She lights a cigarette and Keith makes a growly sound.

We all wait, and finally the guy in the coat shows up.

I can see him closer than I did yesterday. He's old, maybe as old as Smoke. His hair's slicked back and he's got them weird sideburns that go most of the way to his jaw. He smiles at Lace, but I don't like it. His eyes aren't smiling at all.

He puts out his elbow and she takes it. Me and Keith follow.

Smoke taught me how to tail somebody. I don't think he meant to, but sometimes he gets tails on his cases, and he has me watch for them, and he always tells me if they're good tails or bad ones. I told Keith how to do this, how once we get to the sidewalk, it's important to look like we belong and like we ain't watching nothing, but I'm afraid he'll screw me up.

That's why I go first, and when I got to the sidewalk I start walking with attitude, like I'm a Stone. I can hear Keith's boots crunching on the snowy walk behind me. Ahead, the Starlight Café looks just as cheesy as I remember, with its dirty windows and the black steam rising out of the grates on the ceiling, turning that side of the eight-story hotel gray.

I don't see Lace or the guy, but I figure they're inside. It took me and Keith about ten minutes to get there, which I figure gave Lace and the guy time enough to get settled and not worry about the windows or the door.

Just as I make it to the store next to the Starlight, the door opens and Lace comes out. She's smiling. The guy still has her elbow. He's taking her across the driveway and to the front door of the hotel.

My stomach cramps so hard I think I'm gonna puke. But I swallow it down.

I run forward—I'm gonna stop them—but Keith grabs me and makes me near to falling over.

"What're you doing?" I whisper.

"You said not to—"

"They're going to the hotel."

He looks confused. I shake him off. By the time I get inside the hotel, they're on the stairs. The place is old and smells of cigars and sweat and beer. The smell makes my eyes water—not because it's so bad, but because I know that smell. I grew up with it.

I'm shaking real bad. That morning, I thought of taking Smoke's gun out of the glove box in the car, but he told me if I ever did that, even for a good reason, he'd whup me—and that's the only time he's ever threatened to whup me for anything, so I only thought about the gun, I didn't take it.

All I brought was some tweezers and a pen and a screwdriver, just cause I thought I might have to break into Lace's locker or something.

Now I understand though why the Stones have those knives, and I wish I had something because that old guy's a lot bigger than me, and Lace and Keith're next to worthless.

Keith's beside me, breathing hard, and looking confused. The desk clerk don't even look at us. He's probably used to Stones coming in and out. Nobody else is in the lobby.

I point to the pay phone next to the bathrooms. "Call Smoke," I say, handing Keith all the dimes I got. "If he's not at home, try Laura's. Tell her it's an emergency and who you are and she'll get him. If you get him, tell him I said Lace is in trouble."

"Trouble?" Keith repeats and looks at the stairs. "What kind of trouble?"

"You stay here," I say, and run for the stairs. As I fly up those stairs. I can hear Lace asking a question far away, which means she's not in a room yet, so I go past the first floor, then the second, and by the time I get to the third, I see a door close at the end of the hall.

I figure they're down there. If I'm wrong, I'm in trouble, but I'll search this whole place until I find them. I hurry down the hall and try the door, but it's locked.

"Go away!" some guy yells from inside. I never heard the old guy talk, so I don't know if it's him or not.

I don't breathe. I want to surprise him, because otherwise he'll hurt me.

Then I hear Lace say, "I thought there was supposed to be agency people here."

"There will be," the guy says. "Take off your clothes and let's see what you got."

"No," Lace says.

I'm not strong enough to kick the door in, but I do know how to get a door open. I learned picking almost before I learned to walk. The easiest is just to take off the knob, and that's what I decide to do because it looks loose already.

I take out the screwdriver. My hands are shaking so bad I almost drop it. I look down the hall, but no one's coming, not even Keith, so I figure we're okay.

"Listen, cunt," the guy says, "you'll do what I say."

"No!" Lace says, and then there's an awful crash.

My hands stop shaking, but I can't swallow.

Lace screams and there's another thud, and a bang, and it's like I'm back in our apartment in the kitchen where I'm not supposed to leave while Thug is there showing Mom what's what.

I concentrate and force the screwdriver onto the screw and start turning. I make myself focus on the work instead of the thuds and whimpers inside. I'm trying to pretend it's Mom and not Lace, who has no idea what's happening, Lace who I promised Smoke I'd protect, Lace—

The knob falls away and I have to catch it before it hits the floor. I set it down real quiet, keep the screwdriver in my left hand, and pull the door open with my right.

First, Mom would say, you get the money. Then you worry about the guy.

That was when she knew the guy had more money than he was willing to give her, and she wanted it anyway—sometimes for weed, sometimes for rent, sometimes for food.

I ease inside. The place is dark and smells of sweat and Lace's perfume. She's on her back on the bed and she's pushing on the guy who's on top of her, and she's kicking her feet, but it's not doing no good because he's between her legs with his pants down.

She don't see me, which is just as good. I keep a grip on that screwdriver, but first, I get behind the guy and slide his wallet out of his pants just like Mom taught me. I put it in my pocket, then I grab the guy by the belt and yank up.

It shouldn'ta worked. It wouldn'ta worked in Memphis. But I'm spitting mad and it makes me strong. I pull him off. Lace lets out an awful scream and starts kicking him, and I whale on the back of his head with the screwdriver.

"Jesus," he says, covering his head with his hands. Lace keeps kicking and I keep hitting and he grabs his pants, pulling them up as he runs out of the room.

I go to the door, but he's running down the hall, holding his pants up. Blood's dripping off his greasy head and I think that's not enough. If I had Smoke's gun, he wouldn't be moving at all. If—

"Jim?"

Lace don't sound like Lace. She sounds like a baby, her voice shaking. The bed's covered with blood and she's shoved against the wall, her shirt ripped and her bra busted open and her tits hanging out. Her skirt's up to her hips.

"We gots to get you outta here." I take off my coat and wrap it around her.

"No," she says, but she don't fight me. I seen this before too.

"Come on." I help her up. I tug down her skirt as best I can and I pull my jacket tight over her front. She's got a bruise on the side of her face that's gonna swell real bad, and her mascara's run, leaving streaks down the side of her face. One of her eyelashes is falling off, and her hair is coated with some of the guy's blood—at least, I hope it's his.

It takes forever for me to get her to the door, and even longer to get her down the hall. She keeps falling off her boots. I'd make her take them off, but we have to go outside.

"Jim?" she says every few feet, like she can't believe it's me.

I get her to the stairs, and we go down slow, and then I see Keith, who comes running up.

"What happened? Lacey? Are you okay?" And then he screams at the guy at the desk to call the cops.

"Shut up," I say as mean as I can. "A place like this, they won't call the cops."

"You don't know that," Keith says.

"I do," I say. "Shut up, or they'll hurt us too."

I don't know if that's true, but I want out of here fast.

"You get ahold of Smoke?"

"He was at home. He's coming now. I told him here." Keith's hands are fluttering near Lace's face but he don't touch her, like he's afraid he'll hurt her. I'm not even sure Lace sees him.

"Help me," I say, and together we get her the rest of the way downstairs.

We're almost through the lobby when the door busts open. It's Smoke. He's wearing his coat and it flaps around him and his eyes are wild and he's holding his gun. He musta drove like mad to get here so fast.

He sees us and stares for a minute. Then he sticks his gun in the holster he keeps under his coat and comes toward us.

"Lacey," he says in a real gentle voice.

"Some guy hurt her, Uncle Bill." Keith is really mad. He's talking loud. "We gotta call the cops. We gotta—"

"Not now," Smoke says. He reaches for Lace, but his eyes meet mine.

"I'm sorry," I say quietly. "I didn't—"

"Jim saved me, Uncle Bill." Lace says. It's like seeing Smoke made her strong. "He beat the guy up and sent him away. Jim saved me."

Smoke puts his arm around her and she leans against him. Her boots aren't white no more. They're blackish red with blood.

"Uncle Bill," Keith says like he's gonna whine about the police, but Smoke shushes him. Then Smoke lifts Lacey up and carries her out the door, and we follow, like ducklings, all the way to the car.

It's not until we've been in the hospital awhile and Aunt Althea's come and our neighbor, Marvella, who does women stuff and knows how to take care of people who been through what Lace's been through, that Smoke sits down next to me.

"You did great," he says.

"She still got hurt," I say. "If I'd been faster, I could've stopped him."

"You might have been killed," he says. Then he put a hand on my shoulder. "When we're done, I'm going back to the hotel and see if I can get the clerk to tell me this jerk's name."

I reach into the pocket of my pants, and with two fingers I pull out the wallet. I hand it to Smoke.

He frowns at me for a minute, then he opens it, and lets out a small laugh. "This is the guy?"

I nod.

"You got his wallet?"

I don't say Mom taught me how to do that. I don't even say I planned it. I'll let Smoke think it was an accident.

"Son of a bitch," Smoke says, and pulls me close. "You're one incredible kid, you know that?"

I just lean against him. I don't feel incredible. I didn't get there fast enough, and now Lace'll be hurt forever, even though Smoke says she'll get help from the family and stuff.

At least I got the wallet so Smoke can see who the guy is. Because I know what Keith don't. No cop'll arrest a guy like that creep. That guy's probably paying protection. He was prepping Lace to live like my mom. He's got connections.

Smoke don't care about connections. Smoke'll shut him down. Smoke's done it before.

And even though I wasn't able to stop that guy from hurting Lace, at least she won't grow up to be like my mom. If we wasn't here, Lace would've disappeared into that hotel and no one would've known what happened.

But I didn't save her. Not really. I wish I'd gotten that guy before he hurt Lace.

I ain't Smoke.

At least, not yet.

END

JA KONRATH has published several dozen short stories and four books in the Lt. Jacqueline "Jack" Daniels series, including *Whiskey Sour, Bloody Mary, Rusty Nail,* and *Dirty Martini.* He lives in a northwest suburb of Chicago. About Chicago he says, "I love Chicago. The neighborhoods. The people. The music. The food. The sports. The crime. Okay, I don't love the crime, but it sure makes for some interesting stories …"

WWW.JAKORNATH.COM

OVERPROOF
JA KONRATH

THE MAN SAT IN THE CENTER OF THE
southbound lane on Michigan Avenue, opposite Water
Tower Place, sat cross-legged and seemingly oblivious to the
mile of backed-up traffic, holding a gun that he pointed at
his own head.

I'd been shopping at Macy's, and purchased a Gucci wallet
as a birthday gift for my boyfriend, Latham. When I walked out
onto Michigan I was hit by the cacophony of several hundred
honking horns and the unmistakable shrill of a police whistle.
I hung my star around my neck and pushed through the crowd
that had gathered on the sidewalk. Chicago's Magnificent Mile
was always packed during the summer, but the people were

usually moving in one direction or the other. These folks were standing still, watching something.

Then I saw what they were watching.

I assumed the traffic cop blowing the whistle had called it in—he had a radio on his belt. He'd stopped cars in both directions, and had enforced a twenty-meter perimeter around the guy with the gun.

I took my .38 Colt out of my purse and walked over, holding up my badge with my other hand. The cop was black, older, the strain of the situation heavy on his face.

"Lt. Jack Daniels, Homicide." I had to yell above the car horns. "What's the ETA on the negotiator?"

"Half hour, at least. Can't get here because of the jam."

He made a gesture with his white gloved hand, indicating the gridlock surrounding us.

"You talk to this guy?"

"Asked him his name, if he wanted anything. Told me to leave him alone. Don't have to tell me twice."

I nodded. The man with the gun was watching us. He was white, pudgy, mid-forties, clean shaven and wearing a blue suit and a red tie. He looked calm but focused. No tears. No shaking. As if it was perfectly normal to sit in the middle of the street with a pistol at your own temple.

I kept my Colt trained on the perp and took another step toward him. If he flinched, I'd shoot him. The shrinks had a term for it: *suicide by cop*. People who didn't have the guts to kill themselves, so they forced the police to. I didn't want to be the one to do it. Hell, it was the absolute last thing I wanted to do. I could picture the hearing, being told the shooting was justified, and I knew that being in the right wouldn't help me sleep any better if I had to murder this poor bastard.

"What's your name?" I asked.

"Paul."

The gun he had was small, looked like a .380. Something higher caliber would likely blow through both sides of his skull and into the crowd. This bullet probably wasn't powerful enough. But it would do a fine job of killing him. Or me, if he decided he wanted some company in the afterlife.

"My name is Jack. Can you put the gun down, Paul?"

"No."

"Please?"

"No."

That was about the extent of my hostage negotiating skills. I dared a step closer, coming within three feet of him, close enough to smell his sweat.

"What's so bad that you have to do this?"

Paul stared at me without answering. I revised my earlier thought about him looking calm. He actually looked numb. I glanced at his left hand, saw the wedding ring.

"Problems with the wife?" I asked.

His Adam's apple bobbled up and down as he swallowed. "My wife died last year."

"I'm sorry."

"Don't be. You married?"

"Divorced. What was your wife's name, Paul?"

"Doris."

"What do you think Doris would say if she saw you like this?"

Paul's face pinched into a sad smile. My Colt Detective Special weighed twenty-two ounces, and my arm was getting tired holding it up. I brought my left hand under my right to brace it, my palm on the butt of the weapon.

"Do you think you'll get married again?" he asked.

I thought about Latham. "It will happen, sooner or later."

"You have someone, I'm guessing."

"Yes."

"Does he like it that you're a cop?"

I considered the question before answering. "He likes the whole package."

Paul abruptly inhaled. A snort? I couldn't tell. I did a very quick left to right sweep with my eyes. The crowd was growing, and inching closer—one traffic cop couldn't keep everyone back by himself. The media had also arrived. Took them long enough, considering four networks had offices within a few blocks.

"Waiting for things to happen, that's a mistake." Paul closed his eyes for a second, then opened them again. "If you want things to happen, you have to make them happen. Because you never know how long things are going to last."

He didn't seem depressed. More like irritated. I took a slow breath, smelling the cumulative exhaust of a thousand cars and buses, wishing the damn negotiator would arrive.

"Do you live in the area, Paul?"

He sniffled, sounding congested. "Suburbs."

"Do you work downtown?"

"Used to. Until about half an hour ago."

"Do you want to talk about it?"

"No."

"Can you give me more than that?"

He squinted at me. "Why do you care?"

"It's my job, Paul."

"It's your job to protect people."

"Yes. And you're a person."

"You want to protect me from myself."

"Yes."

"You also want to protect these people around us."

"Yes."

"How far away are they, do you think? Fifteen feet? Twenty?"

A strange question, and I didn't like it. "I don't know. Why?"

Paul made a show of looking around.

"Lot of people here. Big responsibility, protecting them all."

He shifted, and my finger automatically tensed on the trigger. Paul said something, but it was lost in the honking.

"Can you repeat that, Paul?"

"Maybe life isn't worth protecting."

"Sure it is."

"There are bad people in the world. They do bad things. Should they be protected too?"

"Everyone should be protected."

Paul squinted at me. "Have you ever shot anyone, Jack?"

Another question I didn't like.

"When I was forced to, yes. Please don't force me, Paul."

"Have you ever killed anyone?"

"No."

"Have you ever wanted to?"

"No."

Paul made a face like I was lying. "Why not? Do you believe in God? In heaven? Are you one of those crazy right-tolifers who believe all life is sacred? Do you protest the death penalty?"

"I believe blood is hard to get off of your hands, even if it's justified."

He shifted again, and his jacket came open. There was a spot of something on his shirt. Something red. Both my arms were feeling the strain of holding up my weapon, and a spike of fear-induced adrenalin caused a tremor in my hands.

"What's that on your shirt, Paul? Is that blood?"

He didn't bother to look. "Probably."

I kept my voice steady. "Did you go to work today, Paul?"

"Yes."

"Did you bring your gun to work?"

No answer. I glanced at the spot of blood again, and noticed that his stomach didn't look right. I'd first thought Paul was overweight. Now it looked like he had something bulky on under his shirt.

"Did you hurt anyone at work today, Paul?"

"That's the past, Jack. You can't protect them. What's done is done."

I was liking this situation less and less. That spot of blood drew my eyes like a beacon. I wondered if he was wearing a bullet proof vest under his business suit, or something worse.

"I don't want to go to jail," he said.

"What did you do, Paul?"

"They shouldn't have fired me."

"Who? Where do you work?"

"Since Doris died, I haven't been bringing my 'A-Game.' That's understandable, isn't it?"

I raised my voice. "How did you get blood on your shirt, Paul?"

Paul glared at me, but his eyes were out of focus.

"When you shot those people, did they scream?" he asked.

I wasn't sure what he was after, so I stayed silent.

He grinned. "Doesn't it make you feel good when they scream?"

Now I got it. This guy wasn't just suicidal—he was homicidal as well. I took a step backward.

"Don't leave, Jack. I want you to see this. You should see this. I'm moving very slow, okay?"

He put his hand into his pocket. I cocked the hammer back on my Colt. Paul fished out something small and silver, and I was a hair's breadth away from shooting him.

"This is a detonator. I've got some explosives strapped to my chest. If you take another step away, if you yell, I'll blow both of us up. And the bomb is strong enough to kill a lot of people in the crowd. It's also wired to my heartbeat. I die, it goes off."

I didn't know if I believed him or not. Explosives weren't easy to get, or to make. And rigging up a detonator—especially one that was hooked into your pulse—that was really hard, even if you could find the plans on the Internet. But Paul's eyes had just enough hint of psychosis in them that I stayed put.

"Do you doubt me, Jack? I see some doubt. I work at LarsiTech, out of the Prudential Building. We sell medical equipment. That's where I got the ECG electrode pads. It's also where I got the radioactive isotopes."

My breath caught in my throat, and my gun became impossibly heavy. Paul must have noticed my reaction, because he smiled.

"The isotopes won't cause a nuclear explosion, Jack. The detonator is too small. But they will spread radioactivity for a pretty good distance. You've heard of dirty bombs, right? People won't die right away. They'll get sick. Hair will fall out. And teeth. Skin will slough off. Blindness. Leukemia. Nasty business. I figure I've got enough strapped to my waist to contaminate the whole block."

All I could ask was, "Why?"

"Because I'm a bad person, Jack. Remember? Bad people do bad things."

"Would Doris ... *approve* ... of this?"

"Doris didn't approve of anything. She judged. Judged every little thing I did. I half expected to be haunted by her ghost after I shot her, telling me how I could have done a better job."

I didn't have any saliva left in my mouth, so my voice came out raspy.

"What happened today at LarsiTech?"

"A lot of people got what was coming to them. Bad people, Jack. Maybe they weren't all bad. I didn't know some of them well enough. But we all have bad in us. I'm sure they deserved it. Just like this crowd of people."

He looked beyond me.

"Like that woman there, pointing at me. Looks nice enough. Probably has a family. I'm sure she's done some bad things. Maybe she hits her kids. Or she stuck her mom in a nursing home. Or cheats on her taxes. We all have bad in us."

His Helter Skelter eyes swung back to me.

"What have you done that's bad, Jack?"

A cop's job was to take control of the situation, and somehow I'd lost that control.

"You're not thinking clearly, Paul. You're depressed. You need to put down the detonator and the gun."

"You have five seconds to tell me something bad you've done, or I press the button."

"I'll shoot you, Paul."

"And then a lot of people will die, Jack. Five …"

"This isn't a game, Paul."

"Four …"

"Don't make me do this."

"Three …"

Was he bluffing? Did I have any options? My .38 pointed at his shoulder. If I shot him, it might get him to drop the detonator. Or it might kill him and then his bomb would explode. Or it might just piss him off and get him to turn his gun on me.

"Two …"

It came out in a spurt. "I cheated on my boyfriend with my ex-husband."

The corners of Paul's eyes crinkled up.

"Does your boyfriend know, Jack?"

"Yes."

"He found out, or you told him?"

I recalled the pained expression on Latham's face. "I told him."

"He forgave you?"

"Yes."

Paul chewed his lower lip, looking like a child caught with his hand in the cookie jar.

"Did it feel good to hurt him, Jack?"

"No."

Paul seemed to drink this in.

"You must have known it would hurt him, but you did it anyway. So some part of you must not have minded hurting him."

"I didn't want to hurt him. I just cared more about my needs than his."

"You were being selfish."

"Yes."

"You were being bad."

The word stuck like a chicken bone in my throat. "Yes."

His thumb caressed the detonator, and he licked his lips.

"What's the difference between that and what I'm doing right now?"

The gun weighed a hundred pounds, and my arms were really starting to shake.

"I broke a man's heart. You're planning on killing a bunch of people. That's worse."

Paul raised an eyebrow. "So I'm a worse person than you?"

I hesitated, then said, "Yes."

"Do you want to shoot me?"

"No."

"But I'm bad. I deserve it."

"Bad things can be forgiven, Paul."

"Do you think your boyfriend would forgive me if I killed you?"

I pictured Latham. His forgiveness was the best gift I'd ever gotten. It proved that love had no conditions. That mistakes weren't deal breakers.

I wanted to live to see Latham again.

Regain control, Jack. Demand proof.

"Show me the bomb," I said to Paul. My tone was hard, professional. I wasn't going to neutralize the situation by talking. Paul was too far gone. When dealing with bullies, you have to push back or you won't gain their respect.

"No," he said.

Louder, "Show me the bomb!"

At the word *bomb* a collective wail coursed through the crowd, and they began to stampede backward.

He began to shake, and his eyes became mean little slits. "What did I say about yelling, Jack?" Paul's finger danced over the detonator button.

"You're bluffing." I chanced a look around. The perimeter was widening.

"I'll prove I'm not bluffing by blowing up the whole—"

I got even closer, thrusting my chin at him, steadying my gun.

"I'm done with this, Paul. Drop the gun and the detonator, or I'm going to shoot you."

"If you shoot me, you'll die."

"I'm not going to believe that unless you show me the goddamn bomb."

Time stretched out, slowed. After an impossibly long second he lowered his eyes, reaching down for his buttons.

I was hoping he was bluffing, praying he was bluffing, and then his shirt opened and I saw the red sticks of dynamite.

Son of a bitch. He wasn't bluffing.

I couldn't let him press that detonator. So I fired.

Thousands of hours on the shooting range meant the move was automatic, mechanical. His wrist exploded in blood and bone, and before the scream escaped his lips I put one more in the opposite shoulder. He dropped both his gun and the detonator. I kicked them away, hoping I hadn't killed him, hoping he'd be alive until help came.

I stared at his chest, saw two electrode pads hooked up to his heart. His waist was surrounded by explosives, and in the center was a black box with a radiation symbol on it.

Paul coughed, then slumped onto his back. His wrist spurted, and his shoulder poured blood onto the pavement like a faucet. Each bullet had severed an artery. He was doomed.

I shrugged off my jacket, pressed it to the shoulder wound, and yelled, "Bomb! Get out of here!" to the few dozen idiots still gawking. Then I grabbed Paul's chin and made him look at me.

"How do I disarm this, Paul?"

His voice was soft, hoarse. "You … you killed me …"

"Paul! Answer me! How can I shut off the bomb!"

His eyelids fluttered. My blazer had already soaked through with blood.

"… how …"

"Yes, Paul. Tell me how."

"… how does …"

"Please, Paul. Stay with me."

His eyes locked on mine.

"… how does it feel to finally kill someone?"

Then his head tilted to the side and his mouth hung open.

I felt for the pulse in his neck. Barely there. He didn't have long.

I checked the crowd again. The traffic cop had fled, and the drivers of the surrounding cars had abandoned them. No paramedics rushed over, lugging life-saving equipment. No bomb squad technicians rushed over to cut the wires and save the day. It was only me, and Paul. Soon it would be only me, and a few seconds later I'd be gone too.

Should I run, give myself a chance to live? How much contamination would this dirty bomb spread? Would I die anyway, along with hundreds or thousands of others? I didn't know anything about radiation. How far could it travel? Could it go through windows and buildings? How much death could it cause?

Running became moot. Paul's chest quivered, and then was still.

I knew even less about the inner working of the human body than I did about radiation. If I started CPR, would that trick the bomb into thinking Paul's heart was still beating?

I didn't have time to ponder it. Without thinking, I tore off the electrodes and stuck them up under my shirt, under my bra, fixing them to my chest, hoping to find my heartbeat and stop the detonation.

I held my breath.

Nothing exploded.

I looked around again, saw no help. And none could get to me, with the traffic jam. I needed to move, to get to the next intersection, to find a place where the bomb squad could get to me.

But first I called Dispatch.

"This is Lieutenant Jack Daniels, from the 26th District. I'm on the corner of Michigan and Pearson. I need the bomb squad. A dirty bomb is hooked up to my heartbeat. I also need someone to check out a company downtown called LarsiTech, a medical supply company in the Prudential Building. There may have been some homicides there."

I gave the Dispatch officer my cell number, then grabbed Paul's wrist and began to drag him to the curb. It wasn't easy. My grip was slippery with blood, and the asphalt was rough and pulled at his clothes. I would tug, make sure the electrodes were still attached, take a step, and repeat.

Halfway there my cell rang.

"This is Dispatch. The bomb squad is on the way, ETA eight minutes. Are you sure on the company name, Lieutenant?"

"He said it several times."

"There's no listing for LarsiTech in the Prudential Building. I spelled it several different ways."

"Then where is LarsiTech?"

"No place I could find. Chicago had three medical supply companies, and I called them all. They didn't report any problems. The phone book has no LarsiTech. Information has no listing in Illinois, or the whole nation."

I looked down at Paul, saw the wires had ripped out of the black box. And that the black box had a local cable company's name written on the side. And that the radiation symbol was actually a sticker that was peeling off. And that the dynamite was actually road flares with their tops cut off.

Suicide by cop.

I sat down in the southbound lane on Michigan Avenue, sat down and stared at my hands, at the blood caked under the fingernails, and wondered if I'd ever be able to get them clean.

END

Formerly a private investigator in Chicago and New Orleans, **SEAN CHERCOVER** is the author of the acclaimed novel *Big City, Bad Blood,* which features P.I. Ray Dudgeon. He lives in Chicago, loves Chicago, and owns more blues albums than can reasonably be justified.

WWW.CHERCOVER.COM

THE NON COMPOS MENTIS BLUES
SEAN CHERCOVER

RAY DUDGEON INVESTIGATIONS
SURVEILLANCE REPORT

Operative: Ray Dudgeon
Date of Surveillance: 07/08 AUG 2005
Time In: 4:30 PM   Time Out: 7:30 AM
Mileage: 43miles

Subject Name	Race/Gender	DOB
GORDON S. HILLS	Caucasian Male	18 FEB 1949
SUSAN TITLEY	Caucasian Female	UNK

Summary of Subject Activity:

4:30 PM: Surveillance commenced in the underground parking garage at 235 North Dearborn Street, Chicago IL. Reporting Investigator (RI) established the location of the subject's green Mercedes 550 (IL license #NJF 823) and parked nearby.

6:36 PM: Subject entered garage from north elevators, carrying a black briefcase and brown overnight bag, and got into his car (photo #1). Subject exited the garage onto Dearborn. Surveillance continued north to Wacker Drive, east to Wabash Avenue, south to Adams Street and west to Daley Plaza. Subject pulled over to the curb and Susan Titley (Caucasian female, app. 5'6", app. 120 lbs, app. 33 YOA, red hair) entered the vehicle on the passenger side (photo #2). Subject drove without interruption to West Webster (route map in case file) and parked at a meter near #447. Subjects exited the vehicle (photo #3) and walked west to Soto le Stelle, an Italian restaurant at #455 West Webster. They entered the restaurant at 7:15 PM (photo #4) and sat at a table near the back of the room. RI returned to the surveillance vehicle.

9:02 PM: Subjects exited the restaurant and walked to the subject vehicle. Primary subject held the passenger door for Ms. Titley, (photo #5) then entered on the driver's side and drove west on Webster, then north on Halsted and parked at a meter near #2519 and then entered B.L.U.E.S. (photo #6). Subjects sat on the raised area near the front door.

11:22 PM: Subjects exited the bar and walked to the subject vehicle (photo #7), and then drove without interruption to the Best Western O'Hare hotel (route map in case file) and parked in the garage. Subject took the overnight bag, locked the briefcase in the trunk (photo #8). Subjects entered the hotel lobby together (photo #9).

12:09 PM: Subjects registered into room 319 (primary subject paid cash) and took the elevator to the third floor.

12:13 AM: RI registered into room 321 and maintained surveillance there, door ajar.

5:30 AM: Telephone in room 319 rang twice.

6:19 AM: Subjects exited room 319 and took the elevator to the lobby. RI took the stairs. Subjects dropped the room key at the desk and walked to the parking garage. Once in the subject vehicle, they kissed for several minutes (photos #10-13). Subjects exited the parking garage (photo #14). <u>Surveillance terminated</u>.

6:40 AM: RI checked out of the hotel.

7:15 AM: RI arrived at home office, 111 North Wabash Avenue.

7:30 AM: <u>Time Out</u>.

END OF REPORT

She'd read the report, looked at the photos, but she still had trouble accepting it. Somehow I knew she would.

"Mrs. Hills, you hired me because you thought your husband was having an affair. He is."

"But some cheap little Italian restaurant and an airport motel? It all seems a little *downscale*, for him." She shot me a look from behind huge Gucci sunglasses. I couldn't actually see her eyes but I caught the abrupt change in the angle of her head. Even without eyes, she shot me a look.

"He's not likely to take her to Charlie Trotter's and the Ritz-Carlton," I offered. "Or any place where he's known."

"And a smoky blues club? *Please.* Gordon doesn't even like blues music."

"Maybe he does."

She shot me another look. "Gordon does *not* enjoy blues music."

Thinking back on the previous night, I had to concede her point. Gordon didn't strike me as a fan of the blues. My impression had been that he'd taken Susan Titley to a blues club in order to impress her. In order to seem hip. When he drummed his fingers on the tabletop, he completely missed 2-and-4, and in fact seemed to miss the concept of any steady rhythm. Susan Titley seemed no more interested in the music than Gordon. They talked a lot, over the music, about how great the music was. And they didn't ever shut up long enough to actually listen.

They missed a hell of a set. Lurrie Bell—my favorite of the current Chicago blues axemen—put on a fine show, complete with searing guitar and heartbreaking vocals. Pearls before swine. But they paid the cover and bought drinks, and I suppose that gave them the right to ignore the musical genius in their midst. Still, I didn't like them for it, and I started to feel something akin to alliance with Mrs. Hills, who now sat flipping through the photos attached to my report.

"Where are the pictures of them fucking?" And now she wanted to see them fucking. So much for our nascent alliance.

"I don't take pictures of people fucking, Mrs. Hills. First, it's illegal. Once they're in the hotel room, they're off limits. Second, it's unnecessary. There's not a divorce court in the state that will believe they were playing Scrabble all night. Now if you can arrange it so they're fucking in public—"

"Just be quiet a minute," she said, "I want to read this again."

So I shut up and let Mrs. Hills read the report of her husband's infidelity for the third time. She was not a bad looking woman, but quite severe. I guessed she'd already had a couple of face-lifts and I put her in her early fifties. She wore a cream Chanel suit, too much gold on the wrists and fingers and three strands of jumbo pearls around the neck. Her ash-blonde hair, cut long enough to caress her shoulders, was her most attractive feature. She made my office smell like Coco, which was okay by me. Perfume—even when overzealously applied—smells better than a guy who hasn't showered in a day and a half. Which I hadn't. Across the oak desk I noticed that her overlong nails were painted to match the pearls. Highland Park *nouveau riche*.

I glanced at my wall of built-in bookshelves. I'd actually read some of those books. Someday I'd read them all. Right now I just wanted to get Mrs. Hills the hell out of my office so I could sleep the rest of the morning away on the familiar burgundy leather couch in the corner. But the tension in Mrs. Hills' ivory jaw said that she was going nowhere for a while. I wished she would just cry, like any normal wife. I reached into a pocket and dug out a half-empty pack of Pall Malls, tapped one on the desk, put it between my lips and fired it up. She forced two sharp coughs to register her disapproval, but didn't look up.

I dragged deep and blew smoke at the ceiling and said, "Coffee?" She waved her pearlescent claws absently in my direction. "Well, I've been up all night and I need some, so I'll put your name in the pot." No response.

I made a pot and came back from the kitchenette with two mugs full of strong, black coffee, put one in front of her and sat and sipped the other one and scalded my upper lip.

"Well Mr. Dudgeon, it appears that you've done your job."

"Not completely. That report, the photos and my testimony will establish that your husband was unfaithful. Once. We need to establish that he was habitually adulterous, or that he was having an ongoing affair."

"She's his secretary. You don't have a one night stand with your secretary."

"Sure. But that logic alone doesn't hold up in court. We need to document three separate occasions of infidelity."

"That's patently ridiculous. I've paid you for three days' work."

"You can't expect me to know when your husband's going to—"

"And your rates are exorbitant. I've checked around." Was she actually trying to negotiate with me?

I blew on my coffee for a while and waited for her to fire me. But she said nothing, just curled her right claw around the coffee mug and took a long, silent sip. Then another. I started to get that uneasy feeling and hit the foot switch under my desk, which activated a video camera hidden in the bookshelf. She read the report a fourth time. I sat and smoked, drank some coffee, and listened to the "L" trains rumble by, twelve floors below, on Wabash Avenue.

Finally she said, "How much would you charge to … well, you know?"

There it was. "No, I don't know."

"To kill him." Only her lips moved. The mug was still in her right claw.

"I'll pretend I didn't hear that, Mrs. Hills."

"I've learned to accept the private humiliations," she said, "but this ... this is the end of it. I'll give you twenty thousand dollars."

I stubbed out the cigarette and said, "I don't murder people, Mrs. Hills. I'm a detective, not a hit man."

"If you're not man enough to save me from his cruelty, I'll find someone who is."

"Wait a second, let's slow down. You've just received some bad news and you're very upset—"

"Do I look very upset?" She didn't.

"Some people hide it well," I said with a good deal of irony.

"I refuse to stage a public performance of my anguish for your benefit," she said. "I want him dead and I'm offering a substantial sum. Now do you or do you not want the job?"

It's amazing how many people think private investigators will kill someone for the right amount of money. Too much television. I stood and picked up my coffee mug, pried hers loose, and went to refill them and give her a chance to think. When I returned, she was standing.

"I've had enough coffee. I want an answer. Yes or no?"

"You want me to kill your husband."

"Yes."

"And you're offering twenty thousand dollars."

She picked up her purse and said, "Stop stalling, Mr. Dudgeon. Yes or no?"

I let out a sigh, almost meaning it. "All right, give me a couple days to work out a few things and then call me if you haven't changed your mind."

"I'll talk to you in a couple of days, then." Her mouth twitched up at the corners. Almost a smile. "I won't change my mind."

And she was gone, her stiletto heels marching off toward the elevators down the hall, probably leaving a trail of dents in the marble floor.

I slumped into my chair and hit the foot switch to shut off the video camera and lit another cigarette.

Then I reached for the Rolodex and flipped to "Holborn."

Special Agent Holborn and I had a brief but intense history. I think Holborn liked me but he wasn't sure if he respected me, while I respected him but wasn't sure if I liked him. Anyway, we'd worked together once and things had turned out okay.

Holborn and his partner Special Agent Jordan watched the videotape in the meeting room at the FBI's Chicago office on West Roosevelt, and I watched them. Holborn was about six feet tall, with sandy hair and a runner's build. Agent Jordan was black, an inch taller than Holborn, with a bald head, a close-cropped beard and a little more muscle on his frame. I'd only met Jordan once, so it was too soon to know if I liked or respected him. The videotape ended and Holborn pressed Stop and the television screen went to blue.

"Looks like we've got a live one," said Agent Jordan.

Holborn said, "Ray, are you sure that you said nothing, prior to activating the video recorder, which could've planted this idea?"

"Well now that you mention it, I may have said something like, 'It sure would be great if your husband was dead.' Other than that, nothing I can think of." Jordan stifled a laugh and I started to like him. Holborn glared at me.

"Don't be a dickhead," he said.

"I've been awake for fifty-two hours," I countered.

Holborn turned to Jordan, "Check with Torontelli and Robertson, in case this turns into something." Jordan nodded and left the room.

I said, "I'd like one more chance to talk her out of it."

"Why? She's an Ice Queen. You can't possibly like her ..."

"No," I said, "but there's something ... I don't know. Offered a way out, she might reconsider. And if she doesn't, it'll help shore up the case against an entrapment defense."

"Holborn considered it. "I'll give you one chance. When she calls back—"

"*If* she calls back."

"*When* she calls back, you record the call. Give her one chance to reconsider, then make the deal."

"Fine."

"And don't get cute, Ray. Play this straight or I'll have your balls in a vice."

"You sure know how to paint a pretty picture, Agent Holborn."

###

Of course she called back. And I recorded the call. I played it straight and gave her the one chance to back out, but she would not be dissuaded. She still wanted the job done and she was growing impatient. We went back and forth on the timing of payment. I said I wanted it up front. She wanted to pay on confirmation of her husband's untimely demise, although she didn't put it that bluntly. Maybe she was being careful because we were on the phone, but her reliance on euphemisms was frustrating. We finally agreed on six thousand up front and fourteen "upon delivery." We arranged to meet that evening at an IHOP diner near the airport.

After we hung up, I called Agent Holborn and we agreed that he would come to my office at nine thirty so he could wire me for sound, go over the game plan and get to the diner ahead of the scheduled meeting time of eleven thirty. I taped that call too, just for the hell of it.

"Now remember, this doesn't transmit, it's only a recorder, so we're relying on you to judge when you've got enough on tape."

"I've done this before," I said as I buttoned my shirt.

"Just don't get fancy. And don't make any assumptions. Check the money. If she doesn't give you money, we're back to square one."

"Yeah, okay." I put on my jacket and tightened my tie. Holborn wore blue jeans, a polo shirt and a black leather bomber jacket. I'd never seen him in anything but a suit. "Is it on?"

"It's on," said Holborn. "There's five hours of tape, so don't worry about it. And don't touch it. If you adjust it, you'll give the whole thing away. Just forget it's there." He seemed tense and it was the kind of tension that can be contagious and I didn't appreciate it.

"Agent Holborn, for a guy who's done this a million times, you seem pretty nervous. Relax."

"I've also seen amateurs like you screw it up a million times."

If he were really so concerned, he'd wire me with a transmitter and have an agent listening in. I smiled. "Since we're doing this on the cheap, I have to conclude that you do, in fact, trust my judgment and all this tough talk is just to keep me in my place."

"As usual, Ray, you assume too much," he said. "I'm watching my budget."

I gave the feds ten minutes lead-time and headed out to Rosemont in a steady drizzle. It had been threatening hard rain for days and the night air had the smell of it, but the drizzle lacked motivation and never graduated to a genuine rain. I spent the drive mumbling obscene stories about FBI agents and their deviant sexual habits into the tape recorder. Something to do with llamas and spandex.

Mrs. Hills was drinking coffee in a booth at the IHOP when I arrived. Holborn and Jordan were sitting at the counter, eating pie. Jordan wore a jean jacket and a faded White Sox baseball cap. The cap looked natural on him and I figured him for a ball fan.

"You're early, Mrs. Hills." I sat across from her and checked my reflection in her sunglasses, thinking *Maybe rich people are more light-sensitive than the rest of us.*

"I wasn't sure you'd come." Her Chanel suit was black this time.

"For twenty grand?" I signaled the waitress for coffee. "You've chosen an appropriate color, if I may say so."

"Let's dispense with the gumshoe humor, shall we?" She said "gumshoe" the way your racist Aunt Mildred says "Negro."

"Sure you want to go through with this?"

Her blood-red nails dipped into her purse and withdrew an envelope. "Six thousand, as we agreed. The balance upon delivery." She slid the envelope to the center of the table.

I took a few seconds to get the wording right. "Mrs. Hills, I'm ready to take your money but you didn't answer my question." The waitress set the coffee in front of me. When she was out of earshot I continued, "You just used the word 'delivery' again, and I don't like it. It sounds to me like you may be sugarcoating this thing in your mind."

"I know what I'm doing," she said.

"Okay." I took the envelope. "But one thing ..."

"Now what is it?"

"I need to be sure that you're not gonna fall apart and rollover on me when the cops come with their questions. Because there will be questions. Probing questions, about your alibi and about your marriage. And another thing ... after it's done, your husband will not look pretty. Are you sure you can handle that?" I knew I was pushing, but I needed her to say the magic words.

"I do not enjoy these childish games," she said, and then stiffened. "Are you setting me up?" A chill ran down my arms. The tape recorder was itchy against my side. I fought the urge to scratch. Thinking, *just play it out, Dudgeon. Play the creep that she thinks you are.* I grinned and spread my arms wide.

"Why don't you come over here and sit on my lap and frisk me," I said, and winked at her. "We can talk about the first thing that comes up."

"Oh dear God, you are a repulsive little man."

"Your loss," I shrugged.

"Shall we stick to business, please?"

"Fine, but you still haven't answered me." I dropped the lecherous grin and sipped some weak coffee. "Mrs. Hills, look at it this way: if you went for a face-lift, wouldn't the surgeon be negligent if he didn't explain the risks?" She seemed to be following me. "Now in a job like this, the risk is that you'll have a change of heart. Once I walk out of here, there's no turning back. Like I said, I want your money, but I've got to know that you're going into this with a level head." I maintained eye contact and resisted the urge to keep rambling.

She nodded her head, at last. "Frankly, I don't care if my husband looks like he's been torn apart by a pack of dingoes, I just want him dead. And there will be no change of heart. Is that level enough for you, Mr. Dudgeon?"

"It'll be done within the week," I said. "Don't come to me with regrets."

"How will I know when it's done?"

"The police will want you to identify the body. It'll look like a mugging." I sipped some more bad coffee. "About the money, it isn't in any way traceable to you, is it?"

"I've had a significant sum of paper money in storage for years." Her nails clicked on the Formica.

"I'll have to trust you on that," I said, and stuffed the envelope into my breast pocket. "I'm going to leave now. You can get the check."

Mrs. Hills fumbled around in her purse and I went to the men's room where I looked in the envelope. It was money, all right. I left the diner without stopping to say goodbye. Holborn had already moved outside. Jordan sat at the counter, waiting to follow her out.

They were easy to spot if you were looking for them, but of course Mrs. Hills wouldn't be. Holborn sat reading a map in a black sedan parked beside Mrs. Hills' Jaguar. Other agents were in a white van, parked directly behind. I couldn't see them but I knew they were there. I got in my car and drove around the building and parked in the shadows. I left the engine running, ready to make my move. With everything by the book, Mrs. Hills would likely strike a plea and I'd be spared the hassle of testifying, so I wanted to get the arrest on tape.

She emerged from the diner, seemingly oblivious to the presence of Agent Jordan, who followed twelve paces behind. As she advanced upon her car, I took my foot off the brake, applied the gas and drove forward, and several other things happened at once: Holborn dropped the map and got out of the sedan; Jordan closed the distance behind Mrs. Hills; the van's headlights came on and its side door slid open and two agents hopped out. By the time they reached her, I was out of my car and coming fast around the front fender.

She froze in place, taking in the fact that she was surrounded. I lit a cigarette.

"Mrs. Francine Hills?" said Holborn.

"Yes."

Holborn flipped his badge. "Special Agent Holborn, FBI. You're under arrest for the attempted murder-for-hire of Mr. Gordon Hills."

"But I ... I ..."

Holborn produced a small card from his wallet and read it, fast and without inflection. "Before we ask you any questions, you must understand your rights ... You have the right to remain silent ... Anything you say can be used against you in court ... You have the right to talk to a lawyer for advice before we ask you any questions and to have him with you during questioning ... If you cannot afford a lawyer, one will be appointed for you before questioning if you wish ... If you decide to answer questions now without a lawyer present, you will still have the right to stop questioning at any time until you talk to a lawyer. Do you understand what I have read to you?"

"Yes I do."

"Having these rights in mind, do you wish to talk to me now?"

A single tear slid from behind Mrs. Hills' sunglasses and down her left cheek. "No thank you. I'll wait for my lawyer." She thrust a finger in my direction. "I'd like a word with him, though." Holborn looked at me. I nodded and stepped forward. She leaned in close and said, "You have no idea what you've done."

"I think I do," I said, and blew a stream of smoke at her hair. Her right claw lashed out and her nails ripped my face, just below the left ear. Holborn grabbed her wrists from behind and held her fast.

"You bastard!" she shrieked, trembling all over. "You fucking bastard! Give me back my money!"

"Mrs. Hills," I said, "I'd advise you to get yourself firmly under control and say nothing until you've spoken with your attorney." I threw my cigarette down and it hissed itself to death on the wet pavement. Agent Jordan handed me a handkerchief and I held it to my face.

"Let's not make this any harder, ma'am," said Holborn. He produced handcuffs from under his jacket and gave Mrs. Hills a new pair of bracelets and loaded her into the backseat of the sedan, sandwiched between the agents who'd jumped from the van. Another agent, still in the van, started its engine. The rain started up again, but it was still only a light rain.

Agent Jordan said, "You better get that checked, it's bleeding a fair bit." I looked at the handkerchief, which was now mostly red but looked purple in the mercury-vapor light of the parking lot. "Keep it," he said, and climbed into the front passenger seat of the sedan.

Holborn approached and said, "The money."

I handed him the cash envelope. "I guess I didn't screw it up, even if I am an amateur."

"We'll see what you got on tape."

I unbuttoned my shirt and ripped the tape recorder off the side of my abdomen, taking some hair with it, and untangled the wire that led to a microphone on the back of my tie. "You're welcome," I said.

Holborn took it from me and nodded. "Come see me tomorrow. We'll need a statement." He got behind the wheel of the sedan and they pulled away.

As I walked back to my car, the real rain began.

Mrs. Hills retained Dermott O'Connor, Chicago's criminal defense attorney to the rich and infamous. O'Connor was one of the most skilled media whores in town and he played the case for full coverage and maximum confusion. And the media had a collective orgasm over the story. After three days of dancing the seven veils for newspaper reporters, talk radio and television, O'Connor had half the potential jury pool thinking that a scumbag private detective had preyed on the emotional vulnerability of an abused wife who came to him for help with a divorce. Naturally, I was being cast in the role of the scumbag private detective. Apparently I'd bullied and persuaded until Mrs. Hills finally broke down in desperation and agreed to my plan to murder her abusive husband. When I felt the heat of the FBI, I framed Mrs. Hills as the architect of the plan. *Sure I did.* And then came the best part: O'Connor wanted everyone to believe that the FBI, although well intentioned, had fallen for my con-job.

The FBI was not commenting, except to say that they were confident they'd arrested the right person and that Ray Dudgeon was not a suspect in this case.

The Federal Prosecutor's office had even less to say than the FBI. They were looking forward to bringing all of the facts to light in the courtroom. Have a nice day.

Mr. Gordon Hills was commenting through his attorney, who had a few points to make on his behalf: "Mr. Hills categorically denies ever lifting a hand to his wife. All marriages have their ups and downs and the Hills' marriage is no exception. Mr. Hills loves his wife but strongly suspects that she may not be of sound mind. He supports his wife's application for bail, with the provision that the court issue a restraining order prohibiting Mrs. Hills from coming within one hundred yards of him, and that she submit to court-ordered psychological counseling."

I was not commenting at all. Not even to *Chronicle* reporter Terry Green, who was my best friend and a former colleague, back when I was a reporter in a former life. I spent my days hanging up on reporters and trying not to read newspapers or listen to the radio or watch television. I wanted to call Terry and howl: *You moron! You call yourself a journalist? I can't believe you're letting yourself get played like this!* But I knew I was being irrational and I could imagine Terry's rebuttal: *This is a newsworthy story and O'Connor is making newsworthy comments. We report the news. You choose not to comment, which leaves those of us who didn't quit on journalism to do the ethical heavy-lifting. And you want to judge us? Fuck that. Get off the cross, you big crybaby.* Of course Terry would've been more diplomatic about it.

On the third day, Mrs. Hills made bail and Federal Prosecutor Alex Cavanaugh beckoned me to his office. I wore a clean suit.

If I'd been there alone, Cavanaugh would probably have sat behind his impressive desk and made steepling gestures at me with his hands. But I wasn't his only guest, so we sat in comfortable leather chairs around a marble coffee table. With us were Special Agent Holborn and Cavanaugh's assistant, Leonard Pritts.

Pritts briefed us on the case and concluded, "We're still back-channeling with O'Connor to work a plea. But the *non compos mentis* angle is bullshit. We'll deal some time but we're not dropping to a lesser charge."

"Great," I said. "But somebody from your office has to make clear to the press what my role in this is. O'Connor's fucking with my reputation."

"So?" said Pritts.

I turned to a friendlier face. "Agent Holborn, I came to you from the start—"

"And we've made it clear that you're not a suspect," said Holborn.

"Just barely," I said. "Look, so far I've been quiet but I have a right to defend my reputation and my livelihood."

Cavanaugh cleared his throat and said, "Do not threaten, Gumshoe." He said "gumshoe" the same way as Mrs. Hills. "You will not even *dream* of speaking to the press about this case, or your career will most certainly be over. And you do not advise us about how we do our jobs."

I felt like a kid in the principal's office. "Not my intention," I said, holding up my hand in apology. "The point that I was so unskillfully trying to make is valid, but my presentation was out of line. I assure you, I have no intention of speaking to the press at this time."

"Good," said Cavanaugh. Then, to Pritts, "I'm sure our office can make a statement that will clearly communicate the fact that Mr. Dudgeon is a cooperative witness who aided the investigation from the start and has never been a suspect in this case."

"Thank you," I said.

As we left the building, I shook my head at Holborn and said, "Thanks a heap for all the support in there."

"Maybe you should be less of a smart-ass," said Holborn, and he walked away. I guess he'd heard my comedy routine on the wire recording.

###

The next day, Mr. Gordon Hills went to his wife's hotel room and beat her to death with a framing hammer. After which he ordered room service and turned on the television and watched *Wheel of Fortune* until the police arrived. He was pleading temporary insanity, according to his defense attorney, Dermott O'Connor.

Small goddamn world.

I took myself out drinking. Thinking *Was Francine Hills really a battered wife, or did Gordon Hills go mental when he woke up to the fact that she'd tried to hire his murder? Beat her to death with a hammer—that's pretty mental for a guy who isn't violent to begin with.*

In memory, Francine Hills' words called out to me: "I've learned to accept the private humiliations ... I refuse to stage a public performance of my anguish for your benefit ... if you're not man enough to save me from his cruelty ..." *Shit. He probably did beat her.* And the sunglasses. Had she been hiding a bruise that makeup could not completely erase? Had I been too quick to dismiss her affectations as vanity?

"You have no idea what you've done," she'd said.

I changed course and made it home relatively sober. There was a message waiting on my machine.

"Ray Dudgeon—Dermott O'Connor calling. As you may have heard, I'm representing Mr. Hills, and I believe you could be of assistance to his defense. I realize we were on opposite sides of this thing until recently, but I know you're a grown-up and you understand how the game is played, and I think our interests now coincide. Right now, I'm sure if you think back, you'll recall something Mrs. Hills may have said which would indicate that she was concerned about her husband's psychological condition ..."

I stopped the machine and erased the message without listening to the rest. Yeah, I knew how the game was played.

END

MAX ALLAN COLLINS, author of the graphic novel *Road to Perdition* that spawned the Academy Award-winning film, has written often about the gangster era in Chicago. Prose *Perdition* sequels *Road to Purgatory* and *Road to Paradise* chart the Nitti and Giancana/Accardo mob eras, and his Shamus-honored Nathan Heller novels follow a fictional Chicago P.I. through the major unsolved crimes of the '30s thru the '60s.

WWW.MAXALLANCOLLINS.COM

SCRAP
MAX ALLAN COLLINS

FRIDAY AFTERNOON, DECEMBER 8, 1939,
I had a call from Jake Rubinstein to meet him at 3159
Roosevelt, which was in Lawndale, my old neighborhood.
Jake was an all right guy, kind of talkative and something of a
roughneck; but then on Maxwell Street, when I was growing
up, developing a mouth and muscles was necessary for survival. I knew Jake had been existing out on the fringes of the
rackets since then, but that was true of a lot of guys. I didn't
hold it against him. I went into one of the rackets myself, after all—known in Chicago as the police department—and I
figured Jake wouldn't hold that against me, either. Especially
since I was private, now, and he wanted to hire me.

The afternoon was bitterly cold, snow on the ground but not snowing, as I sat parked in my sporty '32 Auburn across the street from the drugstore, over which was the union hall where Jake said to meet him. The Scrap Iron and Junk Handlers Union, he said. I didn't know there was one. They had unions for everything these days. My pop, an old union man, would've been pleased. I didn't much care.

I went up the flight of stairs and into the outer office; the meeting room was adjacent, at my left. The place was modest, like most union halls—if you're running a union you don't want the rank and file to think you're living it up—but the secretary behind the desk looked like a million. She was a brunette in a trim, brown suit with big, brown eyes and bright red lipstick. She'd soften the blow of paying dues any day.

She smiled at me and I forgot it was winter. "Would you be Mr. Heller?"

"I would. Would you be free for dinner?"

Her smile settled in one corner of her bright red mouth. "I wouldn't. Mr. Rubinstein is waiting for you in Mr. Martin's office."

And she pointed to the only door in the wall behind her, and I gave her a can't-blame-a-guy-for-trying look and went on in.

The inner office wasn't big but it seemed bigger than it was because it was underfurnished: just a clutter-free desk and a couple of chairs and two wooden file cabinets. Jake was sitting behind the desk, feet up on it, socks with clocks showing, as he read the *Racing News*.

"How are you, Jake," I said, and held out my hand.

He put the paper down, stood and grinned and shook my hand; he was a little guy, short I mean, but he had shoulders on him and his grip was a killer. He wore a natty, dark blue suit and a red, hand-painted tie with a sunset on it and a hat that was a little big for him. He kept the hat on indoors—self-conscious about his thinning hair, I guess.

"You look good, Nate. Thanks for coming. Thanks for coming yourself and not sending one of your ops."

"Any excuse to get back to the old neighborhood, Jake," I said, pulling up a chair and sitting. "We're about four blocks from where my pop's bookshop was, you know."

"I know, I know," he said, sitting again. "What do you hear from Barney these days?"

"Not much. When you'd get in the union racket, anyway? Last I heard you were a door-to-door salesman."

Jake shrugged. He had dark eyes and a weak chin and five o'clock shadow—make that six o'clock shadow. "A while ago," he allowed. "But it ain't really a racket. We're trying to give our guys a break."

I smirked at him. "In this town? Billy Skidmore isn't going to put up with a legit junk handler's union."

Skidmore was a portly, dapperly dressed junk dealer and politician who controlled most of the major non-Capone gambling in town. Frank Nitti, Capone's heir, put up with that because Skidmore was also a bail bondsman, which made him a necessary evil.

"Skidmore's got troubles these days," Jake said. "He can't afford to push us around no more."

"You're talking about the income tax thing."

"Yeah. Just like Capone. He didn't pay his taxes and they got 'im for it."

"They indicted him, but that doesn't mean they got him. Anyway, where do I come in?"

Jake leaned forward, brow beetling. "You know a guy named Leon Cooke?"

"Can't say I do."

"He's a little younger than us, but he's from around here. He's a lawyer. He put this union together, two, three years ago. Well, about a year back he became head of an association of junkyard dealers, and the rank and file voted him out."

I shrugged. "Seems reasonable. In Chicago it wouldn't be unusual to represent both the employees and the employers, but kosher it ain't."

Jake was nodding. "Right. The new president is Johnny Martin. Know him?"

"Can't say I do."

"He's been with the Sanitary District for, oh, twenty or more years."

The Sanitary District controlled the sewage in the city's rivers and canals.

"He needed a hobby," I said, "so he ran for president of the junk handler's union, huh?"

"He's a good man, Nate, he really is."

"What's your job?"

"I'm treasurer of the union."

"You're the collector, then."

"Well ... yeah. Does it show?"

"I just didn't figure you for the accountant type."

He smiled sheepishly. "Every union needs a little muscle. Anyways, Cooke. He's trying to stir things up, we think. He isn't even legal counsel for the union anymore, but he's been coming to meetings, hanging around. We think he's been going around talking to the members."

"Got an election coming up?"

"Yeah. We want to know who he's talking to. We want to know if anybody's backing him."

"You think Nitti's people might be using him for a front?"

"Could be. Maybe even Skidmore. Playing both ends against the middle is Cooke's style. Anyways, can you shadow him and find out?"

"For fifteen a day and expenses, I can."

"Isn't that a little steep, Nate?"

"What's the monthly take on union dues around this joint?"

"Fifteen a day's fine," Jake said, shaking his head side to side, smiling.

"And expenses."

The door opened and the secretary came in, quickly, her silk stockings flashing.

"Mr. Rubinstein," she said, visibly upset, "Mr. Cooke is in the outer office. Demanding to see Mr. Martin."

"Shit," Jake said through his teeth. He glanced at me. "Let's get you out of here."

We followed the secretary into the outer office, where Cooke, a man of medium size in an off-the-rack brown suit, was pacing. A heavy topcoat was slung over his arm. In his late twenties, with thinning brown hair, Cooke was rather mild looking, with wire-rim glasses and cupid lips. Nonetheless, he was well and truly pissed off.

"Where's that bastard Martin?" he demanded of Jake. Not at all intimidated by the little strong-arm man.

"He stepped out," Jake said.

"Then I'll wait. Till hell freezes over, if necessary."

Judging by the weather, that wouldn't be long.

"If you'll excuse us," Jake said, brushing by him. I followed.

"Who's this?" Cooke said, meaning me. "A new member of your goon squad? Isn't Fontana enough for you?"

Jake ignored that and I followed him down the steps to the street.

"He didn't mean Carlos Fontana, did he?" I asked.

Jake nodded. His breath was smoking, teeth chattering. He wasn't wearing a topcoat; we'd left too quickly for such niceties.

"Fontana's a pretty rough boy," I said.

"A lot of people who was in bootlegging," Jake said, shrugging, "had to go straight. What are you gonna do now?"

"I'll use the phone booth in the drugstore to get one of my ops out here to shadow Cooke. I'll keep watch till then. He got enough of a look at me that I don't dare shadow him myself."

Jake nodded. "I'm gonna go call Martin."

"And tell him to stay away?"

"That's up to him."

I shook my head. "Cooke seemed pretty mad."

"He's an asshole."

Jake walked quickly down to a parked black Ford coupe, got in, and smoked off.

I called the office and told my secretary to send either Lou or Frankie out as soon as possible, whoever was available first; then I sat in the Auburn and waited.

Not five minutes later, a heavy-set, dark-haired man in a camel hair topcoat went in and up the union-hall stairs. I had a hunch it was Martin. More than a hunch: he looked well and truly pissed off, too.

I could smell trouble.

I probably should have sat it out, but I got out of the Auburn and crossed Roosevelt and went up those stairs myself. The secretary was standing behind the desk. She was scared shitless. She looked about an inch away from crying.

Neither man was in the anteroom, but from behind the closed door came the sounds of loud voices.

"What's going on?" I said

"That awful Mr. Cooke was in using Johnny ... Mr. Martin's telephone, in his office, when Mr. Martin arrived."

They were scuffling in there, now.

"Any objection if I go in there and break that up?" I asked her.

"None at all," she said.

That was when we heard the shots.

Three of them, in rapid succession.

The secretary sucked in breath, covered her mouth, said, "My God ... my God."

And I didn't have a gun, goddamnit.

I was still trying to figure out whether to go in there or not when the burly, dark-haired guy who I assumed (rightly) to be Martin, still in the camel hair topcoat, came out with a blue-steel revolver in his hand. Smoke was curling out the barrel.

"Johnny, Johnny," the secretary said, going to him, clinging to him. "Are you all right?"

"Never better," he said, but his voice was shaking. He scowled over at me; he had bushy, black eyebrows that made the scowl frightening. And the gun helped. "Who the hell are you?"

"Nate Heller. I'm a dick Jake Rubinstein hired to shadow Leon Cooke."

Martin nodded his head back toward the office. "Well, if you want to get started, he's on the floor in there."

I went into the office and Cooke was on his stomach; he wasn't dead yet. He had a bullet in the side; the other two slugs went through the heavy coat that had been slung over his arm.

"I had to do it," Martin said. "He jumped me. He attacked me."

"We better call an ambulance," I said.

"So, then, we can't just dump his body somewhere," Martin said, thoughtfully.

"I was hired to shadow this guy," I said. "It starts and ends there. You want something covered up, call a cop."

"How much money you got on you?" Martin said. He wasn't talking to me.

The secretary said, "Maybe a hundred."

"That'll hold us. Come on."

He led her through the office and opened a window behind his desk. In a very gentlemanly manner, he helped her out onto the fire escape.

And they were gone.

I helped Cooke onto his feet.

"You awake, pal?"

"Y-yes," he said. "Christ, it hurts."

"Mount Sinai hospital's just a few blocks away," I said. "We're gonna get you there."

I wrapped the coat around him to keep from getting blood on my car seat, and drove him to the hospital.

Half an hour later, I was waiting outside Cooke's room in the hospital hall when Captain Stege caught up with me.

Stege, a white-haired fireplug of a man with black-rimmed glasses and a pasty complexion—and that Chicago rarity, an honest cop—was not thrilled to see me.

"I'm getting sick of you turning up at shootings," he said.

"I do it just to irritate you. It makes your eyes twinkle."

"You left a crime scene."

"I hauled the victim to the hospital. I told the guy at the drugstore to call it in. Let's not get technical."

"Yeah," Stege grunted. "Let's not. What's your story?"

"The union secretary hired me to keep an eye on this guy Cooke. But Cooke walked in, while I was there, angry, and then Martin showed up, equally steamed."

I gave him the details.

As I was finishing up, a doctor came out of Cooke's room and Stege cornered him, flashing his badge.

"Can he talk, doc?"

"Briefly. He's in critical condition."

"Is he gonna make it?"

"He should pull through. Stay only a few minutes, gentlemen."

Stege went in and I followed; I thought he might object, but he didn't.

Cooke looked pale, but alert. He was flat on his back. Stege introduced himself and asked for Cooke's story.

Cooke gave it, with lawyer-like formality: "I went to see Martin to protest his conduct of the union. I told Martin he ought to've obtained a pay raise for the men in one junkyard. I told him our members were promised a pay increase by a certain paper company, and instead got a wage cut—and that I understood he'd sided with the employer in the matter! He got very angry at that, and in a little while we were scuffling. When he grabbed a gun out of his desk, I told him he was crazy, and started to leave. Then … then he shot me in the back."

Stege jotted that down, thanked Cooke and we stepped out into the hall.

"Think that was the truth?" Stege asked me.

"Maybe. But you really ought to hear Martin's side, too."

"Good idea, Heller. I didn't think of that. Of course, the fact that Martin lammed does complicate things, some."

"With all the heat on unions, lately, I can see why he lammed. There doesn't seem to be any doubt Martin pulled the trigger. But who attacked who remains in question."

Stege sighed. "You do have a point. I can understand Martin taking it on the lam, myself. He's already under indictment for another matter. He probably just panicked."

"Another matter?"

Stege nodded. "He and Terry Druggan and two others were indicted last August for conspiracy. Trying to conceal from revenue officers that Druggan was part owner of a brewery."

Druggan was a former bootlegger, a West Side hood who'd been loosely aligned with such non-Capone forces as the Bugs Moran gang. I was starting to think maybe my old man wouldn't have been so pleased by all this union activity.

"We'll stake out Martin's place," Stege said, "for all the good it'll do. He's got a bungalow over on Wolcott Avenue."

"Nice little neighborhood," I said.

"We're in the wrong racket," Stege admitted.

It was too late in the afternoon to bother going back to the office, now, so I stopped and had supper at Pete's Steaks and then headed back to my apartment at the Morrison Hotel. I was reading a Westbrook Pegler column about what a bad boy Willie Bioff was, when the phone rang.

"Nate? It's Jake."

"Jake, I'm sorry I didn't call you or anything. I didn't have any number for you but the union hall. You know about what went down?"

"Do I. I'm calling from the Marquette station. They're holding me for questioning."

"Hell, you weren't even there!"

"That's okay. I'm stalling 'em a little."

"Why, for Christ's sake?

"Listen, Nate—we gotta hold this thing together. You gotta talk to Martin."

"Why? How?"

"I'm gonna talk to Cooke. Cooke's the guy who hired me to work for the union in the first place, and ..."

"What? Cooke hired you?"

"Yeah, yeah. Look, I'll go see Cooke first thing in the morning—that is, if you've seen Martin tonight, and worked a story out. Something that'll make this all sound like an accident ..."

"I don't like being part of cover-ups."

"This ain't no fuckin' cover-up! It's business! Look, they got the State's attorney's office in on this already. You know who's taken over for Stege already?"

"Tubbo Gilbert?"

"Himself," Jake said.

Captain Dan "Tubbo" Gilbert was the richest cop in Chicago. In the world. He was tied in with every mob, every fixer in town.

"The local will be finished," Jake said. "He'll find something in the books and use that and the shooting as an excuse to close the union down."

"Which'll freeze wages at current levels," I said. "Exactly what the likes of Billy Skidmore would want."

"Right. And then somebody else'll open the union back up, in six months or so. Somebody tied into the Nitti and Guzik crowd."

"As opposed to Druggan and Moran."

"Don't compare them to Nitti and Guzik. Those guys went straight, Nate."

"Please. I just ate. Moran got busted on a counterfeit railroad-bond scam just last week."

"Nobody's perfect. Nate, it's for the best. Think of your old man."

"Don't do that to me, Jake. I don't exactly think your union is what my pop had in mind when he was handing out pamphlets on Maxwell Street."

"Well, it's all that stands between the working stiffs and the Billy Skidmores."

"I take it you know where Martin is hiding out."

"Yeah. That secretary of his, her mother has a house in Hinsdale. Lemme give you the address ..."

"Okay, Jake. It's against my better judgment, but okay ..."

It took an hour to get there by car. Well after dark. Hinsdale was a quiet, well-fed little suburb, and the house at 409 Walnut Street was a two-story number in the midst of a healthy lawn. The kind of place the suburbs are full of, but which always seem shockingly sprawling to city boys like yours truly.

There were a few lights on downstairs. I walked up onto the porch and knocked. I was unarmed. Probably not wise, but I was.

The secretary answered the door. Cracked it open.

She didn't recognize me at first.

"I'm here about our dinner date," I said.

Then, in relief, she smiled, opened the door wider.

"You're Mr. Heller."

"That's right. I never did get your name."

"Then how did you find me?"

"I had your address. I just didn't get your name."

"Well, it's Nancy. But what do you want, Mr. Heller?"

"Make it Nate. It's cold. Could I step in?"

She swallowed. "Sure."

I stepped inside; it was a nicely furnished home, but obviously the home of an older person: the doilies and ancient photo portraits were a dead giveaway.

"This is my mother's home," she said. "She's visiting relatives. I live here."

I doubted that; the commute would be impossible. If she didn't live with Martin, in his nifty little bungalow on South Wolcott, I'd eat every doilie in the joint.

"I know that John Martin is here," I said. "Jake Rubinstein told me. He asked me to stop by."

She didn't know what to say to that.

Martin stepped out from a darkened doorway into the living room. He was in rolled-up shirt sleeves and no tie. He looked frazzled. He had the gun in his hand.

"What do you want?" he said. His tone was not at all friendly.

"You're making too big a deal out of this," I said. "There's no reason to go on the lam. This is just another union shooting—the papers're full of 'em."

"I don't shoot a man every day," Martin said.

"I'm relieved to hear that. How about putting the heater away, then?"

Martin sneered and tossed the piece on a nearby floral couch. He was a nasty man to have a nice girl like this. But then, so often nice girls do like nasty men.

I took it upon myself to sit down. Not on the couch: on a chair, with a soft seat and curved wooden arms.

Speaking of curves, Nancy, who was wearing a blue print dress, was standing wringing her hands, looking about to cry.

"I could use something to drink," I said, wanting to give her something to do.

"Me too," Martin said. "Beer. For him, too."

"Beer would be fine," I said, magnanimously.

She went into the kitchen.

"What's Jake's idea?" Martin asked.

I explained that Jake was afraid the union would be steamrolled by crooked cops and political fixers, should this shooting blow into something major, first in the papers, then in the courts.

"Jake wants you to mend fences with Cooke. Put together some story you can both live with. Then find some way you can run the union together, or pay him off or something."

"Fuck that shit!" Martin said. He stood up. "What's wrong with that little kike, has he lost his marbles?"

"A guy who works on the West Side," I said, "really ought to watch his goddamn mouth where the Jew-baiting's concerned."

"What's it to you? You're Irish."

"Does Heller sound Irish to you? Don't let the red hair fool you."

"Well fuck you too, then. Cooke's a lying little kike, and Jake's still in bed with him. Damn! I thought I could trust that little bastard ..."

"I think you can. I think he's trying to hold your union together, with spit and rubber bands. I don't know if it's worth holding together. I don't know what you're in it for—maybe you really care about your members, a little. Maybe it's the money. But if I were you, I'd do some fast thinking, put together a story you can live with and let Jake try to sell it to Cooke. Then when the dust settles you'll still have a piece of the action."

Martin walked over and pointed a thick finger at me. "I don't believe you, you slick son of a bitch. I think this is a set-up. Put together to get me to come in, give myself up and go straight to the lock-up, while Jake and Cooke tuck the union in their fuckin' belt!"

I stood. "That's up to you. I was hired to deliver a message. I delivered it. Now if you'll excuse me."

He thumped his finger in my chest. "You tell that little kike Rubinstein for me that—"

I smacked him.

He didn't go down, but it backed him up. He stood there looking like a confused bear and then growled and lumbered at me with massive fists out in front, ready to do damage.

So I smacked the bastard again, and again. He went down that time. I helped him up. He swung clumsily at me, so I hit him in the side of the face and he went down again. Stayed down.

Nancy came in, a glass of beer in either hand, and said, "What ...?" Her brown eyes wide.

"Thanks," I said, taking one glass, chugging it. I wiped the foam off my face with the back of a hand and said, "I needed that."

And I left them there.

The next morning, early, while I was still at the Morrison, shaving in fact, the phone rang.

It was Jake.

"How did it go last night?" he asked.

I told him.

"Shit," he said. "I'll still talk to Cooke, though. See if I can't cool this down some."

"I think it's too late for that."

"Me too," Jake said glumly.

Martin came in on Saturday; gave himself up to Tubbo Gilbert. Stege was off the case. The story Martin told was considerably different from Cooke's: He said Cooke was in the office using the phone ("Which he had no right to do!") and Martin told him to leave; Cooke started pushing Martin around, and when Martin fought back, Cooke drew a gun. Cooke (according to Martin) hit him over the head with it and knocked him down. Then Cooke supposedly hit him with the gun again and Martin got up and they struggled and the gun went off. Three times.

The gun was never recovered. If it was really Cooke's gun, of course, it would have been to Martin's advantage to produce it; but he didn't.

Martin's claim that Cooke attacked and beat him was backed up by the fact that his face was badly bruised and battered. So I guess I did him a favor, beating the shit out of him.

Martin was placed under bond on a charge of intent to kill. Captain Dan "Tubbo" Gilbert, representing the State's attorney's office, confiscated the charter of the union, announcing that it had been run "purely as a racket." Shutting it down until such time that "the actual working members of the union care to continue it, and elect their own officers."

That sounded good in the papers, but in reality it meant Skidmore and company had been served.

I talked to Stege about it, later, over coffee and bagels in the Dill Pickle deli below my office on Van Buren.

"Tubbo was telling the truth about the union being strictly a racket," Stege said. "They had a thousand members paying two bucks a head a month. Legitimate uses counted for only seven hundred bucks' worth a month. Martin's salary, for example, was only a hundred-twenty bucks."

"Well he's shit out of luck, now," I said.

"He's still got his position at the Sanitary District," Stege said. "Of course, he's got to beat the rap for the assault to kill charge, first ..." Stege smiled at the thought. "And Mr. Cooke tells a more convincing story than Martin does."

The trouble was, Cooke never got to tell it, not in court. He took a sudden turn for the worse, as so many people in those days did in Chicago hospitals, when they were about to testify in a major trial. Cooke died on the first Friday of January,

1940. There was no autopsy. His last visitor, I was told, was Jake Rubinstein.

When the union was finally reopened, however, Jake was no longer treasurer. He was still involved in the rackets, though, selling punchboards, working for Ben "Zuckie the Bookie" Zuckerman, with a short time-out for a wartime stint in the air force. He went to Dallas, I've heard, as representative of Chicago mob interests there, winding up running some strip joints. Rumor has it he was involved in other cover-ups, over the years.

By that time, of course, Jake was better known as Jack.

And he'd shortened his last name to Ruby.

END

"DOUBLE CROSS"

MICHAEL A. BLACK was born and raised in Chicago and has been a cop in the South Suburbs for twenty-eight years. He is the author of six novels, two nonfiction books, and countless short stories. He says: "Chicago is a writer's city. We have everything here ... rich, poor, good, bad, ethnic diversity, a fantastic lakefront and beauty in every season of the year. You want a place to lose the blues (and listen to them, too), Chi-town is the place for you."

WWW.MICHAELABLACK.COM

CHASING THE BLUES
MICHAEL A. BLACK

THE GRAYISH FILM ON THE WINDSHIELD smudged and streaked as the wipers swept over the glass, then gradually, as the pump sprayed more cleaner, our view cleared. I twisted off the dial and the wipers descended and snapped into place. Across the street another car slowed down to ogle the two babes dressed in tight-fitting halter tops and hot pants. Nadine waved to an ice cream vendor driving his truck slowly by, musical chimes playing tunefully. The driver stopped, momentarily blocking our view of the girls.

"What the hell they doing?" I asked, sitting up.

"Ahh, relax," Pat Walsh said from the passenger seat. "They're just trying to keep cool in this damn heat." He glanced over at me and wiped his large face with a dirty-looking hand-kerchief. "Hey, kid, try turning that air on again, would ya."

I twisted the knob for the air-conditioning setting and heard the blower kick in. Hot air continued to emanate from the vents, and the needle of the temperature gauge began a slow and steady ascent.

"It still ain't working, Mr. Walsh," I said.

"Yeah, yeah, I can feel that," he grunted, dabbing at his face again, and heaving a sigh. "Shit, you'd think the fucking brass woulda at least seen to it that we'd have a decent car sitting out here tonight. Ain't nothing more miserable than Chicago in the middle of a July heat wave. And quit calling me 'Mr. Walsh.' You're making me feel older than I am, for Christ's sake." He inhaled some of the hot, stale air through his flaring nostrils and ran his tongue over his lips. "You mind if I smoke a cigarette?"

He was already fumbling one out of his pack.

"No, sir," I said, silently hoping that he'd blow most of the smoke out the window.

"Quit calling me 'sir' for Christ's sake."

"Yes, si—" I started to say.

He replied with an acknowledging wink and stuck the end of the square between his lips. The ice cream truck pulled away to reveal Nadine and Linda both unwrapping something. We watched them. Walsh leaned forward, blowing smoke out of his nostrils, and gave a low whistle.

"Whoooeee, would you look at that," he said, staring at the girls. Both of them had cherry-red popsicles and they were obviously taking their time licking them. "If that don't net us some horny johns chasing the blues, nothing will. Hell, I'm getting a woody just watching 'em."

"Chasing the what?"

"The blues." He frowned. "It was what me and Big Tommy Boyce used to call working vice. You know, like a blue movie?"

"Like a porno flick?"

"Yeah." A wide grin spread across his face. "They used to call 'em blue movies back in the day. Ain't this just like watching one?"

A white Cadillac Escalade slowed down in front of the corner. Nadine lowered her eyes at the driver, and we could see the passenger side window rolling down. She ran the popsicle in and out of her mouth a few more times, then gave it a couple of residual licks. When the car stopped, she sauntered over and leaned her dark forearms on the side of the door, resting her ample breasts on top of her arms. Nadine talked for a few more seconds, then stood up and pointed to the alley about twenty-five feet away. Walsh picked up the mike.

"Looks like we got one," he said. "You guys on it?"

"Ten-four," the take-down unit said. I watched Nadine's tight ass as she walked with that extra little wiggle. Walsh drew in on the cigarette then spoke through a smoky breath. "Hey, Jimmy, you receiving everything all right?" he said into the mike again.

"Got it, boss," came the reply. "They were haggling over the price."

Walsh's face scrunched up with a look of intensity, then seemed to sag with relief as the radio van indicated that the transaction was complete. The take-down cars shot into the mouth of the alley, and we knew they were grabbing the john and pulling him out of his car. Linda had moved back to lean against the building till after the arrest was made and the john's car was taken away before she tried to net another one. Walsh took a deep drag on his cigarette and blew the smoke out the corner of his mouth. We watched as the marked unit drove by, the arrested john's pasty face on the other side of the rear window looking forlorn.

"Look at that asshole," he said with a grin. "Probably a fucking doctor or something. Driving a Caddie. The prick. Don't ya just love these Operation Angel stings?" His teeth were stained very yellow from endless cups of hot coffee and smoldering cigarettes. "These girls are good. Most women coppers got big, fat asses from sitting in the squad car all the time, but these two are tight." He took another drag and blew the smoke out his nostrils thoughtfully.

"They're a couple of babes, all right." I glanced over at him and noticed a far-away expression on his face.

"Chasing the blues," he said almost wistfully.

"What's that?"

"I ever tell you about Celine DuBois?" he asked, tapping the accumulated ash out the window.

I shook my head.

"That blond babe, Linda, over there kinda reminds me of her. Slender, but nice and big on top," he said, holding his cupped hands in front of his chest to mimic a set of large tits. "That's the way Celine was built." He chuckled softly. "Of course, she had a little help, but to stand there and look at her, you woulda never guessed she was really a guy."

I raised my eyebrows, and he continued, caught up in the reminiscence.

"Yeah, she was a real knockout. Like I said, you couldn't tell she was really a guy. Even here." He brought his big finger up to his Adam's apple. "In the old days we used to call 'em he-shes—woman on top, man on the bottom. The first time I ever met her I was on one of those sweeps. We used to go cruising, a bunch of us vice guys, and have a Chicago paddy wagon parked around the corner. We'd hit all those spots up by the bars. Well, in those days I was partnered up with Big Tom Boyce. You ever heard of him?" He paused to glance over at me.

"I think my dad used to talk about him sometimes," I said.

Walsh shrugged and took another drag.

"Tom was the best damn vice cop I ever seen," he said. "I mean, he knew everything about everybody who was in on the hustle. Connections from here to Timbuktu. Whenever the homicide dicks needed some kinda line on a hooker or faggot murder, they'd go running to Boyce." He paused and ran his tongue over his teeth.

"So, like I said, I was just a young rookie in them days. Got transferred to vice after a couple years on the street, and believe me, you were the new guy on the squad, they gave you all the shit details. But you did like you was told.

"In other words, you didn't ask no questions." He spit out the open window. "So this first time I ever met Celine we was hitting the bars looking for faggots and hookers. We go in this one bar and Boyce tells me to go sit next to this blond chick with her hair done up and a real big rack. He says I'm about to get my first vice bust, then he grinned at me.

"So I go over and this babe starts hitting on me right away. And she's got this real sexy voice. A whiskey-tenor they call it. Like Lauren Bacall's voice. You know in that old Bogie movie where she says, 'All you gotta do is whistle'?" He smiled at the memory. "Anyway, she starts putting her hand on my leg, then she's groping my crotch, and asking me if I'm looking for a little action. I barely get time to go into my spiel about being from out of town, and she asks me where I'm from. So I say Cleveland, and she starts gushin' about how that's where she's from too. One thing leads to another and she tells me she really likes me, and she wants to do me. So I say okay, and kind of give her a little sideways look, waiting for her to bring up the matter of price, but she ain't saying shit."

He paused and squeezed a few more puffs off the last bit of his cigarette, and tossed the butt out the window. Then, smiling, he continued.

"So I'm getting kinda nervous, thinking maybe I've blown it, so I whisper, 'Say, is this gonna cost me anything?' And she says, 'Ordinarily it would, but since you're a friend of my Big Tommy, I'll give you a freebie.'" Then she leans over and French kisses me right on the mouth. Well, I wasn't too happy about it, but this was way before everybody got so scared of this AIDS shit, so I just kinda swished a little booze around in my mouth like Boyce had told me to do. Then, I look over and see Boyce laughing, and he winks at me. Then the broad starts laughing too, and we all go out for a smoke. That's when Boyce introduces me to her. 'This is Celine DuBois,' he tells me, and as we shake hands, she gives me another kiss. Then he makes me reach up under her dress and tells me about her extra equipment. Shit, at first I don't believe him, till … After she went back inside, I went over to the alley and puked."

"I'll bet," I said. "Weren't you pissed?"

"Shit, Boyce took it easy on me," Walsh said. "Sometimes he'd have her take the new guy out in the car and really start to get it on. Then he'd tell him." He gave a low, phlegmy chuckle. "Those were the days, lemme tell ya. The stuff we pulled."

"How come the hooker went along with the gag?" I asked. "She owe him, or something?"

"It was a lot more than just that," he said. "She was his snitch, sure. Boyce had rescued her from one of them sweeps. Saved her from being stuck in the lock-up all night." He snorted. "Ever see what they do to one of them queens in a bullpen with two hundred guys? She was so grateful that she woulda done anything for him."

"And Linda made you think of her?" I asked.

"Yeah," he said slowly. "Her and that last john," Walsh said, taking out his cigarette pack and shaking another square out. "You see his face? He kinda reminded me of Matthew Patrick Sheridan." He looked over at me. "Remember him?"

"Name sounds familiar," I said.

Walsh snorted again as he lit the cigarette, then leaned back in the seat.

"He was a special prosecutor about fifteen years ago," he said. "Was trying to make a name for himself by burning coppers. At the time, he was a shoo-in to get on the Republican ticket for Illinois attorney general, but he dropped out of the race."

"Yeah, I do remember that now," I said. "I was in junior high, I think."

Pausing, he took a long drag on the cigarette and let the smoke drift out of his mouth thoughtfully. "I like you, kid, and I've known your dad a long time, so I'll tell you a little story of why Sheridan really dropped out. Like I said, he was trying to make a name for himself burning coppers. Rumor was that he had his eye on maybe running for governor after a couple more years. And he didn't give a shit if he had to step on the bodies of a lotta good men to get to there, either. Well, at the time, I was jocking some gal in personnel, and she tells me that somebody from Sheridan's office came over and flagged a bunch of files, and that mine was one of 'em. I mean this guy Sheridan was a real headhunter. So I started to sweat. The first thing I did was tell Boyce about it. I mean we were partners, and all, so he says he'll look into it."

He turned his head and looked at me, blowing smoke out his nostrils.

"Like I said, in them days, if you was the rookie, you did what they told ya to do. If that meant they sent you into a restaurant in Chinatown to pick up a to-go order, and the owner gives you a bag that's stapled shut, but was too light for food, you just took it and didn't ask what was in it. Get the picture?"

I nodded. Walsh leaned back in the seat and rubbed his lips with his big fingers.

"So, like I said, Boyce had connections everywhere, and the next day he comes to me and says things ain't lookin' too good. Sheridan supposedly had some kinda tape of me making one of them pick-ups in Chinatown, where they was running book outta the back room." He took in a deep breath and let it out with a heavy sigh. "So, needless to say, I started sweatin' bullets. But Boyce told me not to worry. That he'd take care of things.

"Well, the next week they had some big political fund-raiser at one of them big hotels downtown. Hundred bucks a plate, or some shit like that. Well, I'm on my night off when Boyce beeps me and tells me to get my ass downtown right away. When I get there he's standing in the lobby and kinda nods for me to go over by the elevators. I do, and he slips me a key to a room. He tells me to go up there and wait for him. When I get up there, who do I see inside but Celine, and she's dressed to kill. Low cut dress, cleavage hanging out, makeup perfect, just looking like a stone fox. She just smiles at me and keeps right on reading this magazine. *Glamour* or *Mademoiselle*, or one of them fucking girlie things."

He took another long pull on the cigarette and blew out a thin stream of smoke.

"Then the phone rings, and it's Boyce. He tells me to put Celine on, so I do. She purrs into the phone, murmurs something, then hangs it up. She looks at me and says, 'Time to make the donuts,' picks up her purse, and leaves. I don't know what the hell's going on until Boyce comes in a few minutes later. He tells me to go over by the bed and stand there till the phone rings. I ask him what the hell's going on, but he just grins and says, 'Do it,' and takes off.

"So I stand there like a dumb pecker, and after a couple of minutes the phone does ring, and it's Boyce again. He says to come to the room next door, quick. I go in there, and he's got a video monitor set up, with a bunch of wires hanging out of this vent in the wall, and a VCR next to the monitor. Boyce points to a chair beside him, and I sit down.

"I ask him again what's going on, and he says, 'Just think of me as your guardian angel, kid,' and points to the TV screen. Then I realize it's showing the same room I just come out of.

"Well, we sit there for about twenty minutes, then we hear something on the monitor and see Celine come in with this guy. I look at the fucking screen, and I'll be damned if it ain't Matthew Patrick Sheridan himself, stewed to the gills and hanging all over her like a cheap suit. Well, I just sit there watching, and Celine takes off Sheridan's pants and starts to go to work. But the fucker's had so many drinks that he's having some ... you know, problems." A broad grin stretched over Walsh's face as he recalled this part of the story. "So Celine stands up and says, 'Well, if you can't get it up, maybe you can do me first,' and lifts up her dress. She'd left off the duct tape. You shoulda seen Sheridan's face when he seen her extra equipment—" Walsh paused to give a quick, hard laugh. "He gets off the bed and starts to smack her around, but he's so drunk he trips over his own pants. But Celine starts screaming bloody murder, ripping her dress and everything. Boyce tells me to keep watching the tape, and he goes rushing in there flashing his badge. He picks Sheridan up like he was a rag doll, and sets him on the bed. Boyce acts like it's a standard bust, saying that he was moonlighting as a hotel dick, and had a report of a woman being attacked in the room, and came to investigate. "Then he says, 'Hey, don't I know you?' and Sheridan is so shook up that he's practically sober now. He says, 'No, I don't think so.' And Boyce says, 'Yeah, I *do* know you.' He sends Celine into the bathroom to get cleaned up. Then he helps Sheridan get his pants on, and takes him downstairs for a cup of coffee. I get a call from him about ten minutes later telling me to break down all the gear from the rooms, and load it into his car, which was parked in the alley, and then take Celine home. She came in wearing blue jeans and a halter top and helped me carry it all downstairs. Her eye was swelling up pretty bad where that prick had clipped her, but she was a real trooper. Didn't say dick about it."

He rolled the ash on his cigarette against the window frame to form a little cone shape.

"Yeah, the next day at work Boyce comes to me and gives me two video tapes. He tells me to put 'em in my safety deposit box right away, and if I don't have a safety deposit box, to go get one immediately. I grin at him and ask him if the tapes are what I think they are, and he just grins back at me and says, 'Let's just say one's insurance. The other's to remind you about being stupid.' So about a week later I quietly get the word from my squeeze that my personnel file's back in the drawer where it should be, and that I'm no longer being considered as part of any on-going investigation. The next week Sheridan announces that he's dropping out of the primary for personal reasons."

Walsh laughed again, took one more drag, and threw the smoldering butt out the window.

"That night we went out and met Celine and bought her the best Champagne and lobster dinner we could find. I was so happy, I coulda kissed her." He looked over at me with a wry grin and added, "But I didn't."

"Wow," I said. "So what happened then?"

Walsh heaved a sigh. "Boyce retired a couple of years after that," he said, taking out his cigarette pack yet again. "Poor son-of-a-bitch got cancer about a year or so later. He was always a big guy, but he wasted away to about a hundred and twenty pounds before he died. Spent his last few months pissin' and crappin' in a bag." He shook his head as he stared wistfully out the window. "A damn shame. He was the best. A real cop's cop."

He brought his lighter up and flicked the wheel.

"What about Celine?" I asked. "She still around?"

"Nah," he said. "She went out to California right after Boyce retired. San Francisco. Told us she'd finally had enough saved to get the operation she wanted, and figured they'd be more adept at it out there. That was her dream. She came to Tommy's wake though. It was a couple of years later, but she looked finer than ever. I ain't even sure how she found out about it, unless he called her or something before he went. She wore a veil and was crying real tears. Even her mascara was running." He gave a sympathetic cluck. "She bent over the coffin and give him a kiss on the lips."

"I don't get it," I said. "It sounds like he treated her like shit. Used her. Never gave her back anything. Why'd she feel that way about him?"

Walsh gave me a look that make me think I'd farted in church, then shook his head and shrugged. "I think she had a thing for him, though she never admitted it." The smoke drifted up lazily from his mouth, then he abruptly leaned forward.

"What about him?" I asked. "Did he really care about her at all?"

Walsh gave me the sour look again. "Someday you'll learn the score kid. What it's all about in the world of vice."

I grimaced at the thought.

"Anyway, if you remember just one thing …" he said, still leaning forward. He let the rest of the sentence drift off.

I glanced over and watched Linda doing a slow wiggle-walk over to the curb, her tongue doing a slow dance around the rapidly melting cherry popsicle, as a silver BMW slowed to a stop.

"Hey," he said, grabbing the mike. "It looks like one of our angels might have another horny fish chasing the blues."

"What were you gonna say?" I asked.

He kept his eyes on the little drama unfolding in front of us.

"Huh?"

"You started to say something," I said. "About Celine and Tommy Boyce. Something I should remember."

"Oh, that." Taking the cigarette from between his lips, he held it away from his face while he rubbed under his eye with his other hand. He seemed to consider what he wanted to say for a few seconds, then shrugged. "Just that if you're gonna make a name for yourself in vice, sometimes you got to be willing to hurt people. Sometimes even the ones you love."

END

STEVEN B. MANDEL is the author of *Another Lost Angel*, which was released from Thomson Gale/Five Star in May, 2006. He currently resides in the western suburbs of Chicago, with his wife and three daughters. As to why he writes about Chicago, "Chicago is grittiness and violence. Chicago is blue-collar and sweat. It's where the bad guys work just as hard as the good guys, and where it's often hard to tell the two groups apart. It's a city can kick you in the guts, but just as easily give you a hand up. Simply put, Chicago is the most real city I have ever seen and has all the necessary elements of great crime fiction."

WWW.STEVEMANDELBOOKS.COM

BLIND MAN BLUES
STEVEN B. MANDEL

THE ONLY THING THAT KEPT BILLY CALL'S
shoes slapping pavement was the delicious anticipation of
beating hell from the dog-ass he'd been chasing for three city
blocks.

Billy Call goddamn hated running.

Not because he was out of shape or anything. He wasn't
lazy either.

No, he hated running because he had told the fucking
schmuck to stop, more than once. But instead, the ass-clown
took off and beat feet down Ashland.

And if there was one thing that Billy Call hated more than
running, it was being ignored.

Legs pumping hard, Call propelled himself forward. His eyes locked on the guy's dark blue jacket.

The distance between them was shrinking.

The dog-ass careened wide right into an alley just north of Diversey.

However, before Call could make the turn, an enormous clatter exploded past the bricks, followed by stabs of angry chatter.

Heh. Fucker must've tripped himself up.

Call came around the corner cautiously, gun out now. "All right, shit-head, don't—"

"Man, you're sooo slow."

Abby North was standing over the dog-ass, garbage can lid attached to her hand like a shield. The guy was curled fetal, hands covering his head, soft moans gurgling past cracked and bleeding lips.

"Sure, I do all the work and you get all the fun." Call holstered his piece and kneeled behind the dog-ass.

"You can still kick him a little if you want," North offered.

Call looked the guy over. "Nah. It's not the same."

Pulling his cuffs off his belt, Call slapped metal against the guy's wrist. He only had one bracelet secured, when his cell phone chirped. "Excuse me, will you?"

He patted the guy on the head and stood up. "Call."

As he listened, he watched North finish the cuffing.

"Yeah, all right." He rolled his wrist for his watch. "I'll be there in about forty minutes."

After securing their catch, North came up behind Call, her eyebrows plunging in toward her nose. "What? What was that? You're not going—"

Call folded up his cell and dropped it into his jacket pocket. "That was the Kerchoff's maid. Says she has something that might do some damage to Mark Kerchoff's alibi."

"So … you're going?"

"Yeah, I'll help you take in the Running Man here, then I'm gonna—"

North stepped up in her partner's face. Even though she was on the tall side, the top of her head only came up to his eyes. "No, not again. Billy, come on."

"I have to, Abby."

North dug her fists into her hips. "No, that's just it. You don't. It's not our goddamn case, Billy. It's not even our goddamn jurisdiction."

Laying an enormous hand on her shoulder, Call nodded. "You're right. But she was my friend. That motherfucker killed her and I'm gonna prove it."

North reached up and cupped Call's chin. "Billy, you don't even know she's dead. Hell, she could be lying on a beach in Mexico with the goddamn mailman."

Call shook his head, freeing himself from North's grip. "No, she wouldn't do that. She wouldn't leave her kid like that. Not Kasey."

"What do you goddamn know, Billy? You don't know her! You haven't for eleven years! People change! You spent the last eleven years elevating her to sainthood; she could be a serial killer now. She could be a junkie or a child abuser. You don't know, because you don't know her. Not anymore."

"Yes I do! We were in love! Me and her, we were like one person!"

"Yeah, and then she dumped you. She ate your heart and crapped it out. Remember? Remember how she fucked you up so bad that you almost dropped out of the Academy?"

A shadow crossed Call's face. He remembered.

"I have to do this. And you have to understand."

North shook her head. "All I understand is that you hate Mark Kerchoff because Kasey left you for him. And you want so bad for him to be guilty that you won't listen to any other possibilities."

"Abby, I—"

"And I understand that sooner or later the Loo is gonna find out what you've been doing and it's gonna be both our asses."

"Ma'am, I think you should let him go. The poor bastard's obviously dumb in love."

North and Call turned toward the dog-ass, who was now sitting on his rear, hands shackled behind his back. He shrugged his shoulders best that he could. "I'm just saying, is all."

She might be right.

The thought pounded a steady backbeat deep in Call's brain as he ran his truck south down Harlem Avenue, out of the city, toward River Forest.

Maybe North was right. Maybe he was obsessed.

But if he was, it wasn't without reason.

Kasey Flynn Kerchoff had gone missing the morning of Christmas Eve.

Security cameras in the parking lot of the Harlem-Irving Plaza captured her abduction as she was yanked into a late-model cargo van, white with no plates.

And that was that.

No ransom demands, no contact of any kind. No body had been discovered, nor had the van been found.

Her husband, gazillionaire investment banker Mark Kerchoff, was, of course, distraught. And then indignant when he was brought in for questioning, for no other reason than in so many of these cases, the husband turned out to be the offender.

The guy had a pretty air-tight alibi, though. He'd been fishing with a friend in Sanibel, Florida and had returned to Chicago two hours after the abduction. And there were witnesses, airline tickets and hotel bills to back him up.

Still, after some digging, the suburban coppers did find some things to spark their suspicions.

Most damning was the anonymous tip from somebody claiming to be a Kerchoff neighbor, who swore she saw Mark sitting in a black SAAB down the street from his house an hour or so before the abduction.

See, police work was just a matter of burrowing until you hit truth. Problem was, the River Forest coppers didn't seem all that keen to use their shiny new shovels. Money didn't like anybody poking around their secrets.

Solution? Toss a couple bundles of green around and watch how fast people found new hobbies to occupy their time.

And that's why Call took matters into his own hands.

Kasey meant too much to him.

She'd been the only girl he had ever loved.

Okay, he hadn't spoken to or seen her for a long while. But that didn't mean shit. Time and distance couldn't soften up what he felt. And the thought that somebody might've hurt her; it twisted him up inside something awful.

"I found this yesterday morning in the Mister's bedroom."

Call reached over and took the envelope from the pretty Polish girl sitting tight against the passenger seat door.

The girl, Edita, was young and slender. Bright, blue eyes set into a perfectly sculpted face, puffy lips, long, blond hair that dangled past her shoulders. When she spoke, her words danced around a slight European accent.

"I don't know what to do with this, but I don't think that it looks right." She twirled a loose strand of hair with her finger.

Call opened the envelope. Inside was an Illinois driver's license. It had all of Mark Kerchoff's info—height, weight, address, date of birth—yet the picture staring back at Call wasn't Mark Kerchoff.

Oh, it was pretty goddamn close.

Same narrow face with stretched-out nose, smoky eyes and thick, curly black hair.

It was easy to see how somebody who'd been shown a photo of the real Mark Kerchoff weeks after his fishing trip could say that this other guy was the same man who'd flown United Flight 615 from Ft. Myers to Chicago. Or had stayed at the Sun Dial Resort on Sanibel Island. Or had chartered a fishing boat for the week of December 17th through the 23rd.

These people hadn't spent a whole lot of time looking at the real or fake Mark Kerchoff. Mixing them up was a no-brainer.

"It's good, Detective?" The girl was looking at him with wide eyes, an uncertain smile creasing her lips.

Call dropped the license back in the envelope and fished around some more. He pulled out two passports—both for Mark Kerchoff, but one picturing the real deal, the other, his evil twin.

Replacing the passports, Call glanced up at Edita. "And you just found all this?"

"Yes."

The girl's eyes were all over the place. She was trying to appear cool.

"Are you all right?"

"Yes, fine, I just, I have to get back to the house. The Mister will be home very soon."

And there it was. The Mister. She spit the words as if they were poisoned.

"You don't like him? Mr. Kerchoff?"

Edita shifted in her seat, her knees swinging toward the door. She gazed out the window, fingers tapping against her lips.

"Edita?"

"He … the … Mark … said … he promised …"

"Edita, was something going on with you and Mr. Kerchoff?"

Thin, damp lines trickled down Edita's cheeks. "He said that he and I would go live together. That he could make me a U.S. citizen. I would be his wife if I could just wait a little while."

Something hard and cold settled in Call's stomach.

"And he was so handsome and so gentle, he told me that he loved me and that ... and that ..." She sniffled and wiped away her tears with the back of her hand.

"What happened to Mrs. Kerchoff, Edita?"

"I didn't want ... I mean, I wanted to be with him. I loved him, but I thought he was getting divorced. If I knew that he was going to ... I never would have ..."

"Do you know what he did with the body, Edita?"

Edita nodded and leaned toward an oversized handbag with a rainbow print. "After she disappeared, he told me, he said that we couldn't be together. That it would not look right."

Bringing the bag into her lap, she rifled around until she found what she was looking for. When her hand came back, it was wrapped around a white, plastic Walgreen's bag. "Here."

Call took the bag from her and pulled back its edges.

His breath died in his throat as he saw the bulky Sears hammer with a clump of hair and dried blood in its claw.

###

Billy Call watched with tremendous satisfaction as the next few days unraveled poorly for Mark Kerchoff.

His arrest had been very public. Seeing the coppers drag him from his magnificent River Forest manse was even better than watching the White Sox sweep the World Series last year.

The pleasure lasted until the goddamn judge presiding over Kerchoff's arraignment set bail at a piss-in-the-bucket 500K.

The Cook County State's attorney argued about the potential flight risk the accused posed, yet Kerchoff's super-slick, hot-shot attorney pointed out that his client had no priors and was a good-standing member of the community. And, the shark reminded the Judge, there was no body and no motive save for the word of a disgruntled employee who might also be an illegal.

So now Call was on stake-out.

He was sitting Kerchoff's estate, had been since following Kerchoff home from downtown.

Endlessly watching the massive stone house, as leaves, burnt-orange and red, dropped and swirled from century-old oak trees.

And as he watched the house, he tried to imagine what Kasey's life was like there.

Probably perfect, at least at first. Until something ugly shook itself loose, leading Mark Kerchoff to murder.

Call's cell phone vibrated in his lap. He looked at the name floating up on the display.

North.

He opened the phone. "What?"

"So, you ever coming back to work? Or should I put in for a new partner?"

Call rubbed his temples. He was tired of the same old argument. "I'll be back when I'm back. You do what you gotta do."

There was a few seconds of silence from the other end. Then North sighed. "This is crazy. You're crazy. You can't watch him every second of the day."

"Everywhere he goes, I go. Till the day they lock his ass up for good."

"You're going to get fired. Or worse, arrested."

Call gazed up at the house, at the one window that still had light glowing from behind its blinds. "This guy is gonna skate. I can feel it. Judge has his head up his ass."

"Billy, it's over," North said, pleading in her voice. "Let it go. They're going to try him and fry him. You won."

"Yeah, all right," Call replied flatly.

North's tone was suddenly hopeful. "So you'll come in?"

"Yeah. Yeah, I'll come in." He slapped his phone closed and threw it down on the passenger seat. Then he lit another smoke and settled back.

Soon as I watch Mark Kerchoff take a lethal needle up the arm.

Mark Kerchoff disappeared the day that they found the white van.

It had been discovered on the south side of the city, in the rear lot of an abandoned warehouse that sat off California, just under the Stevenson Expressway.

Actually, the van was now flambé-black. A homeless guy had found it, flagged down a cop after discovering the charred chunk of something that used to be human.

And when the police arrived, they did indeed find the corpse of a woman, but it was impossible to tell who the hell it was.

Call showed up almost the same time as the River Forest coppers. But since he wasn't very popular with the RFPD, especially after being so vocal about their incompetence, he hung on the fringes, watched everybody else work.

He had paid a buddy a couple hundred to sit Kerchoff's house while he sped to the scene, but was anxious to get back. Once the news hit, it was sure to light a fire under Kerchoff's ass.

"Hey, over here!"

Call's eyes locked onto the voice. A uniformed River Forest copper was standing by a row of rusty oil drums, holding something red and small.

Walking over, Call peered over the crowd that had gathered around the uniform. A short, fat white guy in a wrinkled suit, Detective Parnell, reached out and grabbed what Call saw was a woman's purse.

Parnell opened the purse and immediately yanked out a red leather wallet. He opened it up and nodded. "Yeah, it's her."

Call couldn't get back to Kerchoff's mansion fast enough.

Already the news was breaking on WBBM. Kasey Kerchoff's body had been found.

Pictures of Mark Kerchoff frantically stuffing clothes into suitcases danced and skipped inside Call's head.

He pressed his foot down on the accelerator, willing the car to go faster.

Parnell had called back to River Forest for a couple of uniforms to go pick up Kerchoff, fuck his bail.

They had a body now.

They had ... oh ... shit ... she was really dead, wasn't she?

Tears, hot and hard, swelled behind his eyes.

Fuck ... Kasey ...

"What do you mean he's not here?" Call pounded the hood of Benno Taddeo's car.

"What were you doing here anyway?" the River Forest uniform wanted to know.

They were both staring hard at Taddeo, a Violent Crimes dick out of Area Three. Call had known Taddeo since the Academy, knew the little Dago was always for moonlight.

"Motherfucker's probably halfway to Mexico by now." Call spit a wad of phlegm at the curb.

The uniform hunched his shoulders against the stiff wind blowing east and tried not to look intimidated by the large and angry-looking Chicago detectives. "You still haven't told me what you guys were doing here."

Call ignored him, looked up at the house. Another pair of River Forest uniforms had gone room to room looking for Kerchoff, had come up empty.

"Hey, I kept eyes on the front door and the driveway. I saw him, he was there. Came out for newspaper. I don't know where he went, but he didn't leave out the front or by car." Taddeo lit a smoke and held the pack out toward Call.

After telling Call and Taddeo to stay put, the uniform trudged up the stairs to join his buddies.

"Go on, take off," Call said, reaching into his pocket and pulling back a small wad of cash. He peeled off two hundred-dollar bills and handed them to Benno. "I don't want you catching heat if heat comes around."

After he watched Taddeo turn the corner, Call leaned against his own car and rubbed a hand over his face.

The day had gone gray, the hawk picking up. High above, it skirted the treetops, bullying down whatever leaves remained.

Winter would be here full-on very soon.

And it looked to be cold, dark and depressing.

The day they buried Kasey Flynn Kerchoff was obnoxiously bright and unseasonably warm for late October.

At least that's what Call thought as he watched the burial from the thin strip of road that ribboned through the cemetery.

Funerals seemed easier to handle when it was gray, cold and rainy. In weather like that, it seemed that the world was sharing in your grief.

When his cell phone blurted out, breaking into the quiet of the night, Call nearly pissed his sweat pants.

He scrambled toward the coffee table, lunging at the little plastic box, scattering the half-dozen empty beer cans that had been strewn over the couch.

"Yeah?"

"Uh … Detective Call?" A man's voice. Hesitant. Unfamiliar.

"Who's this?"

"It's Mark Kerchoff. I … uh … I need to talk to you about … um … Kasey."

###

Call stood next to Mark Kerchoff's black SAAB, which had been backed into one of the handful of parking spaces on the far end of Lower Michigan, just south of where Lower Wacker straightened and reached toward the lake.

The driver's door was half-open, Mark Kerchoff's legs sprawling out. Black slacks, black socks, black leather loafers. Guy liked black.

Used to, anyway.

The rest of Mark Kerchoff had fallen over onto the passenger seat, a large hole, jagged and bloody, where his left temple used to be.

A small, silver revolver was still in Kerchoff's death-grip.

Call leaned into the car, careful not to touch the body. He sniffed, could still smell the gunpowder.

Backing away, he pulled out his cell phone, flipped the lid and was about to dial when he saw the long sheet of yellow paper.

Again he carefully reached into the SAAB and snatched the paper off the driver's side floorboard. As he unfolded it, his stomach jumped and tumbled over itself.

MY NAME IS MARK KERCHOFF.
I KIDNAPPED AND KILLED MY WIFE KASEY.
IT WAS AN ACCIDENT. HONESTLY.
SHE WAS MY LIFE, MY LOVE, MY HEART, FOREVER.
MAY GOD FORGIVE ME.
I KNOW I NEVER WILL.

Confession signed in blood.

###

As Call pulled up in front of Kasey's mother's brown brick Cape Cod, he waved to a young woman with a blond pony-tail who was pulling away from the curb in a black Honda Civic. The maid, Edita.

She didn't wave back, but that was okay. Wasn't like they were best buds. Or maybe it wasn't her. It was kind of far away and Call's eyes were off a bit from all the sleep he'd missed lately.

Call stood at the front door, waiting for an answer to his knock. It was kind of weird. He hadn't stood at that door for a long, long time.

After what seemed like an hour, the door opened a crack, a sliver of Marilynn Flynn's age-creased face filling the space.

"Billy Call?"

"Morning, Mrs. Flynn."

The door opened a bit more, but not enough to be mistaken for an invite inside.

"What can I do for you, Billy?"

For half a second, Call didn't know how to answer. He didn't know what he wanted, what he hoped to accomplish by coming here.

"I … uh, I guess I just wanted to make sure that everything was all right. I hear that you're going to be taking care of Connor, so I just wanted to let you know, if you need anything … um, give me a call."

He peered over her shoulder, trying to see into the house, simply because he had the feeling Mrs. Flynn was trying to block his view.

"We're all right," Mrs. Flynn said wearily.

She must be tired of answering that question.

"Well, if you need anything ..." Call fished a card from his pocket. "Don't hesitate to call."

Mrs. Flynn took the card. "Thank you, Billy. I won't."

He couldn't tell if she meant she wouldn't need anything or she wouldn't call. Guess it was the same, either way.

"Oh, by the way, tell Edita I said hello."

"Excuse me?"

"Kasey's maid. I thought I saw her driving away. I waved, but I guess she didn't see me."

The front door was already on its way shut when Mrs. Flynn said, "I'll tell her, Billy."

"Billy, what the hell happened here? I thought we were going out."

Call looked up at his partner and shrugged. He was sitting in the middle of a mess of photos, papers and boxes. "Sorry, I ... I'm almost ..."

North walked across the living room and kneeled down. "What is all this crap?" She picked up a square sheet of paper that had been folded into threes.

"There was something bugging me about the Kerchoff thing," Call said.

"Gee, you think?"

"It was something ... something about the note, Mark Kerchoff's note. Something he had written ..."

He shuffled around the stacks of letters and photos that Kasey had given him during their twenty-seven month relationship eleven years back.

"I know it's here. I know it."

North was shuffling through a stack of pictures. "I can't believe you kept all this shit." She held up one and showed it to Call. "Look how young you were!"

It was a shot of Kasey and Call at a barbeque in his old partner's backyard. Kasey was wearing a purple tank top and shorts, Call in shorts and a CPD baseball jersey.

They were both holding up bottles of beer and mugging for the camera. It hurt to remember them so happy.

"Oh, look at this one. God, I forgot how pretty she was." She held up another photo, this one of just Kasey, from some wedding. "Man, was she a corn-ball. Listen to this … 'Billy, you are my life, my love, my heart, forever.' Goddamn, that's awful."

Call's head snapped up. "What did you just say?"

North shrugged. "Sorry, no disrespect meant."

"No, no, what she wrote, on the back of the picture."

"Billy, you are my life, my love, my heart, forever."

"That. That was … oh, shit, shit shit!"

North's face scrunched in a question. "What? What's what?"

He stood and went for his wallet and keys. "C'mon. We're going out."

"Okay, so why are we following the maid again?"

Call kept his eye on the black Honda Civic as it moved east down Belmont. He was a couple of cars back, the thick evening traffic providing more than adequate cover.

"Just trust me," was all he would say. He didn't want to tell her what he was thinking. She already thought he was watching a few shows that weren't listed in TV Guide. If he was wrong about this, North would have him committed.

After a few more turns, the Honda pulled into a Western Avenue motel. It was the kind of place where people went to screw when the people they were screwing weren't the people they were supposed to be screwing.

There were two levels, all rooms accessible from the outside. Staircases stood at either end of the building.

Call curbed his car across the street and killed the engine. The pothole-filled parking lot was half-full. He didn't recognize any of the vehicles.

"There." North was pointing across the dashboard. "She's going upstairs."

"Let's wait until she goes in."

A few minutes later, North and Call were standing on either side of room 215.

He looked at North, who nodded back. They drew their guns and Call stepped in front of the door, raised a leg, kicked it down.

As the door flew open, they spilled into the room, North first, going low, Call covering high. They had performed this move a million times since becoming partners, yet it was the first time Call had felt so nervous.

The blond he had seen earlier today at the Flynn house, the same blond they had trailed from there to here, was sitting on the bed.

But she wasn't Edita.

Oh, she looked like her. Hair dyed and cut to look the same. And the bodies were similar, slight and graceful, athletic.

But she wasn't Edita.

She was in fact, Kasey Flynn Kerchoff.

"Holy shit!"

God, Call had never wanted to be so wrong in his life.

"Holy shit," North repeated. "Kasey Kerchoff! Holy shit!"

"Quite the vocabulary," Kasey said to Call.

"Kasey, what the fuck is going on here?"

North still couldn't believe her eyes. "Holy Shit!"

"Kasey, why aren't … what happened …?" Even though he had expected this, he was still halfway to stunned.

"Are you two going to put down your guns?" Kasey sounded completely unflustered. Almost like she had been expecting them. "Put away your guns and I'll tell you what happened."

Call glanced at North, then nodded. North reholstered her piece, but kept her hand hovering just above the grip.

Even with blond hair, even under these incredibly suspicious circumstances, Kasey was like a full-body massage to Call's eyes.

And, just like every time he saw her or heard her name, an electric excitement coursed through his body.

And suddenly he found himself caring less about the hows and the whys. All he wanted was to shove North out of the room, tackle Kasey on the bed and …

But he had to know. He had to check down his feelings and act and think like a cop.

"The story, Kasey. All if it, now."

Kasey sighed and sat down at the edge of the bed.

She shook loose a cigarette from her pack and lit up. And as she smoked, she told about how Mark Kerchoff had been so controlling and abusive. A cheater, too. How the pre-nup she had been forced to sign would leave her virtually penniless if she ever divorced him.

Finally, it became too much. He became too much.

He'd been forcing her to visit underground sex clubs with him, making her do things with other people, both men and women, while he watched.

And when she refused to do something, he would wail on her with a leather strap. She offered to show Call and North the welts.

Kasey knew she had to do something. But she refused to leave that bastard unpunished.

And that's why she decided to fake her own death.

After months of scheming, she hit upon an idea that would place all the blame on Kerchoff. If things worked out, she'd be able to grab all his money, too.

Using some dough that she had stashed away over the years, Kasey began working with the only two people she could trust, her mother and her maid.

Together they obtained a van for the abduction. Mom and Edita dressed like men played the part of kidnappers.

Using a cousin of Edita's who worked for the Cook County Morgue, they were able to get the corpse of some homeless lady and flame-broiled her beyond recognition.

That's why it took so long for the body to be found, Kasey explained. They couldn't take just any corpse and had to wait for a female body that would never be claimed.

The passport and driver's license belonging to the fake Mark Kerchoff, Kasey had produced using PhotoShop and old Kerchoff family pictures. Edita was the one who phoned in the tip about Mark being in his car the morning of Kasey's abduction.

"It was all done to make Mark appear suspicious, then ultimately, guilty. And believe me, the bastard was guilty of many, many things."

Edita played double agent, pretending as if she was aiding Mark Kerchoff, while planting info and evidence with Call.

"You used me," Call spit bitterly.

"No," Kasey replied. "I knew I could count on you to do the right thing."

"So you made Mark call me for a meeting, then faked his suicide. Why? Why not let him just go to jail?"

"Well, then Connor couldn't inherit his fortune."

She explained how once Mark was dead, and with Kasey apparently gone, the Kerchoff's son would go to live with Kasey's mom.

Mark was an only child whose parents had died years ago and nobody in Kasey's family would contest her mother getting legal guardianship.

And with Connor Kerchoff apparently the only living heir, his father's massive wealth now belonged solely to him, to be put in a trust that would be managed by Kasey's mom.

Grandma and Connor would move far away and live off the boy's trust. Edita would be their maid and the other pretty blond woman who lived with them, a distant cousin.

"Wow. That's quite a goddamn plan," North said. "You escape your husband, keep custody of your son and still have access to all that money. Too bad you fucked it up."

Kasey looked up at North, twin streams of smoke cascading from her nostrils. "Yes, how did you find me out, Billy?"

"The suicide note you forced Mark to write," Call answered dejectedly. "You used the same line, the one about my heart forever. You used it on a photo you gave me once."

"And you remembered that? From all those years? Jesus, Billy."

"I know," North said. "He's a regular freak show."

"There isn't a thing about you that I ever forgot, Kasey."

Kasey moved off the bed and came up close to Call. "I was hoping you'd feel that way. Get rid of your friend and we can have a little reunion."

Her scent, that vanilla aroma, swirled around Call's head, forced its way into his nostrils. His head was full of her and her touch made him tingle.

"Make her go away, Billy. I want to be alone with you."

Thoughts were getting more difficult to keep together, like trying to grab smoke.

"Billy, move away from her."

Call looked over at North. She looked like she was a million miles away, standing with her legs slightly apart, her piece out and ready.

"Billy! She's pointing a gun at me! Do something!" Kasey's voice was anger, not fright.

"Abby, put down the gun, let's talk—"

"Talk my ass! Move away from her, Billy! I'm taking her in."

"Billy, don't let her take me away from you!" Kasey's fingers were slipping through his hair. "We can go away together, just you and me. All you have to do is get rid of the bitch."

"You're under arrest. Remove you hands from my partner and place them on top your—"

"NO!" Call launched himself at his partner, his hand locking onto her wrist, twisting until she dropped to the floor.

She lay there, glaring hate, the small automatic pointed up at him. "Are you fucking crazy?"

His head was clearing. He could finally think again. "What? You gonna shoot me?"

"You gonna give me a reason?"

His hand dropped to his holster. The thought of drawing on his best friend made him want to puke, but he needed to be ready.

Yet when his fingers got to where the butt of his gun should've been, they wiggled over empty air. "Where the ..."

"Looking for this?"

Call whipped around. Kasey was standing back near the far wall of the room, his service piece gripped tight in her tiny hands.

Holding his hands out, showing palms, Call shuffled a half-step toward her. "Kasey, give me the gun back. This isn't the way to solve anything."

"Oh?" Kasey arched an eyebrow, a slight smile curling her lips. "What exactly is the way? Let Butch over here throw me in jail?"

"Kasey, this isn't you. Something's wrong." Call tapped a finger against his forehead. "Something up here."

Kasey nodded. "Yeah … yeah, okay. I could plead insanity and get locked up in the nuthouse for most of my life. That could work."

"That's right. Just put the gun down and we'll work this out."

An ugly laugh clawed its way from her throat. "Jesus, Billy. Are you a fucking moron? You think I'm gonna spend the rest of my life doing kitty cat puzzles with brain farts?"

"What are you gonna do, Kase? Kill us? You wanna be a cop killer too? You might be able to make a case for Mark being justifiable. But they'll fry you for sure for killing cops."

Quiet, tense and heavy, permeated the dirty, little room. Finally Kasey nodded toward Call. "All right, Billy. I know how we can settle this."

"How?" Call wanted to know.

"C'mere."

Call took a couple of tentative steps toward her.

"Don't worry, sweetie. I won't hurt you." Her voice had melted into that girly sing-song that used to make his heart flip, flop and fly. "But don't try anything or your friend loses her head."

Keeping her eyes and gun locked on North, Kasey brought her lips softly against Call's ear. She then whispered her secret desires, the sound, smell, the thought of her pushing back all rational thought.

When she finished, she brushed her lips against his cheek, her breath puffing out and spreading over his skin.

"Billy? What did she say?" Apprehension stabbed North's words.

Call's fingers slid against Kasey's as they moved to retake his gun.

"Billy, what are you doing?"

He ignored his partner and brought the gun out, his aim dead on Abby's forehead.

"Drop the gun, Billy. Goddamnit, I will shoot you! You know I will!

North glared up at him, her eyes dusky. "Put the gun down, Billy. You're making a huge mistake."

Something moved just over Call's shoulder. "You're coming with me, aren't you, baby?"

Kasey's words were like candy in his ears, sweet, delectable, making him crave more.

"Call, don't listen to her! She's using you. She broke your heart before and you never recovered. Don't let her do that again!"

"Billy," Kasey purred, "get rid of her for me, please. Then we'll be free and rich and we can stay together forever. Kasey and Billy, just like it was supposed to be!"

Call looked from Kasey to North, then back again.

"Billy, please," North pleaded.

"Don't let them take me from you again, Billy. This is our only chance to be together."

He couldn't get his head clear.

"Billy, please ..." North said.

"Billy, for me ..." Kasey said.

Call leveled the gun, his finger going tight against the trigger. The loud pop bounced off the walls, floor and ceiling.

And Kasey Flynn Kerchoff slumped to the filthy, stained carpet, twitching slightly in an expanding puddle of her own blood.

Call dropped to his knees and watched Kasey bleed out. "It was the only way, Abby. Only way I could get free." He held out his arms. "You can take me in. I won't fight you."

North reached under her jacket. But instead of bringing back her bracelets, her fingers were wrapped around a small pistol, a Beretta M92.

After wiping the gun clean, she placed it in Kasey's left hand. "She's a southpaw, right?"

Call nodded, then North raised the gun hand. "Cover your ears."

As soon as Call did as told, North yanked on Kasey's finger. The shot popped out loudly and thudded into the wall behind them.

North let Kasey's arm drop, then put her own around Call's shoulders. "C'mon, partner. Let's call it in."

END

DAVID J. WALKER is the author of eight crime novels. His most recent, *All the Dead Fathers*, was described as "riveting" by *Publishers Weekly* and "both thought-provoking and entertaining" in the *Chicago Sun-Times*, and was a "Summer Reading" selection on Chicago Public Radio's WBEZ. His new stand-alone novel, *Saving Paulo*, is scheduled for an early 2008 release. A native Chicagoan, he lives just north of Chicago. David writes, "Chicago's famous for just about everything a crime writer needs, and then some. Think drug wars, street crime, white-collar crime, crooked cops, the Outfit, and a political system that's made an art form out of 'connectedness.' Hell, even the weather here's a crime. And I love it."

A WEEKEND IN THE COUNTRY
DAVID J. WALKER

PATRICK MULHANE WAS WORKING THE desk, third watch, at the Twenty-fourth District. At 2200 hours exactly, he turned to Sanchez. "Gotta run," he said. "The old lady's sick. Nothing's going on here, anyway."

Sanchez, who was on the phone trying to talk his brother-in-law out of tickets to Sunday's Bears game, covered the mouthpiece and nodded. "Yeah, fine," he said. "Take it easy, Mull."

Three minutes later, Mull—he didn't much like it, but that's what everyone called him—was out the station door and limping through the parking lot. It was October, and the night was cold, and a constant slow rain had been hanging around all day. Most of the beat cops weren't even back to the station yet, but Mull was meeting Jake Patterson and Karl Krachek—two robbery dicks working Area Three—and he wanted to be sure to get a booth at Malarky's. When he reached his Tahoe he hoisted himself in and fired it up and turned on the heater. The damp cold had his leg stiffened up, and it ached like hell. He sat for a minute to let the throbbing pain ease and catch his breath, then pulled out of the lot.

Mull hadn't worked in uniform in years and he'd had to dig out an old one for the desk job, but what with the leg and his increasing shortness of breath, he'd put in for the assignment temporarily, greasing his request with the right promise to the right guy. After the accident and the compound fracture that never really healed right, he probably could have gotten disability status, but he hadn't put in for it. The fact was he had nearly enough years in to take full retirement, but he wasn't ready for that either. He told everyone that if he spent his time moping around with the old lady all day they'd be divorced in no time, and he couldn't afford that. The truth, though, had more to do with something else. Gambling. Poker mostly. With people you didn't want to owe money to.

He knew better, but he kept falling into debt and having to crawl out again, which was why it was the job, not the old lady, that he couldn't afford to be divorced from. The job—and the access it gave to the unreported cash he'd come to depend on. Plus he was developing what he called his "catering" business, and cops—at least the ones that still had the balls to take advantage of a good time—were the biggest part of his customer base. In the old days there were "watch parties" where guys used to let off steam, but with the new watch system there weren't the same opportunities. So Mull offered something else, a little like an old-fashioned watch party—but with the excitement level kicked up a notch or two.

###

"I don't know," Jake Patterson said, and downed his second shot of Stoli. Jake was way overweight and had the droopy eyes and sagging face of a Basset Hound, and whenever he shook his head from side to side—like he did now—his jowls lagged behind and then, trying to catch up, got caught in a whiplash. "I don't know," he repeated, and poured a third shot. "I don't think you're gonna get enough guys to go way the hell up there."

"Jesus," Mull said, "it's not that far. You shoot up I-94, hop off just short of the Wisconsin line, go west ten minutes to Angle Lake and—"

"Forget the sales pitch," Karl Krachek interrupted. Krachek had a perpetual sour look on his face and everything he said came out like he meant stop wasting his fucking time. He must have weighed as much as Patterson, but was six-four, and not a gram of fat on him. "Jake's in," he said. "He's just gotta put in his usual depressing two cents is all. Right, Jake?"

"Yeah, yeah, yeah. I'm in." Patterson struggled to heft his bulk up and out of the booth. "Gotta hit the pisser," he said, and waddled away.

Malarky's was full of cops and it was noisy enough to make a conversation in a booth private, and when Patterson got back Mull filled him and Krachek in on the deal. He'd been up to see the place, he explained, and rented it right away. Cheap, because it was out of season. The once-elegant two-story summer home was pretty bare bones, and not very well insulated. But it had a wrap-around porch, a partial basement, a big kitchen, a huge living-dining area, two toilets, and six tiny bedrooms—four up, two down. It was remote and private, on wooded lakefront property, well in from the road and with a mowed field around it for plenty of parking—although the ground sloped downward and was pretty uneven and rough.

There was a cable hook-up, but no TV, so Mull would bring one from home. He'd booked the place from Thursday morning till midnight Sunday, for a "fishing weekend." In fact, there were two rowboats available, and if it was warm enough a few of the guys might even try their luck on the tiny lake.

It was Mull's operation, and nothing illegal—except for the prostitutes and some private gambling, and even if these did cross the line a little they were offenses commonly overlooked, except by wives. This was the most elaborate event he'd organized so far, and he'd cut Patterson and Krachek in because he trusted them and he needed help fronting expenses and hauling up supplies—booze and food, the TV and some space heaters, plus the hookers. These last weren't total bottom sludge, and were guaranteed clean; but they weren't exactly Gold Coast, either, and couldn't be trusted to get to the cottage from Chicago on their own. To them, anything north of Howard Street might as well be the goddamn Yukon. Mull was getting them in a package deal from a pimp who was in no position to charge him market rates.

"I saw 'em in person," he said, "and picked five. The two youngest are fresh from Lithuania and speak about three or four words of English, enough to know what the customer wants. There's an Asian—Thai, I think—who's a little over-the-hill, but still has some good miles left on her. The last two are jungle bunnies from the West Side. Only way to tell 'em apart is one's got her hair dyed blonde and the other one red. Oh, and if guys wanna ante up an extra fifty bucks per girl, those two'll stage a cat fight with each other each night."

"How about they go at it with knives?" Patterson asked. "My precinct captain threw a party after the election last year, and had these two banshees who—"

"Yeah ... well ... maybe for a little extra cash." Mull drained his third Heineken. "We charge five hundred a day, based on noon to noon, or twelve-fifty for the whole three days if you pay in advance. Everything's included: hookers, booze, food. By noon Sunday it's all over but the cleaning up."

"No broads but the hookers, right? So who's gonna cook?" It was Patterson again. "You?"

"No way. Everyone's on their own in that department. We provide lots of steaks and A-1 Sauce ... potatoes ... bacon and eggs ... I don't know. I'll figure that out. Half those guys'll be too drunk to eat, anyway."

"Forget cooking," Krachek said. "The problem's getting enough people. We got two weeks to recruit customers."

"Right," Mull said. "It's invitation only. Ask anyone you want, but for chrissake tell 'em no drugs and no cameras or picture phones. Stick to people you can trust to keep their mouth shut. If you're not sure, don't ask. I can get ten or fifteen easy—most of 'em coppers. But even if we only get twenty at the minimum five hundred, that's ten grand. Expenses'll be less than half that, and we split the rest ... with a great weekend for ourselves tossed in. And we'll get more than twenty. Believe me."

###

Mull was right about getting more than twenty guys. It helped that great weather was forecast all week, and that the forecast came true: sunny and in the sixties daytime, fifties night. By Saturday evening they'd collected forty-one guests. Guys showed up and left whenever they wanted, with usually no more than about ten at any one time, not counting a couple of three-dayers who actually came for the fishing as well as the drinking and whoring, and who were given the room in the basement to sleep in. Things went well—as loud and nasty and disgusting as anyone could hope for.

One of Mull's predictions, though, the one about the "great weekend for ourselves tossed in," turned out to be very wrong. The three hosts were on their feet almost non-stop. No booze for them, and very little sleep, with people arriving and leaving at all hours of the day and night.

It was tough keeping track of who was there and whether they'd paid yet; and some people showed up who weren't on the invited list, so they had to make several trips into town for more supplies: booze and food, mostly; and new sheets, too— he'd never thought about that; plus the whores used up rubbers faster than anyone thought they would. Patterson made the supply runs and Krachek handled the money-collecting. His prodigious bulk and forever-pissed-off attitude commanded respect. Meanwhile, Mull played host and tried to keep everyone happy and the place halfway clean, gathering dirty dishes and picking up the garbage that got tossed everywhere and—eleven times in two-and-a-half days by his count—cleaning up vomit.

One weird thing happened late Saturday afternoon. Mull had gone to the basement to get sheets and towels out of the dryer—lucky there was a washer and dryer down there—and when he came back up to the kitchen he heard Krachek explaining the price to a couple of guys who obviously weren't on the list. Krachek let them in, so Mull knew they must be coppers. One of them, a guy in a shiny black leather jacket, came into the kitchen. He said he and his partner worked Bomb and Arson, and had heard there was a party going on. They rode up on motorcycles. "We both got BMW's—mine's a new one—and this may be the last good day of the year for riding," he said. The guy seemed nervous, running on about what kind of bikes they had and all. "My partner's in the bathroom," he added, "but we both wanna know where the broads are."

Mull was explaining things when the guy's partner, carrying a similar jacket over his shoulder, stepped into the kitchen. And that was the weird part. The partner was Mull's own son, Johnny, who'd been a Tac officer in the Fifth District the last Mull heard.

Father and son stared at each other. Mull couldn't tell who was more surprised. Then Johnny and the other guy got a refund from Krachek and left. Mull and Johnny never exchanged a word the whole time, which wasn't too strange since they hadn't spoken in years, anyway. Johnny was a big, husky guy, taller than Mull. Sneaky and sullen ... and mean. Always had been, even as a little boy. God knows Mull had tried to beat that damn mean streak out of him. Time and again. The way Mull's old man had done with Mull. But even the strap didn't work with Johnny, and Mull had to stop when the boy got big enough to hit back. The kid wasn't one to let bygones be bygones.

Except for that little hitch, the weekend went smoothly. The hookers were pros and did their job. The Thai and the two Lithuanians never said a word that Mull heard, and did nothing but sit on their asses whenever they weren't on their backs or their knees. On the other hand, everyone heard from the black chicks. They were loud and low-down and short-fused, but they were also the only ones who helped Mull keep the kitchen and bathrooms halfway clean. And best of all, their barefoot, near-naked "cat fights" were a huge hit.

The fights weren't as bloody as Jake Patterson was looking for, but both girls, besides being tall and strong, were well-endowed in the boobs and butt department. They had high enthusiasm, too, and there was plenty of screaming and cursing, slapping and grabbing, along with the obligatory dragging off of bikini tops and bottoms by the time they finished. It helped, Mull thought, that they were full of real aggression and anger, all of it so close to the surface that even their staged bouts had a reality that the WWE Smackdown people could only dream of. The alcohol-stoked spectators loved every minute of it.

And they loved it even more when, near the end of the finale Saturday night, one of the whores, the redhead, lost it completely. She slipped in a puddle of spilled beer, which made her slow to duck, and she took a truly hard whack to the side of her head. That shook her and made her turn the wrong way just as the blonde's other arm swept through the air. Long, red fingernails raked across the redhead's face, and left two bright, bleeding gashes on her cheek.

The blonde, clearly shocked at what she'd done, stopped short and stared at the damage. "Damn," she said, and reached out as though to stroke the bloody cheek. "Girl, I didn't mean no—"

The redhead howled with rage and grabbed the blonde's outstretched hand and pulled her close … and kneed her in the crotch. The blonde groaned and doubled over and the redhead grabbed her by the hair with two hands and swung her around, lifting her momentarily off her feet and then throwing her to the floor. The blonde ended up on her back, eyes open but the pupils rolled up under the lids. The redhead straddled her and dropped down and half-knelt, half-sat on the blonde's belly. She took the dazed woman by the ears and gave the back of her head a whack against the floor before Krachek and Mull could get over and pull her off.

They dragged both women up onto their feet and Krachek put them in headlocks and muscled them outside onto the porch. The whole event took place amid raucous cheering and laughter and applause.

It was half an hour later, at about one AM Sunday, when more uninvited guests showed up. There were three of them, and even the guys—the cops, anyway—who didn't know them, knew them. The soft leather, hip-length coats, the cashmere sweaters, the sharp-creased pants, the five-hundred-dollar shoes. They were young guys; the tallest one thirtyish and the other two maybe just early twenties. They all had razor-cut hair, manicured nails, and cocky, shit-eating grins.

They were already inside the door when Krachek stepped in front of them. "Sorry, fellas," he said. "Private party."

"We know," the tall one said. "So how much?"

Krachek looked over at Mull and Mull nodded, and Krachek told them the price. The tall one said they'd pay half that, and then peeled off bills for all three, and they walked in. No way Mull could keep them out. The tall one, Chi-Chi DelVecchio, was the goon who collected when Mull got behind in his gambling debts.

The three got the lay of the land in a hurry. To the kitchen for booze first, then upstairs for a chat with the ladies. Then they came down they joined in one of the poker games. Other than acting like they owned the place, which irritated the hell out of Mull, they made no trouble. Still, before very long most of the cops—all but Mull and his co-hosts, and a few guys too drunk to know better—had made their exits, demanding partial refunds from Mull. Time spent drinking and gambling and whoring was one thing, but time spent fraternizing with known mob guys—convicted felons or not—might earn you separation from the department.

###

By noon Sunday, Mull and Patterson and Krachek had counted the money together and split it up—asking each other whether it was worth it for all the aggravation. Then Patterson, who by then was pretty drunk, but still able to drive his van, gathered up the whores to take them back to the city, while Mull and Krachek tried to put the house back together.

Mull was the only one who didn't have to work that night, so Krachek didn't stay long. Mull wasn't left alone, though, because the three mob guys were still there, all snoring with their mouths hanging open like the mopes they were, in front of Mull's TV. He switched it off and they kept on sleeping. The TV wasn't HD or flat screen, but was a big twenty-seven-incher that barely fit on the low, sturdy coffee table where he'd set it. DelVecchio wanted to stick around to watch the Bears game, which started at three, and Mull didn't argue. He wanted to watch the game, too, and he wanted to keep DelVecchio happy. Besides, he wasn't too worried about the "fraternization" problem. He didn't expect anyone to snitch, because no one who'd been there had anything to brag about. If someone did talk, and if IAD came after him, the worst that could happen is he'd have to retire. A cop couldn't lose his pension unless he committed a felony on the job.

He knocked down a couple shots of Jack Daniels, and got out a mop and a pail. As he cleaned up he thought how strange it had been to see Johnny again. His son, the cop. Why would a kid follow in the footsteps of a father he hated? Christ, a question like that called for a little more JD.

By three o'clock he was half-drunk himself, and the place was in as good a shape as it was going to get. He turned on the TV, which finally woke up DelVecchio and his two mopes, and the four of them sat around getting totally wasted and watching the Bears slug it out with Detroit.

During a commercial break late in the fourth quarter, with the score tied at ten all, Mull got up and went through the kitchen and out the back door to take a leak off the porch. When he came back inside he thought he heard something … like knocking. But not very loud. And then not at all. Had it come from the other side of the door by the refrigerator? Not possible. Even drunk, he could remember that the door led nowhere but the basement stairs and that no one had been down there but the fishermen, who'd left after DelVecchio and company showed up. Mull had gone down and checked, and they'd left the area in decent shape. The door always hung open, though, so back when he was mopping up the floor, he'd turned the key on the kitchen side and locked it shut. He knew everyone was gone, and there was no outside entrance to the basement.

"Hey!" DelVecchio called, "bring some fucking brews back with you."

Up yours, Mull said under his breath, but he went over to the refrigerator … and heard the knocking again. Louder now. The basement door for sure. He turned the key and yanked open the door—and the black whore with the blonde hair was standing there ... or trying to. She must have gone down there and crashed, and that damn Patterson didn't even notice he left with only four whores. She looked drunk, or stoned.

"Damn," he said. "What the hell are you—"

"Hey! Hurry up with those goddamn brewskis!" It was DelVecchio again. Mull might be drunk, but that fucker was beyond drunk. "And hey!" the asshole yelled again, "you're missing the best part of the damn game."

"Yeah, yeah, yeah. Gimme a minute," he yelled back. He grabbed a chair from the kitchen table. "Siddown, dammit," he told the whore.

"Head hurts," she mumbled. "Wanna go home."

"Right, I'll take you," he said. "Soon as the game's over." He pushed her down onto the chair, grabbed four MGDs from the fridge, and went back to the living room. There was a Lexus commercial on the screen, with the sound off.

"Took you long enough," DelVecchio said, grabbing one of the beers. "Would you believe it? Fucking Bears get to the Lions' fifteen ... and then hafta call their last time out. Jesus, can't get the damn call straight."

Mull distributed the other beers and plopped down into a sagging easy chair. "I believe it. That's always the—"

"Hey you!" It was the whore, stumbling in from the kitchen.

"Shit," DelVecchio said. "What's she—"

"Said wanna go home." She stumbled across the room toward Mull. "Head hurts."

Mull stood up. "Look, after the game I'll—"

"Shut that bitch up," DelVecchio said. "They're startin' again." He pointed and clicked the remote.

"… into the shotgun," the play-by-play guy said. "Three receivers wide to the—"

"Head hurts!" the whore repeated. "Wanna go fucking home!"

"I told you," Mull said, "after the game."

"… the Lions show blitz. The ball's snapped and—"

"No, now!" the whore said. She turned away from Mull and went toward the TV. "No more game!"

"… breaks a tackle and …" They were all on their feet by now, and DelVecchio and Mull both grabbed at the whore, but they were too late and as the announcer described a pass "lofted toward the corner of the end zone," she grabbed the TV and spun it around on the table, which yanked out the cable connection. Then she pushed on it, hard, and it went off the back of the table and crashed screen first onto the floor.

There was an instant of silence when no one moved at all, and then the whore straightened up and turned. "Wanna go fucking home," she said. "No more game."

"You … bitch," DelVecchio said. "You sorry … stupid … bitch." His voice was surprisingly slow and soft, but also filled with rage. He stood there and swiveled his head and upper body around, as though looking for something—like a wolf sniffing out prey.

Mull was surprised at how the other two goons said and did nothing, and in fact seemed to shrink away from their boss, and he suddenly wondered what this animal DelVecchio had been into besides alcohol.

DelVecchio reached down and grabbed the MGD bottle from where he'd left it beside his chair. He tipped it up and took a long drink, and then said again, "You sorry … stupid … bitch."

The whore just ignored him, though, and kept her eyes on Mull. "Wanna go—"

The bottle caught her full on the left side of her head, and shattered, sending glass and beer everywhere. She stood there for a second or two, beer and blood streaming down her face, and then she tried to walk, but tripped on her own feet and lost her balance. She waved her arms wildly and toppled over backwards, and on the way down the back of her head slammed into the corner of the low table. Her head hung up there for a second, but then her body went limp and the weight of it pulled her head off the table. The final blow, when her skull thumped against the wood floor, was one Mull knew she never felt.

Dead bodies always seem heavier than they ought to, and for Mull it was a real struggle—with his bad leg and his shortness of breath—helping one of DelVecchio's punks carry this one. They had it wrapped in a thin blanket, and were headed across the room toward the front door. Mull could hear DelVecchio out at the kitchen sink, bitching and moaning while his other goon picked little pieces of glass from the maniac's bloody right hand.

Mull had the foot end of the body and was walking backwards. When they got out onto the covered porch they set her down for a minute to rest, and he looked around and saw how dark it was. What light came out through the windows and the doorway spilled onto the floorboards of the porch and seemed to be sucked up by the rough, dry wood.

About the only thing the little bit of light did was to make whatever it didn't reach—which included the bottom two porch steps and everything beyond—look even blacker. There was no moon, no stars, nothing. There was also no driveway up to the porch, since the access drive from the main road just emptied into the large cleared area around the house. According to the punk, DelVecchio's car was parked off to the right, over near the trees. That meant crossing what Mull knew was a sloping, rocky, uneven patch of weeds. Thirty or forty yards away, easily.

"Go get the damn key," Mull said, "and drive the car over here."

"You gotta be kidding." The guy shook his head, and looked genuinely scared. "First, nobody drives that car but Chi-Chi. It's a Jaguar and, like, brand new. Second, I wouldn't ask him for nothing, not when he's into … not when he's like he is tonight. You seen just a little taste."

"Well, then, I'll ask him." Mull started for the door, but the guy stood in his way and pushed him back.

"Uh-uh. You get hurt and we're all in deep shit." He squatted down by the body, then looked up at Mull. "You don't wanna help, I'll drag her to the car myself."

Mull didn't want a bloody body being bounced down the steps and dragged across the yard, so he gave in. He squatted too, and both men shifted their hands around to get the best possible grip. The blanket made it hard to get hold of her arms and legs, so they tossed it aside. When they had hold of her, they stood up together and started for the porch steps.

They hadn't gone three feet when Mull stopped. "This is crazy," he said. "Set her down again, dammit." They did, and he turned and swept his arm out to indicate the darkness they were headed into. "There's been nobody around here but us since Thursday. This could be noon, for chrissake, and there'd be no one to see us." He reached inside the door and switched on the flood lights that lit up the whole yard.

They managed to make it down the porch steps without breaking a leg or dropping the body, and as they started across the yard with it, Mull had to fight the urge to try to move faster than they could. Being out there in the open under the lights made it feel like someone was watching them, and he kept twisting his head around to see who the hell was there, even though he knew better.

By the time they got to the Jag, DelVecchio and the other guy had caught up. DelVecchio's right hand was wrapped in a towel, and with his keyless opener in his left hand he hit the button and the trunk lid sprang open. He seemed a little more calm, but was still in a foul mood. When he saw they'd left the blanket behind, he told one of his guys, "Go back and get the fucking thing ... and hurry up!" The guy ran all the way to the porch and back, and they lay the blanket on the floor of the trunk and then heaved her ... it ... up and in, and slammed the lid.

"None of this ever happened," Mull said, hunching up his shoulders to help himself breathe. "A known prostitute, full of alcohol and who knows what else. No one's gonna knock themselves out investigating. Leave her in a dumpster some—"

"No way," DelVecchio said. "This fucking skank won't be found ... ever." He got into the driver's seat and had to lean and reach around the wheel with his left hand to get the key into the ignition. He closed the door and then lowered the window. "And look here, Mulhane," he said, "nothing's changed. You fall behind, I'll still be the one they send. Understand?"

"Yeah," Mull said. "And you have a nice day."

The Jaguar pulled away, leaving Mull alone to figure out a story for the pimp about how his bitch had split the scene and never come back. He was stone sober now, and first he had to clean up some more. He'd leave the place better than they'd found it—no blood anywhere, for sure—and he'd leave an extra fifty bucks for the missing blanket and towel. He climbed the porch steps and went in and turned off the outside lights.

Maybe five minutes later he heard a car pull up and stop near the porch. But no, not a car. A motorcycle. One motorcycle.

He waited, and Johnny came in.

"Party's over," Mull said.

"I know. I told my partner to go on home, that I wanted to come back and say hello to my father."

"Uh-huh. Well … so … you're with Bomb and Arson these days?" Stupid question. What he needed was to get this son of a bitch out of here before he saw any blood.

"Nope," Johnny said. "Not Bomb and Arson." He made no move to come farther in, just stood by the door.

"That's what your part—"

"Yeah, I know." He reached inside the leather jacket and pulled a business card from his shirt pocket.

Mull took the card. Under Johnny's name it said: Chicago Police Department. And below that: Internal Affairs Division.

He put the card in his own pocket and said, "So you came up here on the job. Did you know I'd be here?"

"Nope. Just heard about a couple of coppers hosting a party that sounded … interesting."

"And now what? I'll be called in?"

"You mean because me and my partner caught you running a traveling whorehouse?" Johnny turned and went out onto the porch, and Mull followed him. The BMW stood at the bottom of the steps, visible because its running lights were on. "My partner says no. He thinks a son shouldn't flip the switch on his own father." Johnny went down the steps.

"Really." Mull stared at his son's back. "And what do you think?"

"Me? I think a lot of things." Johnny lifted the cycle off its center stand, threw his right leg over it, and started the engine. Not like a Harley, the BMW made very little noise as it idled. "Like … I think that limp of yours is pretty bad."

"Yeah … well … I get by."

"And something else I think." Johnny clicked on his high-beam and revved up the engine the way bikers do. Then, using both feet, he pedaled the cycle a little closer, parallel to the bottom porch step. "I think you won't need to turn on those floodlights for me. Not again."

"Not … again?" Mull tried not to hunch his shoulders, but was finding it hard to take in enough breath.

"That's right." Johnny lifted his hand up and out into the dim light and showed Mull a small, chrome-colored camera. "But the thing is," he said, "I don't think I should turn in my own father, either." He held the camera out toward Mull.

"Thanks," Mull said, and reached for it.

"Nope." Johnny yanked his hand back. "Because I think— after all these years—I prefer the crippled-up, vicious old bastard right where he is." The cycle moved slowly forward. "In my pocket."

END

Author of the Jack Caleb/John Thinnes mysteries, MICHAEL ALLEN DYMMOCH is a Chicago resident. Michael's most recent novels are *White Tiger*, nominated for a Lambda Literary Award, and *Death in West Wheeling*. Michael says, "I write about Chicago because I've taken to heart the advice: Write what you know. Write what you love. Write what you must."

WWW.MICHAELALLENDYMMOCH.COM

A SHADE OF BLUE
MICHAEL ALLEN DYMMOCH

"I WANT TO REPORT A MURDER."

Detective John Thinnes looked up from his *Sun-Times*. The man standing in front of him looked and smelled like he'd spent a night in the drunk tank. White male, mid-thirties. Crumpled suit and puke-spattered shoes.

The man pointed back toward the sergeant behind the counter of the Area 3 squad room. "He said to talk to you."

Thinnes closed the paper and pointed to a chair near the cubicle that served as his office. "Have a seat. Mr ...?"

"Quinn. Peter Quinn." He pulled the chair over and sat.

Thinnes took out his notebook. "Spell your name, Mr. Quinn."

Quinn complied. In response to further questioning, he supplied his address—in Wrigleyville; phone number; DOB; and occupation—high school math teacher.

"Social Security number?"

"What do you need that for?"

"The incident report."

Quinn frowned but gave up his sosh.

Thinnes wrote it down, then sat back. "Tell me about this murder."

"It happened last night—I tried to tell the cops. But they arrested me."

"For?"

"Disorderly conduct and public intoxication."

"Who was murdered?"

"A woman—I don't know her name, a singer."

"Where?"

"A blues bar. Somewhere between Elston and Ashland on Irving Park."

"That's more than two miles. And there aren't any blues bars on that stretch of Irving Park."

"Well." Quinn's assurance deserted him. "Maybe it was just a bar with a blues band. They were playing blues."

"Were you drinking?"

Quinn flushed. "That's what you do in bars. Listen, maybe I should just go home. You can look me up when somebody finds the body."

"Take it easy. Tell me what happened. From the beginning."

Quinn seemed to be trying to decide if Thinnes was making fun. Thinnes waited him out.

"I admit I'd had a few too many. I had a fight with my wife and decided to teach her a lesson by tying one on. Luckily, I didn't take the car. I don't remember how I got to the bar, but I'm pretty sure I took at least one cab. I just remember that there I was, and the music pulled me in—'Solitude.'"

Quinn wiped sweat from his forehead with his sleeve. "My ma used to play old Billie Holiday albums. I guess that's what it was. I ended up sitting in a booth in the back. The singer was beautiful—a brunette with dark eyes. She sang a bunch of the old standbys—'Stormy Weather,' 'My Man'—so good it gave me goose bumps …" Quinn trailed off as he remembered.

"Go on."

Quinn shivered. "After the last set, the other patrons left and the musicians started packing up. I was sitting in the shadows—I guess nobody saw me. The bartender poured a drink for the lady. She sat there and sipped it while he restocked. He kept going in the back, coming out with a box that he would empty, then cut apart with some kind of knife. Then he'd throw the knife on the bar, flatten the box and throw it on a pile, and go back for another.

"On one of his trips out, this guy came into the place. Big guy. Mad. So mad he was scary. He started yelling at the lady. She yelled back. Then they were screaming at each other.

"Then the guy grabbed the bartender's knife and slashed her throat."

Quinn stared at the floor in front of him with wide eyes. His breath came faster. Sweat oozed from his pale face.

Thinnes stood up just in time to catch him before he hit the ceramic tiled floor.

###

"What happened?"

"You passed out," Thinnes said. He'd been standing over Quinn with a cup of water, waiting for him to come around.

The paramedic who was bending over Quinn sat back on his heels and said, "You ought to go to the hospital, Mr. Quinn. Get checked out."

Quinn sat up. "Unless they have something to take away horrible memories, it'd be a waste of time. Just let me go home."

The EMT shrugged and packed up his kit. He handed Quinn a clipboard. "Sign here."

"What's this?"

"Just says you refused to let us take you to the hospital." Quinn signed the form and returned it. The medic said, "I advise you to let someone drive you home."

Seeming annoyed, Quinn waved him away and got up. He sat on the chair he'd fallen out of earlier.

Thinnes offered him the water.

He gulped it and said, "Thanks."

"I'll drive you home."

Quinn started to protest, then shrugged.

Thinnes said, "We'll go by way of Irving Park Road."

Thinnes drove as slowly as traffic would allow while Quinn hung out the window studying the storefronts. When they got to Elston, he said, "Nothing."

Thinnes shrugged and turned the car around. They were halfway back to Ashland when Quinn half shouted, "Stop. There!"

He pointed to a two-story building that they'd passed earlier on the north side of the street. The ground floor was boarded up, the upper story looked like apartments. "That's it!"

"You sure? That place has been closed for years."

"It wasn't last night."

Thinnes made a U-turn and parked in a bus stop.

The storefront had a "Coming soon—Brite Boutique" sign posted on the door along with a building permit. No building was currently underway, so Thinnes noted the information on the permit and the building manager's number. Then he dropped Quinn off at his home.

###

"Nothin', Thinnes," the sergeant said. "No murders. No missing women fitting anywhere near her description. No new Jane Does in the morgue or the hospitals. Don't know what your witness is up to, but it sounds like he oughta be writin' for Hollywood."

"I'm gonna check that before I spend any more time on this. But he didn't fake passing out."

###

Quinn turned out to be a solid citizen with a wife, two kids, and a mortgage. Prior to last night's arrest, he'd never had so much as a parking ticket—no mental history. No domestic complaints. No major debt.

Thinnes called the property manager for the alleged blues bar and made an appointment to see the inside.

###

"What's this about?" the manager demanded before producing his keys.

"We had a report a crime was committed here last night."

"No way!"

"Then you won't mind letting me have a look around."

The inside was as clean as a place could be mid-renovation. New drywall was in place but not yet taped. The floor was gritty with dirt and drywall dust, stained but not with blood. There was no trace of violent death or even recent occupancy.

While Thinnes waited on the sidewalk for the manager to lock up, he studied the buildings across the street and to the east and west—a cleaners, a beauty shop, a mom-and-pop bodega, Madame Petrushka's Psychic Readings, an insurance agency, a used book store. None of them would've been open at the time Quinn insisted the murder took place.

A scratchy voice interrupted his study. "You the *po*lice?"

Thinnes looked down the street both ways without seeing a speaker. Then he looked up. A wrinkled, boney woman was hanging out a second-floor window, a cigarette dangling from the corner of her mouth. She grasped it between her thumb and index finger and pointed it at Thinnes. "You the *po*lice."

"Yes, ma'am."

"Murder *po*lice?" Thinnes nodded. "There been another murder? This place is cursed."

"There was a murder here?"

"Thas right. Thirty-some years ago. Singer was cut up by some crazy galoot."

"Do you remember her name?"

The woman shook her head. "Linda. Lucinda. Somethin' like that. Don't the *po*lice keep records? Look it up."

###

The Cold Case detective had the murder on his list—way down near the bottom. "I'll look at it," he said, "but after thirty years, there's zero chance we're gonna close it." He was happy to hand it over, anyway.

Thinnes took the fat file back to Area 3. It was creepy how closely the crime matched what Quinn had reported.

Lucile Reid—stage name Lucile—had performed on the night of her murder at a small storefront bar known simply as "Blues." After the last patron left, the musicians adjourned to the alley out back to share a joint.

The bartender served Lucile a drink and proceeded to re-stock before locking up for the night. While he was in the basement, trying to locate a case of Rolling Rock, someone came in and cut Lucile's throat.

The bartender had called the police. He was in shock after finding the body—probably wasn't the killer.

The musicians all alibied each other.

Detectives couldn't find evidence others were in the bar at the time of the killing or, during the canvass, any witnesses. The follow-up investigation determined that the victim and her husband had fought constantly.

He was a CPD sergeant, on duty the night his wife was killed. Assigned to a one-man car, he was located shortly after the stabbing. There'd been no blood on his clothes or in his car. And it was thought that he couldn't have had time to change because he'd been at his sister's when they found him, engaged in a noisy domestic dispute. The sister's neighbors had called the cops about the ruckus, which confirmed the husband's alibi.

The sister was an actress who'd lived on Pine Grove Avenue at the time. Her statement backed up her brother's story.

The detective in charge of the case liked the husband for the killing, but he hadn't knocked himself out trying to nail a fellow cop. And there hadn't been any physical evidence linking him to the crime.

Supplemental reports made in the intervening years indicated that the bartender and musicians had all died. Only the husband and—possibly—his sister survived.

Thinnes put down the file. Time to reinterview the surviving witnesses.

The guy who opened the door was a heavy-set white male. Typical retired cop.

"Kevin Reid?"

"Who wants to know?" Reid's face gave nothing away.

Thinnes flashed his star.

Reid said, "What's this about?"

"Mind if I come in?"

Reid shrugged and backed into a room that looked like a single man's lair—bare walls and windows with shades at half mast, unmatched furniture, wastebasket overflowing with evidence that McDonald's and Taco Bell catered most of his meals.

Reid grabbed a remote off the scarred coffee table and used it to kill the program on the big-screen TV. He waved at the dingy couch.

"Take the load off."

As Thinnes walked toward it, he could see an unmade bed and piles of dirty clothes through the open bedroom door. He sat down.

Reid sank into his recliner. "What's this about?"

Thinnes shrugged. "We got this new cold case squad taking another look at unsolved murders."

"Lucile."

Thinnes nodded.

"I went over all of it with the dicks back in the day. Nothing I can add."

"It's all new to me, so why don't you start at the beginning?"

Reid shrugged. "I met her in '67. I was a rookie assigned to Uptown. Back then it was the armpit of the city—hillbillies and drunks, mostly. Drunk Indians—the native kind, not the techies. Me and my partner got called to break up a fight in a little dump on Lawrence—turns out over a woman. That's where I first saw her."

He leaned forward and rested his elbows on his knees, staring at the floor. Staring into the past.

"She was beautiful—jet black hair, huge, brown eyes, skin like white silk. And her voice—oh my God …" He glanced at Thinnes as if to judge his understanding. "But she always sang the blues. It was like she was channeling every doomed love affair or failed relationship ever was. Just listening to her could make you wanna go out and get drunk."

He shook his head. "She wasn't like that offstage. She had a brain and a sense of humor. I found myself going back when I was off duty, asking her out. Pretty soon I asked her to move in with me.

"After the convention in '68 her feelings for me changed. Whenever we were fighting—which got to be pretty much all the time—I was a fucking pig. But it didn't stop us from living together.

"When I found out she was pregnant, I did the right thing." Reid stopped and stared at the floor, scrubbing one hand with the other.

When the silence had gone on long enough for Thinnes to be sure he wasn't going to continue, Thinnes said, "Which was?"

"What?"

"You did the right thing?"

"Married her. Neither one of us wanted the kid to be a bastard. He was three when Lucile bought the farm."

"You got any theories about who killed her?"

"Some guy she drove nuts. She had this way of singing like you were the only guy in her life. Took me too long to figure out it was nothing personal—just her shtick."

"Can you tell me how to get in touch with your sister?"

Reid shook his head. "Haven't seen her in years."

"Where's your son now?"

Reid shrugged. "I let him be adopted. Seemed like the best thing. He needed a mother, and I wasn't ever goin' there again."

"So you don't know what happened to him?"

Reid nodded. "Deal was, I gave up all my parental rights. Best for everybody."

###

Actor's equity gave Margaret Reid an address in Andersonville—turned out to be a small house dwarfed by the apartments on either side.

Thinnes pressed the buzzer. The door was eventually answered by a slim woman, five-six, still beautiful in her fifties.

"Miss Reid?"

She didn't confirm or deny it. She waited, cautious or suspicious—Thinnes couldn't tell. He held up his star.

She kept waiting.

"We're taking another look at the murder of your sister-in-law."

She shrugged. "I don't have anything to add to the statement I gave the police."

"Somebody has to have an idea about who killed her."

"Ask my brother," she said—before she closed the door.

###

Reid looked resigned when Thinnes told him, "We need another talk." Just resigned. Not relieved. Not worried.

The former cop shrugged and stepped away from the door.

"At the Area," Thinnes said.

Reid nodded. Thinnes followed him into the living room and closed the door.

"Let me get my jacket." Reid started toward a door Thinnes took to be a closet.

"Hold on." Thinnes stepped around him and pointed. "It's in here?"

"Yeah."

"I'll get it."

There were two jackets hanging in the closet. And there was a holstered Smith & Wesson on the closet shelf. Big surprise.

"The tan one," Reid said.

Thinnes took out the jacket and closed the closet door. He waited while Reid shrugged it on.

Reid started for the door. Stopped before opening it. "This is more than just the standard Cold Case BS. What made you reopen the case after all these years?"

"A witness came forward."

Reid gave him a look like somebody was trying to sell him the Picasso. "The dicks said there were no witnesses."

"Apparently they missed one."

Reid shook his head. "They don't miss—somebody would'a …"

Thinnes let him think about it. He'd been a cop for thirty-five years. There was no way he could be tricked or intimidated into confessing, but …

He seemed to be lost in a memory. Finally he said—so softly Thinnes almost had to read his lips to hear—"I hoped he'd never remember."

"Who?"

"Doesn't matter." He looked straight at Thinnes. "I killed her. I'll sign a statement."

"Why the change of mind?"

Reid just shook his head.

Thinnes took out his cuffs. "Sorry, but I'll have to …"

Reid turned around again and put his hands behind his back.

Thinnes put the cuffs on. "You have the right to remain silent …"

The assistant State's attorney put down Reid's statement and told Thinnes, "Nice work."

"Thanks."

"What made him decide to confess after all these years?"

"Good question."

When Thinnes handed in his paperwork, the sergeant said, "You solve your phantom murder yet?"

"I'm working on it."

"Your brother confessed.

Margaret Reid Quinn stared at him for a moment, then stood back from the door. "You'd better come in."

Thinnes followed her into a bright, attractively furnished living room. She invited him to sit on the couch and took a chair across from it. She waited for him to study the surroundings. He wasn't too surprised to see a portrait of Peter Quinn among the family pictures. Most of the other photos were a time lapse of Peter from infancy.

"Did Kevin say why he was confessing, after all these years?" Margaret asked.

"No. He just gave us enough to prove that he did it."

He pointed at the most recent portrait of Peter. "Your son?"

She nodded.

"You tell him how his aunt died?"

She shook her head. "Never."

"So how did he know?"

"He didn't. He couldn't ..."

Suddenly she was sobbing. Thinnes got up and got the Kleenex box that was sitting on a side table. He put it in front of her and waited for the answer until she'd cried herself out.

"He was there," she said, finally. "I was supposed to be watching him, but I had an audition, so Lucile took him with her to the bar. He was a good kid. Quiet. It was usually dead on a Wednesday night, so she took him along, let him sleep in an empty booth.

"When Kevin stopped in to see her, they got in a fight. He didn't tell me what about, but I think it was the usual—that she wasn't home with her kid instead of singing for strangers in a bar. This time, it went too far, and he killed her. Then he realized Peter was there. And that he'd seen everything.

"Kevin was horrified. He grabbed Peter and rushed him to my place. Started screaming at me—that if I'd been watching the kid, he wouldn't have had to see—

"Kevin wouldn't tell me what. But he and Peter were covered in blood, and Peter was in shock. Kevin told me I had to say I'd been watching Peter all night—to keep him out of it. We got pretty loud; the neighbors called the cops."

"Lucky for Kevin. You gave him the clean clothes?"

Margaret looked at Thinnes. "He used to keep an extra uniform at my place—in case he got dirty at work, so he wouldn't have to go all the way back to the station to change. My brother—what else could I do?"

"What about Peter?"

"He was only three and he didn't remember what happened."

"You adopted him?"

"I made Kevin give me Peter's birth certificate and told him he could never see him again. Then I just told people Peter was my son. We had the same surname, so no one ever questioned it. When I married Quinn, he adopted Peter. And he was a real good dad. Peter turned out all right."

"He never had any flashbacks? Or nightmares?"

"No. Not that he ever mentioned."

"Until today."

END

SAM REAVES is responsible for two Chicago-based crime series: the four Cooper MacLeish books and the current Dooley police procedurals. He thinks Chicago is the quintessential American city and an unbeatable source of material for a crime writer.

WWW.SAMREAVES.COM

THE TEST
SAM REAVES

"YOU CAN HAVE THIS WEATHER. I MEAN, you can fucking have it. Who ordered this shit?"

Me and Terry are going up Harlem, Terry's driving, and this rain is coming down that's like, two degrees away from being snow. I'm like, "That's springtime in Chicago for you. The flowers come out and then bam, they get their asses kicked."

Terry says, "We shoulda broke his fucking windshield. Can you see that fuckwad trying to drive in this, rain blowing in his face?"

I go, "Man, you are a hard case. You don't think you made it hard enough for him to drive, with a broken finger?"

"The guy just pissed me off, that's all. All the money in the fucking world, and he can't come up with my five grand? Fuck that."

I says, "What's he do, that he's got all the money?"

"The fucking guy's a bond trader or something at the Merc. I mean, he's rolling in it. I'm counting on the guy to pay for my mansion down in Aruba."

I have to laugh, thinking about Terry Amonte from the wrong side of the tracks in Melrose Park in a mansion in Aruba. I says, "I hate to see a grown man cry, that's all I got to say."

"He'll get over it. I'll get my money on Monday and by Friday the douche bag will be into me for another five grand, you watch."

We was coming back from visiting one of Terry's customers. The guy had been giving Terry the runaround, and it was time for the facts of life lecture. Terry's got guys that do the lecturing for him when he needs it, but I like, happened to be there that night and he asked me if I wanted to come along, just for like, old times' sake. So I go along, and it turns out I have to hold the guy up while Terry gives him the lecture. Just like old times. Me and Terry been lecturing people since we was snot-nosed punks at Sacred Heart.

So we get to Luigi's without running into anybody in the rain, and we go inside. It's karaoke night, and there's this asshole up on the stage making like he's Tony Bennett. He's trying to sing "The Best is Yet to Come," and I go, "I fucking hope so," loud enough for a couple of old ladies to give me dirty looks.

So Terry goes off to talk to somebody, and I'm standing at the bar trying to make time with Diane, this bargirl Luigi's got that is like a walking wet dream, when Bobby Marino comes up to me and says, "I gotta talk to you, Gino," in that voice of his that he uses when he's afraid the FBI or somebody is listening in, all low and dramatic like. I look at him, this little, pissed-off-looking bald guy with the nose and all, and I almost tell him to go fuck himself, but I could see he was serious. So I take a last look at Diane in her jeans so tight it makes *me* squeak when she walks, and I say, "OK, what's the deal?"

And then he says, "Let's go watch the karaoke," and I says, "Are you fucking out of your mind?" and he just jerks his head that way, and I see what he's thinking, 'cause nobody's gonna hear what we say if we're standing over there by the speakers. So we go and stand there and watch this jag-off singing, and Bobby's leaning over to talk in my ear, like he's making comments about the guy.

And he says, "You're an up-and-coming guy, Gino," like he needs to butter me up for something, and I wonder where the hell he's going. I shrug, and Bobby says, "You ready to move up in the world?"

So I go, "Sure," and then he says, "Casalegno's through," and I get real careful. I take a drink and I says, "What do you mean?" And Bobby says, "I mean he's past it. He's lost it. You happy with the way he's been running things?"

And I shrug again and say, "He's the boss."

Bobby says, "Yeah. But it don't have to be that way."

So by this time, I figure the only thing to do is keep my fucking mouth shut. I'm looking at the guy up on stage, like I'm really watching him, and Bobby says, "If Casalegno goes down, are you with us?"

Well, fuck me, I think. Here's a new one. Fifteen years building up my book, paying my dues, being careful; running my own crew now, things going smooth, money pouring in, and all of a sudden this comes screaming out of left field. "Who's us?" I say.

"Anybody that thinks Casalegno's too fucking old and senile to run the Outfit. Anybody that wants to bring things into the modern world."

So I'm thinking, I knew it was too good to be true. Things are running too smooth. I mean, money's coming in good, nobody's gotten whacked in like, ten years, business is running very peaceful. And if Angelo Casalegno's an old *faccia di culo*, who gives a shit? He'll be dead in a couple of years anyway. I says to Bobby, "What about Salvi?"

"Salvi's a dickhead. You think Salvi can run things? The only reason Casalegno picked him for number two is because him and Salvi's father were friends. Salvi goes down at the same time."

I take a drink and I says, "So who's gonna take their place?"

And Bobby says, "Me. Who the fuck you think? I put in my time, and I can run the show better than anybody else. I understand the modern world like Casalegno and Salvi don't, and it's time for a change."

The guy up on stage finishes butchering the song and everyone claps, and he bows and blows kisses and shit. I says to Bobby, "So what are we talking about?"

And Bobby goes, "A coup. We're talking about a coup. We get the top crew bosses to agree and we tell Casalegno and Salvi it's over. Anybody that don't agree, we make 'em see things our way."

Now there's a fat lady up on stage, and they're farting around with the karaoke machine trying to get a song going, and I'm wishing I was home with Vickie watching TV. I says, "Things have been peaceful."

Bobby says, "Yeah, like a fucking nursing home is peaceful. It's the twenty-first century and there's tons of fucking money out there waiting to be picked up off the street."

I can see the point, because there's all kinds of rackets out there besides gambling, and it's other people that are running them, the spades and the spics and even the fucking Russians these days. Bobby says, "You gotta make a choice, Gino. The future or the past. Casalegno or fresh blood."

Well, that would be Bobby Marino, and that's what explains all this. So the music starts again, and the fat lady starts to screech into the mike, and I make my choice, because I can see I got no good ones. I say, "Well, shit, Bobby. If that's the choice, I gotta go with the future."

And Bobby says, "Good kid." He slaps me on the arm. "One thing," he says. "Keep your mouth shut."

"Like a fucking tomb," I says.

Bobby's giving me the evil eye and he says, "Something like this, everything goes through me and you don't tell your fucking dog about it. I'll let you know what's going down. It'll happen fast, believe me."

Well, I'm like, through for the evening then. I gotta go someplace and think about all this. I find Terry and ask if he's ready to go, and he looks at me like I'm nuts. "We just got here," he says. So I decide to go and talk to Diane some more to take my mind off things, but she's busy as hell and I wind up just sitting there getting drunk and trying to watch a hockey game and even that's for shit, because the Hawks are getting their asses kicked in Detroit, as usual.

The next day I get up and look out the window and the world looks like I feel—like hell. My ma used to call it having the blues, and when she had it she would sit in the kitchen and drink. Whatever it is, I got it bad. It's raining again and dark outside and the wind is rattling the glass, and I just want to go back to bed and never get up. But I get dressed and go out, because I got things to do. I go down Harlem to the deli and go in and get some coffee. Casalegno's Caddy isn't parked out back, so I know he's not there yet, and I'm trying to think of a way to talk to him without anyone knowing I talked to him, and I'm realizing it ain't easy. Finally I remember somebody said he always goes to the senior center in Oak Park in the morning to work out. What the hell working out would mean for a wreck like Angelo Casalegno, I can't quite picture, but I figure I'll go and see.

So I drive down there and find the place and park, and I go in and I find him in a room with a bunch of other old farts, and they're all on treadmills and stationary bikes and shit pretending to exercise. An old lady asks me what I'm doing there, and I say I'm looking for my grandfather. I find Casalegno on a treadmill, going about as slow as you can go on a treadmill without coming to a complete stop, and he looks like he's about to croak. He like, scowls at me and says, "What the fuck are you doing here?" and I tell him I gotta talk to him. I guess he's been waiting for an excuse to stop, because he turns off the machine and then practically falls over from the sudden stop, and I have to help him down off the thing. He's wiping his face with a towel like he's just run a fucking marathon or something. He goes, "Where's Sammy?" And I say I didn't see Sammy, and Casalegno says, "That dumb fuck is supposed to be watching my back and keeping riffraff like you away. What the hell do you want?"

I look around to see if anybody can hear us, and I decide that the only people within earshot are probably deaf anyway, and I just keep my voice down and say, "Bobby Marino's planning to boot you and Salvi out and take over."

See, I had thought about it the night before and some more that morning, and I finally decided to follow the advice old Frankie Palermo gave me when he was breaking me in twenty years before. He said, "The Outfit has rules to keep things from getting out of hand, and you have to follow them. Breaking the rules is what gets people killed." And what I decided this morning was, the rules say Angelo Casalegno's the boss, and he gets to say who's boss after him. And that's the way it is. So that's why I'm standing here watching Angelo Casalegno stare at me like I just knocked his drink into his lap.

And then suddenly Casalegno smiles, which catches me by surprise, and I mean this old man has a scary fucking smile. And Casalegno says, "He is, is he?" And I nod. And Casalegno starts to get back up on the treadmill, and he says, "Come and see me at the deli at four o'clock this afternoon."

So I leave. And I spend the day making the rounds, talking to my bookies and collecting money and passing some of it out again, and all the time I can't stop worrying about what I did, and wondering if Angelo Casalegno is still powerful enough to come out on top in a dogfight, and wondering if Vickie would come with me if I have to leave town all of a sudden. And at four o'clock I go to the deli.

I say hi to Terry's mom behind the counter and go on down the hall to the back, and when I walk into Casalegno's office I get the shock of my life, because sitting there at the table with him is Bobby Marino. And I like, freeze, and Marino grins at me, showing all his crooked teeth, and I'm thinking Jesus Christ what did I do?

And Casalegno says, "Sit down, Gino," and slaps the table in front of him. And I sit down, moving like I'm underwater, and Casalegno says, "Congratulations, you passed the test."

And I go, "What test?" And Marino says, "You passed the loyalty test." And I sit there for a while just looking from one of them to the other, and Casalegno says, "It was a test, genius, to see if you would go for it. The whole thing was my idea."

And I just like, blink at him, and Casalegno shoots Bobby a look like, how dumb is this guy, and Bobby leans forward and says, "Look. Angelo's been concerned about discipline. This was a test, to see who's with him and who ain't. I been going around feeling guys out about taking on Angelo, and seeing who goes for it. And if they come and tell Angelo, they pass the test."

And I start to nod now, and I feel almost like I'm gonna pass out, because I'm realizing what a bunch of fucking maniacs I'm dealing with and how close I came to making the biggest fucking mistake of my life. And I say, "Well, shit. What else was I gonna do? You're the boss, Angelo." And then I look at Bobby, and I'm wondering what the hell to say to him, because what it comes down to is, I snitched on him. And I says, "What if I had just said no and kept my mouth shut?"

And Bobby says, "That would have been good. You would have passed. But coming to tell Angelo was like extra credit. You done good."

And Angelo goes, "You been a good earner, Gino, and you got a future in this outfit. Just keep on doing the right thing."

So I go, "OK," and sit there nodding like an idiot for a while, and I didn't want to ask, but I had to. I says, "You mind my asking you something? Has everybody passed so far?"

And Bobby says, "You'll find out soon enough if somebody doesn't." And I can see that's all I'm gonna get, and so I shut up. And Angelo says, "OK, go on doing what you're doing. And keep your mouth shut about this." And I see that's it and I get up to leave, and Bobby gets up and comes with me.

And out back in the parking lot with the rain crawling down my neck I get this reaction, and suddenly I'm like, shaking, I mean fucking furious. I says to Bobby, "Is he fucking crazy? What kind of a fucking scheme is that, trying to get guys to go for something like that, just as a test? When the G does that they call it entrapment and it gets thrown out of court. What kind of bullshit is that?"

And Bobby goes, "It's something he got from Saddam Hussein, believe it or not. He read about it somewhere. Saddam used to try that out with his generals to see if they were loyal, and guys would say yes, and then Saddam would have them thrown into vats of acid and shit. Angelo thought that was pretty cool."

And I just look at Bobby and say, "That old man is fucking nuts."

And Bobby shrugs and says, "He's the boss, Gino. He's the boss and you did the right thing. Now just keep your mouth shut and wait for developments."

So I go away shaking my head, and I'm wondering again like I do sometimes if I'm in the wrong business, except the money's pretty damn good if you work hard and play by the rules. And I'm hoping like hell that everybody else passes the test too, because the last thing we need is for people to start getting hurt and bringing heat down on the Outfit when things are going so smooth.

That night I'm with Terry at Mangini's in Elmwood Park and we're just fooling around, playing video poker and watching ESPN to see how our bets are doing, and Terry's in a good mood because he made a big score on some heist he and his guys pulled off down on the South Side and he's talking about how him and Julie and me and Vickie should take off for a week or so, the four of us, get the hell away from this dogshit weather and go to Mexico or Aruba or some place warm, because what the hell are we doing all this work for otherwise. And it sounds pretty good to me, and all of a sudden I want to ask Terry about this test thing that Casalegno and Marino are running on guys, and warn him about it. And then I remember Marino telling me to keep my mouth shut, but I think fuck that, Terry's my best friend and rules or no rules I got to tell him. So I says, "Hey, has Marino talked to you yet?" And Terry says, "About what?" And I says, "Has he given you the test yet?" And Terry's looking at me like what the fuck are you talking about, so I tell him. I says, "Casalegno and Marino are running this test on guys, Marino's asking them if they'll go along with him if he takes on Casalegno and Salvi. But it's all bullshit, it's a test Casalegno dreamed up to see if guys are loyal. And if Marino talks to you, you gotta either say no or you gotta pretend to go along and then go tell Angelo. Because they'll fucking whack you if you don't."

And Terry just looks at me for a while like he can't believe what he just heard and says, "That old cocksucker has really fucking lost it, hasn't he?"

And I says, "Yeah, but he ain't gonna last forever. We just gotta play along and wait until he croaks."

And Terry shakes his head and says, "OK, thanks for telling me."

So I'm glad I gave Terry a heads-up on it, and a couple of days go by and I start to think that the whole thing is gonna blow over, because I figure guys are too smart to rock the boat with things going so smooth, and everybody's gonna pass the test and then we can just forget about it and go on making money.

And then Marino shows up at the garage. I'm sitting back there in the office counting the take my guys brought in the night before, thinking about how much money I made off the NCAAs, and Bobby comes in and says, "Gino, I gotta talk to you." And he nods at the radio up on the shelf, and I look at him for a second and I wish to God he would just go away, but I go turn up the radio, even though I ain't worried about anyone listening because I get the office swept every month by an electronics guy I know, and I say, "What's going on?"

And Marino says, "You got a chance to earn big-time points with Casalegno."

I says, "I thought I already did."

Bobby says, "Now you got a chance to do even more."

And I think to myself, shit. I says, "OK, how?"

"You got a chance to make a statement," he says, and I go, "What are you talking about," and he says, "It's time to stand up," and I go, "Don't tell me."

And Bobby says, "Yeah. Somebody flunked."

And I let a few seconds go by and I say, "Who?"

Bobby says, "That ain't important. What's important is you do the job, and that gives you stature. You'll be a big man then."

I'm thinking that stature is the last thing I need right now, with things going so smooth, but I'm also thinking that Bobby Marino bringing me the word from Casalegno is something you don't say no to without thinking long and hard. So I says, "We're talking about hitting somebody, huh?"

And Bobby goes, "Yeah. You got the balls?"

And I like, shrug and I say, "I got the balls. You got a reason?"

And Bobby says, "He flunked the test. He's got to go. It won't be a vat of acid, but he's got to go. He was ready to stab Angelo in the back, so he's got to go."

And I sit there and look at Bobby Marino and I don't like it one fucking bit. We sort of stare at one another for a while, and then I says, "You think that's straight, what Casalegno did? You think that's honorable?"

And Bobby leans forward a little and says, "I think Casalegno's the boss, that's what I think. And I think an organization like this only works if people are loyal to the boss. The Outfit ain't a fucking democracy. The Outfit's like the army, and if the lieutenant says jump, you say, how high? You want to know the truth? That's the only way to run a bunch of fucking criminals like this, with absolute discipline. When the discipline goes, then people start trying to get away with shit, and then it goes all to hell. So in the long run, whacking one guy that gets out of line will save everyone trouble down the line, because it will keep everyone thinking about discipline. And that's why you're gonna say yes."

And I sit there for a while, and I still don't like it, but I can't really come up with anything to argue against it, so in the end I nod and say, "OK, sure. I'm your guy. When does it happen?"

And Bobby says, "Tonight."

And I'm like, "Tonight? Jesus," and he says, "The sooner the better. Get it done."

I says, "OK, it's just like kinda sudden, that's all."

And he says, "It's better that way. It's all set up. Now listen good. What's gonna happen is, we're gonna pick the guy up in a limo. The story is, Joe DiPietro's throwing a party out in Oak Brook and he's sending a limo around for his friends. What it really is, is the limo's stolen, with fake plates, and it's the perfect place to whack a guy. Who's gonna suspect anything in a fucking limo, with a drink in his hand? We hit him and then ditch the limo someplace, and they won't find him for weeks. So we'll get the guy in the limo and then we'll come and pick you up. It'll be Marty driving, with me and the guy in the back. I'll make sure he's up front at the end of the seat, away from the door. And when you get in, we'll hit the road, and when I give the signal, you open the cabinet under the bar, the last one toward the rear door, and there'll be a piece in there. And you take care of business."

And the whole thing sounds insane to me and I'm starting to get a bad feeling in my stomach, but I'm thinking what the hell, I gotta follow orders. So I ask, "What's the signal?"

And Bobby says, "When I say, 'There are too many guys you just can't trust,' that's when you go for the gun. You got that?"

So I repeat it. "Too many guys you just can't trust."

And he goes, "That's it. All you gotta do is reach into that last compartment back there by the door, you know? You been in a limo before."

And I go, "Yeah, I got it."

So Bobby stands up and says, "You do everything right, you'll move way up on the charts, Gino. You'll be a big man in this Outfit. This is how you make your bones."

And I'm thinking, make my bones? This guy's been watching too many gangster flicks. But I says, "OK, I understand. Can I ask you one question?"

He says, "Sure."

So I go, "How come you won't tell me who it is?"

And Bobby says, "It's just security, that's all. In a secret operation everything's compartmentalized. That's Angelo for you. He got that out of some James Bond book he read. You'll know when you get in the limo."

And I shrug and say OK, and Bobby leaves.

And then I go through like the worst day of my life. The weather is for shit, with this freezing rain still coming down, and it's dark as hell, and the wind is blowing old ladies over on the sidewalk, and the radio says the power's out on the North Side, and all I want to do is go home and go to bed and forget about all this shit. And I'm thinking again, maybe I'm in the wrong business and I should have stayed in school like my ma wanted me to. And the thing that's at the back of my mind is, why won't he tell me who I'm supposed to kill. And as the day goes by I keep telling myself, I warned Terry about it, so it can't be him. There's no fucking way it could be Terry. But I still have this bad feeling in my stomach, and I even stand over the toilet for a couple of minutes trying to throw up and I can't, and finally I try and call Terry on his cell phone, but all I get is his voice mail.

I'm supposed to get picked up at ten o'clock, from in front of Luigi's. And Vickie fixes me a nice dinner and all and I can barely touch it, and she says, "What's the matter with you, you sick?" And I says, "I just had a late lunch, that's all," and I can see she don't believe me but she knows better than to ask me questions. So a little before ten I get in my car and go over to

Luigi's and park and go in and stand in the vestibule looking out at the parking lot, the wind shaking the big, lit-up sign and the black asphalt all slick and shiny under the lights, and I'm thinking, can I do this? And it's like, the longest ten minutes of my life, standing there waiting for that fucking limo to show up.

And finally it does, this white Lincoln Town car stretch limo, like, crawling in off the street, and I take a deep breath and go out into the rain. And the limo pulls up and I open the back door, and the first guy I see is Bobby Marino grinning at me, showing all his crooked teeth, and the second guy I see, up at the front with his back to the driver's window, is Terry.

And I almost fucking broke and ran. I'm thinking no, you dumb son of a bitch, I warned you. But I go ahead and get in and pull the door shut, because I'm like a robot by that point, just going on autopilot. And the limo pulls out and Terry's grinning at me and he's got a drink in his hand and he says, "Going in style tonight, dude," and I have to make an effort to smile back at him. I says, "Only way to go," and I look at Bobby, and he says, "What are you drinking?" and waves his hand at the bar.

And I take a couple of minutes making myself a vodka and tonic, and I'm glad to have something to do to cover up the fact that I'm fucking shaking and feel like I'm gonna puke, and and I'm trying not to look at Terry and trying not to look at the door to the last compartment at the rear under the bar, and I'm thinking how you always hear that it's your best friend that kills you, and I'm thinking no, no, no, I ain't gonna fucking do it.

And finally I sit back on my seat with a drink in my hand and I look at Terry and he grins at me again and says, "How in the hell did you sell this to Vickie? Julie told me if there's hookers there, I ain't getting back in the house." And I grin back at

Terry, because in that moment I see as clear as I've ever seen anything in my life that I am not gonna kill my best friend just because Angelo Casalegno and Bobby Marino tell me to, rules or no rules, Outfit or no Outfit. It just ain't gonna happen. And for the first time in days I feel good. Better than good. I feel great, because all of a sudden I know what's right and what's wrong. And I'm looking at the rest of my life and seeing it's all over for me in this town, and me and Vickie and Terry and Julie are all gonna have to book and set up somewhere else; and it ain't gonna be easy, but that's OK because for once in my life I'm gonna do the right thing.

And now all I have to do is figure out what to do about Bobby Marino and how to get me and Terry out of this shit. We're out on the expressway now and Terry and Bobby have been talking and all of a sudden I hear Marino say, "Yeah, it's too bad there's guys in this Outfit you just can't trust." And he looks at me like, that's the signal, remember? And all of a sudden I'm real calm because I see exactly what I have to do. I lean over and set my drink on the bar, and I reach for the handle to the cabinet door, and everything is like, slowing down, because I know exactly how it's going to go, and Terry Amonte is not the one who's going to get shot here in a minute. And I'm thinking about Marty up front driving and how Terry and me are gonna have to pull the wool over his eyes or maybe shoot him too—and then get away clean somehow and get back to Julie and Vickie and pack the bags and run like hell. And I'm thinking, make sure Terry doesn't get hit when you shoot Marino, don't just start firing wild like.

And I open the cabinet door and there's nothing there. I stare into the empty compartment for a second and I can't believe there's no piece there, nothing, and I think shit, I got the wrong compartment; and then I hear another door open and I look over and see Terry opening the compartment down at his end, and he pulls out a big, black fucking automatic. And I can't believe what I'm seeing.

And then as I see Terry raising the gun and pointing it at me, and Bobby Marino starts to scoot up the seat away from me as fast as he can, and I look into Terry's eyes and see nothing at all there, no friendship, no regret, no memories, no nothing, I finally, way too late, realize that Bobby Marino is a lying and treacherous son of a bitch and Angelo Casalegno's day is over, and the coup is for real, and instead of Terry it's me that flunked the fucking test, the real test, the intelligence test, and I am a fucking dead man.

And I open my mouth to scream at Terry that he's the biggest asshole of all, but before I can get anything out he swings the gun over to lock onto Marino, and he looks the old bastard in the eye, and Terry says, "You think I'm gonna kill my best friend because you and Casalegno don't get along? You got another think coming, you putrid motherfucker."

And I start to live again, stepping back from the brink of the fucking grave, and I almost shout for joy, thinking Jesus, how could I ever have doubted Terry. And now I'm the one scooting back on the seat to make sure I don't get hit or get any of Bobby Marino's blood and brains sprayed on me.

And I got to give Marino credit for balls, because the look on his face is like, concentrated, serious, but I don't see him panicking. And then the son of a bitch does what I least expect him to—he smiles, showing all those fucking crooked teeth.

And Bobby Marino says, "You think I'm dumb enough to get in a car with the two of you and give you a loaded weapon? You just flunked the test, asshole." And as Terry pulls the trigger three feet from Bobby Marino's head and the automatic goes click, Marino's hand goes inside his jacket, and the sudden, awful look on Terry's face tells me that I was right the first time, and not just about me, and Vickie and Julie both are widows.

END

"LOVE THAT WOMAN"

MY HEROES HAVE ALWAYS BEEN
   SHORT STOPS   — D.C. BROD
CODE BLUE   — MARY V. WELK
THE SIN-EATER   — SAM HILL
NO ONE   — MARCUS SAKEY

D.C. BROD is the author of five novels in the Quint McCauley private detective series and *Heartstone*, a contemporary thriller with an Arthurian twist. She lives in St. Charles with her husband, Don, a self-described "failed shortstop," and a cat, Travis McGee. "Chicago inspires me—" she says, "its moods, contrasts, and passions. If I'm setting my fiction in Chicago, I feel I'm already starting with a great character."

WWW.DCBROD.COM

MY HEROES HAVE ALWAYS BEEN SHORTSTOPS
D.C. BROD

TONIGHT THE CUBS ARE PLAYING IN
the seventh game of the World Series. In Wrigley Field, no
less. Against the Twins. And instead of sitting in one of the
choice seats behind home plate where I belong, I am watching the game in my condo, my television casting an eerie,
blue-white glow in the dark. I'm alone except for Ernie, my
gray tabby. Last week I took him to a woman who paints
cats. Literally. So, now he's got a Cubs' logo painted on his
right side, and I think it becomes him. I've made myself
some popcorn and have opened a fifty-dollar bottle of pinot

noir. I'd been saving it for after the game, hoping to share it with someone, but now that's not going to happen.

It's the bottom of the seventh and we're behind 6-5. That's not insurmountable, but we're the ones with the catching up to do. I just hope I don't have to leave before I know how this comes out.

I've muted the sound and have my radio tuned low to WGN so I can hear our local guys announce the game. During their chatter they occasionally wonder what happened to Keith, but for the most part they keep their comments on the play-by-play. And that's good, because this game is the only thing in the world that matters right now. Every atom in my body is tuned to it. But sometimes during the commercials my mind wanders, and when it does, it can't help sliding back to that day last winter when Keith McCall first walked into our offices, and once there it can't help but run the bases, so to speak.

I work for a sports agent, so I meet a lot of ball players. My boss, Dave Meyer, is a Chicago boy, and so he's set up his business here rather than New York or L.A., and for that I'm grateful. I will never leave Chicago. At least, not of my own accord. I've worked for Dave for five years. Came to him right out of college. He and my dad were friends, so I had some pull, but I do my job. I manage the office and am learning the fine art of negotiation. Keeping it professional has never been a problem for me. I've got big plans and they don't include settling down with some athlete to raise his progeny. My goal is to be a sports agent by the time I hit thirty. I will learn all I can from Dave, establish some contacts, and then go out on my own. I believe there is a place for women in this field.

I didn't need anything interfering with my goal. I didn't need complications. Also, I guess I've always looked on base-ball players as highly-prized race horses. Beautiful to behold, but too high maintenance to be ridden every day.

But then Dave took on Keith McCall, a promising short-stop, and I found how easy it was to alter my perceptions when appropriately motivated. I'm sure that part of it was the simple fact that he was a shortstop.

I do love shortstops. It's not just the look of them—although I've always found tall, lanky types appealing. It's not simply the fact that for all the infield traffic they manage and the range required to do it, they're arguably the best athletes on the team. No, what really impresses me about a good shortstop is how he bounces back from an error—sometimes a real boneheaded play—and thirty seconds later he's out there fielding a pop-up. I'm not sure how they compartmentalize—where in their heads they put all those errors—but the really good ones excel at it.

My first shortstop was my father. I worshipped him. He died when I was twelve, and so I suppose that just added to this iconic image I had of him. Occasionally, my mother will suggest that knowing him as an adult would have given me some much-needed objectivity, but I never pursue that notion. Heroes are hard enough to come by.

Anyway, there was Keith that day, dressed in a tweed sports jacket over jeans. I am convinced that men like Keith are the reason that jeans exist. He turned on a lopsided smile as he reached across my desk to shake my hand. And there was that grip. Cool, firm and all-encompassing. Well over six feet tall, he didn't slouch at all the way that some tall, slender types do. I'd seen him play before, mainly as the Yankees' backup shortstop, and he was even more impressive up close. Dave saw something better than a backup in Keith and convinced him to sign with us.

Dave placed one beefy hand on my shoulder, gave it a little squeeze and said, "Keith, you ever can't get hold of me, you talk to Abby here. Her word's as good as mine, and she's probably smarter."

"He's right about that," I said to Keith with a grin. Actually, Dave wasn't exaggerating so much. "Abby's the cleanup hitter," he likes to tell people. And baseball players can require a lot of mopping up, so I had plenty of practice.

"Add to that the fact that she's gorgeous and you've got a lethal combination." He gave me a final pat and led Keith back to his office, but not before Keith's gaze stayed on me until long past necessary.

To be honest, I didn't give him much thought after that. I'd seen good-looking men before, and then there was my race-horse theory.

Less than a week later, Dave had signed Keith to a very sweet deal with the Cubs. I'd seen him a number of times as I handled some of the details, and that smile just kept getting warmer. I couldn't have been happier that he was donning a Cub uniform. I guess I'd lost my objectivity, but I didn't realize that until too late. To celebrate, Dave took us to dinner with a couple of his friends. Keith fended off questions and good-natured joking with a deftness I didn't usually see off the diamond.

When asked about his Missouri upbringing, Keith said he'd been a Cards fan his whole life, but the difference was only "a matter of a few miles and mindset."

As per usual, I was the only woman at the gathering. Keith sat between Dave and me and managed to scootch my way during the course of the meal. Afterwards we all adjourned to the bar.

"What're you drinking?" he asked as he slid onto the bar stool next to mine.

"Gin martini," I said, as if he hadn't already seen me down a couple of them. But I didn't mention the brand, just to see how closely he was paying attention.

He called it right—Bombay—and after I took my first sip, I said, "You're an observant man, aren't you?"

"Sure am." He swallowed a gulp of beer and glanced over his shoulder at Dave and his friends who were placing bets on which Bulls' player would get the next three-pointer. He glanced up toward the screen, lingered there for a few seconds, and then I had his attention again.

"I notice you don't wear a wedding band," he said.

"If you're wondering if I'm married, I'm not." Then I shrugged. "You could have asked."

He shook his head. "Not as much fun."

"So, what else can you tell about me?"

Looking down at me with narrowed eyes, he rubbed his chin. Tonight he wore a navy sweater over an untucked white shirt. He'd propped his feet on the stool's upper rung and with his long legs all folded up, he reminded me of a praying mantis.

I crossed one leg over the other as I swung around to face him.

He said, "You're a huge—and I mean huge—Cubs fan."

I snorted a chuckle. "What gave it away? The photos behind my desk? My coffee mug? Business card holder?"

"Well, there's that. But that's run of the mill Cubs' paraphernalia." He paused, and his voice got a little husky. "It's not even that little pendant you wear most days."

I had to stop myself from reaching for my throat.

"So, what is it?"

He glanced down toward the floor, then back up to meet my eyes. "It's the toe ring."

This stunned me on a couple of levels. First, I was both flattered and a little disturbed to realize that he had noticed my toes. They are at the end of my feet, which are at the end of my legs, and therefore quite a distance from his eyes. And that is what really stunned me. The ring is gold, the logo is gold. It is a subtle ring. This man had amazing vision.

"I'll bet you can hit a curve ball," I said.

He gave me that slow smile as he nodded. "I've been known to hit a few."

Later that night, after commenting on my Cubs' bed linens, Keith leaned back onto the blue pillow with a satisfied sigh. I decided it was my turn to pose the "Are you married?" question.

"No," he said, folding his hands behind his head so one of his splayed elbows was inches from my nose.

"Anyone special?" I was a little angry with myself for asking.

He turned his head toward me. "Not here." And then he added, "Not until now."

I crooked my arm and propped up my head with my fist so I could see over his elbow. "I think it's fine you've got someone back home. Or somewhere else. This—tonight—is nice. But I'm your agent's assistant. I don't want emotional attachments."

With a sigh he turned his face up toward the ceiling. "I knew I was going to like Chicago."

Somehow that wasn't quite the response I was hoping for.

When spring training started in February, I spent more than the usual amount of time in Mesa. Keith played well and it looked like Dave had been right in his assessment of the Cubs' new shortstop. He was all over the infield scooping up grounders, shagging pop-ups, and showed an amazing ability to get from one place to another in less time than it took to blink. And, yes, he could hit a curve ball.

One weekend a young woman arrived from St. Louis to see Keith. She was younger than me by a few years and had that scrubbed sexiness that translated well into baseball wife. I could see her raising money for some childhood disease. I flew back to Chicago and spent the weekend watching DVDs of *The Sopranos* and eating pizza.

Neither Keith nor I ever brought up the visiting Barbie.

Once the season started, we settled into a comfortable pattern. I helped him find an apartment, although the time we spent together was usually at my condo, which overlooked Lake Michigan on one side and Wrigley Field from the other. We'd have dinner, sex, and then watch whatever game was on television. Some mornings we'd wake to the glare of the sun off the lake. Keith made breakfast, which usually included his secret-ingredient salsa on an omelet or scrambled eggs. It was the closest thing to an actual relationship I had experienced, and I guess I liked whatever was forming between us.

Dave warned me that Keith was a client, but I assured my boss that I wasn't in it for anything long term. And even if I had been, it would not have been with a guy like Keith. At least that's what I told myself.

We had nothing in common other than a mutual attraction and baseball. He liked country music, hunting and had voted Republican in every election since he'd turned eighteen. I was a vegetarian with eclectic music taste. No one in my family had ever admitted to voting Republican. But Keith and I had great sex and we both loved sports. All kinds. I thought I was addicted, but Keith's enthusiasm could put me to shame.

Not only did he put everything into his ball game, he also put everything into all games—basketball, golf, soccer, you name it. If an event could be scored, Keith was yelling or cheering at the TV. It wasn't long before I noticed that he wasn't consistent on what team he either cheered or harangued. He could be yelling at a Bulls' forward for missing a layup one night and the next he'd be giving the Bulls' opponent a standing ovation.

Finally, I had to ask.

"You're a gambler, aren't you?"

I'd been watching the game from the bed, wearing a short robe with the *Sun Times* laid out in front of me.

Keith had just cast aspersions on some Pistons player's parentage, and it was a moment before my question sank in. When it did, he turned toward me, and I knew I was right.

Before he answered, I said, "That's really, really stupid, you know."

He ran a hand through his hair. "Not like it's against the rules." With an angry shake of his head, he added, "I'm not betting on baseball."

"You better not be."

He got up from the chair and came over to the bed. "What you got against a little gambling?"

I flipped a page in the newspaper and pretended to be scanning an article. "It's just a stupid thing to be doing with your money."

"Not if you win."

I looked up. "Do you?"

"Sometimes."

I turned another page so hard it tore.

"Whoa," he said, taking my hand. "What's the big deal?"

"You're a high-profile athlete. You're good looking, articulate. You know there's already product endorsement possibilities out there. After you win the Series, they'll be offering you top dollar. But if any of these sponsors get wind of a gambling habit, you can kiss those dollars goodbye."

He kissed my neck. "But they're not going to find out. I'm discrete."

I twisted so my neck was out of his reach. "Yeah, well you'd better hope you are."

That was all the discussion we had that day. I guess I knew not to push it, but I started watching him closely, noting his reaction to games we'd be watching together. I didn't think it was my imagination when I saw he was getting edgier. After a while it got so he barely knew I was in the same room when a game was on.

Then one day we were in a neighborhood sports bar sharing a basket of fries and drinking a couple beers. On a large-screen TV, the Mariners played the Royals. I was in the middle of telling him about the merits of a meatless diet when all of a sudden Keith slammed his half-filled mug down on the table and cursed. A little sloshed out over his hand, and he said, "I'll be right back." Then he walked out the door. Just like that. I glanced up at the TV and saw that the Mariners had lost the game. As far as I knew, Keith had no emotional attachment to the Mariners.

I grabbed my purse and followed him.

It was one of those sticky, humid nights that made me think the lake was encroaching on the city. The bar was on the corner, and since I didn't see him walking up the street, I rounded that corner and found him in an alley behind the pub. He was leaning against the building, staring up at the murky night sky.

"You bet on that game, didn't you?"

When he wouldn't answer or even look at me, I knew he had.

I kicked at a piece of gravel. "Do you have any idea how stupid that is?"

He shook his head. "I'm careful. I've got a guy I trust. I don't bet a lot."

"It doesn't matter if you're doing penny ante. Anyone finds out, you're toast, Keith."

"Nobody's going to find out." He finally looked down at me. "Unless you tell them."

That hurt. But all I said was, "I'm the last person you have to worry about."

He looked away again.

"And don't tell me you're getting all worked up over a few bucks."

"I'm not going to get caught."

I grabbed his arm and swung him around so he had to face me. "So help me, Keith. If you don't stop this I'm going to tell Dave. Let him decide what to do with you."

"You wouldn't."

"He will drop you so fast you won't know it happened until you land on your ass. Dave is a respected agent. Do you think anyone decent is going to want to pick you up after he dumps you?"

"After the year I'm having," he grinned, "I don't see that as a problem."

"You know your way around a diamond, Keith, but when it comes to business sense, you're right up there with last year's Derby winner." The grin faded. "And you're a lot dumber than I give you credit for, if you don't see that I'm right."

A muscle in his jaw flexed.

"If you need help," I told him, "I can get you help."

"I don't need help," he said through clenched teeth.

"If you're willing to throw away your career over this, then you do need help."

I dug through my purse until I found the business card of a friend who is a psychiatrist. "Call this guy. He can't tell anyone anything you tell him."

He wouldn't take the card.

"But he is a friend of mine," I continued. "And if I call him next week and learn that you have not contacted him yet, I'm going to Dave."

I can read eyes pretty well, and Keith's were telling me to go to hell.

"And I don't want to see you again until you've got this under control."

I stuffed the card into his shirt pocket, turned and walked out of the alley.

I waited a week before calling my friend, and he told me that Keith had seen him once and had scheduled another appointment.

By August the Cubs had climbed into first place and were four games ahead of the Cards and Reds, who were battling it out for second. I tried to tell myself it was just as well that I wasn't seeing Keith anywhere but at the games. He needed to concentrate on winning. He was hitting better than .300, batting third in the lineup and making some amazing infield plays. Seemed like everywhere I went that summer I saw Keith's number plastered on some stranger's back or chest. Sometimes at the games I'd think he was looking for me in the stands, but that was probably my imagination. I couldn't ask my shrink friend how Keith was doing, but I figured that no news was good news.

We made it into the playoffs and then the Series where we'd be playing Minnesota. I wished I could've been happier than I was, but still, these were good times. But I did miss having someone to share it with. Someone next to me when I woke up or went for a walk along the lake. And the smell of eggs and salsa made my throat knot up. But that sadness would pass and the glow of this year for the Cubs would remain. All in all, I was feeling pretty good. Until the Barbie called, that is.

I'd just brought Ernie back from the cat painter, and I was beginning to think that I'd gone too far this time. The cat had not asked to be a Cub fan. Still, I sensed that he was. When the phone rang, I checked the caller ID, and it was a cellular number neither I nor my phone recognized.

When she said her name, Holly Connors, I still didn't get it. But then she said, "Keith's fiancé," and I said, "Oh." Then I managed, "I didn't know he'd gotten engaged." I swallowed. "Congratulations."

"It's not official yet. We're waiting until after the Series."

"Sure." I was wondering if she knew about Keith and me and thought if she did, it was odd that she'd wait until he had proposed before confronting me.

But then she said, "I wondered if I could talk to you. Not on the phone," she quickly added. "Keith said you were someone he could talk to, and I thought, well, I thought maybe you'd be a good person for me to talk to about him."

So that was how Keith had explained me. I was a pal. Someone who helped him adjust to life in the majors.

"What about?" I asked.

"Can we meet somewhere?"

"Um, sure," I said, and mentioned a pub down the street from me. I didn't feel like traveling far for this woman.

###

She was at Sweeney's when I arrived, sitting at one of the tables with a glass of white wine centered on a napkin. I ordered a draft.

She was smaller than I'd remembered. Could probably tuck herself under Keith's arm with room to spare. Long, blond hair with bangs that were shaped to flatter. Pretty, tan and blond.

She introduced herself, then said, "I think we met in Mesa last spring."

"Probably," I said. "I spent some time there." Then I added, "Dave has a lot invested in Keith."

Her smile seemed a little forced when she said, "He's not disappointing anyone is he?"

"No. Dave knew he'd be good."

"He's got one of the best averages in the league."

The beer tasted flat, and I pushed the glass aside. "What is it, Holly?" Something about this woman presuming to know baseball really irked me.

"It's his gambling."

It felt like something had just crawled onto the back of my neck. "I thought he was seeing someone about that."

"Not anymore."

She must have caught my reaction because she said, "Yeah, I know. I tried to talk him into going back, but he swears he doesn't need it."

"But he does."

"I know." She nodded, and her eyes were shining. "But I can't force him, you know?"

"How do you know he's gambling again?"

"My ring." She raised her left hand and wiggled her bare ring finger. "We had it picked out and then all of a sudden, it's back for adjustments. It didn't need an adjustment." She swallowed hard and shook her head. "I'm finding past due bills in his apartment. I heard him arguing with the landlord." After a deep sigh, she said, "And then last week this guy came to see him."

"What guy?"

"I don't know. Keith wouldn't introduce me to him. But he wasn't a friend. As soon as I got there, he hustled the guy out. The man wasn't happy about it. Said he'd be in touch."

When I let my imagination run with that, I didn't like where it was taking me. And I didn't know if the anger working its way up from my gut was directed at Keith for being stupid and weak or at me for not knowing from the very first that he was.

Holly and I sat there in silence for a few moments and finally she said, her voice raspy, "We're too close. He won't talk to me about it. Will you try?"

I found Keith at his apartment on the morning of the seventh game. If he was surprised to see me, he didn't let on.

He was making an omelet and heating up some of that special salsa. "You're just in time for breakfast. Let me make you something."

"No. Thanks."

He cracked a couple more eggs and added them to the bowl he had going.

"I had a talk with Holly," I said. From the way his mixing stopped all of a sudden, then started up again, I knew that Holly definitely didn't know about whatever relationship Keith and I had had.

I let him suffer for several moments, and then I said, "I didn't tell her about us."

His shoulders relaxed, but then he tucked his eyebrows and said, "So, what did …"

"She's worried about your gambling. She thought, as a 'friend' I might be able to help."

His shoulders stiffened as he turned away, opening a cupboard and pretending to rummage for something. "I don't need your help, Abby."

"You're in deep, aren't you?"

He didn't interrupt his search for the elusive spice.

I continued, "The only way I can figure you're going to settle that debt is to throw the game tonight."

He stopped rummaging, but didn't turn. I'd guessed right. Dammit.

"I have to tell Dave," I said.

Finally he turned, and I was surprised to see he was smiling a little. "You won't." He ground some pepper into the eggs.

I just stared at him.

He didn't need prompting. "You won't tell him because you won't do that to the team. Not the Cubs."

I wasn't sure if he was right, but already my brain was scrambling to see if there was a way to do this and not have to ruin everything for them.

When he saw my hesitation, he smiled and seemed to relax a little. "Besides," he said, "I'm not the only guy on this team, Abby. They could still win." He said that almost as a joke; as though the idea of the Cubs winning without him was ludicrous. Then he put his hand on mine and gave it a little squeeze.

"I've played bad games before and they've won." Again, there was that attitude.

I pulled my hand away. "You're not a part of the team anymore, Keith. You gave that up when you sold them out."

He shrugged. That's all he did. He just shrugged. And then he said, "If Dave is earning his money, I won't even be playing for the Cubs next year. The Yankees want me back, and the Cards are interested." He tasted the salsa and nodded his approval.

Until that moment, I honestly didn't know what I'd do. But now I did.

"C'mon, Abby," he gestured toward a stool at the counter. "Pull up a chair and have breakfast with me."

"Let me wash my hands first."

I used the bathroom attached to his bedroom and made a stop in his closet where I knew he kept his hunting rifle and a couple of handguns. I removed one of these from its case and walked back into the kitchen, holding it at my side.

He was scooping a pile of eggs onto my plate when he looked up. Only when his gaze dropped to my hand clutching the gun did his expression change. He didn't look so much scared as puzzled.

I said, "I thought you were better at recovering from errors."

He opened his mouth as though to respond, but before he could, I shot him.

I couldn't help but notice he didn't bleed Cubbie blue. Apparently it's only the fans who do that.

###

It's the bottom of the ninth now. Ernie is in my lap kneading the soft flesh of my calf with his front paws. We're still down by one, and we've got two out. But we've got a fast runner on second and the backup shortstop at the plate. He's just up from triple A at the end of the season, and he shows promise.

Someone is knocking at my door. I'm going to see if I can ignore it.

END

MARY V. WELK writes the Caroline Rhodes/Carl Atwater mysteries, winner of a 2002 Readers Choice Award for Best Series. Her short fiction has appeared in many national publications. Her first novel, *A Deadly Little Christmas*, will be rereleased by Echelon Press in September, 2007. About Chicago, Mary says, "What better place to stage a crime story than in Chicago? Set it in the past and you have criminals like H.H. Holmes, Leopold and Loeb, or Johnny Torrio. Set it in more modern times and you can model your villain on a crooked judge or politician. From the depths of Lake Michigan to the brownstones of the Gold Coast to the jazz clubs of the South Side, there are hundreds of stories waiting to be told, and Chicago writers are telling them."

WWW.MARYWELK.COM

CODE BLUE
MARY V. WELK

THE HANDCUFFS BIT INTO THE FAT MAN'S wrists, chafing the soft, pink flesh anchoring bone to sinew.

"Don't move."

The blue-jacketed paramedic scowled at the jiggling mound of human blubber he and his partner had dubbed Fat Boy. Ignoring the man's frantic squeals, he let the full weight of his arms fall on the cuffs.

"You're hurting me," Fat Boy whined.

Blue Jacket scrunched his face into a sad puppy look and deliberately dropped the strap's metal buckle on the man's fingers. "Aw, I'm sorry. I wouldn't want to do that." He poked the man with a gloved finger. "Move over, buddy. I'm not breakin' my back trying to lift you."

Mewing like a wounded cat, Fat Boy struggled to heave his three hundred plus pounds off the cot and onto the ER cart.

"My chest hurts, I tell you! It really does!"

"That nice lady over there will take care of your pain." Blue Jacket grinned at the woman leaning against the glass doors of the ER cubicle. "She knows what to do for guys like you."

"Thanks for the vote of confidence." The ER nurse straightened to her full five-foot-five inches and turned to the tech in the doorway. "Hook him up to the monitor. I'll be back after I get the lowdown on our patient." She brushed past the baby-faced cop who'd accompanied Fat Boy to the hospital. "You can cuff him to the siderails, Officer, but we'll need him undressed first."

Baby Face tore his gaze from her ample bust. "The Chicago Police Department is at your service, Miss ..."

"I'm Frankie to my friends." She glanced pointedly at the policeman's crotch. "To you, I'm Nurse Ratched," she said, and walked away.

"That's what you get for being an asshole." Blue Jacket's blond partner shouldered the cop aside and wheeled the empty ambulance cot into the corridor. "Next time, stare at her face, not her breasts."

"He's right, my friend." Blue Jacket emerged from the cubicle and peeled off his gloves. "Frankie can smell bullshit a mile away, especially from a rookie." He waggled a finger at the suddenly red-faced officer. "I wouldn't advise getting on her bad side. She can pack a punch like Ali in his prime."

Frankie's voice rang out from the desk. "Are you boys coming or not?"

"Yes, mother!" Blue Jacket leaned closer to the young cop. "One thing my partner forgot to tell you. Frankie's his sister. Treat her with respect you hear?"

"She said her name was Ratched! I thought ..." Baby Face stuttered, the color draining from his face. "Look, man, I didn't mean ..."

As Baby Face scurried into the cubicle, the blond paramedic rolled his eyes. "If you ask me, the CPD took the training wheels off that kid way too soon. Shit, man. Doesn't he watch TV?"

"*One Flew Over the Cuckoo's Nest* was a little before his time."

"You sayin' we're old?"

Blue Jacket grabbed a gunmetal-gray folder from the cot and rapped it with his knuckles. "Too old for the crap in this report. That son of a bitch deserves—"

"The absolute worst. I agree with you, buddy, but there's nothing we can do about it. Come on, let's grab some coffee before we give Nurse Ratched the bad news."

Frankie was drumming her fingers on the desktop when the paramedics came into view. She glanced at their coffee cups and sighed. "What's the story, morning glory?"

"Same old, same old," Blue Jacket opened the folder. "You know. Guy gets arrested, guy lands in a cell with the usual assortment of Chicago scum. Guy takes one look at his bunkmates and starts worrying about his butthole. Panic sets in. Guy wants out of jail pronto. And what's the best way to get out?" He clasped both hands over his chest. "Officer, I got chest pain! I got it real bad!"

"So you think he's faking it?" She arched an eyebrow.

"Don't they all?" Blue Jacket slumped in a chair behind the desk. "We're always getting called to lockup for some asshole complaining of chest pain. None of them are for real. It's like somebody put up a sign: You Want Out Today, Fake A Heart Attack."

Frankie shrugged. "Maybe tonight is for real. This guy could pass for a sumo wrestler with all the flab he's carrying. He's probably got french fries for arteries."

"I couldn't care less. After what he did ..."

His partner put a hand on his shoulder. "Listen, pal. It don't pay to bust a blood vessel over the likes of him."

"You two are sending out really bad vibes." Frankie glanced from one man to the other. "Why are you so down on this patient?"

Blue Jacket handed her the paperwork he'd lifted from the file. "Check out Fat Boy's name. Then think back to the old lady we brought here Monday night."

Frankie scanned the report. "Harold Ripley." It suddenly hit her. "Ohmygod! You mean this is the fella who—"

"One and the same." Blue Jacket dragged himself from the chair. "I gotta get the hell out of here before I do some major damage." He headed towards the ambulance bay.

The other medic waited until his buddy left the room, then turned to Frankie. "You know what? Sometimes I'd like to bypass the ER and head straight for the morgue. This is one of those times." He shoved his copy of the paperwork under Frankie's nose. "Sign this, doll, while I go rescue the cot."

"Sure." Frankie tried to concentrate on Blue Jacket's scribbled handwriting, but the words on the report blurred into the image of her Monday night patient. An elderly woman, bruised and swollen. She pushed back the memory and considered what she knew of Ripley. The man might be faking pain, but anyone could see he was a prime candidate for a heart attack. As long as you don't go down tonight, she thought, I really don't give a damn.

Still, Fat Boy was no ordinary prisoner. His name had graced the front pages of both city papers recently. Harold Ripley, brother of Congressman John Maynard Ripley. Grandson of May Alcott Ripley, the Ripley candy fortune heiress. Fat Boy was a celebrity requiring careful handling.

Frankie signed the CFD report with an angry flourish. "Just my luck to land this bastard for a patient."

"Talkin' to yourself again?" Rolling the cot to a stop, the paramedic swept his paperwork off the desk and filed it neatly in the gray folder.

"Nursing isn't all it's cracked up to be." Frankie wrote her name next to Ripley's on the ER board. "I should've studied something easier in college, like flower design or basket weaving."

"At least Chicago's finest won't bother you again." He bobbed his head toward the young cop stationed outside Fat Boy's room. "He thinks I'm your brother. My partner threatened him with bodily harm if he messes with you."

Frankie, the only child of Greek immigrants, chuckled as she compared her height-challenged frame, charcoal eyes, and olive skin to that of the big Swede standing next to her. It didn't take a genius to see that his sturdy Viking blood had bypassed her ancestors by half a continent. Now if Soprano-look-alike Blue Jacket had made the threat …

"Gotta run, doll. Duty calls."

The tension in the room lessened with the departure of the ambulance crew. Nevertheless, Frankie shifted into survival mode as she pondered the situation. By now, the press would be aware of Ripley's arrest. So would his congressman brother. Despite the early hour, the congressman's flunkies were probably hard at work doing damage control from their suburban McMansions. Soon one of them would appear to handle the reporters who'd flock to the ER.

A bad night ahead. "Shit and a half," she mumbled.

Baby Face jumped to his feet as she approached Fat Boy's room. "Anything I can do to help?" The cop's eyes were fixed firmly on Frankie's face, never wavering below her chin.

"Tell me something. Has Ripley seen an attorney yet?"

"Not yet, but that slimeball knows his rights. He demanded a lawyer the minute he was arrested. He was in a holding cell when he started blubbering about his chest. Being who he is, the detectives sent him here right away."

How considerate of them, thought Frankie. An ordinary perp would never rate such quick service.

"Guys like him always cause us trouble."

"Cause me trouble, you mean."

Frankie stepped into the cubicle. Fat Boy sat upright on the cart like a cartoon version of Jabba the Hutt. He was swathed in an extra-large gown that drooped low over pendulous breasts. Heart monitor leads dotted his hairless chest. A thigh-sized blood pressure cuff was wrapped around one arm, and an oxygen sensor covered his right forefinger. A plastic cannula fed oxygen to his nose at two liters an hour.

"How's your pain, Mr. Ripley?" Frankie fought a sour taste in her mouth.

Fat Boy's bottom lip trembled. "Please take these handcuffs off. I can't feel my fingers!"

Frankie examined the cuffs binding Fat Boy's wrists to the cart. She motioned to Baby Face. "Loosen them up a little, Officer. He's not going anywhere."

And if he does, you can shoot him, she thought.

She examined Ripley's EKG. Nothing peculiar there, no abnormalities to signal a heart attack. "This looks normal, Mr. Ripley. So do your vital signs. I have a few questions for you, then we'll do some tests. You'll be here a couple of hours. After that, if all's well, we'll release you to the police."

Fat Boy paled.

"According to the paramedic report, you're a diabetic. I take it you're not on a diet."

Frankie's sarcasm missed its mark. "I've got high blood pressure, too," Fat Boy whined. "I know I'm having a heart attack."

Don't I wish! Frankie felt a throbbing at her temples that signaled the onset of a headache. She closed her eyes, willing it away.

"I can't breathe good, either."

Fat Boy droned on while Frankie drew his blood. She shut him off, her mind retreating to a distant past when nursing had appealed to her and caring was easy. Now it was a struggle simply to get out of bed and go to work. She'd struck up a relationship with vodka years before, and it worked for a while. But liquor could no longer inure her to the demands of her job. She hated the slackers who invaded her ER, their pockets empty and their hands outstretched. She hated the fakers, the gangbangers, the jerks. Most of all, she hated the mink coats who treated her like a servant.

"You aren't listening to me!" Fat Boy yelled. "You don't care!"

Frankie adjusted her expression to mask her loathing. "I've listed your complaints on the chart." She pointed to Paula Li who stood in the doorway eyeballing her patient with a marked lack of enthusiasm. "Dr. Li will discuss them with you."

Returning to the desk, Frankie typed the lab orders into the computer.

"Got a new patient?" Harpreet, Frankie's partner on the night shift, sank down in a chair next to her. She glanced at the computer. "That name's familiar."

"That's what I said when I first saw it." Frankie hit the Enter button and watched the screen go black. Turning, she gazed into the compassionate eyes of the young, Indian nurse and saw herself twenty years earlier, a nursing grad eager to save the world. Now all she was trying to save was herself.

"He's a prisoner," she said, leaving it at that. No need to burden someone else with Ripley's unpleasant story.

"You know the code we worked in 9 earlier tonight? His family refuses to leave until the undertaker comes for the body. That won't be for at least another hour."

"That's fine, Harpreet. Let them have their time to grieve."

The security phone rang. Frankie picked it up.

"There's a pair of suits out here in the lobby, one with a briefcase, the other with dollar bills written all over his face. They're lookin' for your jailbird."

Frankie recognized the voice of her favorite security guard, a Brahma bull of a man who maintained strict order in the ER, allowing "polite" visitors in and kicking "nasty boys" out. He was the closest thing to a guardian angel the night staff had.

"Sounds like Congressman Ripley's people. Hold them in the lobby. I'll notify the officer who came in with Fat Boy, see if it's okay for him to have visitors."

Baby Face looked distraught when Frankie filled him in.

"Detective Franklin was supposed to be here by now. I don't think I have the authority to let Ripley talk to anyone."

"Why don't you ring up the station, see if Franklin's on his way. The guard can stall for a few more minutes."

"I don't like being stalled, young woman. Not when my client's life is in danger."

Frankie saw two men pass through the swinging doors at the back of the ER. The shorter of the two she recognized as Congressman Ripley. Balding, in his late fifties, the congressman resembled his brother, minus the belly fat. She'd heard he kept trim by swimming thirty laps in his pool every day. The regimen may have helped his waistline, but it did nothing for his complexion. His face was the sallow shade of a skinned cod.

The man with him was older and more distinguished. Silver hair curled like soft lamb's wool above a high forehead, flat eyes, and a Roman nose. He wore a conservative gray suit, white shirt, and pinstriped tie, and he carried a leather brief-case that would have cost Frankie half a month's wages.

She took an instant dislike to the man. "That's a restricted entrance, sir, for use by hospital personnel only."

Silver Hair waved off Frankie with an impatient flick of his hand. "The guard wouldn't let us in through the lobby, so we found another route. Now, please let us see Harold Ripley."

"And who might you be?" asked Baby Face.

To Frankie's amazement, the policeman seemed not to recognize Congressman Ripley. His attention was focused instead on the man with the briefcase. Maybe like her, he sensed that Silver Hair was the real enemy. Or maybe he didn't read newspapers.

Silver Hair's jaw dropped. Baby Face appeared to take this as an insult and placed one hand on the butt of his gun.

"I asked you a question, sir."

"Please, Arnold. If I may." The congressman extended his card to the officer. "Mr. Ripley is my brother." He gestured at Silver Hair. "This is his lawyer, Mr. Arnold Meyer. We understand that Harold has been falsely accused of a crime. Mr. Meyer is here to clear up the matter."

"Mr. Ripley is in police custody," Baby Face said. "You can speak to the detective in charge ..."

"I want to speak to my client," Meyer cut in, "as is his right—which I understand, he has made perfectly clear." The lawyer shifted his gaze to Frankie. "Who's the doctor in charge? Where is he?"

Frankie glanced over Meyer's shoulder. Dr. Li was making a fast escape into the lounge. She raised both hands in a "not me" gesture and reinforced it with a slashing motion across her throat.

"Dr. Li is on duty tonight. But she"—Frankie emphasized the pronoun—"is unavailable at the moment. Perhaps I can help."

Meyer frowned at her name badge, apparently stymied by the many vowels and consonants in her Greek surname. "Miss, my client needs legal advice. I would like to consult with him now."

"I'm sure you would," Frankie said smoothly. "Unfortunately, hospital policy says I can't grant you access without permission from the CPD. Detective Franklin should be here soon. Until he arrives, I must ask you and Congressman Ripley to wait in the lobby."

"And if we refuse?" Meyer said, his voice cold.

Frankie could have placated the lawyer by turning the whole mess over to her supervisor. But something inside, something too broken to repair, responded to Meyer's smile of contempt.

"Then I'll have no choice but to have you forcibly evicted." She pointed to the security phone on the far wall. "In two minutes I can have this place crawling with security officers."

"No need for that, nurse." Congressman Ripley touched Meyer's arm. "Let's step outside, Arnold. I'm sure we'll be allowed to speak with Harold very soon." He showered Frankie with a politician's smile. "Thank you for your patience."

"That was fun," said Frankie after the two men exited the ER.

"Scumbags," muttered Baby Face.

"Yeah, well, it might have helped if your detective buddy had shown up. You should find out where the hell he is!"

Frankie clamped her lips shut and stalked off to the desk. She spent the next five minutes venting her frustration on paperwork.

"You don't look happy," said Harpreet, emerging from the medication room.

"Lawyer trouble," said Frankie. "What I need is five minutes alone to pull my head together."

"No problem. I'll watch your patient while you take a break."

"Great." Frankie grabbed her parka and fled the ER.

It was snowing when she stepped outside. The cold air felt surprisingly good on her throbbing temples and she lifted her face to the night sky, letting the thin flakes dampen her cheeks and throat. What she needed was two aspirin and a good night's sleep. She lit a cigarette instead.

She was watching the smoke curl around her fingers, wondering how she was going to make it through the night, when she heard Congressman Ripley's voice in the darkness.

"This could ruin my reelection, you know."

"I don't think so. I've gotten him off twice before ..."

"But those witnesses were wetbacks. A Mexican, if I remember, and a Haitian. This time the nurses' aide speaks English. She won't be easy to shut up."

Frankie heard the crunch of footsteps on snow. She ducked into the shadowed doorway of a fire exit.

"I assure you, the case will never reach court."

"How do you propose to stop it?"

"The same way I stopped the others." Meyer chuckled, a short, dry laugh that made Frankie's skin crawl. "This Irish lass has outstayed her visa by a year. One word to the authorities and she'll be back on the Emerald Isle herding sheep."

Frankie sucked in a breath. Was Fat Boy going free?

"Why couldn't my grandmother have died when she had the goddamned stroke? I've had to move her to three different nursing homes—"

"And three times he came in and raped her. You obviously have no control over your brother."

"This time I'll move her out of state where he can't find her."

The men began walking again. Frankie strained to hear the rest of their conversation, but caught only snatches on the wind, then nothing. She slipped back into the ER unnoticed and made her way to Fat Boy's cubicle.

Baby Face didn't look happy to see her. "I contacted the station. Detective Franklin was called out on a shooting. God only knows when he'll get back. The desk sergeant told me to get Ripley's ass back ASAP."

"I'll see what I can do to speed things up," said Frankie. "First, though, I've got a question for you."

"Fire away. As long as it's not privileged information ..."

"I understand Ripley was arrested for rape twice before. What do you know about that?"

Baby Face shrugged. "He was hauled in for questioning, but we could never make the charges stick."

Frankie played back in her mind the conversation she'd just heard. She had to know for sure. "Why not?"

"The witnesses crapped out on us. A Mexican woman reported him the first time. Turned out she was an illegal. She headed south the day after making her statement."

A chill ran through Frankie. She stared at Fat Boy's cubicle.

"Did a Haitian girl lodge the second complaint?"

Baby Face looked surprised. "How'd you know? Turned out she skipped too. Family said she missed Haiti and flew back." He shook his head. "Hard to believe anyone could be homesick for a hellhole like Haiti."

Frankie nodded and turned away, but Baby Face wasn't done.

"The rumor is he may beat this rap, too. The witness went AWOL."

Frankie felt a cold, hard resolve settle over her.

Dr. Li was waiting for her at the desk. "Ripley's tests results are back. Everything's normal, even his glucose, which I expected to be high since he's non-compliant with his diabetes meds. My best guess is that he had a panic attack when he was arrested."

"Could be his nerves affected his stomach. How about we give him a GI cocktail? If it's indigestion, a swig of that might help."

Paula Li smiled. "Not a bad idea. At least he'll stop complaining I'm not doing anything for him."

Frankie entered the medication room and signed out a mini-cup of Maalox, a similar cup containing viscous lidocaine, and two tiny, brown bottles of Donnatal. She mixed the concoction in a large plastic cup, stirring it until the ingredients reached the consistency of a lime smoothie. Then she took a container of orange juice from the room's small refrigerator and partially filled a second cup. She carried the two cups to an empty cubicle where she took a bottle of isopropyl alcohol from a cabinet. She filled the remainder of both cups with alcohol, stirring each to mix the contents. After returning the bottle to its shelf, she carried her offerings to Fat Boy.

He was watching TV, his eyes glued to a comedy about a divorcee and her obnoxious daughter. Frankie glanced at the set before handing him the cup. "Enjoying yourself?"

Fat Boy looked at her wide-eyed, as if suddenly remembering that he was supposed to be sick. "My chest still hurts." He pointed to his bellybutton.

"That's your stomach, Mr. Ripley. Dr. Li thinks that may be what's causing your chest pain. This should help."

She lifted the cup to his lips.

He wrinkled his nose. "Smells bad."

"Medicine often smells bad," said Frankie with a forced smile. "But it does good things. Now drink up."

Fat Boy did as he was told.

"According to the lab, your blood sugar is low. I've brought you some orange juice."

She helped him with the second cup. Again he grimaced but finished the juice.

Her chore done, Frankie left Fat Boy and walked to room 9. Hapreet and Dr. Li were deep in conversation with the son of the dead man. Hapreet nodded almost imperceptibly when Frankie caught her eye, motioned to the crash cart outside the cubicle, and mouthed the word "pharmacy." Frankie wheeled the cart to the desk where the night tech sat slouched behind the computer. He looked up from the book he was reading.

"Want me to get that restocked?"

"Yeah, tell the pharmacist we used it on the Code Blue in 9." She scooped up some opened medication vials from the cart. "His family says he was a good husband and father. He had grandchildren who adored him." She juggled the vials in her hand. "None of these drugs could save him."

"Maybe they'll save someone else," the tech said soberly.

Frankie wondered if he could read her mind.

She dipped her hand over the sharps container and disposed of all but one of the vials. That one she stuffed in her pocket.

Minutes later she walked into Fat Boy's cubicle. She closed both the glass doors and the curtain, then withdrew a syringe from her pocket along with the drug vial she'd taken from the crash cart. "I have something here that'll relax you, Mr. Ripley."

He watched her draw up the drug. "I don't want a sedative. I'm sleepy already."

"I'm glad to hear that, " Frankie said, smiling. "I wasn't sure if the dose of isopropyl alcohol was large enough to affect you. After all, you're pretty big. And I've never done this before."

"Iso what?" Fat Boy hoisted his head off the pillow and glanced nervously at Frankie.

"Isopropyl alcohol, commonly known as rubbing alcohol. I added it to the GI cocktail I gave you earlier. I mixed it in your orange juice, too. Sorry I lied about your blood sugar—it was actually in the normal range—but I wanted a good amount of alcohol in your bloodstream."

Fat Boy's eyes widened.

"Alcohol depresses the nervous system and makes you feel sleepy or inebriated. Desperate drunks will settle for iso when they can't afford real booze. Drink enough of it, though, and you can die."

Frankie squirted a drop of medication onto Fat Boy's bare chest.

"But don't worry. I didn't give you a lethal dose, just enough to show up on a drug screen. Since you said you'd been drinking before your arrest—"

"I never said that!"

"Maybe not. But that's what I wrote on your chart. I had to give Dr. Li a reason for your sudden respiratory failure. Alcohol fits the scenario." She waved the syringe under Fat Boy's nose. "But what's really going to do you in is this. This is succinylcholine, a nice little paralytic we use during Code Blues to intubate patients."

"Intubate?" His eyes were riveted on the syringe. "I don't understand."

"Let me explain. When we intubate someone, we put a tube down his throat to help him breathe. First, though, we give him this medication." She held up the vial of succinylcholine. "It paralyzes him so he doesn't fight against the tube. After intubation, we hook the patient up to a machine that forces oxygen into his lungs." She glanced at the medicine. "This was left over from a Code Blue that ended badly tonight."

Fat Boy reared back in terror. "Where's that cop? I want that cop!"

"I sent Baby Face on a coffee break," Frankie said pleasantly. "And everyone else in the department is busy. There's nobody here but you and me."

"You're nuts!" whispered Fat Boy. He was sweating heavily, beads of perspiration dripping down his cheeks. His eyes darted back and forth from the syringe to Frankie's face.

"I've never been more sane," said Frankie. She injected the medication into the IV line. "In a few seconds you'll be paralyzed by this drug. You'll be awake, your mind fully functioning, but you won't be able to breathe. While you struggle to stay alive, I'll tell you why I'm doing this."

Fat Boy began to gasp. He thrashed on the cart, his cuffed hands rattling the siderails as he reached in vain for his throat. Frankie slipped the oxygen sensor off his finger and placed it on her own.

"The monitor alarm will ring if your oxygen level drops too low. People will come running, and we can't have that."

She watched his chest strain against the neck of the gown in a spasmodic attempt to suck in air. Leaning over the cart, she looked deep into his panic-stricken eyes. "They were going to get you off again. I just couldn't let that happen."

Fat Boy's movements weakened as the drug crawled through his system.

"They scared off the nurse's aide who saw what you did. Three times you raped your grandmother. Three times!"

Frankie bent lower and whispered in his ear. "I was here Monday when they brought her to the ER. An old woman crippled by a stroke. Too sick to defend herself."

Fat Boy's eyes glazed over.

"So you see, I had to step in."

She backed away from the cart and glanced at the clock on the wall. Four minutes had passed since she'd injected the succinylcholine. Fat Boy's brain was shutting down from lack of oxygen, but his heartbeat was steady and strong.

"I don't intend for you to die," she said, staring down at the still form of Harold Ripley. "Instead, I want you to exist in a world where you can't speak or move or defend yourself against the ugliness of others. I want you to be just like her, brain damaged but alive. "

Frankie slipped the oxygen sensor back on her patient's finger. She waited for the monitor to alarm. Then she hit the Code Blue button.

END

SAM HILL has published two critically-acclaimed novels and four short stories, as well as three non-fiction books and dozens of articles for the business press. His work is in at least twelve languages (including Polish, which impresses his cleaning lady). When not writing, he is an executive for a large management consulting firm. He and his family live in Lincoln Square. About Chicago, Sam writes, "I have lived in and around Chicago for twenty-five years. Chicago's voice is in my stories, gruffly promising my characters an almost-fair shot at getting out of whatever it is I put them into, and it's a better deal than they'll get anywhere else."

WWW.SAMHILLONLINE.COM

THE SIN-EATER
SAM HILL

"WHAT'S GOING ON IN THERE?" RONNIE asked, angling his head to look around her and down the hall. Mary Ann looked back at him, but said nothing.

"Who's the woman with the priest?" he continued.

"The priest brought her," Mary Ann answered. "I'll go find out."

"Why don't I ask him?" Ronnie said, putting his yellow plastic helmet and small Igloo cooler-slash-lunchpail down in the dark-wooded hall of the bungalow.

Mary Ann put her hand on his arm. She looked up at his face—broad, solid, high cheekbones over red stubble. People think we're all redheaded she thought, but it's really the Krauts like Ronnie that have the red hair. We Irish are all dark until we reach forty and one morning we wake up and our hair is white as snow. Until then, it's dark hair over pinched, bony faces. "Please don't."

"Then tell me," he persisted.

Mary Ann looked away again, gathered herself. "Mrs. Tunney is a sin-eater."

"A what?" Ronnie looked incredulous.

"It's an old tradition. When you die, the priest recites the major events during your life, and at the end of each year he passes a little cracker across the body of the dying person, and her sins go into the cracker. The sin-eater swallows the cracker and the sin, and that way the dying person is sure of going to heaven, because her sin is gone," Mary Ann said, her voice almost a whisper.

"For Christ's sake, Mary Ann, your family has been here since the famine. Where do you get stuff like this?" he said, turning from her and hanging the dusty jacket on one of the hooks behind the door. He dropped onto a stool and began unlacing his boots. She didn't answer, and he continued. "Anyway, your sister's a nun—I thought that means the whole family goes to heaven automatically?"

"Don't be sarcastic, Ronnie, I know you don't believe, but what can it hurt?" Mary Ann answered.

Ronnie looked back at her. "There's more, isn't there?"

Mary Ann shook her head, "I don't know what you mean."

Ronnie's face turned dark. "The sin-eater doesn't do this for free, does she? You paid her." Mary Ann stood silent.

"How much?" he pushed, standing, understanding flooding his face. "Oh Christ, you used the money we were going to use to fix up the baby's room. You spent the money we had saved up on this bullshit. How much?"

"What does it matter?" Mary Ann asked. "We're not fixing up the room. The baby is gone, Ronnie, and I can't have another one."

Ronnie stood, his face red, anger rippling down his jaw. He started to speak but before he could, Mary Ann continued, "You don't care about the money, Ronnie. You blame Grams because she was watching him, but the doctor said it wasn't her fault. It was crib death. You have to let go, honey." She stepped close to him and encircled his body with her thin arms and pulled him tight, sobbing into the rough fabric of his work shirt.

After what seemed a long time, she felt him ease, and heard him ask, "How long does this go on?"

Mary Ann stepped back and looked up. "For hours sometimes. She's ninety, and the priest is eighty-something and grew up with her before they moved to Beverly. He will put in every detail of her life he can remember, and that might be a lot. I know he christened Mom and buried Daddy Gramps. He'll put all that in, to try to cover as much ground as he can so all the sin will come out. Once it begins, it can't stop. They have to finish before she dies."

"How much of it?" Ronnie said. "Did it take all of it? What was there, almost thirteen hundred dollars?"

Mary Ann nodded, her face wet and swollen from the crying. Ronnie shook his head, "I would have eaten crackers all night long for thirteen hundred. That's every penny we have saved up, honey, and the truck is on its last legs."

"Don't blaspheme, Ronnie," Mary Ann said, "The woman is very pious. It takes great courage to be a sin-eater. Not just anyone can do it."

Ronnie walked back to the open door and looked in. The priest glanced up at him and nodded greeting. He nodded back. His grandmother-in-law lay quietly, her face a sweet, wax mask, hair spread on the pillow like a wispy, blue halo, eyes closed, while the fat, white-haired priest beside her spoke quietly. Ronnie heard the priest say "Bridget," and knew he was talking about Bridget Manders, the old woman's childhood friend, who'd fallen off a bridge into the Cal Sag canal and drowned when both girls were sixteen. He knew they were only into the Great Depression. As he watched, the priest lifted a small, white wafer from the plate and spoke. "Rise up sin, into this wafer, and leave this soul clean and new." He handed it across to a small woman Ronnie vaguely recognized from Christmas mass, also elderly, wearing a black sweater over tan stretch polyester pants. As he watched, she placed the cracker in her mouth and grimaced. Why all this for a nice old woman, Ronnie wondered. Did the sin-eater feel a certain professional responsibility to show some effort for thirteen hundred dollars?

If Grams had slipped on the icy bridge instead of Bridget, would Daddy Gramps have married Bridget instead, as the family story said? Would Mary Ann exist? Ronnie shook the thoughts away. He was not an introspective man, and did not like to dwell on things he did not understand. He turned and crossed the hall into his bedroom to shower. In the bedroom, he undressed slowly, sitting on the bed to tug off his socks. Behind him in the corner rested the crib. He knew he needed to move it to the garage, but could not bring himself to do so. Not yet. Three weeks, and the smell of Brian lingered. He closed his eyes and pulled in deep breaths through his nose.

They ate dinner quietly. After Mary Ann went to bed, he watched a college football game, the sound turned down to a whisper. In the background he heard the continued low rumble of voices. At one point he heard a gasp, and a thud. He jumped out of the recliner and rushed into the back bedroom. The sin-eater was sitting on the floor, the priest's arm around her. He looked up at Ronnie, and said, "1953, Ronnie. The year your wife's aunt Moira drowned in her bath. Your Gram's had a hard life, Ronnie, and it's just too much some times. Mrs. Tunney needs a break, I think." He spoke in a thick brogue, even though Ronnie knew he'd been born on East 103rd in the Chicago neighborhood of Pullman, two blocks from the house where Mary Ann's mother had been born and grown up. Ronnie had never noticed the brogue before, never thought about it.

"Mary Ann's gone to bed, Father. Let me get Mrs. Tunney a glass of water," he said. Ronnie wanted to dislike her for participating in this fraud, but he was a kind man, though rough, and could not bring himself to make her unwelcome. She took the water and thanked him, and he smiled a tight smile of acknowledgement.

Ronnie returned to his game and fell asleep in the chair. He woke sometime later, the football game over and a Sportscenter rerun showing. He stood, stiff, and stretched. The bedroom where the old woman lay dying was to have been Brian's. The plan was to use the savings to fix up the attic for Grams. He remembered her displeasure at the proposed move, hating change the way old people do. As he passed the door, he heard the priest mention Errol, the real name of his wife's grandfather. Daddy Gramps had died in his sleep twenty-five years ago, in the room where Ronnie and Mary Ann now slept. Only up to 1981. He looked at his watch.

Until now Ronnie had never realized that the lives of old people are measured by the number of people they outlive, and for Rose Marie, that was many. Children, grandchildren, friends, husband. She'd lost a son of her own to SIDS, just as he'd lost Brian. He watched as the priest handed the wafer across to the sin-eater, saw her put it in her mouth and press it against the roof of her mouth with her tongue. As he watched, Mrs. Tunney gasped and grabbed her stomach, as if in pain. She folded her arms on the bed and dropped her head onto them. Ronnie started to step into the room, but the priest shook his head, and Ronnie did not enter. The old man looked exhausted, huge, fat, brown raccoon rings set into his red face. Ronnie watched the woman's shoulders shake. His wife's grandmother lay unmoving, her face placid, her breath so shallow he could not see the coverlet move. Ronnie looked back at Mrs. Tunney, uneasy.

He slept poorly and arose at five thirty AM, even though the day was Saturday, his usual day for "sleeping in," which to him meant seven AM He dressed quietly, leaving Mary Ann in bed, her face burrowed down into the pillow, and let himself into the hall. Inside the small room, the priest and the two women were still going. He listened as the priest talked about the unfinished work on the Dan Ryan expressway, the scandal surrounding Richie Daley, and the fire at the parochial school. They were ending then. The arson had occurred just a month ago, the very same day Mary Ann had gone into the hospital to deliver Brian. Healthy, happy Brian. He would have gone to that school, had he and the school survived. St. Theresa's, the last school in Chicago to be integrated. Ronnie remembered the stubborn anger of Grams and her friends at the decision to bring "them" into their St. Terry's. And the two black children had been among the seventeen dead.

Mrs. Tunney reached for the wafer and put it in her mouth. Both sin-eater and priest looked exhausted. Mary Ann's grandmother lay unmoving, expressionless. He heard a shriek, and the woman stood, eyes popping from her face. She grabbed her stomach and rocked forward, doubling over in apparent pain. As he watched, she made a fist, reached over her head, and swung as hard as she could, punching herself in her midsection. Ronnie reached to help but she shoved him aside, stumbling down the hallway, flinging the front door open and staggering down the concrete steps, only to collapse on the cracked sidewalk and dry retch into the frosted grass. Behind her, the pale winter sun peaked through the gap between the twin brick bungalows across the street. She wiped her mouth and tried to stand, but dropped back to one knee. Ronnie stepped outside, but Mrs. Tunney held up her hand to stop him. Without looking back at him, she stood, arm still outstretched, and staggered away. He watched her make her way down the street toward the "L," breath steaming in the cold air. She did not look back.

Ronnie turned and stepped into the dark hallway. At the end, Mary Ann stood in a pale green housecoat. He walked in stocking feet to stand beside her. Inside the bedroom the priest sagged back against the wall, eyes closed. A single, child-sized wafer lay on the silver tray. Grams stirred, and one hand fluttered above the coverlet.

"We have to finish," Ronnie heard the priest say. "Just one more wafer." He looked at Ronnie expectantly.

Ronnie stared back at the priest, then turned to see his wife looking at him. "You said you'd do it," she said. "Just one more."

Ronnie looked up at the bed. The old lady's eyes were open now. She smiled wanly. "Just one more," she whispered sweetly, a single finger lifted toward him. The priest pulled out his handkerchief and wiped his sweating brow. He lifted the tray and set it on the side of the bed. Not even a full wafer. A single, white, child-sized fragment on a silver tray.

"No," Ronnie said. Backing away, socked feet slipping on the dark, polished wood, big working hands squeezed into bricks.

END

Author's Note: Thanks to Museum of Jurassic Technology in Los Angeles, where I first learned of the sin-eating tradition.

Ten years in advertising gave **MARCUS SAKEY** the perfect background to write about criminals and killers. *CBS Sunday Morning* called his debut *The Blade Itself* "the first page turner of 2007," and the *New York Times* selected it as an Editor's Pick. To research the novel, Marcus shadowed homicide detectives, toured the morgue, and learned to pick a deadbolt in sixty seconds. He writes, "Chicago is a city of contradictions, a place where tremendous beauty is made possible by the most offensive corruption, and that kind of dynamic tension makes for great stories. Chicago is alive: vibrant, hungry, and filled with energy, by turns wondrous and cruel. For a writer, it's paradise."

WWW.MARCUSSAKEY.COM

NO ONE
MARCUS SAKEY

IT'S LIKE THE TIME SARA AND I SNUCK into the nature sanctuary in Lincoln Park and went at it in the mossy twilight, both of us bare as the day we were born. There was no one around, but there *could* have been, see? Some evening bird watcher might have caught the motion as she threw her head back; might have raised his binoculars; might have framed them on the softness of her naked body.

That's what this is like. Exhibitionism without risk. No one will hear me.

Of course, they say God is always watching, but circumstances being what they are, I'm guessing not. God wouldn't have made her go. God wouldn't have abandoned me in the shitty basement apartment I rent from Crazy Mildred, who once grabbed at me after I carried her forty-pound bag of cat food into the pantry, old-woman fingers fumbling for my jeans, forcing me to hightail it out of there and quick, locking the stairway that leads to my apartment and pretending not to hear her sobbing through the ceiling.

Mildred crying upstairs, me crying downstairs. No, there's altogether too much crying going on for me to think God is watching. I need a different sort of confession booth. So instead of a kneeling pad, I have a ladder-back chair with a broken slat. Instead of a choir, I've got Etta and Billie and Dinah keeping me company, the radio tuned to blues, the only station I get. There's still a screen separating me from my confessor, but this one shows the keystrokes as I type.

Bless me, void, for I have sinned.

I drove Sara away, and my sadness is heavy and thick, like a choking red fog. Sometimes I can almost see it, the tinges of crimson at the edge of my vision, the way they came in the fifth grade when for no reason Brian Smith twisted the arm off my Luke Skywalker figure, leaving a naked plastic socket. Mr. Jones sent me home for a week for bloodying Brian's nose and blackening both eyes, even though it was all his fault.

But there's no red in my vision now. This confession is doing me good. I don't have anyone to tell about the way Sara broke my heart, so I'm telling no one. No@one.com, get it? I'll type it all here, in this window with its hungry cursor. I'm using one of those web pages that lets you send anonymous email, and when I press Submit my confession will disappear, the server trying to deliver it to an address that doesn't exist. I like to think it will keep bouncing back and forth across Chicago, across the world, an endless digital whisper telling how much I loved her.

And I did. Oh, how I did. From the first moment I saw her sitting barefoot on the field where the jocks play Frisbee, watching the sun settle behind dingy DePaul administration buildings. She wore a sundress the color of fresh cream, not like the short-shorts and belly shirt of most of the skanks around here. The light shone golden through her dark hair, and the dress stuck to the sweat in the small of her back. My stomach turned upside down and I thought to myself, oh man. So this is what it feels like.

And I went right on thinking that until a month later, when I finally got lucky and found myself in the cafeteria line behind her. I was dying for something to say, and when I noticed she had an art history textbook, I asked her if she knew what Van Gogh said when his landlady called him to dinner.

No, she said.

And I cupped my hand to my ear and said, What?

She only laughed a little, but it was only a little joke.

She told me her name, Sara Wheaton, and we chatted while a dour server slapped pale macaroni into Styrofoam bowls. When I asked if I could join her for lunch, she smiled like it was silly question, and that's how we got started.

She was the best thing that ever happened to me. Every guy in college—in the city—wanted her, wanted to be with her. But she was mine. It was the only time I'd ever had something so beautiful.

Our first time, she bled a little, but said she didn't mind. Afterwards, I lay beside her, listening to the shattering rumble of the Brown Line. The "L" tracks ran just above my window, and the train was loud as an earthquake, but not nearly as loud as my heart. I lay in the shitty bed in my shitty basement apartment on a shitty block of Wilton and felt better than I ever had before. Like I could do anything. Just by thinking about it, I could have blown the ceiling clean off and let the sun shine in so I would never be alone in the dark again.

Why did you go, Sara? Oh, god.

It must be evening. On the radio, the blues have given way to a news anchor teasing headlines. Another South Side apartment caught fire, another body was found, another alderman lied. I don't know why they call it news.

It's true what they say about confession, though, how it eases the pain. I even feel strong enough to talk about Mark.

May roaches lay eggs in his eyes.

Mark, who lived in a Lincoln Avenue loft full of furniture his parents paid for. Mark, right wing for the soccer team. Bastard. I knew what went on in his head when they met to work on their class project.

Don't be silly, she said. Trust me. It's just homework. He's just a friend.

But I'd seen the way he looked at my girlfriend, the way he laughed at my clothes. He was just another bully, rich with things he hadn't earned. Like Brian from fifth grade. He had everything, but it wasn't enough. It's never enough for people like that. Not until they have what's yours.

May the brakes fail on the SUV his parents leased for him.

I know, I know. This is supposed to be a confession, and confessions aren't about blame. But if you'd seen the way he looked at her …

Truth, though? She wasn't innocent. Those first months our life was perfect, like a fall day when the sky is so blue it burns. But her group meetings started to stretch longer. And last week she wore a cashmere sweater and the corduroy jeans that fit too tight.

It's the end of the semester, she said. We have a lot to finish.

What about the jeans? What about the cashmere?

I thought you liked the way I dress.

I tried to explain how I did like it, but for me, not for Mark, who was just another smarmy little rich kid from Kenilworth, the same as all the other smarmy little rich kids from Kenilworth. A drone, a suckup, buying round after round at McGee's, throwing down money he hadn't had to earn. He didn't deserve to see her looking this way. That was supposed to be for me, for us, and I tried to tell her.

But it didn't come out right.

You want me to quit? You don't trust me, she said, so I should never leave your basement?

Go, I said. I don't care. Go.

She went.

Maybe I should have been more understanding, but I kept picturing golden-haired Mark, the way he threw his arms in the air when he scored, flashed his idiotic white teeth. How he'd have the same greedy look while he unbuttoned her corduroys. I lay in bed with the curtain closed and the radio on, Etta and Billie and Dinah, and when she didn't call the next day, or the next, I told myself it didn't matter. Lots of fish, and all that. Fell asleep and dreamed red fish in red seas.

Yesterday there was a knock on my door. I was expecting no one, so I figured it was Crazy Mildred, and was feeling so lousy I had my mind half made up to let her grope me with her filthy old fingers.

Rain poured from skies swirling like the end of the world. Sara stood at the top of the steps, framed by the tracks and drooping power wires. She wore ratty jeans and a soaked DePaul sweatshirt, and her eyes were circled in black. I've got something to tell you, she said, and crossed her arms over her belly.

And I knew.

The nerve of the bitch. How could she? How could she sleep with Mark, and then come to me crying, dressed like all the other tramps, and think I'd forgive her? She'd tarnished everything. Red haze filled my world.

She started to lie, to say she hadn't been with him, that it was something else, but I couldn't let her talk. I opened my mouth and freed all the words no one can know I keep inside. I can't even remember what I said, but I know it was red poison. It must have been, because she left, crying and begging at first, then her eyes wide and lips silent as she went away.

After Brian tore the arm off my action figure, I threw it away. It was spoiled.

Now I'm alone in the dark basement that she made brighter, listening to the rattle and clank of the washer, typing with dirty fingers. The radio man is still talking. He's jumped from the apartment fire to the next horror, a body found in the bird sanctuary in Lincoln Park. A woman. Unidentified. Pregnant.

Sara's skin was pale and soft, her freckles constellations in the skies of my world.

The red is creeping back into my vision as the announcer keeps talking, leaving behind the girl in the college sweatshirt and torn jeans, staring open-eyed in the rain. It's time for me to do the same. To press Send and lay down to remember Sara the way I first saw her, swept up by the sun, sundress sticking to her pale, perfect skin. My Sara.

Click.

END

"BIG CITY"

RONALD LEVITSKY recently retired from teaching, having spent the last twenty-six years at Sunset Ridge School in Northfield, IL. He is the author of the Nate Rosen mystery series, and his short stories appear in several mystery anthologies. He lives in Lake Forest, IL. He says, "Raymond Chandler wrote that mystery fiction is an art form, because it contains the quality of redemption. Chicago is a powerful metaphor for redemption—from Lake Michigan saving those who fled the Great Fire, to Governor Altgeld pardoning the Haymarket prisoners, to Ernie Banks cheerfully saying, "Let's play two," after yet another dismal season of the Cubs. Redemption is a theme in the following story."

THE BLUE LINE
RONALD LEVITSKY

IF SHE WAS A SHOT OF CHEAP TEQUILA, I was the worm at the bottom of the bottle. I'm not saying that to make you feel sorry for me. It's just if she hadn't treated me that way, I might've pulled the trigger, and the story would've ended all wrong.

After she dumped me, I was in a bad way for a few weeks, staying in my apartment except for my morning walk to the 7-11 and my evening trip to the liquor store. It was getting darker earlier, and colder; other than that, one hour bled into the next. I slept most of the day and watched TV most of the night—anything to keep from thinking how much I wanted the telephone to ring.

When the phone finally did ring, it was some guy with a Spanish accent. I was about to hang up, when he mentioned my uncle.

Then he said, "My name is Hector Tavares. Perhaps you've heard of me."

"No. Should I have?"

After a long pause, he said, "I need a private detective, and your uncle suggested I call you. Are you interested in some work this evening?"

I focused on the clock—3:34 in the afternoon. I ran a hand through my matted hair.

"Mr. Benes, are you there?"

"Yeah ... okay"

"Good. You'll need to arrive at my home by six thirty. I live in Lake Forest." He gave me the address and directions.

"Okay."

"I suggest you wear a dark suit."

"Anything else."

"Bring a gun. Do you have any questions?"

I looked out the window; the sky was already turning gray. "What day is it?"

He paused, then replied, "Thursday. Today is Thursday."

After hanging up, I walked to the bathroom, stripping off my clothes along the way, and stood under the shower until all the hot water was gone. It took two disposable razors to get through my beard, but the worst was that face staring back in the mirror. The hurt of losing her was still in my eyes, and if the razor had been a straight edge, I don't know what I would've done.

I loaded my gun, put on my only suit, and left the apartment at five fifteen. Getting on the Kennedy Expressway going north, even with the reverse commute, I took over an hour to reach Lake Forest. Tavares lived in an estate a few blocks off Lake Michigan. Great oaks and maples displayed leaves painted blood red and gold and orange; the rest pillowed around their trunks or cartwheeled past my car.

A driveway meandered for about an acre before leading to a detached three-car garage. I parked my Cavalier beside a black Mercedes that stretched like a preening cat. I entered the courtyard of a Spanish-style home with white stucco walls, a red tile roof, and about a hundred hanging plants—all dead.

The front door opened slowly, and a plump Latina housekeeper showed me inside. The foyer, painted white with a crystal chandelier and slate floor, led to an enormous living room. Again the walls were white, as were the carpet, table, leather couch and chairs. A ceiling fan set the whiteness vibrating, blurring the corners of the room, and for a moment the man drinking coffee appeared floating in mid-air.

He was about sixty, medium height but built solid. His broad shoulders threatened to rip the seams of his gray Armani suit. Tobacco complexion, coal black hair brushed straight back, and broad cheekbones revealed his Indian ancestry. He stood and shook my hand with the grip of a stone-cutter.

"Mr. Tavares?" I asked.

"Yes, and you are Mr. Benes. The policeman I spoke to, Lieutenant Priban, called you Bobby."

"He's my uncle."

"You look too big to be called Bobby. Sit down, please. Would you like some coffee? I mean real coffee. *Para un hombre.*"

"No thanks."

Tavares returned to the couch, while I took a chair. On the table between us rested a silver tray with a coffee pot and three demitasse cups. He refilled his cup, which looked ridiculous held by his thick fingers.

He said, "Before his recent promotion, your uncle worked security at some of my exhibits here in Chicago. I asked him to recommend a good private detective." He paused to sip his coffee. "Your uncle told me you once killed a man."

"It wasn't my choice. A man was stalking my client and put a knife to her throat."

"But you shot him. May I see your gun?"

Unbuttoning my suit coat, I pulled back the left side to reveal my holstered 9mm Kel-Tec P 11. When Tavares leaned forward to look, my face grew warm, as if he were standing at the next urinal.

"Your gun is rather small."

"It gets the job done."

As Tavares lowered his demitasse, it slipped from his fingers and fell to the floor. Black coffee splattered onto the white carpet. I stared at it until, like a Rorschach test, it turned into a spider. Reaching for the cup, I noticed other faded stains near one of the table legs. I returned the demitasse to the tray.

Grimacing, Tavares flexed his fingers. "I have more the hand of a peasant, to hold a hammer not a coffee cup. Well, I am proud to say that I am a peasant. What do you think?"

I looked around the room. "I think you've done pretty well for whoever you are."

So, you really do not know who I am?"

"Should I?"

"I'm an artist."

I looked at the bare walls.

"No," he said, "I have nothing exhibited in this room, because I need a place to soothe, not stir my imagination. My imagination is my livelihood. This way."

He led me to an adjacent room where the walls were covered with paintings. They depicted village life in Mexico, but there was nothing idealized. Instead, portraits of young mothers with vacant eyes and shoulders hunched like yoked oxen; ragged children kicking a soccer ball unraveling in tendrils of blood; young men squaring off in a knife fight; and old men in top hat and tails, like figures from Day of the Dead. They shared Latin American themes, bold, dark colors and thick brush strokes, and something unsettling born in the artist's febrile imagination.

I stared at the old men. "I've seen this painting at the Art Institute. It was the poster for the Chicago film festival a few years back. One of my buddies has it on a tee shirt."

Tavares laughed. "Yes, you know you're a success in this country when they put your work on a tee shirt. What do you think?"

"There's a lot of hate."

"One paints what one feels. That kind of feeling, hatred mixed with fear, from my youth so long ago. Yet, like malaria, it never quite leaves the body. You have a favorite?"

I walked to the fourth wall. The setting was Chicago and the brush strokes even bolder and more skillful. "I've seen these kids grabbing purses, sticking each other with knives, sticking themselves with needles. Like the dog in this painting, slung low to the ground and snarling. Too hungry, sick, or stupid to do anything but bite."

"And that last one?"

A large canvas in red and black depicted Jesus on the cross. Only, the face was Mexican—dark eyes and thick black hair falling to his shoulders. A gangbanger's gold chain pierced his neck like thorns, drawing blood.

"It's your best," I said, turning just as she walked into the room.

The woman was maybe thirty, tall with a nice figure and ivory skin against her black evening dress. She wore a diamond necklace with matching earrings and bracelet. She'd put up her golden hair, letting a few wisps curl by each ear. She had yellow-green cat eyes, a turned up nose, and a wide mouth that probably dimpled when she smiled.

"My wife," Tavares said. "Amanda, this is Mr. Benes, the private detective I was telling you about."

He might as well have said "cockroach." She looked away for a moment then said, "We should be going."

"Let them wait. After all, I am the guest of honor. Come join us."

I followed them into the living room. She had the smooth stride of a model on a runway and the same cool detachment. Sitting beside her husband, she replied matter-of-factly to his questions regarding typical household concerns—her Jaguar was running uneven, the maid kept missing spots on the silver, and would Venice be too crowded this time of the season. She seemed a real blue blood, born to an estate such as this and the life that went with it.

Taking her hand, Tavares said, "Enough," and they both sat very still. He was letting it work into my blood the way it had in others for the past five hundred years. A dark man, rich and powerful, possessing a beautiful white woman. Daring me to wonder what his rough touch did to someone so cold and proud.

They might have been one of his paintings, the way I stared at them. Or maybe I was the painting they were viewing—a dog hungry for what it couldn't have.

Finally Tavares said, "Mr. Benes, someone has threatened my wife."

"Who?"

"Six months ago, a young man came up to me in the street. Like me, a Mexican. He was a busboy in a restaurant I often go to. His name is Carlos Lopez. He knew who I was and had some sketches to show me. They were good, especially for one with no training, but that was the way I had started. I let him attend a class I was teaching at the Art Institute. I even gave him some money for supplies. Then ..." Tavares shrugged.

"You invited him home."

"I let him work around the house—gardening and cleaning. We would paint together sometimes. I suppose I was flattered by his attention."

"But he began to pay even more attention to your wife. Mrs. Tavares, how did this man bother you?" When she didn't answer, I repeated, "How did—"

"Really, Hector, this is most unpleasant."

"Mr. Benes, this man not only betrayed my trust, he tried to make my wife betray me."

"I take it that didn't happen."

He flexed his hands slowly. "When I saw him touch my wife, I beat him like the dog that he is. I would have killed him, if the housekeeper had not started screaming. You could see his blood all the way down the driveway. That was two weeks ago."

"That didn't take care of the problem?"

"My wife has received telephone calls. He has threatened to kill both of us if Amanda does not run away with him."

"People make threats all the time. It doesn't necessarily mean—"

"A few days ago he came at me, while I was walking from a gallery in River North. Two of his gangbanger friends were with him. They had knives, chains."

"Did they hurt you?"

"They threatened me, but there were too many people around. He shouted that Amanda would be next."

"Why not call the police?"

"If the police get involved, then it will become public knowledge. I cannot allow that. You understand."

She said, "Hector, we must be going."

"Yes. Mr. Benes, I am speaking at a dinner downtown at the Four Seasons Hotel. It's regarding my exhibit opening next month—the biggest of my career. You will come and watch my wife."

"What makes you think he'll try anything there?"

"The newspapers have advertised that both Amanda and I will attend this dinner. I will be occupied with various people, and he may try to get at her. After tonight, we won't have to worry. In a few days we're going to Italy for a long vacation."

"What if he's still around after your vacation?"

Tavares' mouth tightened into a sliver of a smile. "If he bothers us, I'll kill him myself. I know how to protect what's mine."

He drew his wife close. She neither yielded to his body nor struggled against it. Rather, she waited, gazing somewhere past me. A minute later, she slipped from his grip and rose into the white light as beautiful and delicate as an orchid, before walking toward the foyer.

Tavares' eyes widened, as we both hurried to follow her.

I held the door and waited, stiff as one of those lawn jockeys, while Tavares helped his wife into a long, black coat with a gray velvet collar. We took the Mercedes. I slipped into the backseat and inhaled the rich leather mixed with Mrs. Tavares' perfume drifting from the front seat. I closed my eyes, imagining how she looked with her golden hair hanging down, wearing a slip soft as rose petals. And, when holding her close, what he called her besides Amanda. I also thought about the woman who'd dumped me—how sometimes in bed, just running my hand along her back was enough friction to light her anger—bitter words and clawing nails, so different from the coldness of Amanda Tavares. That poem by Frost came to mind, the one about the world ending either by fire or ice. I wondered which would be worse.

When we arrived at the hotel, the cocktail hour was in full swing. A photograph of Tavares the size of a movie poster rested on an easel at the entrance of the dining room. A dozen tables, each set for eight, were arranged opposite a head table. Most of the guests had already arrived, and the servers kept the champagne flowing. In the corner of the room, a black pianist hunkered over the keyboard and played Duke Ellington's "Satin Doll."

If Tavares was worried, he didn't show it. He pressed enough flesh to make a Chicago alderman proud and knew everyone by name. When people moved to his wife, she nodded politely. Crossing and uncrossing her arms, she kept glancing around the room.

A half hour later, the guests began to be seated. Tavares and his wife were a few feet ahead of me, walking toward the head table. I held back a little, listening to the pianist, and saw them pass a green kitchen door, which was just opening.

I hurried forward, as several women screamed. I knocked an old man onto a table and pulled my gun. Several guests flew past like quail, then Tavares, holding his right arm, fell to his knees.

Above him stood a young Mexican. He wore an old, white shirt and faded jeans that hung on his thin frame, and his long hair spilled over his forehead. As he crouched toward Tavares, I aimed my gun.

The Mexican raised his hands, as if to shield himself, then dropped them. An easy target—I could've popped him through the heart blindfolded. My finger nudged the trigger, while his eyes widened in surprise. I looked into those eyes, seeing something familiar. As I lowered my gun, he ran into the kitchen. Only after the door swung closed did I realize that his hands had been empty.

My own hand was shaking, as I returned the gun to my shoulder holster. Tavares sat on a chair; his wife stood beside him. A cloth napkin, spotted with blood, was wrapped around his right hand. His other hand, clenched into a fist, held a knife.

"It's nothing," he said, his face drawn tight.

A thin man with a gray beard approached. "An ambulance is on the way."

"I don't need an ambulance, Doctor."

"You'll probably require a few stitches, but I want to examine the wound at the hospital."

Leaning back, Tavares stared at me a long time. He bit back the pain, and his lips twisted into that same sliver of a smile.

He lifted the knife; it was a switchblade. "That *maricon* tried to kill me. I had to take away his little toy. You saw him?"

I nodded.

"You took out your gun?"

"Yes."

"What happened?" When I didn't reply, his eyes narrowed. "You should have killed him."

"I didn't have to."

"What do you mean?"

"You hired me to protect your wife. He didn't touch her."

Tavares gave me a jack-o'-lantern grin and laughed hard. He was still laughing as the paramedics took him away.

I said to his wife, "I'll drive you to the hospital."

She hesitated, then fished the keys from her purse.

I kept glimpsing her in the rearview mirror. She seemed preoccupied, her face turned toward the window.

It was the longest fifteen-minute drive of my life. I took the silence for the first two miles, before asking, "You don't like me, do you?"

She shrugged.

"I'm just a guy trying to make a living."

She fingered her diamond bracelet. "So are we all."

"I hope your husband's all right."

She continued to stare out the window.

"Were you frightened?"

"Why should I have been frightened? You were there to protect me."

"You blame me for what happened to your husband?"

She shook her head. I was hoping her hair would loosen, but it didn't. Nothing shook loose, not even another word the rest of the way to the hospital. After parking, I put my gun and holster under the seat. There would be cops, and I didn't want to answer any unnecessary questions.

Already stitched and bandaged, Tavares sat in the waiting area. His coat was draped over his shoulders and his right sleeve rolled to his elbow. His eyes were half-closed, and occasionally he winced at the pain.

Two policemen slouched against opposite walls. A third, holding a notebook, sat beside the artist. "You've given me a pretty good description, Mr. Tavares, but to be honest, this could fit half the busboys in Chicago."

"Yes, I suppose we all look alike."

"I didn't mean that, sir. It's just that there's nothing specific to identify him. Were there any distinguishing features or scars?"

Tavares held up his bandaged hand. "You mean, like this?"

"Sorry. And you have no idea why this man attacked you?"

"None at all."

"That knife is a pretty mean weapon. You're lucky he didn't kill you."

"The day somebody like him could kill me, I deserve to die."

After scribbling the answers into his notebook, the cop said, "The way you grabbed the knife—the man's fingerprints were probably smudged or rubbed away."

"I had no choice."

"Of course not."

Amanda Tavares stepped forward. "My husband is obviously tired and in pain. May we go?"

The cop stood. "Mrs. Tavares, did you recognize the man who attacked your—"

"No. Come along, Hector."

I eased Tavares to his feet.

The cop looked me up and down. "Who are you?"

"The house boy, and I'd never seen the man before either."

He was about to say something but, watching Amanda Tavares frown, changed his mind. Stepping aside to let us pass, he said, "I'll let you know if we find out anything."

This time Tavares and his wife sat in back, while I drove. He leaned against the door; she held his left hand on her lap. I didn't hear a word pass between them all the way home, only Tavares' heavy breathing, as if he were asleep.

I pulled into their driveway a little before eleven. It felt like three in the morning. After I retrieved my gun and holster, I helped Tavares from the car. His wife took his arm and handed me a check.

"For your services this evening."

"If you'd like me to hang around the next day or two, until your trip—"

"That won't be necessary."

"I'd like to help."

Tavares said, "There is one thing you can do. Forget everything that happened tonight."

"Why did you lie to the police? They could pick this guy up."

"And have everybody know what a fool I was to bring such a man into my house? Forget us, Mr. Benes. Forget us."

At that time of night, I made it to my North Side apartment in forty minutes. I fell into bed but, tired as I was, took over an hour to fall asleep. Then the dreams snuck up. Dreams of chasing somebody and being chased at the same time. A dog with fangs sharp as switchblades circling me. I woke up at five AM with my clothes soaking wet and couldn't get back to sleep.

I showered, dressed, and sat at the kitchen table, drinking coffee and staring at Tavares' check. If I hadn't been paying so much attention to the pianist, maybe I could've prevented what happened. Or if I'd shot the man, they'd be safe. She'd be safe.

It was a little after six when I took the long drive back to their house.

A roofing crew was working next door. I parked behind their truck and settled back, putting a Joe Williams CD into my portable player. The odds of Tavares' attacker trying again so soon was unlikely, but at least I was doing something. In a few days they'd be out of the country.

It was peaceful on the street. Occasionally a garage door yawned open; a woman would drive her husband to the train station then return a few minutes later. Even the roofers seemed to walk on slippered feet. I drifted in and out of sleep.

About ten thirty I thought of going for coffee, when a red Jaguar, with Amanda Tavares behind the wheel, glided from the driveway. I followed her onto the expressway heading south. About twenty minutes later, she exited east at Dempster and continued into the parking lot of the Skokie Swift.

I stayed in my car. She'd see me walking to the platform. At that time of day, the train didn't come often, and, despite its name, gave a slow ride before reaching Howard Street in

Evanston, the connection for downtown Chicago. My car could get there easily before she did.

A half hour later, I was waiting behind a pillar on the Howard Street platform as the Skokie Swift slid to a stop opposite the Red Line train bound for Chicago. Amanda Tavares wore sunglasses, a brown leather jacket, jeans, and boots. After she entered the third car, I stepped into the second. The "L" jerked forward to begin its journey into the city.

Passengers trickled on as we continued south; mostly students, a few businessmen getting a late start, and women probably going shopping. That's what I thought Amanda Tavares was doing, getting some things for her upcoming trip to Italy—but why hadn't she driven downtown? It would've been much faster.

I followed as she exited at the underground station at Clark and Lake. I expected her to go up the stairs into the Loop, but instead she hurried to another train. Again I walked into the car next to hers. Only as it pulled away did I realize we were on the Blue Line, the one that traveled through the Northwest Side all the way to O'Hare. Was she meeting her husband at the airport? Were they flying out today?

The only other passengers in my car were a young black woman in a hood who dozed over a magazine and a chunky man with the face of an Aztec, who wore a White Sox cap. We left downtown and passed Division, a working class street that had gone to hell, only to be revitalized by those able to pay a half-million dollars and up for renovated condos. Then Six Corners all meeting at Damen Avenue, the new branch of the public library looking out of place amid the pawnshops, cleaners, and taquerias. We passed, on one side, the old Congress Theater; on the other, bungalows and wooden staircases of three- and four-story apartment buildings. The "L" dipped underground and I had to keep an even closer watch, but didn't have to wait long. She exited three stops later at Logan Square. I followed her up the first flight of metal steps, past the bike rack and Duncan Donuts stand, up the second stairway to the street.

I came up at Kedzie where, to my left, it met Logan Boulevard and Milwaukee Avenue around a circular park. I let her walk a half block ahead of me, past the old Norwegian Lutheran Church built of solid red brick with a jade-colored steeple. The Norwegians were long gone, replaced by Mexicans, Puerto Ricans, and Cubans, as well as some white kids—students and artists—who liked the cultural ambiance and the ten minute "L" ride downtown. But what would interest someone like Amanda Tavares? What was she hiding? Had she taken the "L" into the city, not wanting anyone to spot her car? Maybe, after all, she wasn't the blue blood I'd figured her to be.

She turned at the first street, Wrightwood. I kept my distance, as she took those long strides as if she couldn't wait to get to her destination. Her clothing fit in; she could've been any student coming home from one of the city colleges.

The area was similar to a number of Near North neighborhoods with a combination of graystones squatting like Mayan gods, renovated condos protected by black wrought iron fences, and old buildings with their basement windows boarded tight and signs in the first floor windows: "No loitering" and "We call police." An old car drove by, pumping salsa music into the street.

She jaywalked diagonally across the street and continued down an alley that paralleled an old four-story apartment building. I hurried to follow her, passing a few clunkers parked on the street, including an old van with a feathered serpent, symbol of Mexico, painted from one side all around to the other.

Morning had grown warm and sunny, making the neighborhood seem friendlier. Somewhere a mother shouted in Spanish after her children, and the aroma of *arroz y frijoles* drifted from an open window. Yet, watching Amanda Tavares walk up the rickety steps on the side of the building, I felt my stomach tighten. She stopped on the third floor and entered an apartment without knocking.

I walked through an open security gate, hanging off one bolt like an old drunk, and went up the stairs, past an old black man smoking a reefer. The third floor landing had two back doors. The one to my left was open a few inches with the screen latched. There was a strong odor of paint. I looked through the kitchen window.

A thin man with longish black hair bent over the refrigerator, taking out a bottle of wine. He wore a clean shirt and probably his best pair of jeans. I knew who he was, even before seeing his face, and my stomach tightened again. He grabbed two glasses from the cupboard. Then the man who had stabbed Hector Tavares left the kitchen to join Tavares' wife.

Several canvases had been stacked on the table. The top one, gleaming with fresh paint, seemed a companion piece to the "Barrio Jesus" I'd seen in Tavares' home. Using the same bold strokes, red and black colors, it depicted a radiant Virgin Mary, dressed as a peasant woman, holding a human heart. The face of the Holy Mother was Amanda's.

Leaning against the screen door I listened to them speak in giggles and murmurs. Something about "tonight" and "being happy forever." After a few minutes the conversation grew even softer, punctuated by kisses and sighs, and finally I heard Amanda Tavares melt. I'd thought that she had blue blood, but the blue line flowing through her veins was the "L" that had brought her panting to her lover, the same blue line that had made me crawl before the woman who'd dumped me. The same blue line that drives us all, one way or the other, onto the third rail.

I rode the "L" back to Howard Street then stopped at the nearest bar and played toy soldiers with empty glasses most of the afternoon. I imagined Tavares sitting on his white couch, surrounded by an army of soldiers protecting him. Protecting him from what? What had his wife and her lover said? I rubbed my eyes. I needed to eat, and I needed to sleep. I went home and did both.

I woke about eight PM and, after strapping my gun under an old baseball jacket, went downstairs and got into my car. The night was cool and clean, and I kept the window down all the way to Lake Forest. I parked in the same place as I had that morning. The roofing truck had gone, but half a dozen cars were parked behind me, where a party was going on. I put Thelonius Monk on the CD player and got even lonelier listening to "'Round Midnight."

A half hour later, headlights tickled the back of my neck then swept past to illuminate the hedges along Tavares' home. The van painted with the feathered serpent parked just past the driveway. The door opened and Carlos Lopez stepped out, wearing a cheap suit too big for him. After brushing back his hair, he walked up the driveway. I got to the hedges in time to see him continue past the house, along a path leading to the backyard. He scampered happy as a puppy after a rubber ball.

I looked inside the van, which was unlocked, crammed with boxes of clothes, cheap kitchenware, and about two dozen canvases. I flipped through the paintings. All were in Tavares' style, but several were even more powerful. The van smelled of paint, sweat, and dirt—an earthy peasant smell as old as the Aztec gods. The heart held by the Madonna, like the ones ripped out as sacrifices to the gods. Then I knew. I'd seen it all along only half right, because I'd only been looking with my eyes.

I took the same path along the house and saw Lopez standing on the patio. A sliding door opened, and Amanda Tavares stepped halfway from the house. She wore a frilly, white blouse and black slacks, and she gleamed in the moonlight like an ivory statue. She took Lopez's hand and led him inside. I waited a minute and followed. I moved past a long dining room table toward voices speaking on the other side of the wall. Unzipping my jacket, I walked into the living room.

Track lighting illuminated the white room as bright and cold as a laboratory. Lopez stood in the middle, his back to me. Amanda was a few feet away. Wearing a black silk robe, Tavares stood in front of the couch. His bandaged right hand held a gun.

"Mr. Benes, this is a surprise," Tavares said. "Didn't I tell you to forget about us?"

I angled a few steps to my right, to get Lopez out of my line of fire. "You paid me a lot of money to protect your wife."

"I can protect her myself. This man won't hurt her."

"I don't understand," Lopez said with a thick accent. "I never hurt Amanda. I come to take her away. Tell him, *mi amor*."

The woman looked away, crossing and uncrossing her arms, as she had at the dinner party the evening before. Tonight she was waiting for the same thing.

Lopez took a step forward. "Amanda, I come here like you say. Tell him you go away with me tonight. Tell him we are in love." He turned toward Tavares. "For weeks, she go to my place."

"You're not her lover," Tavares said. "You're something I needed for my work, like my brush or paints. You understand, Mr. Benes."

"Yeah. At first—following your wife into the city, I thought like Lopez did—that they were lovers. But then I saw his paintings, and I remembered how your hand trembled holding the cup of espresso. Just like it's trembling now."

Tavares' left hand reached to steady the gun, while Lopez looked around like a lost little boy.

"They used you, kid," I said, "and now they plan to kill you."

"What?"

"Your paintings aren't just as good as your teacher's; they're better. Besides, your teacher can't paint so good anymore. What is it—Parkinson's?"

Tavares smiled. "Strange how an artist like Lopez can be so blind. You, Mr. Benes, have the real artist's eye—to see beneath the surface. Yes, very good."

"You've got that exhibit coming up. I suppose Lopez's paintings will be a nice addition. And with that knife wound, you'll have an excuse to stop painting. A real tragedy that will drive up the price of your work even more. Almost as good as if you were dead. His paintings in the back of the van out there—that's what you really want."

"You should have killed Lopez at the dinner. That's why I hired you."

"Lopez didn't stab you—you cut yourself with your own switch blade. That's why he looked so surprised. Did your wife persuade him to come to the hotel, saying they could reveal their love in a public place, where you wouldn't make trouble?"

Lopez asked, "*Querida*, this is all true?"

When she looked away, I said, "You surprise me, Tavares, selling your wife for a few paintings—not very macho."

His jaw tightened, and the gun shivered in his hand. It passed, and he allowed himself a sliver of a smile. "You don't know what real poverty is like. I've had to make many sacrifices for all this. I am willing to do anything to keep it."

"And your wife?"

"She is my most precious possession. I must admit, it will give me pleasure killing Lopez, knowing he has touched Amanda. But this all could have been avoided, if only you had killed him at the hotel. Why didn't you? "

How could I tell him the truth—that the look in Lopez's eyes, the agony of losing his woman, was the look I'd seen in my own eyes in the bathroom mirror that same morning?

I couldn't, so instead asked, "You're going to kill me too?"

He nodded.

"You can't make me out to be a stalker like Lopez."

"On the contrary, you tried to protect us. Lopez surprised us. He grabbed my gun and shot you, then he and I struggled for the gun and I killed him. Perhaps not the best story, but who will be alive to disprove it?"

"It might work, except for one thing."

"And that is?"

"I have a gun too."

"Mine is in my hand. Oh, I see—a shoot-out just like your Wild West. That would make it more exciting. But then, you didn't shoot Lopez. Perhaps you don't have the stomach for fighting." He glanced at his wife. "What do you think, *Querida*?"

She said nothing, and when Tavares glanced a second time, I pulled my gun.

Tavares fired first, but his hand was trembling, and the bullet hit the wall somewhere above my left shoulder. I shot back. He fell against the couch then slid to the carpet, grabbing his gut just below the rib cage.

I expected Amanda to run to his side or maybe reach for the gun. But she didn't move, just watched the blood flow from the wound, down his shirt and into the white carpet. Even after I'd called an ambulance and the police, she didn't move. Her expression remained serene, like Lopez's painting of her—the Madonna holding her lover's heart.

END

Suspense novelist **BRIAN PINKERTON** is the author of *Abducted*, *Vengeance*, and the forthcoming Hollywood thriller *Rough Cut*. He has lived in the Chicago area for most of his life. He's drawn to the Blues because, "The Blues is a form of expression drawing a direct line from the heart to art. Unlike the contrivances of pop culture machinery, the blues is personal and true, as poignant and layered as life. If Chicago is 'Home of the Blues,' then the city itself must bleed purest of them all."

WWW.BRIANPINKERTON.COM

LOWER WACKER BLUES
BRIAN PINKERTON

I'M RUNNING IN THE CONCRETE CATACOMBS beneath downtown Chicago, a murky netherworld that hides from the light of day.

As I prowl the subterranean streets, I search for movement in the shadows. I look behind steel pillars, through every chain-link fence, around every stairway. My middle-aged muscles and bones sting in protest, more suited to a chair behind a desk than this pursuit. Wearing new wingtips doesn't help. I resist the urge to wipe sweat from my face with my tie. Already I am coated in grime. I am growing dizzy from the fumes of tunnel traffic.

I dodge a hell-bent cab and jump on a patch of cracked sidewalk. All the real activity, the true glory of Chicago's Loop and

Magnificent Mile, flourishes above in the sunshine and open spaces.

This is another world.

I reach the lower level of the Michigan Avenue Bridge. A rush of cars and buses move overhead, throwing echoes off the beams. The Chicago River flows beneath the grates at my feet. On either side, there are hidden nooks in the enormous gears that drive the opening and closing of the drawbridge. I examine them for a man tucked inside. If I find him, I know what to do.

My search takes me to the other side of the river. Here the trail splits into several directions. I choose a path and keep going. A steady rhythm of yellow lights pulse life into the roadway. I keep an eye on the overpass beams above my head, where someone could lay flat and escape detection.

Several storage trailers are parked against the curb, but they appear padlocked. At a loading dock for one of the big hotels, a delivery man eyes me with suspicion. I veer toward one of the smaller, darker side streets. My instincts tell me my prey has chosen the deepest reaches of these tunnels.

My heart pounds with excitement. I stop and lean against a pillar to savor the exhilaration. I know that my best friend must be feeling the same way.

Suddenly the steel pillar at my shoulder transforms into a gnarled oak tree. The bolts give way to bark. A leafy canopy replaces the low concrete ceiling. Sweet-smelling spring wildflowers sprout through pavement cracks like time-lapse photography, dispersing dirt. I hear the soothing sounds of a bubbling creek and a sleepy chorus of frogs.

Before me is a mosaic of lush woodlands, meadows, and hilltops. The sky dances with birds and colorful butterflies and dragonflies.

I am eight years old.

Kevin runs ahead in shorts and a red t-shirt.

I chase him on a carpet of long grass, weaving through a stand of trees: oak, hickory, cherry and walnut.

The game we are playing is Escape. The concept is simple. One of us has escaped from jail. The "escapee" gets a ten-minute head start into the wilderness. Then the "hunter" seeks him out. Essentially hide and seek, but we hate that term—we're eight years old. Not babies.

"Do you wanna play Escape?"

That was the usual start to a Saturday morning or holiday. Or any day during the summer when we needed an excuse to break away from adult authority, spill outdoors, and run through the sprawling acres of forest known as Spring Pines.

I met Kevin in elementary school in a rural community northwest of Chicago. We immediately clicked, two crazy boys with restless energy and easy laughter. We explored nearby Spring Pines and took turns pursuing each other for hours. The game ended only when dusk lowered its curtain. The hunter would hit the escapee with a pinecone or point a stick at him and shout *"bang."* It wasn't about winning or losing; it was simply a finale so we could retreat to our houses.

Sometimes it was hard to get Kevin to give up the game. Kevin's parents were divorcing and he didn't want to go home. He'd hide in the woods, ignoring my calls, risking punishment for missing dinner.

Those were the times when I panicked. The darkness threatened me with bears, rattlesnakes, and other night terrors. The stakes were suddenly much higher and the hunt for Kevin became desperate.

I am feeling that same desperation on Lower Wacker Drive.

A prickly feeling moves across my skin. As I move beneath the city, my surroundings become claustrophobic. The lighting dims and traffic noise grows distant.

There are real dangers in this secret underworld. Innocents have been murdered and left undiscovered for weeks. I recall stories from the local news: a dead woman found in the trunk of an abandoned car; a man's corpse discovered in a black trash bag in a dumpster, nibbled by rats. The bodies didn't draw attention until the stench gave them away.

I'm searching behind a peeled-back section of chain-link fence that surrounds utility equipment. I find a mound of crusted blankets. Someone has been here, maybe recently. I reach in and touch the top blanket—cold.

I turn around. I head back the way I came. I'm almost back on one of the main roads when I spot him. Kevin slips out from behind a concrete lane barrier, lit for a moment by the headlamps of a passing car. I run right at him. He sees me and allows a mischievous smile. The little boy returns. In an instant, he is short and slender, wearing his red t-shirt and shorts. He quickens his pace. But he does not run fast. He morphs again, the childhood glimpse replaced by someone old and fat, a bald spot on the top of his head. His brown business jacket clings to him. His dress shoes make loud, echoing pops as they strike the pavement.

I chase him. I hurdle the barrier. The pace of Escape has picked up, and I feel the blood rush through my veins. I am so focused on Kevin that I do not see the large truck barreling toward me, white and anonymous, heading for a nearby loading dock. A long blast of horn crashes off pillars and walls. I skip and dance, the truck swerves, and I make it to the other side of the roadway, the breeze from the truck's wake rippling my shirt.

And in that instant, I lose him.

Kevin has escaped. I stand on the sidewalk, bent over, hands on my kneecaps, sucking in air. I start to choke on the exhaust that is trapped here with me. From where I stand, the ceiling must be no more than six feet above my head. I am suffocating in this cold steel and gloom.

Even though these cavernous roadways provide a fast alternative through downtown Chicago, nobody wants to be here, and the sporadic traffic, even at rush hour, speaks volumes. These roads are driven by speeding cabbies, delivery vehicles, and sanitation trucks collecting the city's garbage.

It's efficient, it's progress, and it's ugly.

When Kevin and I entered our teens, the inevitability of progress destroyed Spring Pines, too and stripped away our youth.

The neighborhood fell victim to expansion and development. The mighty trees fell, the land was scrubbed, the natural wildlife fled. Bulldozers opened holes for basement foundations. Skeletons of timber took root and sprouted walls and windows. People, cars, and shopping malls moved in. Soon the town looked like every other Chicago suburb.

Kevin and I replaced our wilderness trail with the automated walkway of adult expectations. Following high school, we attended separate colleges but kept in touch, reuniting afterwards to seek business careers in Chicago.

We found apartments a mile apart in Lincoln Park. We thrived on the hip, young nightlife. We drank too much and slept too little. When Kevin found a job with a Fortune 500 company in the heart of downtown, his number-one priority was finding me an opportunity with the same employer. After a few months, a position opened up and before long, we were on the same floor of a handsome Michigan Avenue high-rise overlooking the Chicago skyline, working side-by-side.

We locked into career paths. We married our long-time sweethearts. We established families. We did everything we were expected to do on our life journey.

I began spending the majority of my waking hours in a six by six cubicle. I worked hard to do a good job. I followed the corporate code of conformity. It was important that everyone like me. The paycheck was good, and so was the lure of promotion and added responsibility. It was all pleasant enough, but I began to view my colleagues as emotionally remote, hiding behind a safe, controlled surface. For a while, I considered myself different. Then I realized I had become one of them. I came home every night with a stress headache. I hugged my young son on his way to bed. I delivered a kiss to my wife's turned cheek. Sometimes we chatted about our days, trading streams of bland, egocentric dialogue that neither of us listened to.

My life was in progress and I had hopped along for the ride. During the day, my routines kept me distracted, but at night, hollowness ached in my chest and my mind wandered restlessly.

Advancing deeper into Lower Wacker, I encounter a community of lost souls, Chicago's homeless. They live apart from sun, moon, rain or shine without addresses or jobs, and hold few possessions. I see evidence of these mole-like inhabitants. Walking down the roadway, I catch glimpses of moving shadows on either side, scurrying from detection like creatures along a river bank.

I want to call out and ask if anyone has seen Kevin. But the shapes slip out of view, disappearing deeper into anonymity.

One man does not run from me. I am frightened, but I find the courage to head directly at him. He lives against the wall in a suite of connecting cardboard boxes. He wears layers of mismatched clothes. He tells me about his makeshift home. He boasts of a living room, bedroom, and eating area. He calls himself Mr. Z.

Mr. Z's face is covered with big, black spots. When he moves closer to the light, I see that the spots are in fact holes in his flesh, holes gouged in his cheeks, forehead, chin, and neck. Some are crusted with scabs. A portion of his left ear is gone, lopped off in a clean, diagonal cut.

I see his arms and ankles. Small chunks of skin are missing. I push back my revulsion. I focus on my quest. I ask about Kevin. Mr. Z tells me that he hasn't seen anyone matching Kevin's description. As he speaks, he tugs at his forearm with long, dirty fingernails. A small pocket knife rests on a fleece blanket nearby. The edge of the blade is stained with blood.

He's doing this to himself.

His eyes lock onto mine. He knows I am watching his actions. His fingernails retreat, pulling loose from pierced skin.

"I don't mean to make you uncomfortable," he says. "But this is something I must do."

He delivers a rambling soliloquy about the evils of above-ground technology: police security cameras on street posts, I-PASS scanners monitoring vehicle movement, satellite surveillance broadcasts on the Internet. He talks about his past, boasting about his glory days. He was once a millionaire with a Lake Forest mansion and a glamorous wife. Until the day his world crumbled.

"They found me," he says.

"Who?" I ask. It will become a recurring question. Mr. Z never answers. Instead he tells me that a small bugging device has been inserted somewhere in his body. It monitors his every move. It sends him unwanted messages. He obsesses over its hiding place. "I don't know where it is," he says. "But every day I reduce the number of possibilities. I must extract it before I can be free."

As he tells me this, he resumes poking his forearm. His fingernails display an uncommon sharpness.

Nearby, a truck parks for a delivery. The glow of its hazard lights splash us in a devilish red. Mr. Z burns a stare into me. "Perhaps this bug will drive me mad. Perhaps it already has."

I tell him I must go.

"They know where I am, what I'm doing, what I'm thinking," he says. I walk away and he continues talking. His words fade. I hear a final anguished cry: "I will rip this intruder from my flesh."

I go deeper, sloping downward, into the jaws of near-total darkness. There is a little-known third level to Lower Wacker, known to the natives as "Lower Lower Wacker." As I advance, I can't get my mind off Mr. Z.

My foot kicks a cell phone across the pavement.

A few feet ahead, I see a BlackBerry.

I follow a series of dropped items. This must be part of Kevin's liberation from the world above. His trail taunts me, like the candy wrappers he used to scatter in Spring Pines.

I find a key chain with half a dozen keys. Beyond the key chain, I spot a Rolodex. Then Kevin's corporate ID.

I pick it up and position it toward the light. I stare at the photo. Kevin is smiling. This must be many years ago. He has more hair, less bloat. His eyes show signs of life. He looks relaxed.

Kevin's wallet is a few feet away, tossed to one side. I retrieve it. The wallet contains eighty-five dollars, four credit cards and various forms of identification. I drop it back to the pavement, drawn to the next item on the trail.

Kevin's wedding ring.

Kevin and I discovered girls at the same time, the onset of adolescence breeding an invasion of hormones. Our earliest relationships followed parallel tracks, swerving at high speeds from crude lust to melancholy crushes. We fell in love for the first time just weeks apart. His girlfriend was a lovely, willowy sophomore named Jenny with a gentle laugh. My girlfriend, Stephanie, was a boisterous, energetic junior who loved to party.

In the years before Spring Pines' destruction, Kevin and I would double date in the forest with blankets and beer. Kevin actually lost his virginity somewhere in those woods. I remember playing my own variation of Escape with Stephanie, catching her under the stars, kissing her against a large oak, feeding off her energy. Sometimes I reflect on those days when I think about the tired, predictable, middle-aged couple we have become. Stephanie's party-girl persona didn't translate well into adulthood. It turned into something sad and destructive.

Even though Kevin and I worked at the same company, lived in the same neighborhood, our paths intersected less and less. Relentless corporate downsizing had stuffed our jobs with extra accountabilities. Any increases in pay were not in proportion to the added hours.

So one afternoon at work, a few weeks ago, the two of us booked a half hour in a conference room. It was the only way we could reserve time in our schedules to catch up on one another's lives. We knew that our half-hour visit would delay our departure at the end of the day by an equal number of minutes. But it provided a much-needed respite from the stifling existence inside our cubicles.

Conference Room B6 held a long table, eight evenly spaced chairs, a white board, and a metal wastepaper basket lined with a clear plastic bag. I paced the floor as I vented about Stephanie's drinking, the debt on the credit cards, the problems my young son was experiencing in school. I told Kevin I felt as though I had lost control of my life. All I could do was cling to the monotony of my job.

Kevin was silent for a while. Then he told me that Jenny had admitted to having an affair. After she had begged for forgiveness, he gave her another chance. She cheated on him again.

Two nights earlier, he had moved out of his house. He was now living in a hotel.

Kevin said he had become so distracted that his job was in jeopardy. He couldn't focus, and his projects were riddled with errors. As his performance deteriorated, he was passed up for a crucial promotion. His new boss was years younger and a lifer, effectively blocking and assuming Kevin's career path.

All I could say was how sorry I was. I asked him if there was anything I could do.

He looked at the carpet. "To fix my career? No. To fix my family? No." After a moment's silence, he said, "I miss who I used to be. I miss looking forward to things and experiencing the rush of life."

Still looking at the ground, he unexpectedly grinned. He reminisced about the game of Escape we had played as kids. He looked up. "Remember how exciting that was?"

"We were eight years old."

His eyes searched the room and landed on a window overlooking Michigan Avenue. "I've got this crazy idea," he said.

As he outlined his plan, he became more animated than I had seen in years. He wanted to revisit our childhood game of Escape. We would play by the same old rules, but stage it in the steel and concrete forest of Lower Wacker Drive. We would start on Lower Michigan Avenue and work our way into the expanding maze of underground tunnels and secret hideaways.

"You can't be serious," I told him.

"I'll bet you can't catch me," he said.

"You're crazy."

"Get crazy with me."

"We're both out of shape. We wouldn't make it past the Billy Goat."

"Just give me a fifteen minute head start."

I shook my head. I looked at my watch. Our conversation had to end. "I have to get to my next meeting ... a real meeting." I started to turn away.

"You've got to do this." He grabbed my arm, hard. I pulled away, intending to leave, but his eyes held tears.

I had never seen him cry in all of our years of friendship. Not when he fell out of a tree and broke his arm in second grade. Not when his sister died of cancer the summer after college graduation. That's why I gave in. I was his best friend.

He perked up, and his voice brimmed with excitement. He planned a date and time. He introduced some new twists to the old rules, claiming he wanted to update the game and bring it into the modern age.

I have to admit the notion was compelling. Could we create a time machine? Revisit the spirit of our youth? I wanted to know as much as he.

In Hollywood movies, flashbacks are black and white, while the present blossoms in Technicolor. But in the real world, the opposite is true. Spring Pines gave us more texture and colors than we could ever experience again. It gave us something bigger than our own lives to get lost in. We believed the forest held no boundaries and if we ran in a straight line, the forest would go on forever.

But every day at Spring Pines came with a night. Every adventure had to end. Every escapee must be caught.

I have yet to find him. The skies are growing dark. As I walk through the forest, an aggressive wind whistles through the treetops. It's getting harder to see. The game needs to end, but Kevin is elusive. We must return. Our parents are waiting.

I'm frightened by a strange rustling in the leaves. Panic and dread settle deep in my gut. I want to scream Kevin's name.

Suddenly, I see Kevin. I feel a surge of adrenaline. I catch a brief glimpse of his shirt. He is hiding behind a large oak.

I run toward him in the twilight. I am running as fast as I can, pumping hard, shoving branches, snapping twigs. Birds flutter out of hiding and soar skyward.

As I rush toward the tree, it becomes a steel pillar, a single object against the darkness. Kevin's brown business jacket sticks out from behind it—just enough to give him away. He picked the best hiding place he could find, but it wasn't good enough. Mr. Z was right. No one slips off the radar. If we stray too far, there is always someone to yank us back.

I have captured my prey.

"*Bang!*" I shout with the enthusiasm of a child. I leap at him, jamming my finger into his chest.

But the face staring back at me is much older, haggard and dirty, with gray stubble and wide, bloodshot eyes. It is not Kevin. It is one of the homeless men of Lower Wacker. He wears Kevin's suit jacket, pants, and shoes.

Cowering, his arm shielding him, he examines me. His body shakes. To him, I must appear crazed.

I don't understand what's going on, but then, very quickly, laughter erupts behind me. I hear approaching footsteps. I turn around. Kevin emerges from the shadows wearing the bum's tattered clothing and wool hat. It is a clever switch. I never would have recognized him

"Looks like *I* caught *you*," he says, proud. The hunter becomes the hunted.

Then I see an object in his grasp—a small gun.

I tell myself the weapon can't be real. Kevin tells me that it is.

The bum wearing Kevin's clothes scampers away, leaving just the two of us alone.

"The game is over," he says.

He points the gun at my chest.

"This isn't funny," I tell him.

"You captured me. I captured you. Now I will set us free."

"What does that mean?"

"You know."

I think about the disappointments we have shared. The futility and despair. But not this. For the first time in years, I think about the things I have to live for.

"Don't do this," I plead.

"It has to be," he says. "We'll leave together. Before we lose the high."

"Drop the gun, Kevin."

"I can't."

I sense his arm locking into position. I charge and slam into his body, grabbing his wrist.

The two of us struggle. A shot lights up the dark, sending echoes crashing beneath the city in a dozen directions.

Kevin steps away. He sinks to his knees, then rolls over on his side.

I stand over him. He brings a hand to his breast. His hand cups a flow of blood. It spills between his fingers.

"Thank you," he says. I realize he only has a few minutes left. The blood drains out and pools on the pavement.

I despise his gratitude. "I didn't want to play this fucking game," I remind him, as he turns pale. "I didn't want to do this."

"You win after all."

"Why did you have to do this?"

He says, "I was already gone."

Those are his last words. The thin smile tells me he has returned to the wilderness.

I go there with him one last time.

The blackness dissolves to blue sky. The steel pillars are once more majestic trees. The pavement is alive with plant life and color. Sweet smells replace the heavy hang of car exhaust.

Kevin relaxes on a pillow of prairie grass, losing the lines on his face, growing youthful again, bringing back the little boy underneath.

I step through the forest in my wingtips, business shirt, charcoal slacks, and tie. I'm trying to find the trail back. Above me, birds float between tree limbs. Small creatures scurry in the brush.

I find the river. Standing at the water's edge, I hurl the pistol as far as I can. It splashes into the river, creating a circle of ripples, and sinks out of view.

I move across the woods, pushing away branches, until I find what I am looking for.

A metal staircase emerges from tangled roots reaching to the sky. I start to climb. I say a final farewell to Spring Pines.

At the top of the staircase, I am met by a rush of reality. The Windy City lives up to its name with a blast of air that wants to pick me up like a kite. Michigan Avenue hums with streams of vehicles. High-rises loom over me, seeming to narrow to a point as they stretch toward the sky. The sidewalks are packed with people, their faces filled with purpose and destination.

I straighten my tie and button my shirt cuffs. I scrub a scuff mark on my shoe. I walk across the sidewalk to my office building. I return to my job. My lunch break is over.

On the 32nd floor, on the way to my cubicle, I pass Kevin's desk. A red light signals that he has voicemail. I hear a "ding" on his PC announcing the arrival of another email. Somebody has dropped a thick binder on his chair with a yellow sticky that carries an executive's request.

Kevin's desktop is covered with a forest's worth of paper. Off to one side, I see a picture frame that has been turned over.

I lift it up. It is a photograph of Kevin and Jenny in happier times. I put it back.

When I reach my cubicle, one of my colleagues finds me. He tells me about a deadline, an upcoming conference call, and a rash of new tasks. He tops it off with a sigh. "We're just going to have to work late tonight."

I sit down. I shove some papers aside. I pick up the telephone receiver. I dial home.

After three rings, a little boy answers.

It's my son.

"What are you doing home?" I ask.

"I have a cold."

"Can't you go to school with a cold?"

"I didn't want to."

"Okay." An honest answer, to be sure. "Where's your mother?"

"She's lying down."

"Oh. Okay." I don't know what to say.

"Dad," says my son.

"Yeah?"

"I made a fort."

"Yeah?"

"It is so cool. I really want you to see it. I had this box that Mom gave me, then I got some of the cushions from the couch, and I used that old blanket, remember the blue and green one? I moved all my superheroes inside. And the cars you gave me. Do you want to see my fort?"

I think about it. "Yes."

I hear Stephanie in the background. She wants to know who's on the phone. "It's Dad," my son says.

"Oh," she says.

When she takes the phone, she asks what's up.

I only have one thing to tell her. "I'm coming home."

END

BARBARA D'AMATO has won the Anthony twice, the Agatha twice, the first Mary Higgins Clark Award, the Carl Sandburg Award for Fiction, the Macavity, the Lovie several times, and other awards. She is a former president of Mystery Writers of America and Sisters in Crime International. D'Amato lives in Chicago and two children and two grandchildren have her. She says, "I love Chicago. It's got everything—every ethnic neighborhood known to humankind, every ethnic restaurant. The Sears Tower, Lower Wacker, which are the highest and the lowest; it has rich and poor; it's a real place."

WWW.BARBARADAMATO.COM

THE LOWER WACKER HILTON
BARBARA D'AMATO

"SO, EIGHT FIFTEEN AM WE GO SCREAMIN' in there," Officer Susannah Maria Figueroa said, "like it's a burglary in progress, and here's this guy—"

"Five-foot-zero," Norm Bennis said, "with four hairs on his head, all four of 'em combed across the top."

"Know the type," said Stanley Mileski, leaning back against his locker.

Figueroa pulled her walkie-talkie off the Velcro patch on her jacket and stuck it back on in a more comfortable position. "So it's eight thirty, give or take, and he'd just got to the office, looked in the back room where the safe was, now he's hoppin' up and down on these little feet and yelping, like, saying, 'It's gone! It's gone!' Pointin' through the door. Well, we go in and take a look and sure enough, the safe's gone. No doubt about it."

Norm Bennis said, "Big pale patch on the wall, clean patch on the floor."

"So he's jiggling and yelping and stuff, and he says, 'This safe's supposed to be burglar-proof, can't be jimmied, can't be opened, can't be blasted, made right here in Chicago, they promised me it can't be opened, and now look!' and he puts these little tiny hands up to his face and he starts to cry."

Stanley "Lead Balls" Mileski said, "Jeez, I hate it when citizens do that."

Kim Duk O'Hara, their rookie, said, "Me too."

"So Norm here," Figueroa cocked her head toward her partner Bennis, who was a black man of medium height and very wide shoulders, now lounging back against the water fountain, "Norm says where in Chicago'd you buy it and the guy tells us. Norm says to the foot officer wait here and we go tearin' over to the safe company. Go in. There's the manager just unlockin' his office. Guy looks like Dwight Eisenhower, manages the Presidential Safe and Security Company."

Mileski said, "I ask you."

O'Hara said, "Who's Dwight Eisenhower?"

Bennis said, "He confirms. Safe can't be blasted, can't be opened without the combination, door's flush so you can't pry it. Set o' numbers on a horizontal dial, you have to slide 'em to the right combination. Can't hear any tumblers fall. Nothin'."

"So Norm says, here it's nine AM, you just gettin' in? Manager says yeah. Bennis says, 'Your company name on the safe?' Manager says yeah. Bennis says, 'Can't be opened? I got an idea.'"

439 \ BARBARA D'AMATO

"Years of experience," Norm said, who was thirty-six to Figueroa's twenty-five.

"Phone rings. Bennis says 'May I?' and picks it up before Eisenhower even had a chance.

"'Why, yes, sir,' Bennis is saying, nice as a cemetery plot salesman. 'We can help you with that. We'll come right on over.' Hangs up, says 'C'mon.'

"We slide on over to North Sedgwick, up the stairs, apartment three-F, ring the bell, door opens, Bennis yells, 'Surprise!' We leap in, Bennis to the left, me to the right, I mean procedure was seriously followed here. And there's the safe and there's the perps."

"You coulda tied a ribbon on 'em," Bennis said.

"And there's the most humongous collection of crowbars and files and hammers and broken screwdrivers and crap you ever saw in your life."

Mileski was all bent over, laughing.

"Turned out," Figueroa said, "brother in law o' one o' the perps just won the lottery. Little lotto or some such. Won twelve thou. Here it is just before Christmas. Our perp was jealous. Wanted to do just as good for his family."

Norm Bennis stood upright, drew down his cheeks and eyelids and intoned, "Ah, yes. Jealousy is a dismal thing."

"Six fifty-nine and forty-seven seconds," Mileski said, looking at his watch. They all piled through the door into the rollcall room and sat down. As the digital clock on the wall changed to 7:00::00 he said, "Ding!"

Sergeant Touhy's face showed expression number four: Extreme Patience with the Behavior of Children.

"Settle down, troops, let's read some crimes."

The rollcall room at Chicago's First District station had its Christmas decorations up. Two loops of tinsel garlands over the door and a plastic wreath near the blackboard. The tinsel had shed as if it had mange and the bow on the wreath was sagging like a weeping willow.

"Figueroa," Bennis whispered, "this needs a woman's touch."

"Screw it, Bennis."

"Somebody to iron that bow, like."

Sergeant Touhy had a raft of pictures of shoplifters. "The stores are crowded. But some of these jerks are after big-ticket items. They're your diamond, expensive-watch gentlemen. You get a call and find the store detective got one o' these babies, hold him."

"There's gotta be a million shoplifters in Chicago, Sarge," Mileski said.

"Hey, these got a history. Career shoplifters."

"But—"

"They're easy to prosecute, Mileski."

"But—"

"Mileski, you see somebody picking up a Honda under his arm and taking it home, be my guest."

"But—"

"Mileski, these are the ones if we don't get 'em, we get criticized, get my drift?" Touhy's voice was taking on a dangerous edge. "You want to bail out Lake Michigan with a spoon, do it on your own time, okay?"

Mileski shut up.

"About yesterday, Bennis and Figueroa?"

"Yes, boss," they said in chorus.

"You were outta your district."

"Two blocks, Sarge," Bennis said.

"Districts is districts, Bennis. Plus you're supposed to leave that crap to the detectives. What's the area commander gonna think when he hears about this stunt of yours with the safe?"

"That they saved some work?"

"Bennis! You're on the edge of a—"

"Gee, Sarge," Figueroa said. "Tell the commander we were in hot pursuit."

"Shit!" Touhy slammed down the notebook. "Okay, you clowns. Hit the bricks and clear."

Figueroa and Bennis were almost to the door when Touhy yelled, "And don't do it again!"

Susannah Maria Figueroa was not in the best frame of mind today. She didn't really like working second watch. Third watch, three to eleven PM was better. Today she was missing her daughter Elena's first-grade holiday play. Elena was going to be half of a reindeer.

Suze Figueroa said, "I'll drive," and climbed into the car with Bennis. After a minute or two the seriously macho mars lights and all the seriously macho dash stuff had her feeling better. Like they always did.

The radio kicked in.

The dispatcher said, "One thirty-one."

"Thirty-one." It was Mileski's voice.

"See the woman at Chestnut and Michigan regarding found property."

"Michigan and Chestnut. Ten-four, squad."

"Thanks."

"Or was that Chestnut and Michigan?" Mileski said.

"Try Chestnut and Michigan and if she's not there try Michigan and Chestnut," the dispatcher said, laughing.

"'Four."

"Someday he's going to go too far at the wrong moment," Bennis said. "With the wrong person."

The radio said, "One twenty-seven."

"Twenty-seven."

"Check the alley behind Clark Street in the four-hundred block. Supposed to be a nine-year-old kid driving a blue Oldsmobile. Citizen called it in."

"Ten-four."

The radio went on with its usual chatter. Bennis and Figueroa cruised their beat, admiring the Christmas lights.

"Cars going to the strongarm robbery at Eight-six-oh North Lake Shore take a disregard."

Silence for a few seconds.

"One twenty-two?"

"Twenty-two."

"Take an ag batt at Seven-one-seven North Rush. One twenty-three?"

"Twenty-three."

"Your VIN is coming back clear."

"Thanks, squad."

The radio said, "One thirty-three."

Bennis picked up and said, "Thirty-three."

"Complaint from a citizen, approximately Two-oh-oh South Wacker. Citizen says somebody's moanin' down in the sewer there."

"Name o' the citizen, squad?"

"Concerned's the name. Concerned Citizen. Not likely to be around when you get there."

"Ten-four, squad."

With the mike key closed, Bennis said, "Shit. Sewers."

Bennis and Figueroa rolled down Wacker, but they didn't see anything. There wasn't any citizen standing around wringing his hands in the two-hundred block. Since Figueroa was behind the wheel, Bennis got out on the sidewalk and stood listening. Figueroa saw him shiver a little.

"Jeez, that was eerie," he said, getting back in the car.

"What?"

"There's a kind of howlin' comin' outta that grate in the sidewalk."

"See anything?"

"Figueroa, my man, wouldn't I let you know if I did? Hang a left and let's get into Lower Wacker."

Two hundred years ago, the place where the center of Chicago now stands was a swamp. Some people think not much has changed.

When Chicago was a young frontier town, the swampy areas were mostly left as they were, filled with water and mud and garbage, and as the town grew, filled with the poor, living in tents and shacks. After the Great Chicago Fire, things were different.

There was big money in Chicago—lumber money, meat packing money, money from making harvesters and combines, money from the burgeoning railhead. Big money went into improving the city. The downtown streets were raised above the swamp or flood level. Whole areas of the Loop were built on iron stilts, the pavements were raised, and gradually the sidewalks were filled in and the vacant land stuffed with buildings until you could walk from one end of downtown to another and not realize it was underlain by swamp.

The only remnant of all this raising of the city was a series of secondary streets below the level where the sun shone. Some, like Lower Wacker, which runs under Wacker Drive along the Chicago River, are regularly used and are favorites of taxi drivers and city cognoscenti for getting places in a hurry.

Others are used primarily by loading trucks and delivery vans, picking up and delivering to the sub-basement levels of glitzy hotels and posh restaurants. Still others carry heat conduits, sewer mains, or parts of the underground transportation system.

Occasionally, one of the daylight-level streets will collapse without warning, leaving a hole at street level, a few cars in the muck at the bottom, pedestrians standing around on top gaping, and the rats underneath scurrying away. The last time this happened a passerby took one look at the hole, which was fifteen feet deep and forty across, and threw himself into it, hoping to collect big damages from the city. Bystanders saw him do it, however, and the ploy failed.

But many of the tunnels and leftovers under the city are unexplored and forgotten. There are homeless living there, and the Mud People. Down in these tunnels it is always dark. They are perfect places for people or deals that don't want to see the light of day.

Figueroa and Bennis slid into the downgrade and pulled up at a stop sign. "That way," Bennis said.

Dimly lit, Lower Wacker stretched away in both directions. They couldn't see any great distance because of the forest of support beams. Vertical iron beams ran down the pavement between the traffic lanes; cement pylons with iron cores held up the fifty-floor hotels that loomed unseen above them. Produce trucks roared out of the gloom from side alleys.

"Go about thirty yards," Bennis said.

Thirty yards in was a side alley. "Let's try this," he said.

"Yeah, it looks like real swell fun," Figueroa said.

The side alley was actually a tunnel, lit by very dim bulbs at hundred-yard distances. Most of it was sunk in gloom. Ahead the pavement was too narrow for the squad car.

Bennis started walking. Figueroa stayed ten seconds more to lock up the car. Leave one unlocked, come back and it's gone. Plus, God forbid you should leave the door open. Get rats in the car.

Figueroa caught up with Bennis and together they picked their way slowly along the tunnel, listening. The tunnel walls were concrete, striped vertically with a hundred years of ooze from the streets above. In some places stalactites of dried road salts and minerals and dirt depended from the pitted ceiling. Puddles of dank ooze lay in the low spots.

They turned down the sound on their radios. They had gone about forty or fifty feet when they heard a howl. For an instant, it sounded animal. Then it broke apart into sobs.

Figueroa and Bennis grimaced at each other, aware that they both had just resisted an urge to hold hands.

There was a still smaller side tunnel nearby. Inexplicably, two "L" tracks ran into this side tunnel on crossties and then ended, dead, having run twenty feet from nowhere to nowhere.

"Kelite?" Figueroa said, very softly.

But Bennis, thinking that a flashlight beam would only give warning that they were coming, shook his head.

The moaning increased.

In the cavern ahead was a dim glow, flickering yellowish on one side and bluish on the other. It outlined a group of figures so mingled in the dimness that Figueroa couldn't guess whether there were two or six. Over the figures loomed what looked like an ancient oak tree. The scene, Figueroa thought, was Druidic. She shivered.

As she and Bennis drew closer, the light seemed brighter. It came from two sources: a squat candle in an aluminum pie tin on the cement floor and indirect light on a part of the wall farther along that looked like it slanted in from an air shaft. The ancient tree became a heat duct that split into three arms near the top of the tunnel.

There was silence now ahead. The people had seen them. Bennis and Figueroa moved closer.

"Jeez," Figueroa whispered. "The Corrugated Cardboard school of interior decoration."

Between the heat duct, which was nearest them, and the airshaft, which was farthest away, were four areas against the wall. Figueroa thought of them as areas, because rooms was too strong a word and beds wasn't quite right, either. They were personal spaces, most separated by corrugated cardboard. The one nearest the heat duct was made from the top of a refrigerator or stove carton, laid on its side. Into this its owner had pushed a cracked piece of foam rubber pad, long enough to make a bed. The carton would enclose the upper half of a sleeper, for privacy. The space next to this was made of a big carton cut lengthwise. This formed a coffin-like bed and inside it were several layers of corrugated board, raising the bottom ten inches or so off the floor, away from the cold and damp. The other two, which were farther away, were also made of portions of corrugated board padded with many layers of newspaper.

In and around all of them were ripped scarves, dirty jackets, magazines, pieces of blankets, shoes, a pink bedsheet, Band-aid cans, soup cans, toilet paper, potato chip bags, duct tape, plastic bags, a saucepan, three or four lopsided pillows, a small pile of maybe half a dozen potatoes, several wine bottles, and a plastic-wrapped package of carrots.

On the pavement against the far wall was a tea kettle, a piece of bread, a small metal trash can, a circle of bricks with a lot of ashes and black coals in the middle, a can of charcoal lighter fluid, a can of Sterno, and a badly dented skillet.

Figueroa took all this in at a glance, at the same time keeping an eye on the human component of the scene.

Two men stood holding a third, who had been crying.

Figueroa said, "What seems to be the trouble here?"

They all stared at the two cops. Figueroa had the impression that a silent message of caution had gone out between them.

The smallest man, whose head jiggled on his neck said, "He's dead."

"Who's dead?" Bennis said.

"Chas. Chas. He's dead. He's dead." He was pointing, his finger trembling, toward the bed nearest the airshaft. It was so tumbled with clothing that they had not seen the body. "Dead,

dead," he said, nodding over and over. The other men shifted their feet and waited.

"Stay here," Bennis said to the three men.

The job of the first uniforms on a scene is to check it out, see if a crime has been committed or if somebody is hurt. If somebody's hurt, call the EMTs. If there's a dead body, close down the scene and call the techs and the detectives.

Bennis went to the body and knelt down. Figueroa kept a watch on the other men.

"Dead?" she asked Bennis.

"Dead."

"Paramedics?"

"He's cooling off already. Dead a coupla hours, maybe."

When Bennis came back Figueroa went and looked at the body. There was no obvious sign of violence. No blood. No knife sticking out. Just a gaping mouth, unshaven chin, and staring, clouded eyes.

Figueroa said to the three men, "Can I see your driver's licenses?"

The man who had been crying giggled briefly. "Don't have any."

"Why not?"

"Got rolled. Inna shelter."

"I have one," the oldest of the three said. Bennis turned to the others and said, "Names?"

Willie Sims was a smallish black man of indeterminate age with white whisker stubble and a coating of dust that made him look gray. Samo Marks was a smaller white man with dark whisker stubble and a layer of dirt that made him look gray.

His head twitched, and when Bennis made a note of his name in his notebook he also made the comment: "Addled."

The third man was slightly cleaner. Louis Papadopolous, who had a driver's license, had washed sometime in the last few days.

Samo hadn't washed recently, but the tears had flowed so freely down his cheeks that most of the lower part of his face was clean, if streaky. Even around his eyebrows, across which he had apparently swiped his sleeve, there was a clean patch.

"Occupation?" Bennis asked, in a tone of voice that suggested he was required to ask it, but thought it was stupid in this case.

Willie Sims shrugged, "I owned a restaurant. Had a fire. No insurance."

Samo Marks said, "Nothin', nothin' a-tall." He waved his head back and forth. "Useta set pins," he said. "Bowling alley."

Papadopolous nodded at Samo as if he were doing very well. "They automated," Papadopolous said.

"And what about you, sir?" Figueroa asked, using her be-nice-to-the-public voice.

Papadopolous said, "Ad exec. We had a few—mm—deep cutbacks."

"Oh."

"I got into the sauce. Not any more." Figueroa gestured at the wine bottles. Papadopolous said, "Samo drinks, some. Chas too."

"Chas was zonked last night," Willie said.

"Zonked! Wasted!" Samo said.

"He 'as real nice, Chas, he 'as real nice," Samo said over and over. "Never hurt anybody." He started moaning again. Emotionally labile, Figueroa said to herself, having just spent four Thursday evenings in Supplemental Sensitivity Training.

"Useta lie there, looking up the air shaft and tell us what went by," Willie said. "Mornings, people on their way to work. Like, just before we'd go to sleep."

"Yeah?"

Samo said, "Tell us all about the legsa the girls on the sidewalk up there. You know."

"Um, legs."

"Yeah, and some of 'em wouldn't be wearing any underwear. Sheet, you shoulda heard some a what he saw—" He stopped, abruptly realizing he was talking to a female-type officer. "Um, yeah, like shoes," he ended up.

"Well, sure."

"Kept us entertained," Papadopolous said.

"No TV here, ya see," Willie said.

"Who sleeps where?" she asked.

"Thas me." Willie said, with some pride, pointing at the piece of foam rubber near the heat duct.

"You got the choice place," Bennis said to Willie.

"Yeah. Nice and warm."

"That's me," Papadopolous gestured at the spot next to Willie, the layers of cardboard.

Samo said, "Over there," pointing to the pile of newspaper and tattered blankets that lay next to the dead Chas. All the while, Samo was moving his head back and forth, as if listening to music.

Chas's bed was a hodgepodge heap of old clothes, including a couple of stocking caps and a shoe. There was a torn plaid scarf over his lower body, though, and while it was a mess, neither that nor any of the bedding looked like it had been kicked around.

"He been sick?" Bennis asked.

"No, just the sauce."

"Well, we'll get the experts on it." Bennis grabbed his radio.

To Figueroa, watching, it looked for an instant like Papadopolous was either going to hit Bennis or run. Her hand moved an inch toward her sidearm.

"One thirty-three," Bennis said. "We've got a downer."

The radio said, "Bagzzt-skeek-urty-three."

"One thirty-three."

"Pzzzzmmmmm."

To Figueroa, Bennis said, "Shit. Reception's cruddy down here." Again he said, "One thirty-three."

Clear as day the radio said, "Thirty-three. You're not makin' it with your radio, sir. Borquat-muzzzzz. Pip."

"Oh, excellent, swell, really sweet. I'd better go up the street and put out the word." He gave Figueroa a glance they'd exchanged maybe five hundred times, him to her or her to him. It meant, "You okay with this?"

She nodded.

"Back in two seconds."

Figueroa believed that Papadopolous's fear had less to do with Chas's actual death and more to do with the possibility that the police would arrest them or move them along to some less desirable place.

"Pretty sheltered here," she said, hoping he'd talk about it.

"We fixed Thanksgiving dinner in that," Papadopolous said, pointing to the small garbage can.

"Store give us a lil' turkey," Samo said.

"You roasted a turkey! In that?"

Papadopolous said, "We made a bed of charcoal briquets and put the can on top." He grinned at her, knowing she was finding it hard to believe they weren't all incompetent morons. "Shucks," he said, laying it on, "anybody'd been a Boy Scout could do it."

"Stores throw out stuff, it doesn't look fresh anymore," Willie said. "Vegetables, like. Pastry."

"How long you been living here?"

"How long?" Willie echoed. "Maybe since November?"

He looked at Papadopolous, who said, "November tenth we came here. The police drove us out of O'Hare."

"O'Hare, yeah," Samo said. "Druve us out."

Willie cackled. "They're bundling us into these buses. So they say, all horrified, 'Do you want O'Hare to look like New York?'"

"Took us a while to find this place," Papadopolous said, obviously uneasy, still thinking they were going to be moved along.

"This is a good place," Samo said, head nodding.

"Yeah, sweet," Willie said, chucking again. "We call it the Lower Wacker Hilton."

"What do you do all day?"

They were all averting their eyes from the corpse.

"Well, day, see, we don't do anything, days," Willie said.

Samo said, "We sleep."

"Stores and all those fancy restaurants, they don't want us millin' around, see?" Willie said. "In daylight."

"They don't mind so much at night," Papadopolous said. "So we get back here just before dawn, go to bed. Get our healthful eight hours. This time of year it's not light until seven, seven thirty anyhow. Sleep to four thirty. It's dark at four thirty, so we get up and go to work. Works out real neat."

Willie chuckled. "Yeah, out there movin' and shakin'."

"Dumpsters!" Samo said brightly. "Garbage cans!"

Papadopolous said, "They don't mind too much as long as you don't throw stuff all over the street."

Samo suddenly broke out, "You oughta see some guys they just dump over a can, throw everything, throw shit all over the sidewalk. We allus been real careful." He grabbed a quick glance at the corpse of Chas and started to snuffle.

Willie said, "Some folks make a bad name for honest street people."

"Basically you're scavengers, then," Figueroa said to Willie.

"Scavengers? No, I don't think we're scavengers."

"What are you?"

"Beachcombers," Willie Sims said.

Bennis came back. Figueroa raised her eyebrows at him. He said, "They will be with us, my man, as soon as is consistent with the pursuit of their other duties."

"Gawd!" Figueroa said.

Figueroa caught sight of two eyes glowing in the darkness behind the head duct. She jumped but covered it by pretending to turn to get a better view.

"Aw, gee," Samo said, seeing what it was.

Papadopolous made a clucking sound.

An animal stepped out of the shadows.

"Jeez, a cat!" Figueroa said.

Papadopolous said, "We feed him. Bring something back for him every night. When we can. Keep him around as much as possible."

"Why?"

"For the mice. And the rats."

"Rats!" Samo shrieked. "Get yer toes."

"Not yours!" Willie said scornfully. Samo's feet were extremely dirty.

Figueroa said, "We got rats down here the size of Toyotas. No cat can deal with Chicago tunnel rats. These rats scare cats outta seven lives."

"Not this one."

It stalked farther forward.

The cat was a marmalade tom with a huge ruff. He had a round face that looked more like bobcat than tomcat and his body was a barrel.

"Weighs thirty-five pounds," Papadopolous said.

"Yeah, okay," Figueroa said. "I guess rats wouldn't scare him."

"Name's Adolf."

There was the sound of heavy feet in the distance, getting closer.

Suddenly Samo started crying. "He kilt'm."

"Killed who?"

"Chas. Smothered'm. Adolf smothered'm. Slept on his face and smothered'm."

"Okay," said Figueroa, "that's enough."

She turned and took Samo's arm.

"Look," she said, "the court's probably gonna say you're not really responsible." Willie and Papadopolous were staring at her as if she was nuts. "You've been drinking crap. You got a can of Sterno over there and a piece of bread to strain it through. You were depressed. You didn't have anything in this world. You wanted something. Any one thing of your own. And you went out of your head. You smothered Chas with your pillow."

"Nooooo—"

"Figured Papadopolous'd help move him, lose the body, rather than have your space here get discovered."

"Nooooo—"

"Come and look up here."

Figueroa dragged Samo over the airshaft. They looked up. There was a vertical cement shaft with light at the top, light coming through opaque glass disks set in an iron grid. There was nothing else to see. Absolutely nothing.

Samo shrieked.

###

"How'd you know, Figueroa?" Bennis said.

"Brilliance."

"C'mon, my man. This is me you're talkin' to."

"Cats don't smother people, Bennis. Useta say they smothered babies, but they don't."

"So the guy was wrong. Chas could of died of natural causes."

"Then why'd he think up an explanation for Chas being smothered? Huh?"

"Beats me."

"Who benefited from Chas's death? What did they have of value, any of them? Two things. The heat pipe and the view from the air shaft. Willie and Chas. They had the prizes."

"Yeah."

"See, they always lie low in the daylight. None of 'em ever had a chance to look up the airshaft. That was Chas's spot. They got back before daylight and everybody had his own space. None of 'em had ever looked up the airshaft, so they didn't know there was nothing to see. They didn't know that Chas was just entertainin' 'em."

"And when Samo realized—"

"I think he was already feeling remorse. When he realized, that was when he really broke."

"Well, I'll tell you what I think, Figueroa. I think you go on workin' at this, my man, you gonna get real good at your job."

END